Henry M. (Henry Morton) Stanley

My Kalulu, prince, king, and slave

A Story of Central Africa

Henry M. (Henry Morton) Stanley

My Kalulu, prince, king, and slave
A Story of Central Africa

ISBN/EAN: 9783743383722

Manufactured in Europe, USA, Canada, Australia, Japa

Cover: Foto ©Andreas Hilbeck / pixelio.de

Manufactured and distributed by brebook publishing software (www.brebook.com)

Henry M. (Henry Morton) Stanley

My Kalulu, prince, king, and slave

MY KALULU

PRINCE, KING, AND SLAVE

A STORY OF CENTRAL AFRICA

BY

HENRY M. STANLEY

AUTHOR OF "HOW I FOUND LIVINGSTONE"

𝔚ith 𝔍llustrations

NEW YORK
CHARLES SCRIBNER'S SONS
1890

RIVERSIDE, CAMBRIDGE:
STEREOTYPED AND PRINTED BY
H. O. HOUGHTON AND COMPANY.

THIS LITTLE VOLUME

is

𝔇𝔢𝔡𝔦𝔠𝔞𝔱𝔢𝔡

TO ALL THOSE WHO HAVE AIDED IN THE SUPPRESSION OF

SLAVERY ON THE EAST COAST OF AFRICA,

BY HENRY M. STANLEY.

LIST OF ILLUSTRATIONS.

PREFACE.

For the satisfaction of those who are always wondering "What on earth ever induced Mr. So-and-so to write or publish such a book," and those who "fail to see what earthly reason" I had in view in the production of this little volume, I quote Prior's lines, and by simply changing one little word I furnish them with a clear and explicit reason :

> Authors. "all the world agrees,
> Write half to profit, half to please;
> Matter and figure they produce;
> For garnish this, and that for use;
> And in the structure of their feasts
> They seek to feed and please their guests."

This book has been written for boys; not those little darlings who are yet bothering over the alphabet, and have to be taken to bed at sundown, and who, when they awake, put civilised and respectable families into confusion with their cries; nor those little dunces, who look at all books with awe, and who begin to scratch their heads as soon as one is mentioned; nor yet those boys who cannot read, though they are tall and strong; but for those clever, bright-eyed, intelligent boys, of all classes, who have begun to be interested in romantic literature, with whom educated fathers may talk without fear of misapprehension, and of whom friends are already talking as boys who have a promising future before them. These boys are the guests for whom I have provided a true Afric feast. The feast provided for them is not over rich, because Africa is not far enough advanced yet to furnish delicacies, such as puddings, cakes, confections, &c. ; but what there is of it, plain rice and curry, dried meat of game, wild fruits of piquant flavour, &c., is healthy and good for such as you, and taken once in a while, between your own regular banquets, you might thrive and be better for it. "And though I say it myself as shouldn't say it," as Mrs. Gamp says, "you might find worse food nor this."

'My Kalulu' is a romance based upon knowledge acquired during my journey in search of Dr. Livingstone, which began in 1871 and terminated in 1872. Within six weeks after my return from Africa I had written the book entitled 'How I found Livingstone.' I had to work hard, because pressing engagements came on thick and fast; and now that the storm and stress of that short period of my life are over, I wonder how I got through it so well as I did. A great many people complained that the book was bulky; that, in fact, there was too much of it. So are newspapers too large, and contain a great deal more reading matter than any one man cares to read. In a book of travels some readers prefer the adventures, the incidents of the chase; others prefer what relates to the ethnography of the country; others, geography; others dip into it for matters concerning philology. The person who reads the whole book through is one interested in the subject, or is attracted to it by its style.

For those boys, and young, middle-aged, and old men, who found my first book rather heavy, I beg to offer something lighter, fresher—a romance. When the customs and ceremonies of the Watuta have been read a pretty fair idea of the customs of the peoples around Lake Tanganika will have been obtained. The geography here described is correct. In any map of Africa published by Stanford or Keith Johnston, the reader may soon find the south-eastern corner of Lake Tanganika, and the great plain country stretching east of this is Ututa.

As a traveller, I dared not venture upon improbabilities. Everything written herein is possible, nay, much of the book contains facts which I have witnessed myself, or which have come to my knowledge.

I will just explain a few things here. The ceremony of the magic drink took place about two miles from Tabora, when Khamis bin Abdullah and his son Khamis, the same as are here described, and several other Arabs of wealth and influence, fell victims to their own reckless courage, slain by the hands of Mirambo and his northern Watuta allies.

The story of the drowning of the poor women and

children in the Rungwa River was given me by little
Kalulu, who accompanied me from Central Africa to
England, as a scene of terror which he remembered he
had witnessed, and could never forget.

The battle of Kwikuru is described from the fatal
day of Zimbizo, when nearly two thousand five hundred
Arabs were routed by King Mirambo.

The Arab youth Selim stands for the son of one
Mohammed, who was captured by the Warori, and
subjected to many indignities, and much of his story
was related to me by Sheikh Thani, my friend.

Some features in Kalulu's character were taken from
Simba, King of Kasera, son of Mkasiwa, the great and
powerful King of Unyanyembe, as related to me by
the gigantic Asmani, my guide, who knew him well,
and was never tired of praising him.

The giant Simba represents Asmani himself, with a
better character however.

Moto represents his friend and constant companion,
the wiry, sinewy fellow, who believed Asmani was the
best man that ever lived.

I had in view, when I wrote this book, the idea that
I might be able to describe more vividly in such a book
as this than in any other way the evils of the slave-
trade in Africa—how it begins, how it is conducted,
and how it sometimes ends.

So it will be seen that I have woven fact with fiction;
and if my readers are pleased with the weaving of the
circumstances into the romance 'My Kalulu, Prince,

Waterlow, Mayor.

A COMMON COUNCIL

Holden in the Chamber of the Guildhal
of the City of London,

On Thursday, the 21st day of November, 1872.

Resolved Unanimously,

*That this Court desires to express its great
appreciation of the eminent services rendered by*

Mr. Henry Morton Stanley

*To the cause of science and humanity by his
persistent and successful endeavours
to discover and relieve that zealous and persevering
Missionary and African Traveller,
DR. LIVINGSTONE,
the uncertainty of whose fate had caused such deep
anxiety, not only to Her Majesty's subjects,
but to the whole civilised world.*

King, and Slave,' the author will consider himself sufficiently rewarded for this his first essay in fiction. Should it turn out as I hope it will, I can assure those interested in Kalulu, that some day, if I live, I shall attempt to take him back to his own country, through numberless adventures, incidents, and scenes, in the hope that he shall enjoy his own again. But if I have failed in this venture, then Kalulu must stop at Zanzibar, where the reader may fancy him, if he likes, eating mangoes and oranges, until I fetch him out. " I have said it."

THE AUTHOR.

LONDON,
September 20, 1873.

P.S.—On my return to England after a residence of some months in Spain, I was not less surprised than gratified to find that the Lord Mayor and Corporation of the City of London had forwarded to my publishers a very beautifully illuminated and handsomely framed copy of a Vote of Thanks which had been previously voted to me. My hurried and wandering life has prevented my personally acknowledging this act of generous consideration, although it has touched me deeply. Partly to gratify, I trust, an excusable vanity, and partly because I know that many of my American friends will be pleased to see it, the accompanying woodcut representation of it has been prepared.

CONTENTS.

CHAPTER IV.

CHAPTER V.

CHAPTER VI

CHAPTER VII.

CHAPTER VIII.

CHAPTER IX.

CHAPTER X.

CHAPTER XI.

CHAPTER XII.

MY KALULU.

CHAPTER I.

ABOUT four miles north of the city of Zanzibar, and
about half a mile removed from a beautiful bay, lived,
not many years ago, surrounded by his kinsmen and
friends, a noble Arab of the tribe of Beni-Hassan,—
Sheikh Amer bin Osman.*

Sheikh Amer was a noble by descent and untarnished
blood from a long line of illustrious Arab ancestry; he
was noble in disposition, noble in his large liberal
charity, and noble in his treatment of his numerous
black dependents.

Amer's wife—his favourite wife—was the sweet
gazelle-eyed daughter of Othman bin Ghees, of the

---

* Amer bin Osman means, Amer, son of Osman.

B

tribe of the Beni-Abbas. She was her husband's
counterpart in disposition and temper, and was quali-
fied to reign queen of his heart and harem for numerous
other virtues.

Though few Arabs spoke of her in presence of her
husband, or asked about her health or well-being—as it
is contrary to the custom of the Arabs —still the friends
of Amer knew well what transpired under his roof.
The faithful slaves of Amer never omitted an opportunity to declare the goodness and many virtues of
' mina, Amer's wife.

A young European, chancing to ride on one of Prince
Majid's horses by the estate of Amer, one afternoon,
casually obtained a glance at the sweet face of Amina,
which made such an impression on his mind that he
continually dwelt upon it as on a happy dream
Some of this young European's phrases deserve to
be repeated in justice to the Arab lady whom he so
admired. "She was the most beautiful woman my
eyes ever rested upon. I felt a shock of admiration
as I caught that one short view of her face. I
felt a keen regret that I could see no more of the
exquisite features of her extraordinary face. If I
were a painter, I know I should be for ever en-
..deavouring to preserve a trace of the divine beauty of
that Arab woman; my brush would ever hover about
the eyes in a vain hope that I could transmit to canvas
the marvellously limpid, yet glowing look of her eyes
or near the finely chiselled lips, tinting them with
the rubiest of colours, or ever trying to imitate the
pure complexion, yet always despairing to approach

the perfection, one glance indelibly fixed on my memory."

Around Amer's large roomy mansion grew a grove of orange and mangoe trees. The fields of his estate numbered many acres, well tilled and planted with cinnamon, cloves, oranges, mangoes, pomegranates, guavas, and numerous other fruit-trees; they produced also every variety of vegetable and grain known on the Island of Zanzibar. By dint of labour, and personal exertion, and superintendence of the proprietor the estate was considered to be one of the most flourishing on the island. A sacrifice of a large amount of ready money had so improved and embellished the mansion, that the oldest inhabitant who remembered Osman, Amer's father, hardly recognised it as the house of Osman. A large marble courtyard, in the centre of which stood a handsome fountain of the same costly stone, was one of the many additions made to the house by Amer after the demise of his father. Marble troughs outside the mansion had also been erected for the use of the Moslemised slaves, that they might wash their feet and hands before attending the prayers in the mesdjid* of the mansion, which were rigidly observed with all the ceremonies usual in Moslem temples.

Amer, the son of Osman, had but one son, called Selim, by his favourite wife Amina. Not less dear to him was this boy than was his wife. In the boy's handsome features, large glowing black eyes, and clear

* Chapel or church.

complexion he saw what he had received from his lovely
mother, and in the boy's graceful vigorous form he
recognised himself, when at his age he looked up to
his father Osman as the paragon of all men upon
earth.

Selim's age, when this story begins, was a few months
over fifteen; and it is at the usual evening symposium,
which takes place near the even sloping beach of the
little bay in front of Amer's mansion, that we are first
introduced to one of the heroes of our story.

It is near sunset, and a group composed of Amer bin
Osman, Khamis bin Abdullah—a wealthy African trader
just returned from the interior of Africa, with an immense number of ivory tusks and slaves—Sheikh Mohammed, a native of Zanzibar, a neighbour and kinsman
of Amer; Sheikh Thani, son of Mussoud, an experienced
old trader in Africa; Sheikh Mussoud, son of Abdullah,
a portly, fine-looking Arab of Muscat; Sheikhs Hamdan
and Amran, also natives of Zanzibar, though pure-
blooded Arabs—were seated on fine Persian carpets
placed on the beach, near enough to the pretty little
wavelets which were rolled by the evening zephyrs up
the snowy sand to hear distinctly their music, but still
far enough from them to avoid any dampness.

Close to this group of elderly and noble-looking
Arabs was another consisting of young people who
were the sons or near relatives of each of the Arabs
above-mentioned. There were Suleiman and Soud,
nephews of Amer bin Osman, gaudily-dressed youths;
there was Isa, a tall dark-coloured boy, son of Sheikh
Thani; there were Abdullah and Mussoud, two boys of

ON THE STRAND NEAR ZANZIBAR.

fourteen and twelve years respectively, sons of Sheikh
Mohammed, whose complexions were as purely white
as black-eyed descendants of Ishmael can well be; and
lastly, there was the beloved son of Amer, son of
Osman—Selim, whose appearance at once challenged
attention from his frank, ingenuous, honest face, his
clear complexion, his beautiful eyes, and the promise
which his well-formed graceful figure gave of a perfect
manhood in the future.

Selim was dressed in a short jacket of fine crimson
cloth braided with gold, a snowy white muslin dis-
dasheh, or shirt, reaching below the knees, bound
around the waist by a rich Muscat sohari or check.
On his head he wore a gold-tasseled red fez, folded
around by a costly turban, which enhanced the appearance of the handsome face beneath it.

While all eyes are directed west at the dark-blue
loom of the African continent away many miles beyond
the greyish-green waters of the sea of Zanzibar, Amer,
son of Osman, remarks to his friends in a musing tone:

"I have sat here, close to my own mangoes, almost
every evening for the last twenty years looking towards
that dark line of land, and always wishing to go nearer
to it, to see for myself the land where all the ivory and
slaves that the Arab traders bring to Zanzibar come
from."

Directing his eyes towards Khamis bin Abdullah,
Amer continued :

"And never has the desire to leave my house and
travel to Africa been so strong as this evening, when
thou, Sheikh informest me that thou hast brought with

thee 500 slaves and 800 frasilah* of ivory from Ufipa
and Marungu.   It is wonderful!   Wallahi!   Five
hundred slaves if they are tolerably healthy are worth
at least 10,000 dollars, and 800 frasilah of ivory are
worth, at 50 dollars the frasilah, 40,000 dollars, nearly
half a lakh of rupees altogether, and all this thou hast
collected in five years' travels. Wallahi! it is wonderful!
By the Prophet!—blessed be his name—I must see the
land for myself.   I shall see it, please God!" and as
he finished speaking he began to wipe his brow violently, a sign with him that he was excited and determined.

"What I have spoken is God's truth," said Khamis
bin Abdullah, "and Allah knows it.   But there are
many more wonderful countries than Marungu and
Ufipa.   Rua, several days further toward the setting
of the sun, is a great country, and few Arabs have been
there yet.   Sayd, the son of Habib, has been to Rua,
and much further; he has been across to the sea of the
setting sun, and has married a wife from among the
white people who live at San Paul de Loanda.   Sayd is
so great a traveller, I should fear to say what land he
has not seen.   Mashallah! Sayd, I believe, has seen all
lands and all peoples.   He says that ivory is used in
Rua by the Pagans as we use wooden stanchions or
posts to support the eaves of our houses, that ivory
holds their huts up, and he believes great stores of it
are known to the savages, where some of their great
hunters have killed a large number of elephants, and
have left the ivory to rot, not knowing how valuable it

* A frasilah is equivalent to 35 lbs. in weight.

is, or where a great herd of elephants have perished
from thirst or disease. However the knowledge came
to these people, or whatever the cause which left such
a store of ivory in that country, Sayd, the son of Habib,
is certain that there is an unlimited quantity of this
precious stuff in Rua, and that we can make ourselves
richer than Prince Majid, our Sultan, if we go in time,
before the report is common among the Arabs   What
money I have made this time on my last trip is so
small, compared to what I might have realised, that I
mean to try my fortune again in Africa shortly, Inshallah!—please God! I intend going to Rua, and if
thou, Amer bin Osman, hast a mind to accompany me,
I promise thee that thou wilt not repent it."

"Amer bin Osman," replied Amer, "goes not back
on his word. By my beard, I have said I shall go, and,
if it be God's will, I shall be ready for thee when thou
goest. But tell us, son of Abdullah, what of the Pagans
of Rua, and those lands near the Great Lakes? Do
they make good slaves, and do they sell well in our
market? Yet I need hardly ask thee, for I have two
men whom I purchased when young, about twenty
years ago, who I believe are more faithful than any
slave born in my house."

"Good slaves!" echoed Khamis. "Thou hast said it.
Finer people are not to be found, from Masr to Kilwa,
than those of Rua and the lands adjoining. And clever
slaves, too! Those Pagans make the best spears, and
swords, and daggers found in Africa. Indeed, some of
their work would shame that of our best Zanzibar
artificers. Near a place called Kitanga—where that

is I don't know, but Sayd, the son of Habib, can tell—there is a hill almost entirely of pure copper, and from this hill the people get vast quantities of copper, which they work into beautiful bracelets, armlets, anklets, and such things. Nothing to be seen in Muscat even can equal the work the son of Habib has witnessed."

"Mashallah!" cried Amer, delighted; "thou makest me more and more anxious to go to the strange land. A hill of copper!—pure copper! The Pagans must really be a fine people, and rich, too. If it were only possible to catch two or three hundred slaves of the kind thou speakest of, I might be able to laugh in the face of that dog of a Banyan Ramji, and old Ludha Damha himself could not hold his head higher than I could then. I owe the dogs a turn, for the heavy usury they exacted of me when I needed much ready money to make my courtyard and fountains. But the women, noble Khamis, thou hast said nothing of them. Tell us what kind of women are seen in those rich lands."

"Ah, yes, do tell us of the women," chimed in two or three others, who had not yet spoken.

"I have seen but one of the women of Rua," answered Khamis, "and she was the wife of the son of Sayd, the son of Habib, a tall, lithesome girl of sixteen years or so. Her lower limbs were as clean and well-made as those of an antelope. She walked like the daughter of a chief. Her eyes were like two deep wells of shining moving water. Her face was like the moon, in colour and form. Oh! the colour was almost as clear and light as thy son Selim's, Amer. She was beautiful as a Peri-banou—God be praised!"

"Thy tongue runs away with thee, Khamis," cried Amer, in a slightly offended tone, "or hast thou imbibed too much of the strong drink of the Nazarenes, for the celebration of thy late success? Light-complexioned women, of the colour of my son Selim's face! Where art thou, Selim, son of Amer, pride of the Beni-Hassan? Thou chief's son by birth and blood, and apple of thy father's eye! Come hither."

"Behold me, my father, I am here," said Selim, who had bounded lightly to his feet, and now stood before his father, after kissing his right hand for the affectionate terms lavished on him.

"Speak, son of Abdullah; behold, my boy, and regard his colour, which is like unto that of rich cream. Is he not as white as any Nazarene? and wilt thou repeat what thou hast said about the Pagan wife of Sayd's son?"

"Khamis, the son of Abdullah, debauches not himself with the strong drink of the foolish Nazarenes. I lie not. I said I have seen a daughter of the Warua whom Sayd's son has taken for wife, and she is almost as light in colour as thy son, Selim, and far lighter than the face of the boy, Isa, son of Sheikh Thani."

"Wonderful! Wallahi!" echoed the group. "It is most wonderful. We shall all go to obtain wives from the Warua."

"Then, kinsmen and friends," cried Amer, "Khamis speaks the truth, and speaks of wonderful things. Is it agreed that we go to Rua with the son of Abdullah, to get ivory, slaves, and copper, and light-coloured wives?"

"It is," they all replied, so deeply impressed were they with what Khamis had said.

"I am glad to hear it, my friends," said Khamis ; "but ye must now agree, before we break up, as the sun is fast setting, upon the day of departure. I cannot wait long, because I am nearly ready, but I am willing to wait a few days, if ye will all promise to be ready by the new moon, twenty-four days from this evening. Ye must also promise to take as many of your slaves as ye can, that we may make a strong party. Tell me, Sheikh Amer, how many of thy people armed canst thou take with thee?"

"Who?—I? I can take two hundred well-armed servants, besides my two faithful fundis, Simba and Moto, as they are called by the slaves, who are worth an army by themselves, and——"

"Let me go, my father," cried Selim, seating himself on the carpet close to his father's knees, and looking up to his face with eager, entreating eyes, "I can shoot. Thou knowest the new gun which thou didst send for to London, in the land of the English, and which the good balyuz* taught me how to use. The balyuz told me the other day that I would be able to shoot better than he could, by-and-by. I can shoot a bird on the wing already with it. Give thy consent, and let me accompany thee, father. I will be both good and brave, I promise thee."

"Hear the boy!" said Amer, admiringly. "A true Bedaween could not have spoken otherwise. But why dost thou wish to leave thy mother, child, so soon?"

* Balyuz is an Arabic word for consul, or rather embassador.

SELIM.

"My mother will regret me, I know, but I am now strong and big, and it is not good for me to remain in the harem all my life. I must quit my mother some time, for work which all men must do."

"And who gave thee such ideas, son Selim? Who told thee thou wert too big to remain with thy mother?"

"The other day I went out with Sulieman, son of Prince Majid, and the young son of the American balyuz—I can't pronounce his name—to shoot wild birds. The young American boy, who is smaller than I am, and already thinks himself a man, though he is no bigger than my hand, laughed at me; and when I asked him why he laughed, he said to me, 'Truly, Selim, thou appearest to me to be like a little girl! whose mother bathes her in new milk every day to preserve her complexion. I cannot understand the spirit of an Arab boy which contents itself with looking no further out-doors than within sight of a mother's eyes.' These are the words he spoke to me within hearing of Sulieman, Majid's son, who also laughed at me, while I felt my cheeks were red with shame, they tingled so."

"Tush, boy! What is it to thee what the thoughts of a forward Nazarene lad are? Thou art not of his race or kin. But I must own to ye, my friends," said Amer, turning to the elders, "that the youths of the Nazarenes* are bolder than ours, though they do not possess higher courage or loftier spirit than our own children. Who would have thought that such large independence could hide within the little body of the

* Nazarene is the Arabic term for Christian.

American balyuz's son? That small child cannot be twelve years old, yet he talks with the wisdom of a man. All the Nazarenes are wonderful people—wonderful! Who are stronger, richer than the Nazarenes of England?"

"Ah, but, father," said Selim; "do you not think the Nazarenes are accursed of God, and of the prophet Mohammed—blessed be his name? The American boy told me the Arabs are wicked, and are accursed of God. Said he to me that same day in hearing of the Sultan's son, as if he was not a bit afraid of the consequences, 'The Lord God makes his anger known against the Arabs by refusing knowledge and the gifts of understanding unto them, because they are wicked, because they go forth into Africa with armed servants a-plenty to destroy and kill the poor black people, and to take slaves of parents and children, whom they bring to Zanzibar to sell for their own profit.' Is he not an unbeliever, father?"

"Peace, Selim; let not thy tongue utter such words against the true believers, though they may have been said by a young dog like that. Cast them away from thee entirely, and let not thy father hear thee utter aught against thine own race and kindred. To the unbelievers God has said, 'Woe unto them; they shall be the prey of the flames.'"

"But, father, thou art not offended with me? Thou hast not yet given thy consent to my going with thee and my kinsman."

"Dost thou know, my child, that the Pagans are fierce, that they have great spears and knives, and will cut that slim neck of thine, and perhaps eat thee without compunction?" asked Amer, smiling.

"I fear them not," answered Selim, tossing his head back proudly. "When did a son of the great tribe of Beni-Hassan show fear? and shall I, the son of a chief of that tribe—the son of Amer bin Osman—look upon the faces of the Pagans with fear in my heart?"

"Then thou shalt go with me, were it only for those last words. But fear not, Allah will care for thee," said Amer, solemnly laying his broad hand on his son's head.

"Let us end this before the sun sets," said Khamis impatiently, watching the descent of the sun. "How many men canst thou take with thee, Sheikh Thani?"

"Thani has a son — Isa," answered that worthy trader. "Thani is poor compared to Amer, but he can call round him fifty well-armed slaves, who will stand by him to the death."

"That is answered well, and Isa is a likely lad, though his skin is dark; but he has the soul of an Arab father in him. I see we shall have a glorious company; and thou, Mussoud?" said Khamis, to that florid-faced chief, who was proud of his intensely black and handsome beard, "How many canst thou muster?"

"About the same as my friend Thani," replied Mussoud, caressing his beard. "All my people are Wahiyow, docile, and good; and, if cornered, brave. They will follow me anywhere."

"Good again!" ejaculated Khamis, evidently pleased. "And thou, Sheikh Mohammed?" he asked of the chief so named, who had a terrible reputation in the interior among the Wafipa and Wa-marungu, and of whom many tribes stood in awe, — "how many of thy people wilt thou take to Africa this time?"

"Well," said Mohammed, in a deep voice, which resembled the bellow of a wild buffalo, "for such a grand project as this I think I can take one hundred men from my estate; my head men can take charge of the rest with Rashid, my brother, very well. I shall also take these young lions— Abdullah and Mussoud— with me, to teach them how to catch slaves and claw them, as I have done often."

"Thanks, father," replied the grateful youths, who as soon as they had said these words looked up slyly to Selim, who smiled appreciatingly at his boy-friends.

"Sultan, son of Ali," said Khamis, "thou art a strong and wise man. Wilt thou be one of us?"

Sultan, son of Ali, was a man of about fifty, or perhaps fifty-five, of strongly-marked features, who had keen black eyes. Strong and wise, as Khamis bin Abdullah had said he was, indeed no one looking at him would doubt that he was one of the best specimens of a hardy Bedaween chief that ever came to Zanzibar. Besides, Sultan had been an officer of high rank in the army of Prince Thouweynee of Muscat, who had often eulogised Sultan for his daring, obstinacy, forethought, and skill in handling his wild cavalry. He was still, as might be seen, in the prime of mature manhood, which age had not deteriorated in the least.

Sultan answered Khamis readily. " Where my dear friend Amer bin Osman goes, I go. Shall I remain at

Zanzibar eating mangoes when Amer, my kinsman, is in
danger? No! Son of Abdullah, thou mayest count
me of thy party for good or for evil, and I can raise
eighty slaves to shoulder guns for this journey."

"Good, good," the Arabs said, unanimously.
" Where the stout son of Ali goes, the road is straight
and danger is not known."

" Well," said Khamis bin Abdullah, " we have now
four hundred and eighty men promised; I will take
with me a hundred and fifty men with guns, and I
dare say Sheikhs Hamdan and Amram and a few other
friends will bring the force up to seven hundred. Isa,
son of Salim, Mohammed son of Rashid, Rashid bin
Sulieman, tall young men, and kinsmen to me, have
already agreed to follow my fortunes. A large number
of Arabs is always better than a few. I have one thing
more to say before we rise to prayers—the sun is just
sinking. I see—Ludha Damha, the collector of customs,
has told me that if a strong party went with me he
would let us have any amount of ready money at 50
per cent. annual interest, which is half the usual price
he asks—the old dog!—and if any of you desire money,
go to him for your outfit, for I will speak to him
to-morrow morning and give him your names."

" That is well-spoken, by my beard," said Mohammed.
" I was thinking that we could not raise money under
100 per cent. interest from the Banyan usurer."

" Very well, indeed," added Amer bin Osman.
Ludha Damha must be sure of a speedy return to let
his money go so cheap. My mind is now perfectly
made up; and, friends, the sun has set and we must

to prayers." Saying which Amer rose—a signal which the Arabs readily understood.

After the usual salaams, courtesies, and benedictions had been uttered, the Arabs departed each to his own home, at a slow and dignified pace, while Amer and his son Selim retired into the mesdjid of their own mansion.

When Amer and Selim had ended their evening prayers, and had left the mesdjid or church belonging to the mansion, Selim asked, pulling at his father's robe:

"Father, I see my mother at the lattice; may I go and tell her that I am to go with you to Africa?"

"Ah, poor Amina! I forgot all about her," said Amer, stopping and speaking in a regretful tone. "Selim, my son, this is sad. Amina will never permit thy departure. It would break her heart."

"But I must go sometime from home, father. Why not now? With whom can I be safer than with thee? I am not going with strangers, nor am I leaving my kindred. I am going with thy kindred, thy household, and thyself. What can my mother object to?"

"Thou art right, Selim—thou art right! She cannot object. Our slaves, our kindred are going—but—but—poor Amina, she will be left alone. Go, Selim, tell her kindly. It will pain her." And Amer turned shortly away, as if he had sudden and important business in another direction.

Selim, on the other hand, bounded lightly away, arrived at the great carved door of the mansion, ran up the broad stairs, and made his way to the harem, or the women's apartments, where Amina reigned queen and mistress.

Few boys of Selim's age could have approached their mother with the earnestly-respectful manner with which Selim approached Amina. I doubt even if the Queen of England's children ever observed such courteous respect towards their august parent as Selim observed now, and as most well-bred Arab boys do observe always toward their parents.

Selim left his slippers outside, and lifting the latch quietly, walked in with bare feet, and, approaching his mother, kissed her right hand, and then her forehead, and at her invitation seated himself by her side, and suddenly remembering the all-important secret he had to communicate, looked up to his mother, with his handsome features all aglow.

"Mother, canst thou tell me what I have come to say to thee?"

Amina looked for an instant fondly on her son, and then answered with a smile—

"No, my son. Hast thou anything very important to tell me?"

"Very important, mother," and he pursed his lips as if he would retain it for a long time before imparting it, and as if it were worth some trouble of guessing.

"I wish thou wouldst not task my skill of divination too much. Thy face tells me thou art happy with it, but it does not assure me that I shall be equally happy. I divine only on the Kūran, and though thy face is innocent and without guile, yet it is more difficult to read than the Kūran. Tell it me, Selim, I pray thee."

c

"Then, my mother, I am going with my father to Africa!"

"To Africa, child! To Africa! Where is that? Thou dost not mean the mainland, surely?"

"Yes, I mean far away into the interior of the mainland," replied Selim, still looking at his mother smilingly.

"To the interior of Africa!" cried the poor woman in dismay, her face assuming the hue of sickness. "Why, what can thy father want in Africa?—he was never there before. What can he want there now?"

"He is going to Africa with Khamis bin Abdullah, Sheikhs Mohammed, Thani, Mussoud, Sultan, Amran, Hamdan, and many others, to a far country called Rua, to buy ivory and slaves, and come back rich."

"Going to Africa! To get rich! Oh, Allah!" cried out Amina, in accents of unfeigned surprise, mixed with emotion. "And thou art going with him—thou, a child? Art thou going to get rich too?"

"I am to accompany my father and kinsmen, not to get rich, but to see the world, and learn how to be a man, to shoot lions, and leopards, zebras, and elephants, with my new English gun."

"Cease thy prating, child; thy tongue runs at a fearful rate. Thou shoot lions and leopards! Thou! Why thou art but a baby, but lately weaned! Thou and thy father must be dreaming!" said Amina sharply, and with an attempt at a sneer.

It was a brave attempt on the part of a nearly heart-broken woman, who would fain suppress the cry of anguish that struggled to her lips, but as she said the last words, one glance at Selim's face showed to her that such tactics would never answer. The eaglet had been taught that wings were made to fly with. The boy had been rudely laughed at, and his latent manliness aroused, by the son of the American consul, who had sneered at him. Selim had found that a head was on his shoulders which teemed with daring thoughts; that he had arms to his shoulders, and legs to his body, made on purpose, as it were, to execute such thoughts as the head conceived. With the culmination of such knowledge fled unregretfully the pleasant days of the harem, the memories of his romps with the girls, days upon days of effeminate life.

Achilles was found out by the sight which he obtained of some war weapons. Selim had found out that he was a boy by a sneer. Charming as was his mother's company, happy as he had been with his feminine playmates, proud as he had been of his golden tassels and embroidery, fond as he had been of being loved and embraced as an entertaining young friend by little girls of his own age—all these experiences became inane and stupid compared to the overpowering consciousness he felt that he was a boy, and might in time become a strong man. A man! perish all other thoughts and memories, feelings, and reminiscences save those which tend to lead him to the goal of manhood, which he has set himself to reach by a journey to Africa, to the land of cannibals and lions, leopards and elephants, to the land of adventure, undying fable, and song.

"Mother," said Selim, removing his turban and fez,

as if his head-dress compressed the grand thought
which filled his brain, "my childhood is passed. I have
been thoroughly weaned from all things belonging to
a child. I am now a strong boy, and in five years I
shall be a man. Allah made the world, and made it to
grow. It has been growing ever since it was made.
Allah made infants; infants grow if they live; they
become boys—boys become men. When I was an infant
I had no understanding nor strength. Thou, my mother,
didst point out to me my nourishment. I flourished
on it, and in time was weaned. In a little time my
strength availed me to put my own food into my own
lips. I flourished on that food, and I became stronger
still. Later I understood language, and answered thee
with childish love and affection. I romped in the
harem, and was happy. Then I was permitted to go
out of doors unattended by my female attendant. I
bathed in the sea. I learned to swim, and acquired
games which boys learn one from another. I learned
to ride on horses; I learned to shoot, and day by day I
was getting stronger in body and limb, and with my
strength has begun to grow my thoughts. These
thoughts are thoughts of manhood, of duty; and the
business of life, which I am beginning to learn, is
serious. Mother, dear mother, my health required,
when I was strong enough to enjoy out-of-door life,
that I should run about and leap. Mother, my
happiness demands that my thoughts should be humoured as my strength was. I find I am made of
two parts—body and mind. Neither may be longer
neglected—both must be humoured, or I die. If my

body is not exercised out in the open air—if I be imprisoned in a harem, I shall become dwarfed. I shall not grow. If my mind is not exercised by seeing, and talking with many people—if I see no more than my mother and my mother's slaves—my mind cannot grow. I shall know nothing, and I shall become a fool. I, the son of Amer, the son of Osman, will be sneered at. It may not be, dear mother. I must go away, and learn the lesson of a man's life."

"But, my dear son," said Amina, entreatingly, for she had been astonished and amazed at the amount of logic which the boy, to her surprise, had put forth in his statement. "Consider, thou art yet young, and that thou mayst wait awhile yet before journeying to that horrid land of negro savages. What canst thou find there to learn? Seeing lions and leopards, and elephants and ugly crocodiles, will not ripen thy mind. Surely thou art cruel to think of leaving me alone here—both my lord Amer and my son at one time!"

"Nay, my mother, what I shall see in Africa will be new and strange. The sight of new and strange things is like the lessons which the good Imām used to give me at school from the Kūran. Every day I shall see something new, and every day I shall grow in wisdom and experience; and my mind will be enriched by each new thing, and in time will become a store of wisdom, to be applied to my advantage in affairs of life. Thou art surprised that I talk so, mother. I have been talking with wise white men. The consuls, who know everything, have been dropping strange ideas to me every day, not because I asked them, or that they dropped them for my benefit. Being permitted to play with their children, I have been in their presence while they were conducting their business, and the amount of wisdom the white men know is wonderful. Great thoughts--too great for me to understand—dropped from their mouths—from one to another—just as those pearls which thou dost play with are passed from thy right hand to thy left."

"It is well, my son. I have heard thee through. Thou art already older by many years than I took thee to be yesterday. Thou mayst tell my lord Amer how Amina received thy news. I will have something more to tell thee, before thou goest to Africa," and Amina arose to leave the apartment for another, humbly, and with her head bowed down.

"My mother," cried Selim, springing up, and seizing her hand, which he conveyed respectfully to his lips, "be not offended. It is not my doing, but Allah's, and Allah's will be done!"

"Ay, truly! Allah's will be done!" said the poor mother, embracing him, but with more restraint than usual.

We are now compelled to leave each of the Arabs engaged to accompany Khamis bin Abdullah to Rua in search of ivory and slaves to make his preparations as he best knows how. It is not our duty to peer too closely into the small details of this business of preparation. It absorbs all one's time, and we feel sure if we troubled them to give us too minute an account of the manner in which they get along, some impatient expressions might escape to our regret.   Therefore we think it better to leave each Arab alone, to the cunning of his own devices, to his calculations, and purchases, to his ever-recurring vexations, to the fatigue and anxiety which belong to the task of fitting out ; merely observing, as we pass by, that each Arab purchases such beads, of such colours, as he thinks proper, such cloth as he deems suitable for his market, so much powder and lead as will sufficiently provide his men for the defence of his goods, should such be ever necessary, so many guns as he has men, such luxuries in the shape of crackers and potted sweets, sugar, tea, and coffee, as the chief of the caravan deems it necessary to take   " Nothing in excess, but enough of every necessary thing," is the golden rule adopted by all people about penetrating Central Africa.

The Arab chiefs and their followers, though they generally take a long time to prepare a caravan, were in this instance, however, much to our pleasure, punctual to the day named, and at the beginning of the new moon of the sixth month of the year of the glorious Hegira 128-, or the year of our Lord and Saviour Jesus Christ 186-, the ships containing the expedition and the vast amount of stores requisite for the consumption of a large and imposing caravan for about three years, set sail in the morning from the open harbour of Zanzibar, for the port of Bagamoyo, on the mainland, distant twenty-five miles.

Let us wave our snowy handkerchiefs to the travellers, for we have one or two young friends who accompany them.   Let us wish them a cheery *bon voyage*, and a happy issue out of their enterprise, if it so happen that the Lord of Moslems and Christians looks down upon its purpose with favourable eye. Let us at least bear them good will until they have forfeited our good opinion by acts contrary to Christian charity and the good will to all men which that most loving God-Man, Jesus, preached unto us.

CHAPTER II.

Bidding Farewell — Amina's Farewell to Selim—Selim in Tears—
Simba's Feats of Strength—Moto's Character described—Little
Niani, the boy, called Monkey—Moto meets Elephants—Moto's
daring Adventure—A narrow Escape—The Story of Moto—Kisesa
prepares to attack—The King's son, Kalulu—What Prince Kalulu
said to Moto—Simba praises Moto.

On the fifteenth day of the sixth month, the members
of the last caravan, under the command of Amer bin
Osman, were taking farewell of their friends, who had
arrived at Bagamoyo from Zanzibar that morning for
last words.

It was a most affecting scene, as all such must be
when young men are about to sever themselves from
their connections for the first time, and fathers and
husbands are commending to the care of the good God
those whom they are about to leave behind, perhaps for
ever.

Who knows how many of these stalwart and stout-
hearted people will return to those from whom they are
now almost tearfully withdrawing? Will the brave
and noble Amer son of Osman, who is now bending over
his beautiful wife, in earnest conversation, ever come
back? He appears so strong and robust in health;
two hundred well-appointed servants of his household

are round about him ; his Arab companions, with their powerful retinue, who have gone before him to Sim-bamwenni, we may be sure, will be faithful to him. Yet who can insure his return? And thus doubt, fear, and anxiety alternate in his wife Amina's eyes, as she raises them appealingly, regretfully, towards his own.

"Yes, Amina, please God, I shall come back within two years, with so much ivory, and so many slaves, as will make me the richest man in Zanzibar. Inshallah! Inshallah!" said Amer, in a sanguine tone.

"Amina, say thy farewell to Selim, the pride of the Beni-Hassan. He will some day return to Oman, a rich and powerful chief. Dost thou not think he looks a warrior in his marching dress? But hasten, or we shall have nothing but women's tears, which perhaps will drown us before we begin our journey."

As Amer turned away after a still but fervent embrace, Amina turned to Selim, with a look which revealed the love her maternal heart bore him, and so steadfastly did she regard him, that it seemed she was fixing a life-long picture of his features in her memory which time would in vain attempt to efface.

"Thou, Selim," she said, drawing him nearer to her, "thou joy of my heart, and jewel of my eyes! Thou art really about to depart! Thou to leave thy mother's heart desolate! What joy is left for me—my son and lord both going? Wilt thou not let thy mother's voice plead, and prevail with thee, Selim? Look, Selim, on that dancing sea! Beyond the narrow strait lies the Zanjian isle! Over its fair shores the gentle winds waft the perfumes of citron and orange! The sweet

scents of the jasmine flowers, the cinnamon and clove
vie with the fragrance of the orange! Rare odours and
sweet strains of bulbul lull the senses into perfect
felicity! The sweet air is pregnant with fragrance!
Where canst thou meet with a land so fair, my Selim?
Wilt thou leave thy mother, these delights, these joys,
for the cruel heat, and thirst, and jungle-thorn of
negro-land? Oh, Selim! Oh, Selim! Wilt thou leave
thy mother, the orange-groves, the palms, the cool
fountains, for scorching days and arid plains? The
road is long—oh, so long—for weeks, months, and years
it lies to the west! Stay one moment longer, my
Selim, and let thy mother read thee what the Kūran's
sacred page, which I've divined, reveals. Remember,
it is the sure decree of Fate, to which God has affixed
his own heavy seal. Hear these words, and stay with
me:—

> A day will come, a day of saddest woe,
> A day when Arabs meet the savage foe,
> And Arabs vainly cry for strength and might,
> And vainly strive to save themselves by flight.
>
> It is a day of woe, a day of doom,
> A day surcharg'd with black and bitter gloom;
> And sons shall mourn for Arab fathers slain,
> And Arab wives shall shed their tears like rain.

Wilt thou stay with me now? No! Proud boy, shun
the death and misery which wait this venture! Despise
not the warning of Allah! Why wilt thou, oh Selim,
shake thy head so stubbornly? Speak."

"Dearest mother, it may not be. If Fate decrees
my death and misery, then why should I try to escape
its sure laws by remaining behind? If death awaits my

father, Selim's place is by Amer's side, to die as becomes the son of an Arab chief. But these are but trivial fears of thine, my mother. Why shouldst thou fear for me? Am I not with my father, the brave Amer son of Osman? Have I not my gun and long sword? What can the Pagan dogs do against all the great Arabs, and my father's kinsmen, when Khamis bin Abdullah, and Amer bin Osman lead? Trust in Allah, mother. Believe me, I shall return to thee, tall and strong, with plenty of ivory and slaves to make thee rich—to hang such jewels on thy neck as befits a chief's wife. Hark! the horn of the guide sounds the signal of departure. My father is impatient, and I must go to him. Embrace me, mother, and bless me ere I go."

Amina, seeing persuasion useless, needed no command for such an affectionate duty. A full mother's love rose responsive to the call of her son, but her son's impatience rendered the embrace, though fervid, short.

"Allah go with thee, my boy!" cried the mother.

"And with thee also, for ever!" responded Selim.

They were parted at last, one to join his father, who was striding forward with his caravan, the other to turn to a friend's house, to sob and weep, and think of the loved ones now fast retiring towards the west.

For a long time father and son were silent. Amer strode on quickly, with an impassive countenance, whence all expression was banished save firmness, and a lofty air of determination.

Selim, thorough son of a thorough Arab, with his head bent down mechanically followed his father's footsteps, and allowed the strange birds to rise, and sing, and fly unheeded about him, the sun to sink unheeded to the west, and the twilight to approach, without seeming to be at all conscious that he was marching to that grand, fabulous, awful heart of Africa, about which he had heard so much, and which he had craved in his heart of hearts to see.

The silence was unbroken until the caravan had halted on the banks of the Kingani, then Selim recovered himself, and a copious flood of tears caused by a feeling of tender melancholy which came over him at the thought that he had really and actually left the pleasant happy home for that sable, ominous, forested land that stretched deathly still across the river.

The father turned as he heard the deep sobs of his boy, and on approaching him laid his hand kindly on his head, and said :

" What! in tears, my son? Art thou sorry thou hast left thy home — eh, Selim ? "

" No, father, I am not sorry, but home seemed so beautiful as I thought of it compared to that still dark land beyond. There are nothing but black-looking forests across the river, even the sky looks black and desolate, and my heart seems to have caught some of its desolation."

" The forest looks sombrous and dark, my son, because night approaches," said Amer, tenderly. " That black-looking sky which hastens from the east is but the counterpane earth draws about it before folding its arms to sleep. When we shall have crossed the river we will camp, and in the tent, which thou wilt learn to love as thy home, thou wilt forget thy present misery ; and in the morning, when earth is wide awake, and the sun comes out as gay as a bride from the east, and the birds have all left their nests and fill the air with their joyous songs, and the fleet-footed antelope browses in the open glades, thou wilt wonder that thou couldst find it in thy heart to weep."

" Oh, father, I shall weep no more. See, my eyes are already dry;" and Selim raised a brave face towards his father, which was tenderly kissed.

The caravan was soon across the river, and every man and woman was engaged in cutting down young trees and branches to form a stockade, a duty not to be omitted by well-conducted caravans in Africa.

When this was done the people gathered within the camp and prepared their evening meal. The tents were all disposed in a circle, with their doors open towards the centre, where stood Amer bin Osman's tent. Close by the master's tent, on either side, were two or three of the most faithful slaves, who were styled fundis, or overseers, to whom were given the orders for the conduct of the caravan by the chief.

Over these overseers, for their fidelity and peculiar qualities, were placed two men, who are intended to figure conspicuously in this narrative; their names were Simba (Lion) and Moto (Fire). Where Amer bin Osman the chief went Simba and Moto followed. To these two Amer was as dear as their own hearts, and the boy Selim was their delight; his slightest wish was law to these faithful creatures, who looked upon him as though he were something immeasurably superior to them, as though he belonged to some higher world of which they had no comprehension.

Simba was a giant in form, and a lion, as his name denoted, in strength and courage. He was originally

SIMBA AND FAMILY.

from Urundi, a large country bordering the north-eastern part of Lake Tanganika. He was the son of a chief, and was captured when a boy in battle when Moeni Khheri's father sided with the Wasige against Makala, a quarrelsome king living in the northern districts of Urundi. Being a chief's son he of course belonged to the Wahuma, a superior race of bronze coloured people who formerly migrated from Ethiopia, and from whom only chiefs are selected in the countries of Urundi, Ruanda, Uganda, and Karagwah.

Simba was now in the prime of manhood, and he had lived in the household of Amer bin Osman for twenty years, for Amer, after his arrival at Zanzibar, within a year of his capture, had purchased him, and seeing him to be docile and good-tempered, though uncommonly strong, had almost adopted him as his son.

Some of Simba's feats of strength bordered on the marvellous. Taught by the young kinsmen of Amer the use of the long, sharp sword of the Arabs, and being apt, he had acquired a terrible proficiency with it. He had often walked up alongside of a full-grown goat, and had with one well dealt blow halved the animal from head to tail. Many of his negro admirers verily believed he could perform the same feat upon an ass, so extraordinary was his strength, but he had never attempted it, as the experiment was too costly for his means. He had once carried a three-year-old bullock on his back half way around the plantation of his master, Amer. He had often taken one of the large white donkeys of Muscat by the ears and by a sudden movement of his right foot, had prostrated the animal on his back; and once, upon an extraordinary occasion, had actually carried twelve men on his back and shoulders and chest around his master's house, to the intense wonder of a large crowd of spectators. He could toss an ordinary man ten feet high into the air, and catch him as easily as an ordinary man would catch a small child. But manifold were the stories related with awe of the feats of strength performed by the brave lion-hearted Simba, chief overseer of Amer bin Osman's caravan. By measurement he stood six feet and five inches in his bare feet, and from shoulder to shoulder he measured thirty-two inches.

Moto, or "fire," could not have been better designated. His name, which his master had given him, had been bestowed upon him for his peppery, irascible temper. He was from Urori, as almost any one acquainted with the peculiarities of the various tribes in Central Africa would have sworn. A small wiry frame, indicating cat-like activity, strength, indomitability, capable of enduring great fatigue, characterised the form of Moto. He had also been brought to Zanzibar when a child by a slave-trader, and from a mere caprice had been purchased for twenty dollars by Amer. But his master had never regretted the purchase, for next to Simba, Amer bin Osman preferred Moto. To serve his master Moto would have thrown himself into the fire or leaped into the sea. He was a great hunter, he could track the soft velvet foot of the leopard upon a rock, could tell what animal had broken a blade of grass if a single hair but adhered to it, could stalk an elephant and tickle his belly with a straw without letting the enormous brute know what deadly foe intruded on his presence; and a man slightly inclined to exaggeration, and not at all noted for his veracity, declared by this and by that, that Moto had at one time dragged himself into a jungle after a lion, and, finding the lion asleep, had from sheer bravado walked noiselessly up to him and stepped over his body before he shot him through the head.

If you knew Moto as well as his own best friends knew him, you would describe him as being as brave as a lion, active as a cat, keen-eyed as the fish-eagle, hot as pepper, as hardy as an ass, and faithful as a dog. If you will add that he was a little vain, and never disposed to resent any kind friend boasting of his prowess, you will have a perfect picture of Moto the Mrori.

The first night on the road with some caravans is not very lively; the people are engaged either in thinking of the joys they have left behind them, or they are shy, and are sounding one another's qualities before making advances. But in the camp of Amer bin Osman there was no regret at parting from Zanzibar, since the great master and little master were with them, and every man knew his fellow and mate; thus there was no disruption of friendships, associations, and congenialities. Most of those who were married had their wives with them; those who were not married had their intimate friends and saw time-endeared faces around them. They were all of one household. It was like unto the migration of an entire settlement.

One glance within the huts and at the squatting forms informed you that they were all happy—if not happy, contented. No eyes like the coal-black, the pure well of jet undefiled, of the native African, when the firelight is reflected in their quick sparkles, can so well

D

represent merriness. Those people with those sparkling eyes were merry; they were interesting each other
with their trite stories of very trite lives; but when
a peal of laughter louder than usual startled the camp
and rang through the forest, you may be sure it was
either at a story of hearsay or at something that Simba
or Moto had been saying.

Such a laugh was heard, and instantly all eyes and
mouths were uplifted, and ears seemed to be quickened,
to catch a few words of the story that had caused an
interested group to so loudly vent their delight.

The interested party of laughers were seated around
a miniature bonfire, which Simba and Moto had
kindled some thirty feet or so from the chief's tent.
Selim had lately arrived before it, and Simba had
rolled a mighty log behind his young master and had
asked him to be seated, himself seated on the ground,
attentive and alert to please him; and Moto, not to be
outdone in assiduity by Simba, had just begun to draw
from the recesses of his memory, or from the cells of his
imagination, one of his best stories, when a ludicrous
incident occurred and Selim had laughed heartily.
Their young master had laughed, and of course when
he laughed Simba laughed; then seeing Simba laugh
Moto laughed; and, as real genuine laughter is contagious, all hands laughed, and the outer circle, the
entire caravan, smiled sympathetically.

Moto had commenced his story thus: " One day, when
I was in the caravan of Kisesa—(Abdullah bin Nasib—
you know Kisesa is a great friend of my master Amer,
and if Kisesa liked to have me accompany him, Master
Amer would never say 'No.' It is in his caravan as

fundi I finished my education as a hunter)—travelling through Ukonongo, I—— "

" Have you been to Ukonongo, Moto?" asked Selim.

" Oh, yes, and much farther. Well, I was saying, I—— "

" But, Moto," broke in Selim again, " Ukonongo is the best country for shooting, is it not?"

" At certain seasons only. In the dry season, yes. Then all kinds of game travel to the neighbourhood of the Cow River, and shooting is plenty then, but for elephants give me Kawendi. I was just going to say, I—— "

" But, Moto," broke in a naked youngster called Niani,* or the Monkey, a nephew of Moto, " are there lions in Kawendi? because—— "

But he was not permitted to finish, as Moto sprang up furious, with his kurbash (a hippopotamus hide whip) in hand. Niani noticed the movement, and with the activity of his namesake, took a flying leap over the fire, and alighted in a huge dish half full of rice that was slowly simmering over some hot embers. There was a loud shriek, and clots of hot rice splashed in all directions, several falling on the nude shoulders of the group, which started them all to their feet. Then Selim laughed heartily at the catastrophe. Simba followed, then Moto stayed his hand and laughed, and the laugh was taken by all, and this was the cause of that which startled the camp and drew our attention.

" That is what some people get for interrupting a good story," said Moto, sententiously addressing unfortunate Niani, who was rubbing his scalded feet and

* Niani is a Kisawahili term for monkey.

moaning piteously in a low tone; but the words were
said as more of a hint to Selim.

"Well, go on, Moto; I will not disturb you another
time," said Selim.

"Ah, I did not mean you, dear master," replied
Moto. "You may disturb me as often as you like."

"Well, well, go on with your story, and let it be a
good one," urged Selim.

"All right, master. Well, I had just said that I was
in the caravan of Kisesa, travelling through Ukonongo,
when that little monkey Niani interrupted me, and so
got——"

"No, no, Moto, it was I that interrupted you; but
go on with your story, and never mind poor Niani; he
has got his punishment, and you punish me too by not
telling me the story," asked Selim.

"Yes, yes, Moto, go on!" said the deep-voiced Simba.
"Do you not hear the young master ask you? Heh,
what is the matter with the man to-night?"

"Oh, well, if you are all going to interrupt me, the
story will last from here to Rua," said Moto in a careless tone.

"Moto," said Selim, "I will never disturb you any
more—there's my hand on my promise."

Moto's pride and vanity being gratified by this ready
promise of Selim, cleared his throat, and commenced
this time in earnest, as follows:

"We were travelling through Ukonongo, and had
reached Sultan Mrera's village, when Kisesa asked me
to go to the forest along the river to look for game,
adding that if I brought a Kudu antelope to the camp
he would give me four yards of cotton cloth.

"After a good breakfast of rice and curry, which Kisesa sent me from his table to make me strong, I started. It was then about noon, and the sun was very hot, though once in the forest it would be cool enough. In a short time I was by the river, a crooked little stream of delicious and clear water. I walked along, looking to the right and left constantly for hours, when just about two hours before sunset, I heard a hollow sound, as though the earth was shaking; but I knew, after listening, that the sound was caused by a herd of elephants walking in filo along the hard-baked road, and that they were approaching the stream to drink.

"In a moment I was down on my face like a dead man. The grass was about two feet high, and very thick, so that I was quite safe, if I did not stir, and I am too old a hunter not to know what to do in the neighbourhood of elephants. As the elephants passed by I lifted my head up cautiously, and counted them. Two—four—six—eight—ten enormous beasts, who tossed their trunks aloft, as if they were masters of the forest, and knew it. Careless and confident, they passed on, and I wriggled out until I was some distance away; then I jumped up and leaped across the stream, and on all fours crept across a deep bend of it; then lying flat along the ground, I moved forward towards a great tree, a baobab, that stood between me and them. If the elephants had all stood in a row drinking from the river I could never have come up to them unseen, but one greedily thirsty fellow was standing in the middle of the stream, almost touching the baobab tree with his side, so that he completely hid me from the others.

"I thought that Kisesa, though he had not told me to shoot elephants, would not mind my bringing him two great ivory tusks, which would be worth at Zanzibar 500 dollars, since he had come to Ukonongo to get ivory, and that if he gave me four yards of cloth for a Kudu antelope, that he would give many more yards of cloth for 500 dollars worth of ivory.

"This thought gave me confidence to proceed, and imperceptibly I was drawing nearer and nearer to the monster near the baobab. After a few minutes, which seemed to me to be hours, I was lifting myself to my feet, girding my loins tighter, and preparing myself for a run for life. But just at the moment I ought to have fired, a mischievous idea came into my head; the hind quarters of the brute were so close to me that I thought it would be great fun, and a good story to tell afterwards if I tickled the brute's tail. Cutting a long straw, I extended the point towards the tail, and then traced a line across the leg to the belly. It was delicious to watch the flurry of the short tail and the circles it described, and to watch the brute half leaning against the tree, and rubbing it with his ponderous form. When this play had lasted a short time, I brought down my gun, and pointing it about three inches or so behind the left fore leg, on a level with the position of the beast, I fired. The elephant sprang forward, and by doing so disclosed to the astonished eyes of the others my retreating form, which, I assure you, was bounding over the low bushes and grass tops as if I were an antelope.

"The elephants got over their surprise in a second then a wild snort of rage greeted my ears, and I knew

by the crash of bushes and splash of water that they
were after me. Never an antelope bounded over the
plains of Ukonongo, when chased by a lion, as I
bounded then; never a timid quagga's fleet feet carried
him away from the hunters as my feet carried me over
that ground. But it seemed to me for a time as if it
were of no use—the awful crashing got nearer and
nearer, and as I turned my head to measure the distance the foremost was from me, I saw the lord of the
herd was but thirty paces from me. He seemed to
tower up to three times his usual height, and to swell
out into proportions three times as vast as his natural
size; his great ears stood straight out as flat as a
board, as if they were wings, and his eyes were like
coals of fire; his trunk was lifted up, as you sometimes
see the deadly forest snake before it strikes his victim;
his head was stretched out, as the head of a giraffe
when chased by a beast of prey, and the two long,
mighty, gleaming teeth seemed awful just then. His
eyes caught a glance of mine as I turned them towards
him, and that instant he uttered another snort of rage,
which was as fearful as the war-horn of the Watuta.
But it gave me greater speed; if I ran before, I now
flew; yet closer and closer the monster came. I suppose he was about fifteen feet from me when the
tricks of the elephant hunters of Urori came to my
mind. I had noticed that though the big elephant was
the foremost, he was also the outermost on my right —
the other elephants were to my left, and they seemed
to be following the lord of the herd rather than any
particular object. In an instant after observing this,
I shot out straight to the right from the direction I

was first going as hard as my feet and legs would take me. The elephants passed on, the rushing sound of their feet going through the grass was like unto the wild pepo of Ugogo, accompanied by thunder, when it comes sweeping over the plain, with a moan and a rush, whirling and tossing bushes, and even small trees about sometimes, and darkening the air with what it tears from the earth.

"I had got fifty yards away before the elephants could turn about. Only an instant, however, they stopped. They caught sight of me again, and with loud, furious snorting again they charged in a mass. I am a pretty swift runner as you all know, but the best of us seem to crawl compared to the speed of an elephant for the first few hundred yards. The elephants, especially one or two of the foremost, were gaining on me rapidly; the stubborn grass whipped my legs severely as I ran, and was a sore distress to me, but the thick hide of my pursuers was proof against it. A little distance off before me, and to the left, was a clump of brushwood. I thought if I could gain it, I would be comparatively safe, as I could find somewhere to hide. In a few moments I reached it, and looking sharply about, I discovered, a little distance off, half hidden by grass and brush, a hole in the ground, which I knew to be that of the wild boar. I thought it would be a capital place to hide, provided the boar was out of his hole, and in a second I was on my face crawling backwards into it. I had barely crawled in when I heard the elephants' thunder overhead, and at the same instant I heard a deep grunt behind me, and immediately after I was shot out of that hole, like a bullet out of a gun, and I lay on the ground a few paces from it like a dead man. I had just consciousness enough to know that I had been grievously wounded in one of my hams by the furious owner of the underground excavation in which I found shelter; that the boar had darted off in the direction the elephants had taken, then I lost all knowledge of everything for many hours.

"When I recovered it was night. And soon I heard shots in the distance, fired at regular intervals, and thinking perhaps that they were my friends looking for me I fired my gun, which was immediately answered by another. By firing thus every few minutes I succeeded in guiding them to where I lay, for I found myself unable to move.

"When my friends found me, and were acquainted with my condition, they lifted me on their shoulders and bore me to the camp, where I lay unable to move for about three weeks. The marks that savage boar gave me I have yet, and shall have to my dying day. I have spoken."

"Well, what became of the elephant you shot?" asked Selim, when Moto had concluded his graphic and interesting story.

"He was picked up next day, about two hours' distance from the place where I had shot him. His trail was easily known by his blood. Kisesa made quite a sum of money from that elephant, as the tusks were as large as any that were ever seen."

"How many cloths did Kisesa give you?" asked Selim.

"Only forty."

"*Only* forty? That was a good deal, was it not?" asked Selim.

"Forty cloths for what brought him three hundred at Zanzibar! Do you call forty cloths a great deal?" asked the offended Moto.

"But you forget, Moto," said Selim, "that you were a slave in the employ of Kisesa; that the gun you carried was his, that the powder and shot you used to shoot the elephant with were his, that the clothes you then wore were given you by him, that the food which gave you strength was purchased with his money, that the men who carried you from the forest to the camp were his slaves, that the men who looked after you when you were sick and wounded were his men, that the man who found the elephant dead belonged to Kisesa, and that without Kisesa's aid you would have died in the jungle, perhaps, and never have seen the elephant again. What do you say now, Moto?" asked Selim.

"You are right, young master, as you are always," said the humiliated Moto, which remark was echoed and applauded by everybody around the camp fire.

"But, now," said the hitherto quiet Simba, "tell us about that battle Kisesa had with the Warori—your own people—and how you saved the king's son."

"Ay, do tell us that. It must be an interesting story," said Selim. "I shall sleep all the better for it this first night of my life in Africa."

"Well, when my friend Simba asks and my young master commands me, Moto is always ready," said Moto, adding a huge log to the already cheerful fire-pile. "It is not such a long time ago but what I can remember every detail of it. It may have happened

three or four years ago; Kisesa was then in Unyanyembe. He was mortally offended with the Arab chief
Sayd bin Salim, the Wali of the Sultan of Zanzibar at
Unyanyembe, and most of the Arabs took sides with
Kisesa, as they knew he was a brave, powerful, and rich
chief, who might defy even the Sultan of Zanzibar if he
chose to do so.

"When Sayd bin Salim requested the Arabs to assist
him in fighting the black chief of Kahama in Ugolo,
Kisesa refused to go, and most of the other Arabs did
the same, as they said that Kahama was but a small
village and that the son of Salim had soldiers enough
paid by the Sultan of Zanzibar to do that kind of
fighting. Now the son of Salim, though he knows how
to govern Arabs and keep the peace with peaceful
merchants, has neither head nor heart for fighting. (It
takes Kisesa to do that work.) So two or three weeks
after Sayd bin Salim had gone to the war we were not
at all astonished to see the Wali come back well beaten
by Kahama; and Kisesa and the other Arabs had a
good laugh at him.

"When soon after the war with Urori broke out, and
Sayd bin Salim was requested to call every Arab to the
war, Sayd bin Salim refused; but said that if Kisesa
desired to go, he, as king's governor of Unyanyembe,
would empower Kisesa to lead the Arabs to war, and
make him chief of the army. Kisesa accepted at once,
and the principal Arabs at once volunteered to go with
him. Within a very few days Kisesa left Unyanyembe
with nearly a thousand men for Urori, so that Unyanyembe looked like a deserted place.

"I think it was on the twentieth day—I am not
sure—of the march, that after travelling through

Unyangwira and Kokoro we came near Kwikuru, the capital of Urori. We slept on our arms that night until about the eighth hour, when at a given signal we all crept through the bushes for about an hour, and by the moonlight we saw just ahead of us the boma (palisade) of the king's village. I assure you we did not stop long to look at it, for our horns gave the signal and we all ran for the boma. Quick as a flash of powder in the musket-pan, as you may say, the men of Kisesa were at the palisade, and had their guns pointed at the village through the bars; but not a gun was fired, as Kisesa knew how to make war.

"Kisesa blew his horn, and a voice from the village shouted out to ask who we were, and what we wanted.

"Our chief replied, 'Come out to fight, for Kisesa is at your gates.'

"'Kisesa!' said the voice, in an astonished tone. 'Kisesa! it cannot be Kisesa from Unyanyembe!'

"'It is Kisesa, and no other man. I am Kisesa, and I have come to kill you.'

"The man said then, 'Kisesa has been in a hurry to lie to come so soon to Kwikuru, the capital of the King of Urori. Does Kisesa usually fight in such a hurry? It has been our custom to talk first before we fight. What does Kisesa mean?' asked the King, for it was he, though we could not see him, as he took care not to let himself be seen.

"'Thou art a dog, and a son of a dog!' answered Kisesa. 'Hast thou not been making war upon our merchants, killing them in the forest for the sake of their ivory? Hast thou not been mutilating their young sons by cutting off their right hands? Hast thou not been beating the prisoners with sticks until

many of them have died under the torture? Hast thou
not asked for Kisesa, the great Arab warrior, that thou
mightest flay him alive and make clothes of his skin
to cover thy nakedness? Lo! Kisesa is here at thy
gates; come and take his skin.'

"'Kisesa, thou hast done well to come to me before
I came for thee. Kisesa, thou art a good man, but I
will flay thee alive nevertheless, and thou shalt know
what it is to come to the gates of Mostana, like a thief
at night. They told me thou wert brave. Is it brave
to do what thou hast done? My young son Kalulu,
who is but a child, is more than a match for thee.
Halt where thou art until daylight, that we may at
least see him who is said to be brave, but is but a night
prowler!'

"'Mostana, if that be thy name,' said Kisesa, 'I will
wait for thee until the sun appears in the east. Thou
shalt then look on my face and die. I have spoken.'

"So we all laid down close against the palisade outside. Every fifth man was to stand watch while the
others slept. As soon as the sun appeared in the east,
over the tops of the trees, the horns of Kisesa were
heard, calling us all to be ready; and at the same time
the drums of Mostana were heard. I had been sleeping soundly, and I now looked in between the posts of
the palisade to see what kind of a place we were about
to attack. It was a large village, circular, like all in
Urori, but the palisades were strong, and but lately
put up. There were scores of huts inside, but what
struck me as something very uncommon in Urori was
an inner enclosure (like that in the King's village at
Unyanyembe), which surrounded Mostana's quarters,

so that he could from the inside hold out as long as we could outside if we were not more numerous or better armed than he.

"We were not long before we were at it like lions, shooting into one another's faces, or as near them as the defences would permit. It was evident that Mostana was getting the worst of the fight, for we were far more numerous and had better guns, and farther apart from each other, while Mostana's people were crowded together, and every bullet that went in through the palisade wounded or killed some one, and the cries of the women and groans of the wounded were frightful.

"After shooting at each other for an hour Kisesa gave notice to have the two gates opened, and into these we poured in crowds, and as fast as we got in we took advantage of the huts that were outside the king's quarters. Then, working ourselves gradually, shooting as we went, we sprang at the other palisade, and putting our guns through, fired into the crowds. I assure you the scene was horrible; the people dropped to the ground as fast as we could count them, so that in a short time the few that were left began to cry for mercy, shouting 'Aman! Aman!' The gates of the inner defences, or the King's quarters, were broken open at once, and Kisesa's men bounded in, making such noise that might be heard a day's march from the village. They fired their guns, they hooted, they shouted, they sang. Were they not victors? I was carried in with the crowd which poured in towards the King's house. Old Mostana—he was not very old either—was fighting to the last, firing his arrows so fast into the crowd that many of Kisesa's men, even while they were singing the songs of victory, fell dead, pierced to the marrow with the deadly arrows which flew unerringly from his bow. At his side was a young lad, younger by three years than Master Selim is; he was tall, straight, and slender as one of the light assegais he threw so dexterously and quickly into the crowds who were pressing onward towards the King. Kisesa himself was with us, and on seeing the matchless spirit and bearing of the boy, he shouted, 'Kill Mostana, but save the boy. Fifty cloths to him who brings me Kalulu alive.' I am a Mrori, and I loved that boy for his bravery the first time I saw him, and I determined to save him if possible for Kisesa and at the same time get the fifty cloths. A shield belonging to one of Mostana's men lay on the ground; I snatched it up, and defending my body with it, I cried out to Kalulu in Kirori that I was his friend and wished to save him. The boy, surprised for a moment, desisted, but seeing me advance hurriedly towards him, and fearing that I only wished to do him harm, he hurled another light spear at me. So true was the boy's aim, he hit the centre of the shield and pinned my hand to it, and at the same moment I saw his father fall across the threshold of his house. I heard the boy give one wild shriek, and then saw him disappear inside; but darting forward, heedless of the pain in my arm, I arrived at the door of the house, only in time, however, to see him escape by another door, that led outside of the royal quarters. I saw him take a hasty look, and, as if the coast was clear and no danger to be apprehended, shoot off like an arrow, and the head-dress of fish-eagle feathers he wore streamed behind him straight, so swift were his feet. I permitted him to spring to the palisade, but before he could well clear himself of its tall posts I laid hold of his feet; but not for long, however. As the fiery lad clung with one hand, he used the other in threatening to strike me, and the spears of the Warori are sometimes dangerous. When I released him, quicker than the black leopard of the jungles of Kawendi, or the ever-jumping monkey of Sowa, he sprang over the posts, and picking himself up, he raced away for liberty as if for life. But I am a Mrori too, and I am not to be outdone by a boy, even though he were sired by Mostana; so snatching the assegai, which hitherto had pinned my hand to the shield, I tossed the shield over to the other side, and sprang after it myself. It did not take long for me to catch the fugitive; he had just entered the belt of wood when I caught hold of his arm and bade him, in the Kirori tongue, not to run away from a friend. He turned round to me with such a look in his large eyes— eyes that truly were like unto those of the young Kalulu, his namesake, which, as it bounds over the low brush or grass clumps in the plains of Urori and Ubena, seems never to touch the ground as it leaps lightly and swiftly away from the cruel hunter. Perhaps it is because I am a Mrori that I was rather partial to the son of Mostana, captive of my bow and of my spear, but when I saw those large, soft, pleading eyes turned up to me, I wept for him who was a king's son yesterday, and to-day was Moto's slave.

"'You are a Mrori,' said the boy, 'and will you make Mostana's son a slave to those robbers?'

" 'My lord, the Arabs are not robbers ; they are rich merchants trading for ivory, who, when angered by wrong done to them, band together to fight. Mostana is dead ; the Arab chief, Kisesa, wants you for himself. Will you submit ?'

" 'You are not a Mrori ; no Mrori warrior would talk of submitting to be the slave of an Arab dog, however great or rich he is. Mostana has warned me often how it would all end. But Kalulu, his son, will never be a slave. Listen, my brother * I was born in that village ; I first drew breath within that palisaded enclosure ; there I first learned to lisp "baba," "mama ;" there I first learned to distinguish friend from foe, light from darkness, good from evil ; there I first learned how to handle the spear and the bow, how to throw the war-hatchet and the knob-stick ; under those trees I have sucked at my mother's paps, and when older have listened to the elders of the village and counsellors of my father relating the traditions of my great warrior tribe ; in those fields now green with corn I have played with friends of my own age—with Luhambo, Lotaka, Rorata Natona, Kahirigi, and others ; in the pleasant stream which is now before us I have bathed and caught the great fat fish ; in this forest I have chased the honey-bird, and searched for the sweet treasures the wild bees stored for me ; here the antelope and fleet zebra invited me to the chase ; even the very trees seem to know me, and recognise me as belonging to this portion of earth. But now Mostana, my father, is dead, my village will be burnt, my

* All strangers are addressed in "Urori" as brothers. All travellers are hailed as brothers.

E

kins men are either dead or bound captives, the fields will be left desolate, and what I have hitherto known as home will become a wilderness. Yet for all this, when Cruelty would even pause before going farther, I am pleading to a Mrori for the only thing left for me to ask—my liberty! Mrori, speak; must I ask twice for that which was never yours to give? Will you not let me depart to my uncle, to remember the friendly Mrori who scorned to take advantage of a boy?'

"'Go in peace, my lord, go in peace: I did but try you. Moto is your friend, and if you can remember Moto when you live happily amongst your uncle's tribe, Moto will ever be grateful.'

"'Is Moto your name?' he said delightedly, taking my hand, while his eyes danced with joy. 'Then let the Warori of my uncle's tribe ever remember your name with pleasure. Katalambula, my uncle, shall remember your name for future benefit, should we ever meet again. Kalulu has spoken.'

"He embraced me as if I were his father, and then snatching his weapons and the shield which I gave him, he turned away and, light as the jumping antelope,* bounded away from sight.

"Come, my friends, the night is far spent, let us retire," said Moto, when he had ended his really interesting story.

"What, Moto! I am surprised that you let the fellow go, when you might have got fifty cloths for him," said Selim.

"And I am not," said Simba, "for I know Moto, and it is for that I love him as my brother. Why, he was

* The springbok.

a king's son ! Should Moto take that from Kalulu which
was not his to take ? Ah, Moto! thou art good as
the yellow metal which all the rich Arabs at Zanzibar
love so much, and which the Banyan women love to
hang on their yellow breasts. Master Selim, you know
not what it is to be a slave ; pray Allah that you never
will know," said Simba as he rose and yawned.

"I a slave! you are dreaming, Simba. An Arab
cannot be a slave, but a black man was born to be an
Arab's slave," replied Selim, with some tartness in his
tones.

"Well, well, we will talk of this another time," said
Moto quietly, "eh, Simba, my brother? Master, the
journey is far to-morrow; before the sun rises, your
father has said, we must be on the road to Simbamwenni. It is now late. Good night, young master."

"I shall go to my father's tent to dream of Mostana's
son, Kalulu," said Selim, recovering his temper, saying
which, he walked away.

CHAPTER III.

THE next morning the caravan of Amer bin Osman was
afoot at an early hour, all hands feeling in a more
excellent mood, if possible, than they were when they
retired to sleep. They shouted, they sang merrily, and
enjoyed themselves in much the same manner that all
caravans do, when fresh and cheery they start on a
trading campaign.

On the tenth day, on coming from under the shadows
of the great scarps of the Uruguru range, the walled town
of Simbamwenni lay before them, and on a green grassy
slope, trending to the River Ungerengeri, were the white
tents and the huts of the caravans they were to join.

As is customary in Africa, the new comers made
their presence known to their friends by repeated discharges of musketry, which brought out the Arabs and
their people by the hundreds.

The greeting which Amer bin Osman received from
his friends was warm and cordial. The chiefs all

embraced him after the manner and custom in vogue amongst the Arabs, while their followers were not a whit less expressive to Amer's people. Selim was received with extraordinary cordiality by the younger Arabs, some of whom were of his own age, and after interchanging the long list of greetings customary in Arab countries, they all adjourned to Khamis bin Abdullah's tent, who had by acclamation been elected chief of the expedition, where in a short time dishes of curried chicken and rice, kabobs, and sweets of various kinds, with nice biscuits, were served as a substantial repast for the hungry travellers.

Though conversation was animated and varied enough before Amer and his son Selim had satisfied their hunger, it did not touch upon the object of the expedition, but simply as to what events had transpired during the journey from the coast to Simbamwenni; but when the repast was ended, and the dishes were cleared, Khamis bin Abdullah broached the subject near and dear to each heart just then—the future journey or route of the expedition.

"The great question, Amer bin Osman, about which we have been attempting to decide," said Khamis, "is, shall we take the road to Mbumi, in Usagara, and skirt the Mukondokwa mountains to reach Uhehe, and strike a straight line to Urundi, thence to Marungu, south of the Tanganika, for Rua, or shall we follow the old road through Marenga M'Kali and Ugogo to Unyanyembe, thence to Ujiji, and across the Lake Tanganika to Rua? I should like to have thy opinion, for thou art a man of age and experience, though thou hast never been to this land before."

"Allah knows," responded Amer bin Osman, " that I know very little of this country. If thou dost not wish to decide thyself, as chief, which is the best road, I should like to hear from thee, or others, about the differences between the two roads, and the kind of countries which they traverse."

"Well," said Khamis bin Abdullah, deliberately, "if I were by myself I should prefer the old road, but there are some here of my friends who know the country as well as I do, who think we are strong enough to be able to march along the southern road.

"If we," continued he, " take the old road we shall have the Wagogo to pay tribute to, or fight, as we like, between here and Rua; but if we take the southern road, those thieves, the Wahehe, will have to be looked after closely when going through their country; then we have the Warori, a more powerful people than the Wagogo, to meet, whom we must make friends or fight; then beyond Urori we have the Watuta, a tribe related to the Warori, who speak their language and are more than the Warori, whom we shall be obliged to pacify or make war against, just as we feel, and beyond the Watuta is a straight road to the ivory country of Rua. I will admit that the southern road is by three or four months the shortest, but I cannot admit that it is the safest."

"And what do my friends think of the two roads? What does Sultan bin Ali say?" asked Amer.

"I say," replied old Sultan, "that it would be far more prudent in us to take the northern road. The Wagogo are far more mischievous and insolent than any I know, but we need not fear them if we are wise, and do not provoke war."

" Well, if Sultan bin Ali and Khamis bin Abdullah
think that the northern road is the best, I would prefer
to be guided by their judgment; but what do the
majority of the chiefs think of it ?" asked Amer, directing his glance to the others who had not yet spoken of
this matter to him.

Said Khamis : "There are ten chiefs of us, including
thyself; seven of us are for the southern road, and thou,
and I, and Sultan bin Ali are for taking the northern
road."

"Yes," said Sheikh Mohammed, "for this reason.
We are over 600 strong, all armed with guns. It is
true we shall have to pay tribute to the Warori and the
Watuta, and may experience some trouble from the
Wahehe, who are dogs and sons of dogs; but the tribute,
if we pay any, will not be much, and will be cheaper in
the end than the three months we would lose on the
southern road ; besides, we save the cloth we would
have to pay the Wagogo, who are insolent besides
being extortionate. Three months on the road cost us
altogether about 900 doti, or fifteen bales of cloth. Put
the Warori tribute against the Wagogo, and we have fifteen bales of cloth, out of which we can pay the tribute
to the Watuta. It is evident we effect a saving, besides
gaining three months time."

" That is a very good way of putting it," said Amer,
" but what dost thou say, Khamis, about the comparative
safety of the two roads ? Is there more danger to be
apprehended from the Warori and the Watuta than we,
a trading caravan, would care to meet ?"

" That is the view we should take of the matter, and
not of the little cloth we should save," responded

Khamis. "Experience tells me to avoid the Warori, if possible, but above all the Watuta. The Warori are brave and strong, and sometimes very dangerous; but I have always heard the Watuta were dangerous, that they are a fierce tribe who live by robbing caravans, and I should not like to undertake to decide for the southern road without the concurrence of every chief here present."

"Well, thou hast my consent if thou dost require it, and if God pleases he can guide us in safety through any tribe in Africa. Far be it from me to disagree with those who know better than I what roads to take, and what will best serve our interests," said Amer.

"And if thou dost require mine for thy decision," said old Sultan bin Ali, "I shall not deny the right of any of the other chiefs to have as much a voice in the caravan as I have; so now, friend Khamis, thou hast the liberty to agree or disagree, and hast a right to decide whether thou wilt lead us through Urori or through Ugogo to the ivory country."

"I have only one voice in the matter, and if ye are all of one consent that it is better for us to march by the southern road, and still of one mind that I shall lead ye, I have nothing more to say," responded Khamis.

"We are, we are," they all replied.

"Very well, the march begins to-morrow," said Khamis bin Abdullah, "at one hour before sunrise. We follow the old road as far as Mbumi, when we shall turn south."

The news was soon communicated through the host of followers, and each knot and group had their own opinions, which they discussed with as much acumen and wisdom as their superiors had evinced.

But not to lose sight of our friends Simba and Moto, let us listen to what they have to say concerning the unusual line of route about to be adopted.

It is night. The camp fires are blazing by the score; huts are ranged around the immense circle, which is more than 500 feet in diameter, and scores of huts dot the centre of the circle, with their doors opening according as the taste, fancy, or caprice of the builders suggested. The huts of the Arab chiefs are arranged in a line close to one another, but still far enough to insure the privacy and exclusion which every Arab so much loves for the female portion of his household.

Near the tent of Amer bin Osman are seated before the usual fire-pile the faithful slaves Simba and Moto with the fundis of the other Arabs; and on carpets of Oman manufacture are placed Selim, the son of Amer, Khamis, the young son of Khamis bin Abdullah, the leader, Isa, the son of Sheikh Thani, and Abdullah and Mussoud, brothers, aged fourteen and twelve respectively, the sons of Sheikh Mohammed.

We hear Selim's voice first, as we pay him this attention for personating the hero of this veracious romance.

Said he : " Well, Simba ;— ah, Isa, you do not know what a treasure Simba is ; he is so great, so wise, so strong !— what do you think of the southern road ? do you think we shall see more fun ?"

" My young master, I fear so," answered Simba, while at the same time he never lifted his head, so apparently intent was he in keeping his flint-lock musket clean—a favourite occupation with Simba.

" You fear so !" said Isa, in a tone of surprise. "What, you fear that we shall see some fun ! Fie, Simba ! did you not hear your young master say you were brave and strong, and why should you fear we should have some fun?" he asked, in a sneering tone.

Simba, turning his wise and large eyes upon Isa, said: "Ah, Master Isa, you are a boy, and cannot understand."

"Hear the slave!" shouted Isa, laughing boisterously at Simba's solemnity. "Hear the man!" he repeated. "Isa, son of Mohammed, is a boy and cannot understand—and cannot understand what—will you tell me, brave Simba?" he asked.

"You cannot understand, child, that what may be fun to some people will be sorrow to others; that we may meet with fun of a kind that neither you nor any of us will much like," said Simba, still rubbing away at the already excessively clean gun, and looking graver than before.

"Why, what is the matter with you to-night?" asked Selim of Simba.

"The truth is, master, I do not like the course the Arabs have taken. I think they have been too hasty in adopting the southern road. None knows it better than friend Moto, and if the great masters had asked of Moto something about the road, my mind would be more easy concerning you and the great master Amer."

"What do you know of it, Moto?" asked Selim. "Speak, and tell us all you know."

"What Simba says is truth," replied Moto. "The Warori are bad, bad, bad, and the Watuta are worse—very bad—and I think we shall have very serious times of it."

"How serious?" asked Selim again.

"I mean that we are very likely to have war with

them. Ever since Abdullah bin Nasib or Kisesa had
that battle with Mostana, the Warori have been wicked.
They have Arab slaves now. They formerly used to
kill their prisoners or torture them, but now they treat
them in the same way that the Arabs treat the Warori
chiefs — they make slaves of them."

"Make slaves of Arabs!" shouted young Khamis, a
sinewy youth of sixteen, and brave as the bravest of men.
"You lie, cur dog ; you lie, slave !" he added furiously.

"Ah, Master Khamis," said Moto, deprecatingly, "if
they are slaves, it was not I who made them slaves ; but
I speak the truth."

"A Bedaween !—a free Bedaween, who owns no
master—a slave ! Moto, you are a liar ; it is impossible.
A Bedaween cannot live in slavery."

"But there are slaves with the Warori, and some are
Arabs. I swear it," he added solemnly.

"Then for my part," said young Khamis, "I am
glad that my father has taken this road. The torments
of Eblis light on the unbelieving dogs ! An Arab a
slave ! Then let every Mrori look to himself should he
fall into my power, for, by Mohammed's holy name, I
will torture the reptile to death."

"Hold, young master," said the deep-voiced Simba,
halting a moment in his work, and raising himself to
his fullest height, which, as the firelight danced on his
gigantic form, seemed to add vastness to that which
was vast already.   "Listen to me, Khamis, young son
of Khamis bin Abdullah ; the Warori are bad, as you
heard Moto say, but the Warori are men, and I have
heard a good Nazarene, one of the white men at Zanzibar, say that all men are equal. If the Warori are

men, and are lords of their own soil, and if Arabs
trouble them, or will not do them justice, what great
wrong are the Warori guilty of if they fight; and if
they catch Arabs prisoners in war, why should they
not treat them as the Arabs would treat the Warori?
Answer me that."

"Why, Simba," asked the eldest of the sons of Mussoud, "do you know what the sacred Kūran says? I
remember what the good Imam has told me often:
*Verily the fruit of the trees of Al Zakkum shall be the
food of the unbelievers, as the dregs of oil shall it boil in
the bellies of the damned, like the boiling of the hottest
water. When ye encounter the unbelievers strike off their
heads until ye have made a great slaughter among them,
and bind them in bonds, and either give them a free dis-
mission afterwards or exact a ransom, until the war shall
have laid down its arms.'* And in another place the
Kūran says, according to the holy and learned Imam,
*' And as to those who fight in defence of God's true religion,
God will not suffer their works to perish; he will guide
them, and will dispose their heart aright; and he will lead
them into paradise, of which he hath told them."*

"There, Simba," said Isa, triumphantly, "what do you
think now of slaves and true believers? Do you not think
it right for us to take and capture those who waylay us,
and make them slaves for their perfidy and savagery?"

"I think the same as before," answered Simba. "I
do not know the Kūran so well as Abdullah, it is true,
but I know that the same God who gave you sense and
feeling gave the savages of Urori some sense and feeling as well; but I should like to know what my young
master Selim's thoughts are upon these subjects."

" To tell you the simple truth would be to tell you that I never thought much of these things," answered Selim, in a mild tone. " My father has slaves, and my relations own a great number They are all well looked after, and I have never heard that they were much astonished at their condition. I have seen slaves punished and killed ; but they had done wrong, and they deserved their punishment. Neither my father nor my relations ever gave me to suppose that by keeping slaves they were committing wrong, and you surely cannot expect me, who am but a boy and the son of my father, to say anything against my elders. Whatever Amer bin Osman does is right ; at least, so I have heard men say, and shall I, his son, judge him ?"

" Bravely spoken," said the impetuous Khamis. " Bravely said, my brother Selim ; but, instead of speaking to Simba as thou hast done, thou shouldst have taken thy kurbash (whip) to him, and taught the dog to watch the doorstep of his master, and not be teaching the son of Amer."

" You are over hasty, Khamis," replied Selim, in a deprecating tone. " Simba is good and true to me and to my father's household. My father loves him, and I love him, black though he be, as if he were my brother. Simba and Moto are worth their weight in the yellow metal which our women love to adorn their necks with ; yet, did it depend on my voice, a thousand times their weight of gold would not purchase them."

Both Simba and Moto were so affected at this that they both fell on their knees, and crawled up to their young master to embrace his feet, thus testifying the great love they bore him; but Selim would not permit this, and said:

"Nay, my good Simba, and you, Moto, rise. I think you men, not slaves, and you need not kiss my feet to show me how much you love me. You are my friends, and I shall ever esteem you as such."

"My good young master," said Simba, in a voice broken with emotion, "we are your servants, and we are proud of it. Are we not, Moto?"

"Indeed, we are," said Moto.

"What Arab tribe can boast a lad of your years with so much beauty and heart? Your eyes, young master, are blacker than the richest, ripest singwe (a species of wild plums) of Urundi, and as large as those of the sportive kalulu (young antelope); and when they are covered with your eyelids, we have often compared them while you were asleep, and Moto and I watched you, to the lotus which hides its beauty at eve from the fell touch of night. And your flesh, though not white like the bloodless pale children of the white races, is like the warmer colour of ivory, and beautiful and clear as the polished ivory ornaments of my people in Urundi: your limbs, clean and shapely, are firm and hard as ivory tusks. You are like a young palm-tree in beauty and strength. He is a happy man who calls you son, and your mother laughs for joy in her sleep when she dreams of you. Your slaves are proud to call you master."

"Amen, and amen," responded Moto, while tears descended his cheeks. "Simba has spoken nothing but the truth; he never utters lies. Master Selim knows what Simba and Moto say they mean. Evil cannot

approach him while we are near, nor can danger lurk
unseen. Rocks shall not wound his feet, neither shall
thorns prick his tender skin. If the journey is long
Simba is as strong as a camel, and Moto is fleet of foot
as the zebra, and enduring as the wild ass of Unyamwezi. Moto has spoken."

"Eh, Khamis, and thou, Isa, hear and understand,"
said Selim, smiling. "Where is the Arab who does
not love the Nedjid mare, which partakes of his food, as
the wife of his bosom? But in Simba and Moto I have
two faithful friends. I have a camel, a zebra, and an
ass, and you tell me to beat them, Khamis. Fie, boy!"

"Boy, indeed! I am older than thou, and taller and
stronger. Thou art a child, or thou wouldst not
believe the fulsome words of these lying knaves. I
have seen the world more than thou hast, and I assure
thee on my head I never saw the black man yet who
could keep his hands from stealing and his evil tongue
from lying. I—Khamis, the son of Khamis, the son of .
Abdullah—know whereof I am speaking."

"What a dear little child he is, to be sure!" laughed
Isa. "Is it Selim, the son of Amer, whose eyes are
like the singwe of Urundi, and whose limbs are like
ivory? Eh, Khamis, my brother? Is Selim, the son
of Amer, turned a girl, that his ears court such music?
And if thou art of the complexion of ivory, what are
we, I wonder—I, Isa, son of Mohammed, and Khamis,
son of Khamis?"

While Selim was blushing crimson from shame at the
mocking words of Isa, little Abdullah spoke up, and
said, much to everybody's amusement except Isa's:

"Why, Isa, dost thou mean to say that Selim is not

good-looking? I have often heard my father, Sheikh Mohammed, say he wished I was as good-looking as Selim the son of Amer, though he thought I was every bit as good. And, Isa—now—don't be angry. I—I don't think thee good-looking at all. Thou art almost as black as Simba, and——"

"Liar!" thundered Isa, directing a blow at Abdullah, which was happily warded by Khamis, who, though ever ready to lift the whip against stupid slaves, was averse to see an Arab beaten. Isa, however, darting behind Khamis aimed another blow at Abdullah; but Abdullah, probably seeing that he was very angry, and would strike a serious blow, took to his heels running round the fire, chased by the infuriate Isa. As Isa passed near one side of the fire, Niani, the little negro boy called Monkey, who had hitherto been very quiet, seeing a chance to assist Abdullah, who had praised Selim, thrust his foot forward; and Isa, too much occupied in watching the manœuvres of Abdullah, struck his shins against the obstacle, and came heavily to the ground.

A shout of laughter greeted his fall; but the amusement of Selim was soon changed to real concern as he saw that Isa had quickly recovered himself, and had sprung upon Niani, and catching hold of him by the throat and legs, was carrying him to the great log-fire, to warm him, as he said.

Niani struggled and screamed, but in vain. Isa's ears were closed against a little slave's cries, and he would probably have made good his threat had not Selim, Khamis, and Mussoud, aided by Simba and Moto, interfered, and cried out, "Enough, enough, son of Mohammed. Be not wrathful with a little slave."

As Arabs dislike to see scuffling, or at least always interfere in cases of this kind, it is not to be wondered at Khamis taking the part of Niani, or Simba and Moto exerting their manhood to prevent cruelty; but Niani was not released scot-free; he received several energetic slaps and kicks, which accelerated his departure to a safer distance.

This incident broke up the meeting. Simba and Moto withdrew to their mats on each side of their master Amer's tent. Khamis, Isa, and Mussoud retired to their respective parents' tents, and Selim entered the tent of Amer bin Osman.

Sheikh Amer was seated on his mat in the tent, writing by the light of a single tallow candle on a large broad sheet of stiff white paper; but as Selim entered he put his papers by, and bending on his son an earnest and melancholy look, said:

"My son, light of my soul and joy of my heart, come to me, and do thou sit by me that I may feel thy cheery presence. Dost thou know that my soul feels heavy to-night, as if some great affliction was about to visit me?"

"And what, my father," replied the boy, bending a loving look on him, "couldst thou fear? Art thou not surrounded by kind friends and servants who love thee as their father?"

"Nay, my son, it is not fear that I feel, but a vague foreshadowing of evil which none can feel save those who have much to lose. On whose head the evil will fall I know not, nor do I know from what direction the evil may come; but that evil is nigh in some indistinct

F

shape or another my soul knows, and it is that which has cast this passing cloud over it. But let us speak of other subjects. I have been occupied in writing letters to Zanzibar to my friends, telling them of the new route these wayward companions of ours have adopted, and giving directions about the disposition of my property. Thou knowest, Selim, my child, how I have always loved thee and treated thee, for thou art my hope and joy, and I may not hide it from thee. Should accident happen to me it will be well for me to warn thee now that thou hast an uncle from whom may Allah guard thee. He is a deep, designing man, though he is my brother. Should I die, thy uncle will endeavour to do thee harm, and it is against him I wish to guard thee."

"But, father Amer, what harm can my uncle do me, and why should he wrong me, who have never done him wrong in word, or thought, or deed?" asked Selim, surprised at the tone of his father's voice and this revelation.

"Thou art but a child of tender years and but little aware of the amount of wickedness in this world. Thy uncle is an avaricious man, who would rob thee of thy birthright could he do it, and I believe him to be bad enough to injure thee in some covert way if it were possible. My property amounts to about fifty thousand dollars in slaves and land, and if I die, this property, by right of thy birth as eldest son, is thine wholly, and under no condition or restraint. Wert thou and thy mother to die it would become the property of my brother Rashid, who is a cunning and unscrupulous man."

"Thou dost surprise me, my father; but thou art well, and in good hopes of a long life. I hope thou wilt live a thousand years; I am happy only in being thy son," answered Selim.

"I know it, my son; and if ever a dutiful child made the years of his father seem light, I have that child in thee, but it is well to be provident for those whom we love. For the rest, the will of God be done. There is another subject I wished to converse with thee upon, and that is thy marriage. Dost thou know Leilah?"

"What! Leilah, the daughter of Khamis bin Abdullah?" asked Selim.

"The same," answered Amer.

"Surely, I know her. Have we not played together when we were children, and, now I bethink me, she is the loveliest girl at Zanzibar."

"It is well," said Amer. "Leilah, the daughter of Khamis bin Abdullah is wedded to thee, and the settlements are made between friend Khamis and myself. Should evil happen to me—which God forefend—on thy return to Zanzibar, if thou art of age, seek thou Khamis or, in Khamis's absence, his kinsmen, and claim thou thy wife according unto the custom of thy tribe. I have prepared this future for thee that thou mayst not, like the degenerate Arabs at Zanzibar, seek a wife among strangers to thy race and tribe, and bring disgrace upon the name of my father Osman. Thy kinsmen are proud and belong to the pure Arab race, and they would not think well of my memory if I had neglected to warn thee of thy duty to me and the tribe of which Osman was so loved. Bear thou my words in

thy mind, write them upon the tablets of thy heart,
and obey. Dost thou promise?"

"As God liveth, and as thy soul liveth," responded
Selim earnestly, "to hear is to obey. I shall cherish
as a holy thing thy wish "

"Then do thou retire and rest. These papers are to
be committed to the care of two of my servants, who
will return to Zanzibar to-morrow, when they will, upon
arrival, present them to the Imam. God shield thee
from evil, and may He avert it always from all of us,"
said Amer, as he resumed his work.

"Amen and amen!" replied Selim ; and, after embracing his father, he quietly retired to his carpet to
sleep the sleep of the innocent and young.

At early dawn next morning the horns of the several
kirangozis, or guides, of the respective caravans blew
loud and cheerily, calling on all to prepare for the
march.

Before an hour had elapsed, the tents had been
struck and folded, and each carrier, bearing his burden
of cloth or beads (which were to be used for barter
for ivory with the tribes in the far interior, or
were, in the meanwhile, to purchase food as the caravan
journeyed) or bearing the beds, and carpets, and
rugs, cooking utensils, and despatch-boxes, was following his leaders as he stepped out briskly for the
march.

The Arab chiefs remained behind to bring up the
rear, and then, giving their rifles in charge to their
gun-bearers or favourite slaves, followed on the road
their caravans had taken.

The country before them broke out into knolls and

tall cone-like hills, whose slopes were covered with here
and there patches of dense jungle, or nourished young
forests whose umbrage formed a most grateful shade
during the heat of day.

Soon they had passed the healthy, breezy hills which
are but offshoots of the Uruguru range, and the land
now sloped before them into the low, flat basin of the
Wami river, which during the rainy season becomes
one great swamp.

But the season, at the time our travellers passed
over the Makata Plain—as the basin is called—was
soon after the effects of the violent monsoon had disappeared, in July, when the land presents an unusually
bleached appearance ; the grass is crispy, ripe, and extremely dry, the ground is seamed with ugly rents and
gaps, and the rivers, Little Makata and Mbengerenga,
are but little better than small rivulets. The caravans
were therefore enabled to cross the breadth of the
Makata Plain within two days, and arrived at Mbumi in
Usagara on the evening of the second day.

From Mbumi, in the same order as before, avoiding
the Mukondokwa Valley, the steep passes of Rubeho,
and the desolate, forlorn-looking plains of Ugogo, the
lengthy file of men—carriers, soldiers, and slaves—
skirted the eastern end of the Mukondokwa range, and
on the third day from Simbamwenni, arrived in a
country which differed materially in aspect from that
which they had just left. Mountains of a loftier alti-
tude, in peak upon peak, in tier upon tier, range upon
range, met the eye everywhere. Green trees covered
their slopes in an apparently endless expanse of vegetation. The sycamore, the tamarind, the beautiful

mimosa and kolqual vied with each other in height and beauty, while a thousand other trees, shrubs, plants, and flowers aided to give verdancy and freshness to the scene.

Down the hard, steep, rocky beds of granite and sandstone, with here and there basalt and porphyry, flint, and quartz, foamed the sparkling streams, which, when encountered on an African journey, give zest to the travel and add something to the pleasures of memory. A deep gaping fissure in a high jutting wall of rock, through which bubbled the clear water in volumes, or a great towering rock, with perpendicular walls, to which clung, despite the apparent impossibility, ferns, and plants, and moss, thick and velvety, or a conical hill, which ambitiously hid its head in clouds, were scenes to be treasured up when the march should hereafter become monotonous through excessive sameness of feature.

When they were in camp and had rested, our young friends went into raptures over the bold beauty of mountain scenery, and Selim, and Abdullah, and Mussoud were constantly heard uttering their exclamations of admiration. Selim especially, imbued as he was with the religious faith of his father, was filled with a loftier feeling than that youthful glow and exhilaration which his companions felt. Had he the power, he would like to have poured out his soul in fervid verse about the grandeur, the indescribable beauty of Nature in her wildest and most prolific mood. But being as yet a boy, in whom the poetic instinct and feeling is strong, he said to his father, one day, as the scenery was unusually picturesque :

" Hast thou ever, my father, during these days of
travel over these great mountain-tops, thought that
Palestine, the promised land, must be something like
this ? The land flowing with milk and honey. Why,
honey is already plentiful here—we need but the cows
to furnish milk ; but if milk means the richness of
earth, the never-dying fertility of the soil, look but
once on this view now before us, and tell me, think you
Palestine can be richer than this ? Why, I feel—I do
not exactly know what—but it is something that if I
have never been good or thankful to Allah for his goodness to men, that I could be good for ever in future.
Do you understand this feeling, father Amer, or is it
singular in me ?"

" No, it is not singular, my dear son ; but go on, tell
me what is in thy mind," replied Sheikh Amer, himself
gazing on the revealed might of Nature.

" I have also a feeling—as if I knew it for the first
time—that this earth is large, very large, that it is
immense, without limit or boundary, and that, consequently, God, who made all this, must be truly great.
With the mountain air which I now inhale I seem to
have imbibed something purer, more subtle ; yet that
thing is capable of giving me more expansion. Why
was it that, before coming to these mountains, I never
thought upon this subject? Why was it that, before
to-day, I had no one thought of what might happen to-
morrow, beyond what might happen to our caravan, or
beyond what I should see on the road? Yet at this
moment, though my eyes seem to rest upon this view
of loveliness, I know I do not look upon its details or
any particular object, but they seem to drink it all with

one look, and more, infinitely more, than is contained in
the area before me.   I seem to have eyes in my mind
which have a keener sight, more extended vision, greater
power than the eyes of my head, which can see so far,
and no further.   Yet to the sight of the inner eyes,
which see not, yet can see a thousand times vaster
scene, a thousand times greater prospect is revealed.
Hills, dales, mountains, plains, valleys, forests, rivers,
lakes, seas, all lovely, and lovelier than what we see
now, are comprehended within the scope of my hidden
and unseen eyes.   What is this new sight or feeling,
my father ?   Canst thou tell me ? ”

“ Ah, my child, it is simply the awakening of the
hitherto latent mind; or thought, exercised by but a
faint experience, has been touched by Nature, and
begins to dawn,” replied Amer.   “ God had endowed
thee with the power of thought and of mind when he
gave thee life.   It was impossible that it could remain
for ever hidden.   The hour that a child begins to exercise his mind seeth him advanced a step nearer to
manhood.   It will kindle and expand as thou growest
in years, and in each day’s march thou wilt find fresh
food for it.   It remains with God and thine own nature
to improve it with every breath of air thy lungs inhale.
By diligently reading the Kūran and studying the pre-
cepts of Mohammed—blessed be his name !—thou wilt
so protect that thought pure from evil as the tiny germ
God implanted in thy breast at thy birth.”

“ But tell me, father, one thing—it is different from
that which thou hast been just telling me,” asked
Selim.   “ Thou knowest Simba and Moto are thy slaves.
Is it right, or is it not, to own slaves ? ”

"It is right, certainly, my son. The Kûran sanc-
tions it, and it has been a custom from of old with our
race to own slaves. What has prompted thee to such a
question? Is it another sign of the growth of thy
mind?" his father asked, with a smile.

"I know not," replied Selim, bending his head like
one who hesitated to speak his mind or was unable to
comprehend the drift of his own thought. "But thou
knowest Simba and Moto are good; they love thyself
and me exceedingly, and as I know better than others
that thou art just, and lovest justice for its own sake,
wouldst thou think it right to retain thy slaves in
bondage if they thought it injustice to them?"

"Ha! where is it possible thou couldst have gained
such ideas, child? But, never mind, since thy thoughts
run so wild, I will answer thee," replied Amer. "No,
it is not right in me, or any living man, to retain a
slave in his possession, if the slave thinks it injustice,
or if his slavery galls him; neither is it fair that, after I
have purchased him with my money, I should give him
his liberty for the mere asking; but strict justice would
demand that I set a price of money on his head, or a
term of labour equivalent to the money I paid for him;
and, on the payment of such money, or on the conclusion
of such labour, that he be for ever freed from bondage.
So says the Kûran, and such is our law, and such has
been my practice, and I would advise thee to do likewise
when the time shall come."

"I thank thee, my father; it is all clear to me now.
But stop! harken to that sound! What may that be?
Can it be the hyæna?"

"Yes, the hyænas are out early this evening. They

are hungry; but, Selim, my son, haste to tell Simba and Moto to set the tent on that flat piece of ground near that great tree, and bid them to be sure to turn the door of the tent to-day towards the east."

"Yes, my father;" and Selim, the fleet-footed youth, agile as a young leopard, leaped over several bushes, as he ran to do his parent's bidding.

The camp was situated on a limited terrace or shelf of ground rising above a body of water which more resembled a long narrow lake than a river. Yet it was the river Lofu, or Rufu, as some call it, which in the dry season, like many an African river, loses its current, and becomes a series of long narrow pools, which in some places may be compared to lakes for their length, according to the nature of the ground wherein these depressions are found. If the ground is rocky, or of clayey mud, the water is retained instead of being absorbed, in which swarm multitudes of the *silurus*, or bearded mud-fish. Wherever mud-fish are abundant, crocodiles, the great fish-eating reptiles of the African water, are sure to be found; and wherever crocodiles are found one is almost sure to find the hippopotamus, the behemoth of Scripture; not because crocodiles and hippopotami have any affinity with each other, but because the soil, which retains the water during the hot days of the droughty season, is almost sure to produce in the vicinity of the pools abundance of rich grass and tall cane, the food of the hippopotamus.

About two hours before sunset, soon after camping, Selim, accompanied by Simba and two other men, named Baruti and Mombo, sallied out of the camp with his faithful rifle on his shoulder to hunt for game.

The party travelled towards the upper end of the narrow lake the caravan had camped by. Matete cane, spear, and tiger grass, in profusion, grew near this end, and beyond lay a thin jungle, the borders of which touched the water line. It was to this jungle they directed their steps, for Simba had judged that it was a promising place for such sport as Selim desired.

When the party arrived in the jungle they found the place so delightfully cool, that they could not resist the inclination to rest awhile and cool themselves after the labour and toil of going through the long grass.

Simba and Selim sought the deeper shade of a mammoth and far-spreading tamarind tree, while Baruti sought a place about thirty yards from the tamarind, and Mombo, fatigued with the long journey over the mountains that day, reclined under a young mimosa near the water's edge.

The coolness of the retreat, the silence which prevailed, and the weariness which had come over their tired frames soon induced sleep.

They had not been in this condition long, before the reader, had he or she been there surveying the scene, might have heard the faintest sound of a ripple on the water, and have seen a crocodile's head stealthily rise above the surface, the eyes, cold and fixed, gazing over the slightly protuberant nose, to the spot where Mombo lay. A few minutes the crocodile thus lay still as a heavy sappy log, more than three-fourths buried in the water, but almost imperceptibly the heavy body became buoyant, until the lengthy form, with great ridgy scales marking the line of its spine, lay half uncovered. Without a movement of the long powerful tail, and with but the faintest motion of his heavy, broad, short legs, he propelled himself towards the shore.

A minute he rested there, still as death. One could not have sworn that it was an animal, though one might have been sure, provided no one suggested a cause for doubt. He then lifted his long head, but with the same cautious movement which always characterises this stealthy, cowardly creature of the African deeps, then his enormously long body, until he resembled a huge log, propped up by four short pins—the legs appeared so out of proportion. Anybody at first glance would have seen that in the great, unwieldy form lay tremendous power. The trunk of the largest elephant that was ever born would not equal in size that long tail, which seemed, on account of its length and weight, slightly bent towards the ground at the tip.

Having again halted, he moved forward silently, with a slightly waddling motion; and as he approached the sleeping form of Mombo, his movements were as slow and cautious as those of a leopard before springing upon its prey; but the monster made one hurried, convulsive movement forward, the lower jaw was run under the sleeping man's leg, and the upper jaw came down with a sound like a well-oiled and sound steel spring, and the crocodile swung the limp, warm body around, as a man would swing a cat by the tail. But this swinging movement proved to be poor Mombo's salvation, for he was thus swung against a strong young tree, to which he now clung with the strong tenacity of a man who clings for life, while he gave vent to the full power of his lungs in cries so alarming

RESCUE FROM A CROCODILE.

and shrill that they were heard at the camp of the caravans two miles off. Selim, Simba, and Baruti realised the scene in an instant; they saw the great reptile, horrible and hideous as a nightmare, tugging violently at the leg of the unfortunate man, whose screams pierced their ears, and whose arms almost cracked as he held on with such a fierce grip to the strong young sapling, and they saw that had it not been for its fortunate proximity to him they had never seen Mombo more.

Simba was the first to recover himself, for Selim and Baruti stood as men transfixed.

"Now, master," said he, "your gun—quick! or he will run away. Aim at once; but be cool, or you will kill Mombo. Aim just at his throat, as you see his head lifted up. There, son of Amer, you have slain the brute! Ah! he is trying to escape. Hyah! on, Baruti; your spear, man! Run! come with me, and catch hold of his tail. Two of us can hold him, I think, or delay him at least until he dies. There—take that, you beast!" he shouted as he hurled his broad-bladed spear full through his side, behind the fore leg, into his vitals, which stretched the monster lifeless after one or two convulsive efforts.

Baruti, encouraged by Simba's powerful voice, which roared through the wood in accents so cheery, had at first boldly dashed at the crocodile's tail; but receiving a tremendous thwack on his side from the mighty tail, which was swung about as though it were a well-handled flail—which almost fractured every rib in his body—now stood by, looking fearfully punished and sore.

When the monster had ceased to breathe, Selim and Simba, attracted by the moans of Mombo, hastened to him to examine his condition.

"Poor fellow!" said Selim. "See Simba, the leg is stripped to the bone. What a savage reptile the crocodile is! Do you think Mombo will live, Simba? For after this I should not like to see him die; it would seem as if my big bullet had done no good after all."

"He will live, Inshallah! Inshallah! (Please God! Please God!) Mombo will live to tell the story to his children on the island when he is an old man and past work. You know the hakim (doctor) with us is wise and learned, and, Inshallah! Mombo, after a few days, will be all right. Sho! Mombo die? No, master; Mombo will live to laugh at this. But we must carry him to the camp that the hakim may dress his wounds. Come, Baruti, man—cease your cries. Take your hatchet and cut young straight trees down while I prepare some rope whereon Mombo may be carried. You, young master, may cut a piece of the crocodile's tail to show your father Amer, who will be proud of what you have done."

They all three set to work. Baruti cut two young trees, which he barked. Simba made use of the bark as rope, and in a short time a comfortable bed had been made, on which Mombo was carefully lifted, and in a few moments, Selim having secured his trophy, the three friends set out briskly on their return to camp.

Young Selim, who had "bagged" his first game, was highly gratified by the praise bestowed on him by his father and his father's people, and the braggart Isa was the only one of his boy-fellows who refused to say a kind word in commendation of the feat. Noble young Khamis, on the other hand, did not stint his appreciation of it, and youthful Abdullah and Mussoud hung about Selim as though he were some suddenly-discovered hero. The chieftain Khamis bin Abdullah, the noble leader of the united caravans, took from his waist a gold-hafted curved dagger as a token of his esteem, and Sheikh Mohammed presented him with a crimson silk sash to put around his waist. Sultan bin Ali, the patriarch of the expedition, who was the very type of a venerable Arab chief, gave him out of his treasure a red fez-cap with a golden tassel, and Sheikh Mussoud gave him a Muscat turban of a rich cherry pattern, so that Selim, before night, was arrayed in costly garments.

The slaves among themselves did Selim honour by praising him around the camp-fires, and Halimah, the black woman-cook of Amer bin Osman, as she turned her ugali (porridge), declared, by this and by that, that Selim was the noblest, sweetest lad she had ever seen.

Selim would have slept that night the sleep of those who do praiseworthy actions, had he not been awakened at midnight by a loud shriek from one of his father's slaves, whose right cheek was completely ripped off by a prowling hyæna. The disturbance in the dead hour of night alarmed some of the younger slaves, but they were calmed by the wise and experienced Moto, who said sententiously that "the hyæna is a cowardly brute, who would run away at the sight of a child in the daytime, and who could only fight sleeping or dead men."

After these incidents, which occurred at the stagnant pools of the Lofu, the caravans continued their march uninterruptedly until they arrived among the Wahehe, a tribe of predatory people who live south of the great arid plain country of Ugogo.

The first night, before going to sleep after their arrival in Uhehe, the kirangozi of Khamis bin Abdullah rose up at the command of his master—and spoke out in a loud voice to the united caravans:

"Words, words, words! Listen, ye children of the Arabs, sons of the great chiefs, Khamis bin Abdullah, Amer bin Osman, Sultan bin Ali, the Sheikhs Mussoud, Abdullah, Rashid, Hamdan, Thani, and Nasib! Open your ears, ye people of Zanzibar! Ye are among the Wahehe. Ye are in the land of thieves, and night-prowlers. Be wary and alert, my friends; sleep with one eye open; let not your hands forget your guns. When ye meet the prowling Wahehe in your camps at night, shoot and kill all such. Do ye hear?"

"We do," was answered by six hundred voices.

"Do ye understand?" he again asked.

"Yes," they all replied.

"It is well; the kirangozi Kingaru, slave of Khamis bin Abdullah, has spoken."

For two days they travelled through Uhehe without molestation, but on the evening of the third day Sheikh Amer commanded his tent-pitchers to set his tent close against the hedge of brush and thorn (which always surrounds a camp in Africa when it is procurable), for the convenience of his household, the members of which could thus by a slight gap pass in and out freely to the pool to get water or to procure wood for the fire, without being compelled to traverse the length of the camp.

A couple of hours before dawn, when people sleep heaviest, and their slumbers are supposed to be soundest, Simba, who always slept lightly at night, because of the responsible cares which a just and faithful conscience ever imposed on him, was awakened by the crushing of a twig. He never stirred, but continued his regular breathing as before, and compelled his ears to do their duty to the utmost. After a little time his quickened hearing was rewarded by the sound of a human foot pressing softly, yet heavily, the ground near him. The gap, left imprudently open, which fronted the tent door of Amer bin Osman, was that to which his cautious gaze was directed. By the light of the stars, which shine in Africa with unusual light, he saw the very faintest resemblance to a human figure, which held in one hand something darker than its own body, yet not so long, and in the other a long staff, at one end of which there was a cold glimmer of faint light, or reflection of light, which he supposed at once, and rightly, to be a spear. That human figure was that of an intruder. A friend had never stood so long in that gap, or advanced so stealthily. A wild beast would have advanced with as much circumspection and caution—why not a human enemy? The instincts of both man and beast are the same in the silence of night, when about to act hostilely.

Simba still lay seemingly unconscious of duty—unconscious of the danger which menaced the occupants of his master's tent; but could that human enemy have seen through the gloomy mist of night those large,

G

watchful eyes of the recumbent form stretched almost within reach of him, he had surely hesitated before advancing another step towards that open tent-door.

All seemed still, and the figure bent down and moved in a crawling posture towards the open door, wherein lay Selim and his father, unconscious of the dangerous presence of an armed intruder. But Simba's eyes were not idle, though silent. What thing on earth does its work so quietly as the eye? They followed the crawling form unwinkingly, until it had half entered the open door; then Simba raised his head, finally his body, upright to its full gigantic height. The feet of the daring intruder were within tempting reach of those long muscular arms if he but stooped, and Simba knew it. He stood up one short second or so, as if he summoned threefold strength with the lungful of air he but halted to inhale; then quickly stooping, he caught hold of the robber's feet, and giving utterance to a loud triumphant cry, swung him two or three times around his head, and dashed his head against the great flat stone on which, a few hours before, the woman-cook, Halimah, had ground her master's corn, and then tossed him lifeless over the hedge of the camp as carrion!!

In an instant, as it were, the camp was awake, and fires burned brightly everywhere. The cause of the disturbance was soon made known all over the camp, and curious men came rushing by the score to the scene of the tragedy, to gaze upon the victim of his own savage lust for plunder or murder. Amer bin Osman, when he heard the explanation of Simba, took a torch, and followed by Selim and others, went to gaze upon the dead man. One look satisfied him that the

man was a Mhehe, who had armed himself with a long
oval-shaped shield, broad-bladed spear, and battle-axe,
for a desperate enterprise.

When Amer raised his head, he seemed to be studying what the intention of the man might have been,
and he retraced his steps backwards to the tent-door,
and looked in, as if to consider what might have been
done, or stolen, had he succeeded in his attempt.
Then, looking at Selim's pale face, who had also arrived
at the same opinion as his father, a grateful look stole
over his features; he said to his son with a smile :

" Well, boy, thou hast to thank Simba for thy safety,
for thy head lay uncomfortably near that door; and
hadst thou awakened, thy life had not been worth
much.   What hast thou to say to Simba, Selim ?"

The boy turned his large bright eyes upon Simba's
face, which glowed with honest pride and affection, and
then they measured the giant limbs, the tremendous
arms, and the broad heaving chest, and to his father's
question propounded another, which rather startled his
father :

" Simba is a great strong man, but whom dost
thou value more, father—thy son Selim or thy slave
Simba ?"

" Why, son of mine, what a question ! Art thou not
the child of my loins, and of my dear Amina ? and have
I ever failed in my love for thee ?"

" Never—no, never, dear father ; but Simba has given
thy son back again to thee, else had I been dead.   Has
Simba paid thee full valuation for the purchase-money
thou didst pay for him when he was a child ?"

" Simba is good ; but had I lost thee, I had surely

lost all. Thou hast said it, my child. Simba is free, and is no longer a slave of Amer bin Osman."

"Simba!" cried Selim, "good Simba, do you hear the words of my father? You are a man, and no longer a slave!"

Simba at first did not seem to comprehend the full meaning of the words addressed to him, but as the words of the boy whose life he had saved were repeated to him, a proud smile lit his features, and as he tossed his head back, while his nostrils dilated, he said:

"A slave! It is an ugly word; but Simba, of the Wahuma, of Urundi, was in his own mind never a slave, so the word troubled him. Simba might long ago have been free, had he wished it, but he loved his master, Amer, and Sheikh Amer's son; so he remained their servant, and while being their servant he never forgot that he was a man. Simba is grateful to Amer and his son Selim, and while he remembers that he is free, Simba will be happy only in remembering also that he is their servant;" saying which, he bent his knee and kissed the right hand of father and son.

"Ah, Simba, my friend!" cried Selim, "I shall call thee friend in future, and thou shalt say 'thou' to me, and I 'thou' to thee, as my father and I say to each other; and if thou art grateful, Selim has also a heart, and can feel."

"Then, boys," said Amer, breaking in upon this interchange of compliments, "to bed, and sleep your sleep out. Let a watch be kept, lest the Wahehe robbers come to avenge the dead dog of a thief, and upon the first appearance of anything suspicious, sound the alarm instantly."

The night passed without further alarm or disturbance of any kind, and at the usual hour of the morning the signal horns aroused the camp for the fatigue of another day's march.

As the caravans were about leaving their camp, a group of Wahehe strolled up carelessly, similarly armed to the one who had met his fate so suddenly at the hands of Simba. As they were advancing towards the central gate of the camp, their quick eyes caught sight of the dead body of their comrade, and hastening towards it, they regarded it with wonder depicted on their faces. On stooping down to examine the head, they found it elongated into a hideous, formless shape, and not being able to contain their surprise, they questioned as to why and how it all came about.

Said Moto, who had keenly noted these signs, and had approached the group to answer their expected queries, "Ah, my brothers! some men are bad, very bad, and fools. What could have possessed this man to try and rob a caravan of 600 armed souls, I cannot say, unless it was the evil spirit. Do you see that big man with the great battle-axe in his belt, and a long ivory horn slung to his shoulder? That big man caught this thief in the tent of Amer bin Osman : he seized him by the feet, and whirling him around, he brought his head down flat on that stone."

"Eyah! eyah!" said the astonished Wahehe. He must be the evil spirit himself; but all thieves should die, and if, as you say, this man was caught at night in the camp, he has earned his death."

"Say you so, my brothers?" said Moto; "then it is well. But listen to me; if the wind came to steal in

our camp that big man would know it. He seems
never to sleep, never to rest ; he could smell a Mhehe
at night afar off."

"Eyah, eyah, ey—eyah !! He must be the evil
spirit." Saying which they departed, muttering to
themselves and looking very much crestfallen.

The caravans journeyed on for several days after the
incidents just related without meeting anything worthy
of note in these pages. The western part of Uhehe is
very uninteresting ; one march follows another through
the same *triste* scenery. A long reach of country to
the right and the left, covered with short ripe grass,
dotted with a ragged clump of thorn-bush here and
there, or a solitary baobab stem, unbending in its vast
girth and thickness of twigs, alone met the wearied
eyes of the travellers. The Wahehe, the southern
Wagogo, mixed with a stray Wakimbu family or two,
permitted such a large caravan to pass without molestation, so that the march was getting exceedingly monotonous. But when, after crossing an unusually arid
plain of some extent, they saw before them a long line
of white rocky bluffs, the people began to whisper
among themselves that "beyond those bluffs lay the
lands of the populous Warori, who are mostly shepherds, and will not, if in the mood to quarrel, regard
our numbers or strength."

It was the tenth week of the departure of the
Arabs from Simbamwenni when the above-mentioned
bluffs were crossed, and the pastoral country of the
Warori extended far before them in a succession of
wooded hollows, bare uplands, and jungle-covered plains.

Those who knew Moto, the slave of Amer bin Osman,

were startled at the remarkable physical resemblance
he bore to the majority of the shepherds and villagers,
who grouped themselves along the road to wonder at
the wealth of the Arab caravans, and to make their
rustic comments upon what they did not understand.

The Warori, however, did not seem disposed to dispute their advance, but stood contentedly gazing at
the strange sight of some of the whiter faces among
the Arabs. For instance, Khamis bin Abdullah and
his son Khamis, Amer bin Osman and his son Selim,
and the boys Abdullah and Mussoud. This paleness
of complexion became often a matter of eager specula-
tion, and as those who, fortunately or unfortunately,
possessed white faces passed by, the straining of eyes
and the narrow scrutiny were amusing to witness, and
afforded Selim more especially some discomfort at first.
The shepherds and villagers furthermore willingly
bartered whatever the Arabs wished for red beads and
American domestic. Milk, butter, and eggs were
plentiful, which, to the Arab boys, were rare treats
after the dry heat and desolate aspect of Western
Uhehe. The arms which these shepherds carried were
far more formidable than anything they had hitherto
seen in the hands of savages. Their bows were longer
and heavier, and their arrows longer and more cruelly
barbed, and besides a lengthy broad-bladed spear,
which resembled a broad Roman sword fastened to a
staff, and half a dozen lighter spears—assegais—and a
battle-axe, they carried a knife which might be likened
to a broadsword for length and breadth.

On the sixth day after their entrance into Urori, the
caravans came within sight of a large palisaded village

called Kwikuru, or the capital. It contained about eight hundred huts, strongly protected by a lofty fence of hard red wood. This village was protected on one side by a stream of considerable magnitude. On the other side of the village was a grove of fine trees situated from it a distance of about 1000 yards. Into this grove the Arabs marched to encamp.

Kwikuru, or the capital, was a good distinction awarded to the village, or town rather, for its size and importance; for, next to Simbamwenni, it was the most populous place they had found in Africa. Cattle grazed by the thousand a little distance off from the grove, attended by watchful and well-armed herdsmen. The lowing of the cows, and the bleating of the sheep and goats, and the braying of a few large donkeys, were welcome sounds to travellers, to whom such sights in Africa were rare. And the long extent of well-tilled ground, in which grew the Indian corn, the manioc, the *holcus sorghum*, the sugar-cane, and plantain, with abundance of vegetables and melons, enhanced the pleasure the Arabs' people naturally felt, unaccustomed as they were, since leaving Zanzibar, to feast their eyes upon such scenes.

Late in the afternoon, after the Arab chiefs had, with commendable caution, constructed a dense hedge of bush and branches around their camp, they called a meeting to discuss the measures they should take to open friendly communication with the formidable citizens of Kwikuru.

When they were all assembled, the leader Khamis said to them:

"My friends, we are at last in Urori, where I

suspect we shall have to conduct ourselves differently from what we have been accustomed to. I mean that I fear that tribute may be exacted by the King, and I have called you here to advise prudence, and to ask you to use tact in all your dealings with them. We may have to pay a heavy tribute, for this King is evidently powerful and rich, and a mean present of cloth I expect he will refuse."

"Khamis," said Sultan bin Ali, "thou hast done well to advise us upon this beforehand. What amount of cloth dost thou think will suffice this man's greed? We may be liberal, for we can afford it, but we have not one doti (four yards) of cloth too much."

The chief answered, "I do not know as yet what amount will suffice, but let us begin prudently, for in that course is wisdom. I suggest that six doti be made up; two doti (eight yards) of Joho cloth for the King, two doti of light checks for his wife, one doti of Muscat check with the red and yellow borders for his eldest son, and one doti of good Kaniki (blue cotton) for the principal elder."

"That idea seems excellent to me," said Sultan bin Ali, "and Amer, thou hast a cunning slave called Moto, a Mrori, I believe; let him and another good man take the cloths to the King with words of friendship from us, that we may pass through the country in tranquillity and peace with all men."

This advice meeting the approbation of all the chiefs, Moto, accompanied by the kirangozi of Khamis bin Abdullah, who was learned in all the languages of Eastern Central Africa, sallied out of the camp in the direction of Kwikuru, while the Arabs sat in the tent of their leader, hospitably entertained with the best that the larder could furnish.

An hour had barely elapsed before Moto and the kirangozi, or guide, returned to the camp; and going directly to the principal tent, kneeled before the door and said to the Arabs:

"Salaam Aleikum!" (Peace be unto you.) To which greeting the Arabs responded with one voice:

"Aleikum Salaam!" (And unto you be peace.)

"Well, Moto, speak," said Khamis. "Why, you have brought the present back! You have been unsuccessful?"

"These are the King's words, which he commanded me to tell you: 'Why have you come to my country? Know you not that there is enmity between the Warori and the children of the Arabs? Mostana, the great chief whom the cruel traders slew, was my friend; and can I forget his death with such a contemptible present as that which you have brought to me? Go slaves, and tell your masters that, unless they send me fifty bales of cloth, and fifty guns, with twenty barrels of gunpowder, they must return the way they came.' These, my masters, are the words which Olimali bade us tell you."

A deep silence followed this declaration of the King of Kwikuru, and the Arabs instinctively looked at one another in surprise and dismay.

Sheikh Mohammed, the black-browed Arab, resolute and determined as he always was, first broke the silence with the question, directed to Moto:

"Have you regarded well this village of Olimali?"

"I have, master," said Moto.

" Is it strong? Speak, for I respect your opinion, Moto."

" It is strong, master, much too strong for us to attack it with our people. If the Warori come out of their village they could not take this camp while our men remained within.

" That is well spoken, Moto," replied Mohammed; and turning to Sheikh Khamis, he asked:

" Hast thou decided what to do, son of Abdullah?"

" Mashallah! my friend, can I decide upon so important a subject as giving away thy property to this greedy infidel? May his soul perish in Al Hotamah! Does he think that cloth, and guns, and powder grow in the jungles of Africa? But this is serious, and we must set on our heads the caps of wisdom and understanding to consider the determination of Olimali. Speak, friends, Arabs of Muscat and chiefs of Zanzibar, my ears are open."

Out spoke Amer bin Osman: " Do you think, Moto, if we offered half he would accept?"

" No, master, I do not. I think Olimali desires war and not peace, and if he thought you would send fifty bales of cloth, he would ask for fifty more. I heard the people talk, as I left the King's presence, of war. My ears are very sharp."

" War!" shouted Mohammed, " then war he shall have, and I shall have the pleasure to put light through his body with my good Shiraz sword;" and Sheikh Mohammed looked as fierce as his threat.

" Peace, Mohammed, my friend," said Sultan bin Ali. It is not every one who trusteth in his sword flourisheth. I think there are more ways of tiding over this evil hour than by war, even if we were doubly strong with men and guns. Let us act prudently in the hour of danger."

"Sultan bin Ali is right," said Sheikh Thani. "Rather let us try all pacific measures first, and let war be the last resource. We have slaves, and women, and little ones in the camp, besides much property. We must remember this before we act hastily."

"Thani has spoken well, and with understanding; and I propose that we send forty good cloths and forty ordinary cloths, besides an odd gun or two, with half a keg of powder to Olimali by Moto and the kirangozi, who will speak him fairly and with due respect," said the leader, Khamis.

"I do not go again," said Moto. "What I have seen in the village, and what my ears have heard are no light things, and I would ask permission from my master to remain."

"Well, never mind, any man will do who has a smooth tongue and fair speech," said Khamis. "Let the kirangozi choose whom he will take, and let him go with the cloth."

A man was readily found, who, ignorant of the danger, had no reason to refuse to go upon the errand which the always bold Moto had refused.

But even as the guide and his companion were leaving the camp Moto saw he had acted wisely, for the cattle were being driven towards the village with far more expedition than the time of day warranted; but he held his tongue, not wishing to alarm the camp unnecessarily.

He followed the movements of the kirangozi and his

companion with exceeding interest until they had arrived
at the gate, where they were halted; and after a short
pause, he saw the two men returning towards the camp.

Proceeding to the gate of the camp, he there awaited
the arrival of the kirangozi, and when he was near
enough Moto quietly asked of him:

"Is it peace, or war?"

"War!"

He needed to hear no more, for he had been certain
of it, and he went directly to his friend Simba to communicate the news, who received it with surprise.

"War, Moto? Then our fears, my friend, have turned
out true, and it is because of the battle which thou wert
in with Kisesa against Mostana, eh?"

"Yes, Simba; and wouldst thou believe it? I saw two
or three fellows eye me pretty hard, and it was for that
I refused to go the second time; for if they had known
to a certainty that I was in that battle thou wouldst
never have seen Moto again, friend Simba."

During the greater part of that night the Arabs sat
in council, debating how to proceed; but not agreeing,
they separated for the night, not, however, without
posting sentinels all around the camp under the charge
of Sheikh Thani.

CHAPTER IV.

Khamis's Address to the Arabs—Proposals for Attack on Kwikuru—
Simba splits the Gato from Top to Bottom—The Warori Chief
shot—Death of Khamis bin Abdullah—Amer bin Osman pierced
by an Arrow—Selim made Prisoner—Selim brutally lashed by
Tifum — The three Arab-boys brought before Ferodia — Selim
refuses to drink or dance—Abdullah refuses to be called a Slave
—Flight of Sultan bin Ali—Division of the Spoils—The Magic
Drink: Mutilation of the Dead—The Chant of the Magic Doctors.

THE young people who have been fortunate in buying
this book may not have experience of the battle-field, and
therefore may not know what the feelings and thoughts
of those who are about to stake their lives against the
lives of others for the victory in the bloody contest are.
The feeling is the same in all men, whether white or
black, though some natures are so constituted that they
are enabled to hide feelings which some say partake
largely of fear. But I deny that such indicate fear,
though, left to themselves, they might create fear. In
the Arab camp, as report and rumour had been busy at
the camp-fires, a feeling of dread predominated in all
minds, but had there been one chief of resolution, with
power unlimited over all, a few words of cheer had done
wonders in improving the tone of their minds.

Khamis bin Abdullah was a brave man; no man
might deny that; but his bravery was undisciplined; it
was uncultivated; it was the bravery of a wild but

noble heart. He had not seen so many battle-fields that he could afford to smile at the declaration of Olimali; he had not the experience of war which would have satisfied him that, however large and numerous the force of Olimali was, he had resources enough in himself to defeat them all. Khamis bin Abdullah could die himself, but he could not bring others to look upon death with calmness and courage. So that, despite the high-spirited courage of his race, which he eminently possessed, the truth must be told without any disparagement to himself; a feeling of depression, some undefined dread, remained settled in his breast, though his outer aspect, his mien, or behaviour, did not betray this.

As it was with Khamis, so was it with the other chiefs. Amer bin Osman was as brave as a lion, but he could not depend upon his people as he could depend upon himself personally, and this thought created the dread, and doubt, and apprehension of something undefinable, which all the chiefs at this critical moment felt.

Sheikh Mohammed, Sultan bin Ali, and the rest were as brave as any living men. Had there been only one hundred Arabs, a doubtful issue of the war would never have been entertained; but there were only twelve Arabs and six hundred black men; and how long would the black men stand together?

At sunrise, another meeting was called, and the Arab chiefs, with their sons, hastened to the council.

Khamis, the leader, when all had been seated, said:

"My friends, the last words of Olimali, according to my kirangozi, were that the Arabs need not try to tempt him to forego his revenge, but that we must prepare for war. We can easily prepare for war, for we are always ready; but we must endeavour to sustain each other by friendly counsel and cheering words; for in a fatal issue to us of this war we know what the fate of us true believers will be. We can hold out in our camp against four times the number that Oli- mali may bring against us. We are weak, however, in this country, because we have no friends to supply us with food, and it is not a little that will suffice to feed six hundred souls. The men had no food yester- day, they have none to-day; they cannot hold out long in the camp against hunger. In this case what do you propose ?"

Sultan bin Ali spoke and said, "Our answer has been given to us, and there is no longer any doubt of what we have to do. We must fight, but how fight is the question. Shall we await here in the camp the coming of the infidel savages, or shall we sally out of the camp and attack them in their boma (palisade) ?"

Sheikh Mohammed answered, "We cannot remain in the camp to starve and eat each other; we must go out and get cattle, while a few of us stop inside here to strengthen the camp with branches. I would suggest also that a trench be dug all around the camp, and the earth thrown against the hedge as a parapet. Wallahi! I have seen such things done in Unyanyembe, and the enemy beaten."

"Mohammed's words are well spoken," said Amer bin Osman. "I would advise eleven of us sally out with our men, and one Arab remain with one hundred men, who will stir themselves to strengthen the de- fences with our cloth bales and baggage; and if we have to fall back, we shall find a strong place ready for us. We can harry those infidels; though they may be hidden behind triple rows of palisades, some of our bullets will reach them. Thanks to Allah! we have enough ammunition with us."

"Very good indeed," said Sheikh Thani, a wiry, cautious old man, who had had much experience in Africa; "but supposing we are beaten in our attack upon the palisades of Kwikuru, we shall not be any better off than we were before, but worse; our men will get disheartened, and starvation will stare us in the face. I propose that five hundred men, divided into two parties, make for the gates as quickly as possible, and break open everything with all the speed we can. It is only in this way that we can succeed."

"The oldest among ye have spoken," said the leader Khamis, "and ye have spoken well. But I have been in Urori before, and know the customs of the Warori. If we succeed in taking this village of Kwikuru, we cannot hope to be permitted to march through this country any more; but as soon as we take it we must strike along the road to Unyanyembe. It is useless for me to tell ye that I advised ye at first not to take the Urori road. I shall not quarrel with ye about that now, but will try to do my best for our general safety. If we succeed in destroying Olimali and his people, we must begin our march north to Unyanyembe to-night, for in two days the fugitives will carry the news from one end of the country to another."

"Excellently spoken, brave Khamis," said Amer bin Osman "Thou hast a wise head, and art a worthy

H

leader. Do thou, with thy men and other chiefs, attack one gate, and I, with my men and other chiefs, will attack the other gate, and whosoever takes a gate first, let him blow on his horn once. I advise now that whatsoever we may have we shall eat, and that after we break our fast we sally out."

"Praised be Allah for his goodness! Let us eat; then fight!" all shouted.

In half an hour breakfast had been despatched, and every chief sallied out with his men under his respective flag, except Sultan bin Ali, who was left with one hundred men to prepare the camp for defence in case of failure.

Simba and Moto had also had their little council together; and as they marched by the side of Amer bin Osman, various signs might have been seen by the observer to pass between them, accompanied by many ominous shakings of the head.

A deep silence prevailed near the village; not a soul was seen, not a dog was heard to bark; but the sun shone as usual with its summer heat, and the sky was perfectly cloudless and beautiful in its azure purity.

But little did the approaching Arabs and their followers heed the beauty of the sky, the brilliancy of the day, or the heat of the sun.

When they had advanced within 300 yards of the village, the force under Amer bin Osman separated from that of Khamis bin Abdullah, and marched at a respectful distance from the village towards the southern gate, and when he had gained his position, at a preconcerted signal both forces began their firing, advancing rapidly as they fired.

The village stirred not; not a sign of life was visible for some time, until the Arabs had approached within fifty yards; then clouds of arrows were seen to issue from the village, and furious yells were heard, which seemed to rend the sky. Numbers of the Arab followers fell pierced to the core by the arrows; but the animated shouts of their chiefs spurred them on towards the palisade.

In a few moments, after repeated discharges of musketry, the Arabs gained the outer defence of the village, and, intruding their guns between the tall posts, were soon firing right in the faces of the astonished but not dismayed people of Olimali. But at this juncture, a long blast on a deep-sounding horn was heard from the interior, simultaneously with a shorter and shriller sound which proceeded from the southern gate. The shriller horn belonged to Amer bin Osman, and was blown by Moto; but what did the bass horn from the interior of the village mean? But there was no time to lose in conjecture.

Amer bin Osman had advanced with resistless impetuosity towards the southern gate, and the gigantic Simba had, with one blow of his heavy axe, split the gate from top to bottom, and, giving it a strong push with his foot, had sent it flying open, through which, accompanied by his master Amer and Selim, who carried his rifle, he had bounded into the interior, firing his musket with the utmost rapidity.

Amer's followers, animated by the valour of their master and the immense strength of Simba, now became as brave as lions, and vied with each other in noise and bravery. Not being able to make their way rapidly enough by the gate, which was thronged by the besiegers, they climbed over the palisades like monkeys, and little Niani's agility might have astonished his namesake. Abdullah, Mussoud, and Isa were with their parents, Sheikhs Mohammed and Hamdan, and they crept through the gate much behind Selim and his father Amer, owing to the press of besiegers.

So quickly had Simba gained the gate and destroyed it, that all the fugitives were not able to enter the inner inclosure which surrounded the king's quarters, and a body of them, numbering about fifty, under the leadership of the king's eldest son, now stood with their backs to the palisades, resolutely confronting Simba and his companions, with heavy spears in their hands.

Simba, at this time before a foe on whom he could exert the full power of his arm, became transformed into the embodiment of a black Mars, the god of war. He was no longer the humble and obedient servant of Sheikh Amer and the true friend of Selim. He was more; he was their irresistible leader. In his eyes glowed the ardour of fierce battle; the terrible savage spirit of the Warundi, hitherto constrained for faithful, though menial, service, had burst its trammels, and he now stood, with uplifted musket,—confessed—the bronze Achilles of the war. His fierce eye caused the doomed fugitives to quail with cowardly dread; and when aimed at him, the heavy spears of the Warori fell harmless at his feet. Giving vent to the hitherto latent passion of the savage's soul in a loud bellowing cry, he sprang forward, and the rapidity with which he dealt his blows with his clubbed musket awed even the warrior soul of his Arab chief. But not for long

did Amer pause to regard even the prowess of Simba.
Calling to his followers, he raised his long two-edged
sword, and darted at the enemy, plying the weapon
best known to him and his race with a power which
elicited as much admiration as Simba's strength of
arm and dexterity of stroke had done.

Rendered desperate by the knowledge of their situation, the remaining Warori, headed by their chief,
made a rush towards their enemies and used their
heavy spears with frantic energy. In front of the
Warori chief stood Selim, firing and loading his rifle
with a coolness and method which would have won
applause from his father's people had the combatants not been so busily engaged. He was in the
act of re-loading when the desperate rush of the
Warori was made, and their chief stood with uplifted
spear above him; but well was it for him that the
watchful eye of Moto was on him, else had our story
been ended here, ere it is hardly begun. When it
seemed that Selim could not have been saved, and he
stood expectant of the blow which would have ended
his young life there and then, he saw the chief's head
fall back with a cruel jagged wound in the temple,
through which the bullet of Moto had sped home.

The Warori no longer resisted when they saw their
chief fall, and attempted to fly, but the force of Arabs
was too numerous; they fell dead to a man.

Khamis bin Abdullah had also been successful.
Cheered by the news which the horn of Amer conveyed, he soon effected an entrance, and, accompanied
by his followers, he had entered the village, and almost
similar scenes awaited him though not so sanguinary.

When they had succeeded in forcing the outer inclosure, they had still a hard struggle before them to
conquer the village ; but they, no doubt, would have
done so had not a new enemy come upon the field.

Unknown to the Arabs, a few miles west of the
village was stationed a large body of Watuta, whose
chief had been sent by Katalambula, brother of the
dead Mostana, to pay his respects to his brother's
friends, and to renew "assurances of his esteem and
consideration" for them, as the old letters used to say.

This body of Watuta was one thousand strong, and
as soon as the Arab caravans hove in sight, Olimali
had despatched messengers to Ferodia, the Watuta
chief, telling him of his intentions, and bidding him
hasten to the neighbourhood to watch events, and to be
ready for the signal, as he intended to attack the
Arab camp. But the attack of the Arabs upon his
village had caused him to give the signal earlier than
he had at first anticipated, and the easy entrance of
the Arabs into the outer village had been partly effected
through the connivance of this wily chief, though in
the loss of warriors and in the death of his eldest son
he had paid dearly for his treachery.

While the Arabs and their followers now devoted
their attention to the attack upon the inner inclosure,
which was vigorously defended, the major number of
the Watuta had risen, in response to the deep-sounding
war-horn of the Warori, from among the corn-fields to
the west of the village and camp of the Arabs, and
had hurried to the rescue.

They came upon the outer inclosure just as the Arabs
commenced their attack upon the inner palisade, and

the first time the Arabs knew of their presence was
when they were first fired upon before and behind.

The followers of the Arabs, before so valiant, now
became panic-stricken, and they simultaneously made
a rush for the gates, while the defiant yells of the
savages completely drowned their cries; but the cunning Watuta had closed the gates, or had so barricaded
them that egress was impossible. They now saw
nothing but death staring them in the face—savages
in front, savages behind; both parties defended by
palisades, while they stood exposed between, to be shot
to death in their tracks. It was useless for the Arab
leaders to attempt to encourage them, for one after
another of these brave men fell and died. Khamis
bin Abdullah fell, pierced by a dozen arrows, and his
son, the noble young Khamis—the proud-spirited
young Arab—fell also across the body of his father at
the hands of the people whom he so much despised.
Mussoud, and Thani, and Amram died also bravely,
and one after another of their followers fell to rise no
more, until those who were left threw down their guns
crying "Aman, aman!" (Mercy, mercy!) upon seeing
which the Watuta and Warori desisted from further
murder, to make slaves of those who cried for quarter.

The force under Amer bin Osman, Sheikh Mohammed,
and Hamdan, and the other chiefs, fared as badly.
They were engaged in vigorously attacking the inner
defence in front of them, when they heard a loud
gurgling shriek issue from Sheikh Mohammed, who had
been pierced in the nape of the neck from an arrow
behind, and on turning to see whence it came, they
were dismayed to find an enemy of another tribe

behind them. Moto, on seeing them, shouted "The Watuta! the Watuta! Olimali has betrayed us into their hands." Simba, hearing the words of Moto, desisted from further attack, and came to Amer bin Osman, counselling him to fly with him, and handing him a shield to cover his body, which, from the dress he wore, was a prominent mark. Moto also held a couple of shields before Selim, while Abdullah and Mussoud were ordered to do the same.

"Fly!" said the astonished Amer—"fly! Ah, Simba, my friend, had we wings, we might fly. See you not the gate is closed?"

"The gate is closed, I know, great master, but Simba's arm is strong, and I will force it open."

"No, Simba, I cannot fly to be butchered like a bullock outside. I shall meet my fate here. Ha! do you hear that? See! the savages are within. Khamis bin Abdullah is dead! Save my boy Selim, for his mother's sake! Ho, my son, come to me! One embrace before we part for ever; but, my son, remember, I shall meet thee in Paradise!"

The father and son were united in a fervent embrace when Amer received an arrow in the back from within the inner inclosure, which caused him to fall, with his son in his arms, to the ground. The arrow had been driven by a strong hand, for the point projected in front and slightly wounded Selim in the chest, the blood of father and son commingling in one stream.

"Brave Simba and faithful Moto, where are ye? Save my boy!" cried Amer, looking up with glazed eyes at the two who bent over him, heart-stricken with sorrow. "Save my darling Selim! Save him for

the love I bore you! Ah, Selim, my son, kiss thy
mother for thy fa—— Amina!—Sel—— Ah!"—and
the great soul of Amer hastened upward to the Judgment Seat.

Simba and Moto, when they saw their master had
breathed his last, stretched his form out evenly, and,
placing a cloth reverently over his face, caught hold
of Selim, and pressing the heart-broken boy to the
ground, close by the body of his father, said to him:

"Lie still, young master. Nay, but you must. Your
father commanded us to save you, and we will; but you
must do what we advise you. Think of your mother,
of many happy days yet in store for you. Lie still as
death, and they will take you to Katalambula's village,
and there you will meet us. Here, Abdullah! Mussoud! Isa! lie down here, alongside of Selim. What,
all the chiefs dead already! Wallahi! but this is a
sad day for the Arabs at Zanzibar!"

Having given these instructions to the Arab boys,
which had been given in much less time than we have
taken to record them, Simba and Moto also fell to the
ground, but retaining their spears and shields in their
hands.

By this time the Watuta were within the village,
crowing triumphantly over their success; but Ferodia,
the chief, after giving orders to bind the captives, hastened away with nearly all his force to attack the camp,
which, under old Sultan bin Ali, held out still against
the force that had been detached to attack it.

While the few remaining Watuta were binding the
captives, Simba and Moto rose to their feet, and, using
their spears right and left, soon cleared a passage to

the gate, before the astonished savages could recover their senses.

Once outside the gate, Simba and Moto exerted their powers to the utmost, and by their extraordinary speed soon left their pursuers far behind.

Finding it useless to pursue the runaways, the Watuta began to examine the wounded, and especially the Arabs, whom they surveyed with astonishment. The group formed by Amer bin Osman, Selim his son, Abdullah, Mussoud, and Isa, attracted them most for their rich dresses. They began to strip the bodies, but their astonishment was very great when they perceived Isa sit up and fold his hands, asking for mercy.

Suspecting that others shammed death, they laid hold of Selim, and he also sat up; then Abdullah and Mussoud, and they also sat up, looking very sheepish, or like guilty people caught doing a mean action. Angry at the cheat, as they imagined, to have been practised upon them, they snatched the cloth from the face of the dead body of Amer bin Osman; but there was no mistaking him—he was dead.

Some were for slaying the boys at once; but the majority interposed, and said in an inquiring tone, " Why slay boys, when you can make slaves of them ?" which shortly met general approbation.

Upon agreeing to this, they began to strip Isa, who shortly found himself as naked as when he was born; but being extremely dark of colour, there appeared nothing remarkable about him to attract any special attention, and he was taken at once to the other captives, where he was firmly bound with strips of green bark.

They then laid violent hands on the others, on Selim, Abdullah, and Mussoud; and despite their struggles and tears, they were soon denuded of their finery and of their rich embroidered dress. When they saw the pale and clean colour of their bodies, the fierce Watuta gathered about them, and wondered what strange beings these were who were all over white, while they themselves were all black. They looked at the wound in Selim's chest, and on pressing it saw the red blood flow, which only increased their astonishment; for how could people with white skins have red blood? But Selim's proud heart was rebelling against the indignity of being stared at as a curious specimen of humanity, and he had endeavoured to hide his blushes with his hands; but when they pulled them down, and ordered him to show his tongue and teeth, and began to feel the muscles of his arms and legs, then he could bear no more; and flinging himself across the dead body of his father, he wept aloud, and prayed to God that he might die. Abdullah and Mussoud were as yet too terrified to do more than cry silently; and they were accordingly led away and bound without resistance. They then took hold of Selim to tie him, but he would not rise; and, angered at what they deemed his stubbornness, two warriors brought the shafts of their spears full upon his body, which had well-nigh broken the high courage of the young Arab; for so great was the pain his pride suffered, and so indescribable were his emotions, that he lay like one stunned.

While the boy lay fainting in the hot sun amid the dead and the blood, the chief of the party in charge of the prisoners, casting his eyes around, saw a whip of hippopotamus hide in the waist-cloth of one of the dead fundis, or overseers, of the Arabs. This pliant and formidable whip the chief—a man of stern and forbidding aspect, whose name was Tifum (pronounced Teefoom),—Tifum Byah, or the " Wicked Tifum," and who was evidently a traveller—handled like a man who knew its uses, for he made it fly about his arm in black circles, and made it hiss its menace in the ears of the sorely-tried Selim.

"Proud Arab boy, arise! Tifum Byah speaks but once, else you will feel the pains of this whip, with which your cursed race torture the backs of your slaves. Many days lie between here and Ututa, and you will suffer more than this ere you see our plains. Arise! No? then words are light as air, and seldom go into the ears of the stubborn;" and as he spoke, he lashed the prostrate youth with all his might, while the shrieks which the pain elicited at last from him were responded to by the mocking laughter of the brutal crowd, who pointed at the marks which the whip made in high glee.

When Tifum fancied he had punished him enough, he ordered the boy to be assisted up to his feet and bound ; and when this was done Tifum lowered his face to Selim's, and said, "Mark my words, child of the pale race! You shall be Tifum's slave, to hoe his field and bring him wood and water. You shall nurse his children, be a herdsman of his cattle, and I will break your heart, and make your ears open to his slightest breath. Do you hear me, white face?"

So strong was the nauseous and hateful repugnance he felt towards this man that Selim could not repress the expression of the loathing that filled him, and almost unconsciously he spat in his face, which was instantly retaliated by Tifum with a tremendous box on the ear, which prostrated the boy once more across the dead body of Amer, where he lay like one deprived of life, and not all the brutal lashing which the almost lifeless form received evoked one groan from him; and it was in this unconscious state that he was carried to where the other prisoners stood huddled together like frightened sheep.

Then, directing his attention to the dead bodies of the Arabs, these were ordered to be denuded of their clothing, and to be laid in a row together, Sheikhs Khamis, Amer, Abdullah, Mussoud, Thani, Hamdan, Mohammed, Amram, and young Khamis, and two others of lesser note—an honourable company truly, even in death!

There seemed to have penetrated into the brain of the unconscious Selim some idea of what was about to occur; for as soon as the dead had been gathered together, he raised his head and sat up, with his eyes fixed upon the dishonoured bodies of his father and his father's friends, which were laid side by side. He heeded not the taunts of the Warori who had collected to menace and insult the prisoners, and feast their curiosity with a sight of the noble dead; he heeded not the groans of his boy-companions Isa, Abdullah, and Mussoud, nor the wailing of the little slave Niani, who had been born on his father's estate, and who was now crying his eyes out for the loss of his master Amer, and for the more pitiable condition of his young master Selim; he heeded not the hot sun which was blistering his back with its fierce heat, nor the scores of flies which troubled his numerous wounds; he sat heedless of all, with his great eyes fixed sadly on the remains of his father.

But night was approaching, and Ferodia had not yet returned. Volleys of musketry were heard incessantly all the afternoon; but as the sun set the musketry ceased, and Ferodia returned with all but a few of his people, when it was reported that the camp still held out, but that in the morning all the fighting men of Olimali and Ferodia would take the camp at a rush. Until then he had left a few of his men to watch it, lest they might abscond at night and take away the most part of the great wealth which must be stored within the camp. The losses of the Watuta had been excessively heavy, as, when Ferodia darted out with his victorious men, it was expected that the camp would have surrendered at once; but it seems that Sultan bin Ali had so well fortified it that it was almost impregnable, and that the Watuta had been punished severely.

The Warori of the village of Kwikuru had prepared food in a great quantity for the warriors of Ferodia, who were too much engaged with satisfying their ravenous hunger to display much interest in prisoners whom they knew were secure; and when they had finished, they had so gorged their stomachs with food and pombe, that they were too indolent to stir. But when Tifum, who was obsequious enough to Ferodia, though cruel to his subordinates, had told the latter of the interesting character of the white slaves, as he called the three Arab boys, and how he had found them shamming death, he commanded him to bring them before him and Olimali that they might be amused.

Tifum hastened out obedient to his chief's mandates, and, arriving before the prisoners, searched for the Arab boys, who had already forgotten their misery in a deep sleep. Finding that they were in a too un-interesting condition to amuse his master, he had several gourds full of water brought to him, which he threw over them to cause them to cast off the disposition to sleep. This being done, he led them to the presence of his chief.

Ferodia was holding forth to Olimali upon the pro-spects of the great riches they should share with each other on the morrow when the young prisoners were ushered before him. By the dim light which the torches gave out, they appeared much more pallid and strange in a land where white people had never been seen; indeed, one might say they were rather alarm-ing; and it is no wonder that Ferodia started as the three were pushed towards him.

But, quickly recovering himself, as he remembered who they were, he burst out into a laugh, saying, "Ah, I remember, these are the Arab youths thou didst speak to me of, Tifum. This pombe, Olimali, is strong. I think it has made me light-headed,"—speaking these words aside to the Mrori chief.

Then attentively fixing his gaze upon the prisoners, and looking them all over, he said, half to himself, "What strange people these Arabs are—all white! Their hides are as white almost as the yolk of eggs; but how came the tallest one, I wonder, to have so many wounds?"

"Tifum," said Ferodia, aloud, "what ails this tallest lad? These wounds are not the wounds of arrows."

Tifum, bending his back almost double, said, "My chief, this boy is as stubborn as an ass. When I remembered the cruelties the people of this boy have practised upon those of our colour, my blood boiled within me, and when I told him to arise and be bound like the other prisoners, he spat in my face, and I flogged him."

"Pah, pah, Tifum! he but acted as the Watuta boys would have done; but lay not thine hand on him again. I take him for my slave. The boy is half dead already. Here," said he, addressing Selim, "drink this," handing him a good ladleful of sparkling pombe; "it will put life in thy dull veins."

Selim shook his head and curled his lips in scorn, and looked at the half-inebriated chief with contemptuous indifference.

The chief regarded him for a moment in silence, with the cup still stretched, and then said, "Thou art right, Tifum; no Mtuta boy would have had the courage to refuse a cup of pombe from a chief, nor regard his future master with such a look. He is a fool, and stubborn as an ass, truly. But I will tame him, or I will kill him. How Kalulu, the nephew of Katalambula, will wonder at him! Why, he must be of the same age as Kalulu; but Kalulu is taller and stronger; but I doubt if he has this lad's high courage, though he is proud as if he were already king of the Watuta. Kalulu would act differently from this youth if he were in his place; he would have taken the pombe and then killed me as soon as he had the opportunity. Ah!

Kululu is a true Mtuta. But here I am with the cup still in my hand. If this boy will not drink it, perhaps the others will. Here, you!" addressing himself to Abdullah, "drink, young one. No? And you refuse it, too? Well, you smallest one," to Mussoud. "Not even you? Strange youths! Dost thou speak their language, Tifum?"

"A little, my chief."

"Ask this tallest one why will he not take this cup of pombe from the hand of Ferodia, chief of the Watuta warriors."

"Boy," said Tifum, addressing Selim, "Ferodia, chief of the Watuta warriors, demands to know why you will not accept the drink at his hands."

"Then tell thy master," said Selim, without even turning his eyes towards the man, "that I may not accept anything in kindness from his hands, since he gives it to me while he believes me to be a slave. Tell him I am not his slave, and never shall do his bidding save under constant compulsion."

When Tifum had communicated this to his chief, Ferodia burst into another loud laugh; then said:

"This boy is verily proud; but, Tifum, ask him to dance."

"Dance!" said Selim, when the order was communicated to him—"Dance! when my heart is breaking, when my father lies dead and dishonoured before yonder gates! Sooner would I die than obey!"

"Then tell him to sing," shouted Ferodia, laughing.

"Sing!" replied Selim. "How long, oh Allah! shall I suffer these tortures? Sing! As well might you ask the dead to sing!"

I

"What, will he do nothing, then? I will wait until the marks of thy rough hand have been cured, when I will make marks of my own on that hide of his," said Ferodia, with a wrathful glance in his eye. "But where is that whip of thine, Tifum?"

"Here, my chief, at the door of the house," said he, rising to fetch it.

"Give it me." And giving Selim a severe stroke with it across his shoulders, he ordered him to stand back, and Tifum to cut the bonds of the boys Abdullah and Mussoud.

Then, commanding the youths to be brought before him, he told Tifum to tell Abdullah to dance and Mussoud to sing.

For awhile Abdullah hung down his head in confusion, not seeming to understand or to realise that *he*, the son of Mohammed, was actually required to dance by the slayer of his father; while Mussoud looked from Abdullah to the chief Ferodia's face in quite a foolish way.

"Ask him, Tifum," said Abdullah, in a trembling voice, "if Ferodia understands what he requires of me."

"Why need I ask him? Do I not tell you that he commands you to dance, and the other slave to sing?"

"Slave!" shouted Abdullah, recovering quickly firmness of tone in his voice. "Slave! Lying dog! Do you call my brother a slave? Am I a slave?"

"What does he say?" thundered Ferodia.

"He says he is not a slave, and calls me a liar. They are all asses and sons of asses," replied Tifum. "Verily, though they own hundreds of black slaves at

Zanzibar, they don't seem to know that the chance of war has made them slaves."

"Tell him, Tifum, that I say he is a slave, he and his brother; that they shall be my slaves; that they shall do whatever I bid them, and if not, that I will punish them until they do.   Ferodia speaks."

"Do you hear and understand, asses and sons of asses?" asked Tifum of Abdullah and Mussoud.   "Do ye hear, children of the Arabs ?   Ferodia the chief tells you that you shall be his slaves to do his bidding, and if you do not, he will punish you.   Listen to the chief's words, and obey him."

"We are Arabs," said Abdullah, proudly tossing his head back, while his chest seemed to dilate with the great thought.   "We are Arabs, and children of the Arabs of Muscat.   A chief of the free Bedaween was my father Mohammed, and I am his son Abdullah.   The desert wind is not freer than our never-conquered race, and every child of that race is free.   We, therefore, cannot be slaves.   Ferodia has lied."

"Tell him, Tifum, that I will beat him until he is bleeding on this floor—until he confesses himself my slave."

"Ferodia says he will beat you, Abdullah, if that be your name, until you bleed on this floor."

"Tell him from me he may beat me until I die, but he cannot make me a slave.   Has he not slain my father, and has he not dishonoured me by causing me to stand naked before him ?   Can he punish me more ?   He is a strong man—you call him a chief; he has in his hand a whip; he says he will use it.   I am but a child, but he cannot make me a slave.   See, I go to

him nearer, and turn my back to him. I will not cry,
though he tear my flesh;" and the indomitable young
Arab walked up nearer to the chief, looked at him in
the eye for a second, then slowly turned his bare back
to him, and with bended head and folded arms waited
for the blow.

Ferodia, though a chief and a Mtuta warrior, was a
true savage; he had never heard of that rare quality
which belongs to races civilized and semi-civilized, and
is called magnanimity, or a generous forbearance to a
conquered foe. He beheld the defenceless boy who was
fully in his power standing within reach of the lash he
held in his hand,—that delicate youth with the fair and
faultless skin, on which an angry blow had never descended, which a whip had never dishonoured, – and the
savage could not restrain his instincts of cruelty or
the delight to torture and rend which is the instinct
of wild men as well as of wild animals. So, when
Tifum explained to him what Abdullah had said, and
what he meant by thus turning his back to him,
Ferodia, as though it were an every-day matter in
which no principle was involved, lifted his whip, and as
he saw the tender flesh shrink and redden, and then
bleed and gape, it but kindled the desire to hurt; but
a powerful antidote and corrective,—even subjugator,
you may say,—was the resolute passiveness and determined silence of his victim; and without being aware
himself of what lessened the power of his blows, and
weakened his anger, and finally conquered the desire to
torture, his arm was stayed, and still the boy stood up,
now confronting him, with the same steady gaze and heroic
mien, to ask the astonished savage with a curling lip:

" Well, have you made me a slave now ? Am I more a slave than before ?"

"Stand aside, fool, else I will do thee a greater harm ; and thou, Tifum, away with them, treat them as slaves ; and when we are on the road, give them loads to carry. Since they think it such a terrible thing to be naked, let their nakedness be seen of men and women, and if they suffer through it, so much the better. Slaves were made to suffer. Are my words nothing ? Shall these baby-faces beard me before my own people ?" So saying, Ferodia threw his whip from him, and drowned his further reflections in a mighty gourd-bowl full of strong pombe; and as he sighed his content, all traces of anger vanished ; and as he observed his friend Olimali had long ago measured his length upon the clay floor of the hut, he laughed heartily ; but the fumes of the pombe he had already drunk were rapidly conquering the conqueror—even Ferodia, chief of the Watuta.

The first news Ferodia and Olimali received, when they had recovered in the morning from their drunken stupor, was not calculated to content them. This was the flight of Sultan bin Ali and his men by night from the camp, with but two or three bales of cloth, so that a party flying for their lives, and so lightly laden, were not easily to be overtaken, and could not be done before they would reach a country friendly to the Arabs. Still, when the two chiefs, after venting a few angry expletives, came to reflect, to converse, and turn over coolly, calmly, and deliberately the news, it was found not to be so bad after all—rather the reverse ; until, finally, it was settled that the news was the best that could be heard of what might concern them, and they felt accordingly very gratified.

Four hundred bales of cloth and beads, one hundred kegs of powder, a vast number of bullets, rugs, carpets, counterpanes, feather pillows, richly embroidered caps, knives, looking-glasses, despatch-boxes, a few guns, kettles, cups and saucers, sugar, coffee, tea, spices, curry, and numberless little things which go to make the miscellaneous sum-total of the plunder of a large and wealthy caravan—in short, the sum of fifty thousand silver dollars would not have covered the cost price of the articles found in the Arabs' deserted camp.

In the possession of these articles, what a difference had been made within twenty-four hours in that small area contained within the compass of a square half mile, a spot in Africa that might be covered by a pin's point on an ordinary school-map of the world! How much noise, confusion, blowing of gunpowder, did the fact of possession comprehend! How many lives had been destroyed! What noble men had died! How much misery had been created! And on such a very small spot in this world, that no one would ever have heard of it, had I not been elected the historian of the battle of Kwikuru! Yet who will dare deny my right and duty to relate truly and clearly how it all happened—what dashing bravery Simba showed; how Khamis bin Abdullah and his lion-hearted son and the noble Amer bin Osman died; how our proud, high-spirited heroes, the Arab youths, Selim, Abdullah, and Mussoud, endured their sad misfortunes—to illustrate the high and noble principles involved in all these things, and to point with bold finger the moral which adorns this chronicle?

Happy are ye, my young readers, if your eyes fall upon these few pages; for ye shall be counted as those to whom a new world of human life has been revealed, where exist passions and joys so akin to our own that none may be so blind as not to perceive our relationship to them!

Putting by moralising for the present, let us glance at the incidents which transpired on the news of the desertion of the Arab camp becoming generally known.

Ferodia and Olimali became exceedingly elated when the rich store of plunder was described to them. They rubbed their hands, like two children rejoicing gleefully over a nice Christmas present; they laughed, and giggled, and said so many tender silly things to one another, that the historian of these events finds his patience too exhausted to relate them.

Trusty men were at once despatched to the camp to superintend the removal of the riches to Kwikuru, and when they were all conveyed into the inner inclosure and exhibited to the view of the chiefs, they could barely realise that they were the actual possessors of all this immense wealth until they had peered into every box, and felt over and over again the texture of the gaudy cloths before them. The palisade was lined by men, women, and children, who endeavoured to thrust their over-large heads for such intentions through the narrow spaces between the poles. Their cries of admiration were irrepressible. They hummed, and hawed, and heyed, and coughed their immeasurable satisfaction.

The division of the spoils was made with religious justice. Ferodia retained half of everything, and to

Olimali, his friend and ally, was given the other half. But their respective halves were so large, that there was no room for quarrel, and the most ambitious African could never have dreamed of such abundant store as had now fallen into the hands of these fortunate chiefs. When Ferodia, assisted by ten favourite head men, had reckoned up, after much mental calculation, how much cloth he had, he could only express it by saying that there were belonging to him one hundred hundreds of dotis and sixty hundreds of dotis of cloth, including all kinds ; or, as we should say, with our expressive terms, there were 16,000 doti, or 64,000 yards.

Ferodia caused his warriors to be drawn up in line. Though a few had been killed, still there were enough men in the line to warrant the statement that there were 900 men where originally there had been 1000 of them. To these warriors the head men delivered six doti each of mixed cloth, which left in Ferodia's possession 10,600 dotis. The odd 600 were for himself and his head men and doctors of magic—himself, as may be supposed, retaining the lion's share. The remaining 10,000 dotis, and the beads and other things, were for the king Katalambula and his prospective heir, Prince Kalulu.

The 10,000 dotis of cloth were made into 200 light portable bales containing fifty dotis each, which weighed about forty pounds. The beads were distributed for the like purpose, as well as the fifty barrels of powder, &c. &c.

The distribution having taken place, and each warrior made perfectly satisfied with his share, there remained one more duty to perform—a religious duty—which might not be neglected long, and this was the religious ceremony of making each warrior magically strong in arm and limb, by giving him to drink of the consecrated drink.

This ceremony took place the evening of the day after the battle. First, fires were lighted around a large circle outside the boma, or outer palisade of Kwikuru, with only one entrance left for the passage of the sacrificial bodies of the dead Arabs. The bodies, being all denuded of their clothing, were laid diametrically across the circle. Then earthen, tin, and copper pots full of water, with some millet flour in each, were placed over the fire, and then small bottle gourds (with numbers of small pebbles in them), two for each magic doctor, were prepared and placed near the heads of the bodies. Everything being thus ready, the magic doctors took their sharp knives in their hands and began their work. To the sound of a low crooning song, or rather chant, the words of which could not be distinguished, the knives were set to work on the bodies of their enemies, first in cutting the tips of each nose, then the lower lip, then the flesh under the chin, then the ears and the eyebrows, which, when ended, they conveyed to the pots over the fires. Continuing their work, the nipples of the breasts were then cut, the muscles of their arms and legs, and, lastly, the whole of the flesh covering the abdomen, which they took and placed in the pots over the fire. Then the hearts were extracted, and, finally, the fat of the entrails of each body. After this mutilation and disfigurement of the dead, the head of each body was cut off and placed on the end of pointed poles, to be borne around the camp during the ceremonial song.

Within half an hour the water had boiled sufficiently, and the magic doctors, taking the wonderful gourds filled with pebbles in their hands, began to shake them to the tune of a monotonous chant, in the chorus of which the warriors, bearing the heads aloft on poles, joined, marching slowly as they sang around the circle. The words ran thus, as well as they may be translated:

> Oh, the horrible, fearful battle,
> Where warriors slew and were slain,
> Where dead lay unnumbered, and wounds were made,
> Till the field ran red with blood that was shed
>   In the horrible, fearful battle.
>   *Chorus.*   With the blood that was shed
>   In the horrible, fearful battle.

> Ferodia the chief, Ferodia the strong,
>   The lion and leopard in war,
> Tifum Byah, Maro, and Wafanyah,
> Great chiefs of the unconquer'd Watuta,
>   In the horrible, fearful battle,
>   *Chorus.*   In the horrible, fearful battle.

> They heard the loud note, the war-horn's note,
>   Olimali, their friend, was distress'd;
> They rose from the bush, they rose from the ground,
> They rush'd to Kwikuru, and hemm'd them round,
>   For a horrible, fearful battle.
>   *Chorus.*   For a horrible, fearful battle.

> The Arabs and blacks who came from afar,
>   Who came from near the sea,
> To give the Warori and Watuta,
> King Olimali and Ferodia,
>   A horrible, fearful battle.
>   *Chorus.*   A horrible, fearful battle.

> Warori were brave, the Watuta were strong,
>   'Gainst those who came from afar.
> The Arabs lie dead by hundreds around;
> They will hear never more the war-horn's sound,
>   For a horrible, fearful battle.
>   *Chorus.*   For a horrible, fearful battle.

THE MAGIC DRINK.

Then, drink, warriors! drink the true magic drink!
      The strength of your enemies slain!
Drink of the blood, of the fat, and the heart,
Drink to commemorate before we part,
      The horrible, fearful battle.
    Chorus. Before we part
      The horrible, fearful battle.

Then, drink, warriors! drink the true magic drink!
      The strength of your enemies slain!
Be strengthened in heart, in limb, and in arm,
Be strong, be swift, be wise, and safe from harm
      In each horrible, fearful battle.
    Chorus. And safe from harm
      In each horrible, fearful battle.

When this chant was over, which has been rendered into English as faithfully as possible, the poles on which the ghastly trophies had been placed were planted in the ground before each gate of the village. But the young Arabs were spared this fearful scene, as they had been sent ahead with the loads, escorted by a strong guard. Then, the ceremony over, the chief Ferodia embraced in a loving manner his friend Olimali, and departed to the sound of booming horns and drums, and a general grateful look from the young women of Kwikuru—he and his warriors.

At sunset they camped in a forest, through which the road led towards the south-west.

CHAPTER V.

SIMBA and Moto were men as capable of enduring
fatigue as the Watuta were, as good runners also; so
that even had their enemies pursued them with a
greater determination than they showed, the two men
might have laughed securely, as night would soon have
shrouded them with its friendly mantle.

For a long time, however, the two held on their way,
raising their eyes every now and then toward the
bright Southern Cross, which shone so clearly, and
pointed their future road so plainly. They travelled
with their figures half-profile to the Cross, or in a
south-westerly direction. But at midnight the two
halted in the denser portion of the forest; and there
they built two fires and prepared their resting-places
with leaves and tender twigs; and having done so, they
breathed a long sigh of relief, sat down, and gradually
their eyes lost the eager, intelligent look in vacancy.

But after a while Simba said in a deep, low voice,

half to himself and half to Moto : "Wallahi! but this
has been a sad day for us. That large and costly
caravan and the brave men and leaders are gone. It
was but last night I stood at their tent-door, looking
at my noble master Amer and his friend Khamis, and I
was thinking that there never lived finer and nobler-
looking men. Ah, Arab sheikhs! where are ye now,
chiefs of Zanzibar?" Then, raising his head, he said,
"Answer me, thou black, blackest night! Answer me
if ye can, oh twinkling stars! Answer me, dark and
dread silence! Shall I never see dear master again?
Moto, where dost thou think Amer is now?"

To which Moto answered : "Amer, the noblest of his
tribe, the worthiest master that ever lived, the man
with the kind heart and liberal hand, is not dead—he
sleepeth."

"Sleepeth! Ah, would it were so! then this great
heaviness of sorrow within me would vanish. But
what meanest thou, Moto?"

"Hast thou forgotten already the words of our noble
master, the son of Osman, how that he said to us
often, a man cannot die ; the body may remain on the
ground to moulder, and rot, and become dust, but the
life that was in him cannot die? Hast thou never
heard him mention the word SOUL—that unseen, unfelt
thing, which is as light as air, yet is the most important part of a man? For a long time I laughed at
Amer's words in my secret heart, but when I heard all
the Arabs say the same thing, and the Nazarenes at
Zanzibar say it also, I was obliged to believe, though I
could not tell what the soul was like, or who had seen
it, or if anybody had ever seen it. But now Amer's head

lies low on the ground and a cruel wound has found his kind heart, I shall keep thinking of his words, and believe in them ; and I believe truly that Amer's soul looks down upon us through this darkness from above."

"I remember me now much the same thing," said Simba, "though my sorrow of heart had blinded my memory. Is it not a happy thought, Moto, that master Amer is not quite, quite dead, and that we shall see him again ?"

"Yes, very happy. Thou knowest, Simba, that he cannot be dead with us either, for we shall carry him in our memories like a valued treasure, and will never cease talking of him when we are together."

"Ah ! thou hast a good memory, Moto ; but who, thinkest thou, is the happiest—master Amer, up above there, or young master Selim, a prisoner ?"

"Oh, Simba ! while I was beginning to think myself happy, thou hast made my heart black with sorrow, by making me think of what that boy must suffer. If it were not for his future good I would never have left him. Amer is happiest in Paradise, but Selim, his son, living on earth, must be miserable."

"It is just as I thought also," said Simba. "Poor child ! Do you not remember how pretty he looked when he hinted to his father, that perhaps Simba would like his freedom ? How his eyes, always beautiful, seemed filled with softness, and love, and gratitude to me ? Ah, Selim, young master of everything that Simba has, it will go hard with some of these savage Watuta if they harm thee !"

"They will not harm Selim or the Arab boys ; they

will keep them as curiosities, unless some of them have seen Arabs before going about to buy slaves, in which case I pity them all," said Moto.

"Moto," shouted Simba, raising himself up, "art thou revenging thyself on me for making thee unhappy with the mention of him? Speak. Selim a slave! That petted, tender Arab boy a slave! Answer me, Moto."

"It is as I tell thee; if any of the Watuta understand, as we do, what the word Arab is, all the Arab boys will be made slaves, and be beaten like dogs," answered Moto.

"We are not obeying master Amer by running away from the camp of the Watuta. He told us to save his son Selim. I am going back;" and Simba snatched his spears and gun.

"Fool!" said Moto. "We cannot save him from the Watuta by going into their camp. We can only do it by finishing as we have begun. We must go to Katalambula's village and see Kalulu. He only can save Selim and ourselves."

"Well, I believe thou art right," said Simba. "Let us go to sleep, and at dawn let us be off to see this Kalulu." Saying which, he lay down between the fires, but sleep did not visit his eyes for some time afterwards.

For fifteen days they marched long and far towards the south-west without any incident worthy of notice. Now and then they left the forest occasionally, to follow a road leading to some village and obtain information as to the whereabouts of the village of Katalambula of those people whom they might meet, with little danger to themselves.

On the sixteenth day of their flight they came to a large plain, extremely populous and rich. The dun-coloured tops of huts arose above the tall corn and millet everywhere. At midday they came to a deep river flowing north-west, which the people called Liemba. On the opposite side of the river they were also told was Katalambula's village.

They were rowed across, for which Simba paid the canoe-man with a couple of arrows, having no other means of paying him. Then, following the right bank of the river for a few minutes, by fields of splendid corn, they came in sight of the village.

It was substantially built; and was constructed in the same manner as the Kwikuru of Olimali, except that the king's quarters were flat-roofed tembes, sur-rounding a square of large dimensions, where the king kept his cattle and goats, and two or three donkeys, which were preserved more as curiosities than for any use that were made of them, and where he himself lived with his numerous family of women; for, strange to say, Katalambula, with all his wives, had never been able to obtain a son.

The principal gate was, as usual, decorated with the only trophies savages respect or regard, viz., glistening white skulls of their enemies.

When Simba and Moto arrived near the gate, the former's gigantic height of body and breadth of shoulders soon attracted attention, and drew crowds towards him of curious gazers.

"Health unto you," was his greeting to them.

"And unto you, strangers!" they replied. "Whence come you?" they then asked.

"We are travellers," said Moto, "who have heard of King Katalambula, and have desired much to see Ututa's king." This was said in good Kirori, which, excepting a few words, is the same as Kituta.

"Your words are well, strangers. You are Warori?" a chief, who now made his presence known, asked them. "Though your garb is different, and the punctures on the cheek and forehead are wanting."

"I am a Mrori," answered Moto, "but my companion is not; he is a stranger from a far land."

"Then do the Warori carry guns nowadays? And how is it that you wear such fine clothes?" he asked, regarding them suspiciously.

"We were successful in hunting, and shot an elephant, whose teeth we sold for cloth and two guns."

"And where did you meet elephants?"

"On the frontier, near Urori."

"And where did you meet the Arabs?"

"In Ututa, two days from Urori."

"Did you ask them where they were going?"

"They were going to Uwemba."

"Perhaps you can tell us where they came from?"

"From Ubena."

"Strangers," said the chief, "you are liars. No Arabs have been in this country for a long, long time. You are our prisoners, and must come before the King in our company;" and, as he spoke, the men that had gathered near rushed at them and disarmed them.

In a short time they found themselves within the inner square; and under a large sycamore in the centre was seated, on a dried mud platform, raised two feet above the ground, and which ran around the tree like a

K

circular sofa, covered with kid and goatskins, and over
these skins of wild beasts, an old white-haired man,
whom, by the deference paid to him, the prisoners knew
was King Katalambula.

The King had on his head a band of snowy white
cloth, and his dress was a long broad robe of crimson
blanket cloth. He was a kindly-looking old man, and
he was evidently at the time being much amused with
something that a tall young lad of sixteen, or thereabouts, was saying; but as the group of warriors guard-
ing Simba and Moto entered the square, the old man
looked up curiously, and when they drew nearer he
demanded to know what the matter was.

"My sultan, my lord," said the principal man to
whom we were first introduced at the gate, "these men
are suspicious characters. To every question I asked
them they replied with a lie; wherefore we brought
them to you to judge."

"Speak, strangers, the truth. Who and what are
ye?"

The quick eye of Moto had seen the young lad standing by Katalambula when he entered, and he suspected
that he was the object of his search, the young friend
of bygone years.

"Great king," said Moto, "I did lie; but to you I
will give the truth. I am a Mrori, who was taken
when a child by the Arabs of Zanzibar. Years after
that time, when I was a man, I accompanied an Arab
chief, called Kisesa, to Unyanyembe; but soon after
arriving, he declared war against the Warori, and——"

"Kisesa!" said the young lad, advancing towards him
with the stride of a young lion. "War against the

Warori!" he added again, with an angry glitter in his eyes.

"Yes, young chief," said Moto, humbly; "and I accompanied Kisesa to this war. After a long march we came before a village near Ututa, governed by——"

"By whom?" asked the young chief. "Tell me his name—quick, dog!"

"Mostana," said Moto, deliberately.

"Mostana!" shrieked the boy, and the word was echoed in a tone of surprise by all.

"Yes, Mostana was his name," said Moto, unheeding the menacing looks or the angry murmurs which arose from all sides, but hurrying on with his story. "We took the village after a short time, though Mostana's men fought well, and numbers of our people were killed. Mostana's men were nearly all killed, and those who were left were made slaves, according to the custom of the Arabs."

"Yes, that is true," said Katalambula. "Those cruel people make clean work of it when they fight, but I——"

"Were they all made prisoners?" asked the boy chief, in a curious tone.

"All, except one, and——"

"And his name was—— ?"

"Kalulu!" replied Moto, in a clear tone.

Again rose a murmur of astonishment from all sides, but, apparently heedless that he had said anything very strange, Moto continued:

"Yes, Kalulu, the son of Mostana, was standing by his father's side, when Kisesa, observing him, said he would give fifty pieces of cloth to whoever would take him alive. On hearing that, my soul felt a feeling of pity for him, as you must remember I was a Mrori; and, though I liked the Arabs, I could not kill my own people at their bidding, nor did I like to see such a brave boy as Mostana's son in danger of being made a slave by Kisesa. So, on hearing the offer made by Kisesa, I snatched up a shield and rushed forward to whisper to him to follow me, but the boy thought probably that I was about to kill him, as he put a spear clean through my shield and pinned my arm to it."

A loud cry of admiration greeted this, while the boy already advanced nearer to Moto and regarded him affectionately; but Moto heeded nothing of this, but continued:

"Seeing me still advance, the boy sprang back just as his father fell dead by a bullet from some gun behind me. I hastened after the boy, saw him look cautiously around, and spring over the palisade; but I was right behind him; and when he was a little distance off in the forest I chased him at my best speed, and soon came up to him. I explained to him who I was, and why I chased him, and told him I was his friend; upon which he told me that he was going to his uncle, a great king in Ututa, and that if ever we met again he would be my friend."

As Moto finished this part of his story, the boy chief sprang forward and embraced Moto, saying:

"Dost thou not know me? I AM KALULU! And thou art my friend Moto! I shall keep my promise, and the King must thank thee," said Kalulu, as he drew Moto forward towards Katalambula.

As they heard these words from Kalulu, the chiefs

and elders clapped their hands, and saluted Moto, while the King took hold of Moto's right hand and said:

"Kalulu has told me the story which related how the Kirori slave would not take him when he might have done so; and though I never expected to see the man, I promised him that if any of my people met him and they should bring him to me, I should be his friend; that he should have one of my daughters for wife, and that I would bestow on him anything else he asked, for Kalulu is as dear to me as though he were my son. Speak, Moto, and tell me what I can do for thee."

Then Moto, after a seat had been given to him, repeated briefly the story which we have already given to the readers, while murmurs of approbation at the wonderful good fortune of Ferodia rose from every side; then, when these had subsided, Moto said:

"Oh, Kalulu, if what I have done for thee deserves kindness at thy hands, and if thou wert sincere when thou didst promise to be my friend, speak to the great King of the Watuta for me, and let him give my young master Selim, the Arab slave, as well as the three other slaves their freedom, and let them depart to their own land, and to the friends who will mourn for them."

"Kalulu has already given his promise to thee, Moto. Kalulu is the friend of thy friends, and the enemy of thy enemies. Katalambula, the King, hears my words, and will do this kindness for thee for what thou hast done for me. Speak, great King," said Kalulu, advancing to him as he spoke.

"Ah, Kalulu!" said the King Katalambula, "thou

knowest not what thou askest, but I will do for thee
what may be done. I can intercede with Ferodia for
them, but I may not command him. Those Arab
youths are the slaves of Ferodia; but if he is willing to
exchange for them, I will give him two female slaves
for each of the Arab boy-slaves. Will that content
thee, Kalulu?"

"I will wait until he comes here. I will then give
thee my answer. But I think thou givest way too
much to Ferodia in all things; he likes me not too
well, because I stand between him and thy favour. If
I were king of the Watuta, I should give Ferodia a
lesson."

"Tush, boy! be not too hasty with thy tongue.
Ferodia is chief in his own right of a large tract of
country. Dost thou wish me to take that from him
which he has won by his spear and his bow?" asked
Katalambula, slightly frowning.

"He has not won by himself, with his sword and his
spear, the battle against the Arabs. Eight hundred of
the ten hundred warriors he has with him are thine,
taken from thy country. Wilt thou that he shall
choose for himself what he shall please to reserve, or
wilt thou choose what he shall have and what thou
wilt keep?"

"Boy, boy, Ferodia is the chief warrior of the
Watuta; he knows every art of war. He has never been
beaten in the battle, either by the Wabena, or the
Warungu, or the Wawemba, or any other; and though
I have furnished him with men, he has always given me
the greater and the most valuable share. Why wilt
thou, who art but a boy, tell me these things concern-

ing Ferodia? Be patient; I will ask him when he comes for these slaves for thee. But had it not been for the good deed this man did for thee, I should have ordered Ferodia to roast them all alive. Go thou, rather, and do thy duty towards these travellers; give them food and drink; and when they have rested, give each a house. Then let my daughter Lamoli be given to Moto for wife; and to this tall man give one of my female slaves for wife. Katalambula has spoken."

While the King was speaking he was evidently getting more peevish, for he was old and soon tired; so Kalulu refrained from taxing his patience further, and beckoning to Moto and Simba, he walked away with his guests, leaving the King to be assisted by his chiefs to his quarters.

When young Kalulu arrived at his own house, or rather room—for the entire square was surrounded but by one house—he again embraced Moto, and promised to leave no stone unturned until he had secured the freedom of the Arab boys. "But," said Kalulu, "it is well for them that you are my friend, as I do not think I can ever forgive the Arabs for murdering my father; and the King finds it very hard to do this thing for you, because in Mostana he lost a brother; and those of our tribe who have travelled far to hunt and kill elephants always come back with tales of their cruelty. I fear if Ferodia insists on their being slaves my uncle will not resist him; for, but for you, nothing would please him better than to torture them, and I should have liked it too."

"Oh, Kalulu," said Moto, "you do not know Selim. He would never have treated a man badly, neither did his father. Simba and I were proud to be slaves of such a man as Amer bin Osman, and we were proud to call Selim our young master. Do you know that Selim is just your age, though you are taller than he is, and you are thinner than he was; though, poor boy! he will be thin enough when he comes here. But how you have grown, Kalulu! yet you cannot be more than sixteen years old!"

"I do not know how old I am," Kalulu said, laughing. "I was little when I saw you, or you would never have caught me. But I must do what the King has commanded me to do." And Kalulu darted out, spear in hand, his ostrich plumes trailing over his head far behind.

Perhaps here would be a fit place to intercalate a description of the native youth whose name forms the title-page to this strange historical romance.

Since ancient Greece displayed the forms of her noblest, finest youth in the Olympian games, and gave her Phidias and Praxiteles models to immortalise in marble, all civilised nations have borrowed their ideas of manly beauty from the statues left to us by Grecian and Roman sculptors, because civilised nations seldom can furnish us with models to compete with the super-excellent types designed by Greece. While American and English sculptors go to Rome to play with marble and plaster, and borrow for their patterns of an athlete or perfect human form, the vulgar, low, and uncouth lazzaroni of Rome, the centre of Africa teems with finer specimens of manhood than may be found in this world; such types as would even cause the marble forms of Phidias to blush.

Kalulu was one of the best specimens which the ancient sculptors would have delighted to imitate in stone. His face or head may not, perhaps, have kindled any very great admiration, but the body, arms, and limbs were unmistakably magnificent in shape. He had not an ounce of flesh too much, yet without the tedious training which the modern athlete has to undergo, and following nothing but the wild instinct of his adopted tribe, he was a perfect youthful Apollo in form. The muscles of his arms stood out like balls, and the muscles of his legs were as firm as iron. There was not one of the tribe of his age who could send a spear so far, or draw the bow with so true and steady aim as he, or could shoot the arrow farther. None had such a springy, elastic movement as he, none was so swift of foot, none followed the chase with his ardour, none was so daring in the attack; yet with all that constant exercise, the following of which had given him these advantages, his form lost nothing of that surpassing grace of movement and manly beauty for which he was styled by me, just now, a perfect youthful Apollo.

If I give him such praise for his elegance of form and free graceful carriage, I may not continue in the same strain in the description of his face. Kalulu was a negro, but his colour was not black by any means, it was a deep brown or bronze. His lips were thick, and, according to our ideas, such as would not lend beauty to his face; his nose was not flat, neither was it as correct in shape as we would wish it; but, with the exception of lips and nose, one could find no fault with his features. His eyes were remarkably large, brilliant, sparkling,

and black as the blackest ink, while the whites of his
eyes were not disfigured by the slightest tinge of
unhealthy yellow, nor seamed with the red veins
common to negroes of older growth. His ears were
small and shapely, and, strange to say, the lobes were
not as yet distorted out of all form with the pieces of
wood or gourd-necks, which, unhappily, with the
Watuta, are too common among their ear ornaments.
His ears were simply decorated with two Sungomazzi
beads,* one to each ear, each bead suspended by a piece
of very fine brass wire. His hair, though woolly, hung
below his shoulders in a thousand fine braids, adorned
with scores of fine red, yellow, and white beads. His
ornaments, besides those already mentioned, consisted
of three snow-white ostrich plumes, fastened in a band
which ran around his head, and which, besides holding
the plumes, served to hold his hair; a braided necklace,
ivory bands above each elbow, and ivory bracelets, and
broad bead-worked anklets.

While the author has been endeavouring to portray
Kalulu, that the reader may become acquainted with
his excellence, the youthful hero had hastened to bring
Lamoli to her husband; and he now appeared on the
threshold of the door with his cousin, who at once
pleased Moto as much as the King expected she would.
We will say this, however, in passing, that though she
was not by any means the loveliest of her sex, she was
neither ugly, toothless, nor old; nor was she young,
pretty, or one calculated to charm our fastidious tastes.
But Moto did not refuse her; on the contrary, he

---

* These beads are as large as a pigeon's egg, and are either of
coloured porcelain or coloured glass.

thought it a high honour to marry the daughter of a king, and became lavish in his praise, with which Lamoli was not at all displeased.

Having performed this marriage according to the customs of the Watuta, Kalulu remembered that he had still another marriage on his hand, and at once asked Simba what kind of a wife he fancied. Simba was not at all displeased with the idea of another wife, though he and Moto had each a wife at Zanzibar, who had borne them children; and he at once replied that Kalulu might choose for him. After an absence of only a few minutes, Kalulu returned with a young woman who might have drawn crowds in London and New York, as the "Great African Giantess."

As he saw the gigantic couple together, Kalulu clapped his hands in high glee, and danced about them as if he were about to receive a magnificent gift, and laughed as he burst into a mock rhapsody.

"Lo, Kalulu has seen strange things! he has seen two trees drawn together from a great distance! he has seen them walk together arm-in-arm!! Behold how the trees, the sycamore and the mtambu, the great baobab, and the mbiti, how they nod their heads, and are pleased!! For they rejoice that two great trees are married, and a forest of young trees will soon sprout up. As they move, the ground shakes and the huts reel. Verily this is a great day; both the ground and the huts have been guzzling pombe—they are drunk, rejoicing over the marriages Kalulu, the future King of the Watuta, has performed!

"Lamoli, my sweet cousin, daughter of Katalambula— of Katalambula the great King—was sorrowing for a husband. She was thirsting, like a pool in the middle of the plain in a long summer. She, the flower of Katalambula's household, was sick for a husband. But the day came—ah, happy day! A man from afar— from the island in the sea—he came, he saw me, I knew him. He was my friend; and in him Katalambula—Katalambula the great King—found a husband for his daughter—a mate for Lamoli.

"Ah, Lamoli! Lamoli! Lamoli! weep no more; but laugh until thy mouth reaches from ear to ear, and I, Kalulu, thy cousin, can see the joy welling from thy throat, like living water springing from a rock! Laugh, Lamoli, sweet Lamoli! so that the unmarried women of all Ututa may hear and envy thee; so they may rend their bosoms with rage, or crush themselves to death with the over-weight of their ornaments. Laugh, Lamoli, sweet Lamoli! until every foot of man and woman moves to the sound of thy happy laughter! And thou, tall woman of Ututa! do thou laugh and sing, until all the tall trees of Ututa will become jealous of thee! we then may have rain. And thou, Simba, tall man from afar, well named the Lion! roar for joy, and thou wilt hear the wild lions of the forest roar in concert with thee, and each will be roused to fury, roaring for their loving mates. But enough; be happy, and raise warriors for your tribes. Kalulu is not a singer; he is a young warrior, who is learning how to throw the spear and shoot with the bow. The singers are coming with drums to do you honour, for such are the King's commands."

While Kalulu had been thus employing himself, a company of drummers, eight in number, two tumblers,—

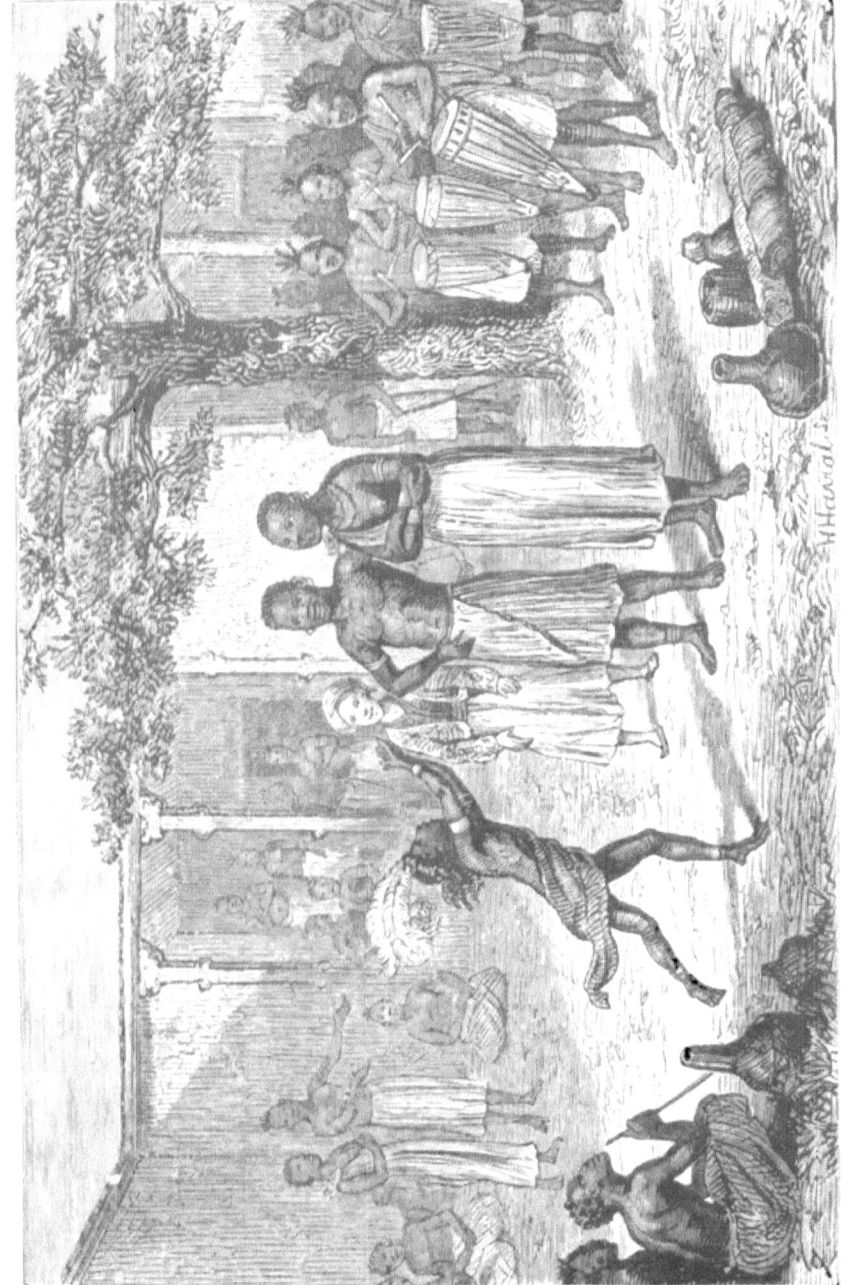

or, as we should call them, two mountebanks,—and fifty couples of young men and women had formed themselves in a circle; and as Kalulu ceased speaking, the Magic Doctor, or Mganga, as the natives called him, raised his voice and sang the marriage song, while he danced in an ecstatic manner as he sang. I should also say, before giving the song, that the smallest drums only accompanied his voice, while the great drums thundered together when the chorus was given by the dancers. The words were, as near as they can be translated:

> We sing the happy marriage song,
> We sound the drum, and beat the gong
> > In honour of Lamoli!
> She is the daughter of a king,
> Yet she spent her days in weeping,
> Being left alone and sorrowing.
> > Poor sorrowing Lamoli!
> > *Chorus.* Oh, Lamoli!
> > Poor Lamoli!
> > Sorrowing Lamoli!
>
> A day has come, ah, happy day!
> That brought a stranger in the way
> > Of sorrowing Lamoli!
> Long ago the stranger did a deed,
> A friendly deed, in time of need,
> Which won for him the lover's meed.
> > Sweet Lamoli!
> > *Chorus.* Oh, Lamoli!
> > Sweet Lamoli!
> > Charming Lamoli!
>
> This stranger sav'd young Kalulu
> From cruel bonds at Kwikuru.
> > The good stranger!
> Kalulu swore to this brave man,

As long as life-blood in him ran,
To praise the name to every man
             Of this brave stranger !
      Chorus. Oh, stranger !
             Good stranger !
             Brave stranger !

This man has come to 'Tuta Land,
This man who sav'd with friendly hand
             Our young Kalulu !
Shall we deny him our faint praise?
Shall we refuse him wedlock lays?
Shall we not wish him happiest days?
             Who sav'd Kalulu?
      Chorus. Oh, Kalulu !
             Young Kalulu !
             Brave Kalulu !

Our great King heard the stranger's name,
And nearer to him the stranger came,
             To Katalambula !
He said, "I've known this story long,   .
A Mtuta's memory is strong.
I love the good and hate the wrong,"
             Said Katalambula !
      Chorus. Oh, Katalambula !
             Good Katalambula !
             Great Katalambula !

Give him house, give him home. You boy !
Give him pombe and food. Give him joy !
             Give him Lamoli !
Brave man ! take the pride of our race ;
Take the dearest girl with the loveliest face.
Live in the shade of our kingly mace
             With good Lamoli !
      Chorus. Oh, Lamoli !
             Good Lamoli !
             Sweet Lamoli !

We sing the happy marriage song,
We sound the drum and beat the gong
             For joy with Lamoli,

Now a wife, no longer weeping,
No more to spend her days in mourning,
She will be for ever laughing,
                    Happy Lamoli!
        Chorus.   Oh, Lamoli!
                    Charming Lamoli!
                    Happy Lamoli!

The music accompanying this song was slow and sweet, worthy of the great occasion on which it was given. During the chorus, the dancing became more lively, and each man and woman lifted the voice high, which created a grand and majestic volume of sound, while the drums were beaten with a terrific vigour. The festivities lasted all the day and night, until sunrise next morning; but during the night they were better attended, nearly a thousand souls joining in the song and chorus. Kalulu and many others were hoarse from over-exertion of voice, when they retired next morning to rest.

Having brought Simba and Moto to their temporary home and through their difficulties, let us now withdraw from this scene for a while, and see how it fares with the Arab boy-slaves and Ferodia's caravan.

CHAPTER VI.

ALTHOUGH the caravan started the day after the departure of Simba and Moto, it could not of course travel
so fast as two fugitives; so that the journey, which only
occupied a few days with our two friends, lasted nearly
a month with Ferodia's caravan.

Ferodia, the chief of the Watuta caravan, had besides
four Arab slaves—three of whom were perfectly white
—nearly three hundred black slaves, who had been
captured in the battle of Kwikuru. If the report was
spread abroad that he possessed so many slaves, as
would undoubtedly be the case, he would soon be visited
by traders from Unyanyembe and from Kilwa, and perhaps, if he waited long enough, from Tette, on the
Zambezi river; so it was for his advantage to travel
slowly, not only that the rumour might have time to
spread, but also to give the human cattle plenty of
time to recover from their wounds.

The marches were, therefore, commenced at six

o'clock in the morning, and seldom lasted longer than noon, as the first part of the country through which he now travelled was extremely populous and rich, and each chief was friendly to him and his men ; but after the tenth day he neared the debatable ground, consisting of extensive tracts of forest and jungle, lying between Urori and Ututa, and inhabited by no living being, except wild beasts. From the farthest westerly point of this debatable tract, there were three long marches, or say ninety miles, to Katalambula's country.

Having explained so much, let us glean what may be interesting to the general reader of the incidents of this march relating to the slaves.

Besides suffering intensely from the heat, Selim, Abdullah, and Mussoud suffered excessively from the loads which they were compelled to carry, and which chafed their tender shoulders frightfully. For the first three days they went entirely naked, as it must not be supposed that, because the Watuta were rich in clothes, they possessed one yard too much, or that they could have dispensed with a yard for the comfort of slaves.

Slaves are cattle, are supposed too often to be able to live like cattle, and are therefore treated like cattle. So these three hundred slaves were chained—for chains, it must be confessed, were part of the plunder which the Watuta had found in the Arab camp—by twenties ; an iron collar ran around the neck of each adult, while the boys, Selim, Abdullah, Mussoud, Isa, and the negro boys, among whom, it must be remembered, was our mischievous Niani, or the monkey, and others,

L

were tied by ropes around the waist, about six feet apart, the tallest first. Of the adult slaves there were fifteen herds, or gangs of twenties, each gang being superintended by a sub-chief or a trustworthy warrior, and there was one gang of boys which were looked after by Tifum Byah.

I have already said that the slaves were cattle. The word cattle must be understood by the reader in its most literal sense. Decency was therefore out of the question. If one needed to wash his face in camp, the whole gang, accompanied by the chief, were obliged to march out for the convenience of this one. If from any cause a man required to fall out of the line, there was a halt and a constant worrying of the unfortunate wretch until the caravan had been overtaken. If one needed a drop of water all had to stop. In all gangs and crews of slaves there is always one calling for something or requiring something more than his fellows; and this to the others is a source of vexation, because the chief who has charge is soon irritated if such a proceeding is carried too far, and he is not slow to avail himself of the rod to quicken the footsteps of the lagging gang.

In the boy's gang, Isa was one of those who continually required to halt, and all the boys suffered in consequence, especially Selim, whose file-leader was the lagging and unfortunate Isa.

Niani saw through the trick of Isa in a very short time, and no doubt he would have remained silent about it, had he not seen that his young master Selim suffered through it. For two or three days of the march Niani held his peace, but when Selim received a more than usually severe beating from Tifum Byah, Niani exploded, and told the chief, to his surprise, that he was whipping the wrong boy, that it was Isa who was the cause of the stoppage; whereupon Isa received a severe punishment with the ever-ready kurbash (hippopotamus-hide whip). While Selim had been whipped Isa had never expressed any great sympathy with him, but when he was punished himself his cries and groans were dreadfully long and loud, and in the camp he was constantly bewailing his hard lot, and always threatening that supple-minded and tough-bodied little negro Niani for his expose of him.

On the evening of the fifth day after their arrival at camp, Niani, who knew how to like and how to hate, said aloud to Selim, as soon as he had an opportunity, that he would much prefer if Selim took his waist-cloth. Selim refused it upon the ground that he would have none left for himself.

"Oh, but, Master Selim," said Niani, "I am but a little nigger; no one will mind me. I wanted to give it to you before, but I did not like to offer my cloth to you, because it is dirty."

"Anything is better than nothing. I will take it with thanks, since you say you don't want it; but won't you keep a little of it for yourself?"

"Not an inch," said Niani, resolutely. "I don't want a cloth anyhow—never did want it; besides that is the cloth you gave me that night I tripped Isa, and cruel Isa was going to put me on the fire."

Selim then rose up to put this filthy piece of torn cotton cloth around his waist; but as he was about to put it on, he saw his friends Abdullah and Mussoud looking wistfully up; and their colour, as well as his own, made them look all too nude for a country where all skins were black. Without saying a word he measured the cloth in three equal pieces, and tore it into three equal strips, one of which he presented to Abdullah, another to Mussoud, and the other he reserved for himself. The two boys rose up, blushing gratefully, and Abdullah said to Selim:

"Thy heart is as soft as fine gold. The cloth is not six inches wide, but I feel more grateful to thee than ever I did when I received fine daoles (rich gold-worked cloth) at the hand of my father, Mohammed, whom may God preserve! A pure heart like thine will not long go unrewarded at the hand of Allah."

"Thou mightest have given me a piece," said Isa to Selim, in a complaining tone.

"How can you talk so, Master Isa?" asked Niani. "Your skin is as black as mine; sure, you look as though you were clothed already. You should be happy in having a black skin, instead of wanting a piece out of nothing."

"A truce to your insolence, Niani, or I will come and break every bone in your body," said Isa, angrily.

"You had better not, Isa, because I am a slave of Ferodia, the Mtuta chief; and if you kill me, Ferodia will kill you," answered Niani

"Well, then, hold your tongue, and don't torment me. I am sick of life already, and sick in mind and body," said Isa.

"Dost thou suffer much, Isa?" asked Selim.

"Indeed I do. My head aches as if it would split, and all down my back run sharp pains. They are not the pains which that savage dog Tifum made, but something else. I think there is something serious the matter with me," moaned poor suffering Isa.

"I hope not," said Selim. "Cheer up, Isa, my friend; we have only to reach Katalambula to have rest. This march cannot last for ever."

"I shall never reach the country of the accursed Watuta," said Isa. "My illness is too serious."

"Why, what can the matter be with thee, my friend?"

"Don't start, Selim, and don't curse me when I tell you that I have the *jederi* (the small-pox)."

"The small-pox! What makes thee think that?" Selim asked.

"I have seen it often enough, and have seen the men die on the road from it, and I fear I shall die too," said Isa, mournfully.

The next morning Isa was very much worse, and it was obvious to every one that the boy had it very badly, but he was not permitted to halt or to be carried. Slaves are not carried: there are no means of carrying sick slaves in Africa, and so he was driven along with the rest; but about ten o'clock, after four hours' march, as they were approaching a forest, the sick lad became delirious, and he began to reel like a drunken man, and after a short time the load fell from his head, and as Tifum came up raging furiously at this weakness, Isa fell across his bale with his eyes half protruding from their sockets, and his tongue hanging out. But Tifum had no sense of kindness in his heart; so he began to flog the unfortunate wretch with all the force that an unnatural cruelty alone could have impelled, until Selim, unable longer to bear the disgusting sight, hurled the load he carried on his head full at the head of the savage ruffian, and while he was down he snatched the whip from his hand, and began to belabour him with all his might until he was overthrown himself on the ground by the infuriated Tifum, and belaboured in his turn until Tifum was obliged to desist lest he might kill him.

Cutting the rope which joined the prostrate bodies of the boys, the one insensible from violence, the other from a deadly sickness, he called for a gourdful of water, and pouring it on Selim's head, soon restored him to consciousness. Then the refined cruelty of the slave traders, and the utter abomination of the inhuman traffic, began to be exhibited. Trembling with rage and merciless hate, he called for the long, heavy, wooden yoke, which, furnished with two prongs a little apart from each other, is used for the most refractory slaves. When green, this yoke-tree weighs about thirty pounds, but dry it generally weighs about twenty pounds. One of these tree-yokes had been prepared but a few days before, so that it could not be much reduced in weight from what it weighed originally. This was the clumsy, heavy instrument of torture with which Tifum designed to encumber Selim's body.

After the neck of the half-unconscious lad was placed between the prongs, the ends of the prongs were drawn together by means of a strong cord, so that the head remained firmly imprisoned, while the huge unwieldly tree of the yoke sloped behind him about ten feet off from his shoulders.

In order to avoid employing a guard to carry the tree,

the end was lifted up and tied to Abdullah's shoulders and arm.

When things had thus been prepared for the continuance of the march Tifum proceeded to the dying Isa, and seeing it was hopeless to expect further work from him, as the look of death was already on his face, the savage fiend bestowed a kick on the body, and swishing his kurbash warningly, gave the hint to Selim, who was now the file leader, to proceed. In a short time the caravan was out of sight, while the unfortunate Isa was left in the middle of the road to gasp his last, unseen, unwept, and unhonoured.

On the twentieth day of the march it was found that little Mussoud was attacked with the small-pox. Numbers of the slaves had already perished from this fell disease; for as fast as they fell from the ranks and could not rise again, despite repeated applications of the staff of a spear, or a rod, or a kurbash, they were left to die the miserable death of deserted sick where they fell, and not one thought was ever directed to them again.

Thus when Mussoud became sick, the alarm of his brother Abdullah and his friend Selim was extreme. They requested permission to share the burden of his load by having it tied to the yoke-tree with which Selim's neck was still furnished, but the slight request was refused, and when the latter's eyes again flashed a dangerous light, Tifum, who saw that he had a stubborn soul to deal with, replied with another dose of vigorous lashing on the boy's shoulders until they were one mass of weals and bruises.

Selim uttered not a word nor moan; he was getting

to be past all feeling of bodily pain, though his heart
was keenly alive and sensitive. While plodding along
in this manner under the burning sun, no sound breaking the soft shuffling sound of the tramp of naked feet
of the slaves, except a low moan now and then from
poor little Mussoud, and Tifum had retired to vent his
spite upon those in the rear, it struck him as a sudden
idea that he was being punished more cruelly than the
others because, despite the fine religious education he
had received, he had of late, since he had been in
bondage, forgotten the God of his fathers, whom Amer
had counselled him so often never to forget. His conscience was not a whit more hardened; the reason of
this neglect was the delicacy he felt in approaching his
God with unwashed hands and feet; but now he determined to avail himself of the first opportunity of a
halt, and prepare himself for prayer.

After repeated prayers from the sick boy Mussoud
to Tifum to give him one little halt to rest, it was at
last granted; more, however, to give Tifum an opportunity to light his pipe than for the sake of the sick
boy.

No sooner had Tifum turned his back, than Selim
bent down and began to scrape together the dry, white,
sandy dust from the road, and to rub his feet, and
hands, and face, and body with it, as if he were wash-
ing himself; then turning his face to the north-east,
in the direction of Mecca, he began his prayer in a
whisper:

"Oh, Thou who art the light of heaven and earth,
whom all creatures praise, unto whom all things be-
longeth, thou bounteous, wise, and compassionate God!

be gracious and merciful to one of the true believers, who now standeth before Thy footstool.

"Thou art great, Thou art holy, Thou art almighty, Oh God! and unto those who invoke Thee Thou hast promised, through Thy prophet Mohammed, blessed be his name! to be attentive and to lend assistance.

"Thou all-knowing and gracious God! avert from me the torments of Jehenna, which I suffer at the hands of these infidel savages.

"The unbelievers have laid cruel hands upon me, a true believer, and a son of a true believer. Lo! they have bound me like unto a sheep about to be slaughtered; they have laid their whips upon me, the cruel thongs have cut into my bones, and with their sharp spears have they gashed me.

"Thou Powerful and Self-sufficient God! Thou hast promised to protect the fatherless and the orphan, and to be solicitous for him, and to punish those who oppress him.

"Thou compassionate and loving God! let the orphan's cries take the form of prayers, and suffer them to ascend unto Thee before Thy footstool, and do Thou bow down Thine head, and let them penetrate Thine ear.

"Thou one, only, and eternal God! hearken compassionately unto my prayers, and rescue me from the unbelievers.

"Thou Lord of men, King of men, and God of men! save me from mine enemies, by the promise Thou hast given unto all true believers through Thy holy apostle Mohammed, and be Thy heart softened toward the orphan, and hear his prayers."

When Selim had finished this urgent, sincere appeal to his God, he prostrated himself to the earth, and then rose refreshed in body and spirit.

Turning to Abdullah, who had been attending to his brother, he said:

"Abdullah, my friend, I feel refreshed and strong. I have a bright idea in my head."

"I have seen you pray, Selim, and have wished that I could pray, too; but my heart is too bitter for prayer. I feel as if I could curse all men, and myself, and die. Poor Mussoud's days are numbered, I fear: and if he dies, I do not care what becomes of me."

"But, my dear friend, the Kūran says: 'When thou art in distress pray to thy God and He will hear thee; His ear is open to the oppressed.'"

"I know it, Selim, but I cannot pray now. I fear I should curse God for permitting his faithful to be treated as we have been. Listen to the moans of my brother, and think of his being left to die all alone in the road, because, if he cannot march, they will not let me remain with him!" But what is thy bright idea, Selim?"

"My idea is to run away to-night, and go to the depths of this forest. Far better to die there than lead this life so wretched. If one of these people can trust himself in the forest, why may I not do so? They have not been able to kill me with all the weight of their cruelties. The forest were far kinder than these inhuman Watuta."

"And my brother, what of him?"

"We will take him with us; and when we are alone, safe from our pursuers, we will be able to nurse him.

We will build ourselves a strong little hut near some nice stream, where we shall be safe and quiet; and while you are watching your sick brother, I will take my spear and go out to gather wild fruit and honey. But, hush! Here comes Tifum. Help Mussoud to his feet, and let him hold up until to-night."

Just then the stern signal to march was given, and the boys turned industriously and submissively to their bales; and Mussoud feeling relieved by the rest, the caravan set out at its usual pace.

About noon they halted in the forest, and, knowing that no danger from men was to be feared in the forest, the Watuta were heedless of the usual boma or brush fence around the camp.

The boy-gang being tied together, were of course inseparable, and Abdullah, in his usual place, sat next to Selim, as they munched their roasted Indian corn or their half-boiled holcus grains. Mussoud was accustomed to sit next to Selim, but owing to his illness he was placed outside the camp, as all the Watuta knew this disease was contagious, and what danger lay to the whole unvaccinated camp by the dread presence of the small-pox.

At night they were still together, Selim and Abdullah. Inside the circle of the camp were men seated in circles near the fire, discussing various topics. Outside the camp, in the deep, deep night was perfect silence; not a sound broke upon the ear, save now and then the uneasy growl of the hyæna.

"Well, Abdullah," said Selim, "the night has come, and thou must decide what thou wilt do."

"Dear Selim, I cannot go and leave my brother. Poor Mussoud will not live till to-morrow morning. I am afraid he is very ill to-night. His head was so hot, and he did not seem to know me. If thou goest away I shall be alone of us all. Poor Isa is dead already; Mussoud is dying; and thou wilt be gone; and I shall be alone."

"Well, Abdullah, if thou dost not go, I shall. I am tired of this life. I wish to die. I am not afraid of death, but it shall never be said that Selim, the son of Amer, died like an ass in the road, to be spurned by the foot of that dog Tifum, like poor Isa was. If I am to die, let me die like an Arab, with none but my God to pity my wretchedness, with none but the birds of the air around my bed. Do me this favour, Abdullah, friend of my heart. If Mussoud still lives in the morning, tell him Selim is gone, and give him one kiss for me; and before thou goest to sleep thou must give me one, for when thou wakest up in the morning, Selim, the son of Amer, will be gone. The lashing of this clumsy yoke around my neck is already loose; it only requires a second to be free."

"I thank thee, Selim, for this thought of my brother. I wish thee God's peace and blessing. If I live after this hard march, I shall dream and ever think of thee, and shall sometimes whisper thy name in my prayers, that the angels may carry it to thy ear, and that some memory of Abdullah, thy friend, may be preserved in thy heart. Thou art a true Arab, son of Amer, a true friend; thy soul is a jewel, brighter and purer than the diamond. On the road to thy home look up at night to those seven stars which thou seest together, and say to thyself, 'Abdullah thinks of me. Poor Abdullah!' May the holy Mohammed take thee to thy mother, and when thou art welcomed back to thy friends, think of my mother, and bear to her the kindly remembrance of her son. Selim, dear friend, I am about to compel myself to sleep, that I may be ready for my morrow's work. See! I kiss thee with the kiss of lasting friendship, and, since thou goest, be strong with Abdullah's faith that Allah will save thee!"

They then both lay down, and, after a few uneasy tossings, Abdullah fell asleep, while Selim also lay down to plan out his march. Suddenly he remembered the parting words of Simba and Moto, and wondered to himself how he had not thought of them before, as they would have enabled him to bear up with a little more patience and fortitude the trials he had undergone. But they came not too late; he felt that with such friends as those he was not alone in the world, and he resolved on leaving the camp to strike south, then wait a day in the woods, and afterwards strike off through the forest until he came near to a village in Ututa, and then lie in wait for some one who would direct him to Katalambula. A cruel thought came across his mind once, to stab Tifum with his own spear, but he instantly rejected it as unworthy of an Arab and the son of Amer bin Osman.

The hours passed by, but not wearily, as Selim's thoughts had been busy. All slept soundly, and the fires also seemed to have fallen into drowsiness, for nothing but dull red embers marked the places where the fires stood.

He muttered a short prayer to God for courage and strength, and the lashings of the cruel yoke fell apart, and he drew his head through, free. Free! not yet.

He stood up silently, walked straight to a tree deliberately but noiselessly, chose a couple of spears, a gun, a powder horn, and a cartouche box, and began to withdraw as stealthily as he had advanced.

It seemed an age to him, the time before he began to congratulate himself that he was safe; for so precious were the articles in his possession, and so rich seemed the prospect of freedom.

A few long strides brought him from tree to tree, and the more he counted of these trees the more certain was he of safety. Tree after tree was passed, their tall thick columns—taller and thicker by night—formed a denser rampart between him and his enemies, an impenetrable protection against pursuit.

Finally, he was free! Free he felt, freely he walked, freely he thought, and the new idea, as it settled in his mind, seemed to fill him to strangling, it had such power of expansion; the lungs were more inflated, the stride became firmer, the head assumed a prouder air, and the back of him straightened rigid!

He was impelled forward, fatigue seemed to fly from him, an eager urgency of movement seemed to have come upon him; he was walking against time for freedom!

An endless number of dark solemn trees were passed, countless numbers of acres in front, behind, and around him, of this tree-covered upland, and still it remained night. To darkness there seemed no end, nor did he want it to have end; he wished it would ever remain night and his enemies ever sleep.

But though the night was long, and friendlily sheltered him with its kind mantle of impenetrability, through which a fugitive was not visible, it had an end, for all things have an end; but Selim and the Watuta camp were far apart!

Daylight—a dull grey mantle seemingly, which night had put on for a fickle change—appeared, but greyer and greyer it came through the foliage above; it then came pale, and then a steely blue. A streak of silver light shot athwart his path; the foliage was a bright green, and the leaves moved responsively, gently sighing to the morning wind!

How cool, how fresh it was! How newly-born seemed the world, while the hum of busy insect life told him there were other creatures, after their rest, rejoicing in the new light of day!

It became full day, for the sun, a round globe of living fire, or like a fiery balloon, surged upward light and airily. But oh! with what different feelings he gazed upon it now. Yesterday it was hateful with its dry heat and blister, and its thirst-begetting warmth; to-day it was like a huge lamp hoisted up to the sky to light the dim and lengthy aisles of the forest. There was no heat nor thirst in its appearance, nothing but strengthful vigour and cheery light!

At noon, Selim came to a quiet pool in the forest; the lotus flowers rose like yellow cups above its surface, while the leaves lay languidly flat. All around the rim the pool was garnished with these water flowers of Africa; and, so decked, it looked like a great shallow dish adorned with a pictured border!

How delicious did the water taste! How cool and tranquil the spot! What deep silence pervaded the forest at noon! How soothing to the fugitive soul!

A little distance off he espied a large baobab, which had a hole in its body. Walking to it and looking in, he saw the hole led to a large hollow in the tree, as large as a small chamber. He crept in, for it was empty, and there he laid down to rest, and finally he slept. He had escaped, and was safe!

It was night when he awoke; he must have slept eight or ten hours; there were no means of knowing how many. It was evidently a hard task to wake up, for after the first movement indicating life, he lay still, and tried to compel the sodden brain to recover its duty, and the eyes to aid it by piercing that thick darkness of the natural chamber in which he found himself. Bit by bit, the senses resumed the old order of things. Mind stirred up, and gave its master to know that he had run away from a most cruel slavery. Ah! yes! and, the keyword touched, all became clear.

"The Watuta!—that torturing yoke-tree, and the sleepless nights it caused me! my galled shoulders, my wealed back, my racking head! that monster Tifum! that fierce man-animal whom pity never touched! that pariah dog-face, repulsive in its animal malignity! those thick lips which uttered such horrible blasphemy! that always-ready whip! Who can forget him? May the foul mother who bore him, and her fouler son, perish like one of those whose fate will be Al Hotamah!

"All is clear to my mind now. I am free! Arise, my soul, for further freedom; the dark night is kinder than day. The wilderness will take more pity on me than man. Shake thyself, son of Amer, thy mother is patiently waiting for thee; thy kinsmen at Zanzibar still look for thee. Courage, my heart, there is nothing to fear."

He rose to his feet and looked out. "Is that a beast, or is it my timid fancy which creates such a shape? Hush, that was a step! a slow, stealthy step of padded feet; no man alone in the wilds would walk on all fours. Hush, but a moment. Ah! what is it?"

For just then an unearthly laugh—terrible in its satiric wildness of tone—rang through the forest. It was startling for a moment, because it was unexpected, and fearful, because it seemed to challenge all the denizens of the wilds. "What beast can it be?

"Ah! I remember now. Moto has told me of it. It is only a hyæna, and the hungry fellow has scented a prey. Not yet, my friend, can I be thine. Selim is safe from thy jaws. He must see Zanzibar first, before any of thy species can eat him. Oh God!——"

The satiric laugh of the hyæna was succeeded now by a roar which echoed through the forest, and another and another succeeded it, which almost deafened the lad with its volume and power. No animal but the dread king of the forest could have emitted such sounds, and there is nothing more startling than the first sudden bellowing outburst of his lungs—it is so deep, so protracted; but, as if he expends the concentrated power of his lungs in the first roar, the others which succeed it come out in short, gasping, rasping sounds, which seem to chase one another as they peal through the forest in quick succession. Though the first sudden outburst is startling, even appalling, when

M

unexpected, a certain feeling of admiration quickly suc-
ceeds the first fear, at the volume and the force of it,
and at the echoes which it wakes up.

"It is a lion!" said Selim to himself when he had regained his bewildered senses; "the king of beasts. I
have often desired to see thee and to hear thee, but I
may not venture too near thee, as I fear thy claws and
thy cavernous mouth. Halt where thou art until
dawn, my friend, and I will look at thee well, but just
now I will remain here. Ah, that is right; thou comest
nearer, but I have a gun, and there is a bullet in it,
O lion, so thou hadst better keep a respectful distance.
The window through which I look at thee is too small
for thee to enter; besides, king of beasts, I need no
companion like thee in this small chamber with me.
How my bones would crack under thy strong jaws, and
what a delicious morsel thou wouldst deem me. The
*hulwah** of Muscat were as nothing to it; the honey of
thy native wilds were bitter compared with my flesh,
and bones, and warm blood. Nay, I beseech thee keep
thy distance, O lion. If thou art hungry catch that
laughing devil of a hyæna; but me, poor me, thou wilt
surely not harm me!"

But the lion had advanced nearer to the tree; he
had also scented a prey, and while he knew that the
prey was contained within the tree, he was doubtful
whether he could obtain the wherewithal to satisfy his
hunger, and this was why he advanced roaring.

Arriving at the foot of the tree he halted, and stood
looking up at the tempting morsel. As if he heard and
understood the low-spoken words which the Arab youth

* A species of sweets made in Muscat, Arabia.

SELIM AND THE LION.

addressed to him, he uttered another terrific roar. This
caused Selim to draw in instinctively and seize his gun,
but at the same instant the lion's form came bounding
in at the hole through which Selim had entered, where
he clung tenaciously with his claws, and endeavoured
to drag himself in. Then Selim, with his heart in his
mouth at the dreadful presence, put the muzzle of the
gun against the lion's head and fired, and the monster
fell dead outside.

Selim, finding it dangerous to leave his friendly
shelter, resolved to remain where he was until morning,
and after he had listened a long time at the aperture
of the tree, and became satisfied that the lion was dead,
he laid down again on the floor of his natural chamber,
and, happily for one in his situation, fell asleep once
more.

About two hours after dawn he awoke, and immediately going to the window, he looked down, and
when he saw the dead lion stretched stiff at the foot
of the tree, he said to himself:

"He would have it; he would not listen to me.
Like Tifum he revelled in his strength, and was conscious of his might, and, like him, he wished to rend
and tear me, but I have a gun, and I would that Tifum
came after me, so that I could give him the same answer
I gave this lion."

As he spoke, he placed his spears outside, then his
gun, then went out himself, and, taking his weapons
up, he stood by the body of the lion.

The following thoughts, though unexpressed, ran
through his mind:

"Behold! how strong this lion was early last night

—how proud his pace as he roamed through the silent
forest looking for his prey! All the animals ran from
before him, and left him lone in his proud strength.
As if they knew his power, the echoes submissively sent
his voice pealing through the long colonnades of the
forest, like the heralds trumpeting the approach of a
king. His eyes pierced the darkness and searched the
night, his nostrils scented prey and blood, and he came
and stood before me, the relentless tyrant of the
wilderness! His great, flaming eyes glowed red
with rage, his nostrils dilated wide as he thought of
his hunger and the prospective feast; he pawed the
ground and whirled his tail in fury, and tossing his
mane back impatiently, he sprang at me and met his
death.

"Now, how weak! An unarmed infant might play
with his mane and pull at his great teeth. There lies
no more danger in him; and as he is, so may all my
enemies be! Farewell, thou lion! I would have preferred thou were not so unclean. My hunger is now
sharp, and woe befall the hoofed animal I meet, but
thee I may not eat."

Then Selim, shouldering his gun and spears, having
observed the sun, and found out the direction he intended to go, strode on, looking keenly to the right
and left for any game that might promise him relief
from the gnawing pangs of hunger he began to feel. He
had been now thirty-six hours without food, for he had
disdained to steal the rations of his comrades, as he
might have done, knowing from experience that the
slave who lost his rations or consumed them before
the next distribution of food was very apt to suffer, as

none of his fellows, having nothing too much for himself, could find charity enough in his own destitution to share with him.

Thirty-six hours is a long period for a growing boy to be without food, and Selim began to feel it. There were none of those wild fruit trees, so common in Ukonongo, and Kawendi, and Usowa, the mbembu, the singwe (the wild wood-peach and plum); no wild grape nor nux vomica fruit, as in the south-eastern forests of Urori. The long, extensive plain south of the Cow River seems to have made two zones, different from each other, of Southern Unyamwezi and South-Western Urori. The trees in this forest were more adapted for building purposes; but had Selim understood the ways of wild life in the forest, had he been anything but the tenderly-nurtured and pampered youth from Zanzibar, even here he might have found plenty of eatable roots. There was no lack of these about him; the roots of those long, slender, primate-leafed plants, on which he trod, he would have found to be as nutritious as the yams of Zanzibar. But the boy was innocent of this knowledge, and so he kept on, seldom looking on the ground, except when he began to feel disheartened.

As it was approaching sunset, however, he espied a small antelope crouching behind the bushes about fifty yards from him. Lifting his gun, with a prayer for success, he fired, and the animal, after making two or three convulsive leaps, fell wounded on its side. Hurrying up, he caught it as it was about to rise to its feet, and using one of his spears as a knife, looked towards the north-east, in the direction of Mecca, and uttering his fervent "Bismillah"—(in the name of God!) the pious youth cut its throat.

Then, proceeding with the work of preparing the meat, he cut off the head, skinned the animal, and extracted the inward parts, which he left for the hyænas, while the eatable portions he conveyed to the fork of a great tree, where he intended to rest that night.

Hastily collecting some dry leaves, twigs, and sticks, he conveyed these also to the fork of the tree, and with the aid of some powder, he succeeded, after much patient work, in making a fire, over which he placed whole pieces of the antelope to roast, or rather to warm, for his ravenous hunger would not permit him to wait for the roast.

Had Selim understood the art of travelling, he would, of course, have cut the meat into thin strips, and have dried them slowly over the fire, and by this means have furnished himself with sufficient food for two or three days. But not knowing the art, he had placed all the pieces over the fire at once, believing, doubtless, like many other hungry people, that he could eat them all at one meal. Before, however, he had eaten half of one leg, he felt gorged; and feeling tired, put out the fire, raked all the ashes away, and when the fire-place had cooled somewhat, he laid himself down, with his legs coiled, and went to sleep.

In the morning, before starting on his journey again, he ate the other half of the leg, out of which he had formed his supper, and tying the other three legs together, he descended the tree and resumed his march.

During that day he was more bent upon walking

than upon anything else; consequently he made a good day's march. At night, when he began to eat his supper, perched, like the night before, in the fork of a great tree, he perceived the meat was tainted, but as he had no other means of gratifying his hunger, he suppressed the rising nausea, and contentedly ate the ill-smelling meat.

In the morning the meat swarmed with maggots, and he tossed it from him with disgust, and, without breakfast, resumed his journey. During the morning he travelled, at noon he rested; and for a couple of hours in the afternoon he contrived to hold on, until, faint with hunger, he was compelled to halt and go to sleep supperless also.

Another day dawned, and Selim, descending from his perch, resolutely determined upon prosecuting his journey. The forest was unusually silent and deserted; not an animal crossed his path; a few kites alone hovered above. Hour after hour he dragged his weakened legs along till the sun was sinking over the western horizon. He had seen no water on this day, and thirst sharply and severely attacked his frame.

And still another day dawned. Hunger and thirst had made great inroads on his strength, and had begun to sap his resolution. If he had but known that a few hours ahead of him lay the cornfields of the Watuta villages, or if he had but known that only a mile north of the line he traversed lay the road over which Ferodia's caravan had travelled two days before! But enveloped round about by the great forest, to which there seemed to be no end, he knew nothing,—tiny mite that he was, alongside of one of those straight-stemmed and towering trees,—beyond the thin line of vision which his low stature permitted him. Could he only have seen one foot above those trees, he had been safe, and could have directed his steps whither he desired. But he could barely see the sky, so dense was the foliage and so closely did each tree's branches embrace the other. How hard it is to strive to attain the end of the interminable! What a seeming waste of strength is it to ever work and work to span the infinite! How disheartening it is to one to feel that he can never live to see the end of the endless! Interminable, infinite, and endless seemed this forest to the wearied, hungry, and thirsty Selim. He strained his eyes ever in his front, hoping that every low swell of the ground would enable him to see something encouraging; he looked in all directions for anything bearing the semblance of a living creature, of beast, or fowl; he looked upwards, striving to gain a glimpse of the serene face of heaven, which, in his present state of mind and body, would have afforded him momentary relief. Had he been more experienced in African travelling he would have known how to procure water; he would have known that in any one of those hollows a few hours' excavation with a pointed stick would have procured him water, and that if there were not roots to satisfy a craving stomach, then the land would be poor indeed. Knowing nothing, however, of these things, he wasted the precious hours in resting, and then plunging nervously on his way, until his body was obliged to confess its weakness and his starved legs refused to go. When much time was thus wasted, again he would rise to again fall; and, finally, he fell fainting to the ground. Poor boy! he was paying dearly for the desire of his father to increase his riches by the bartering of cloth and flimsy beads for human creatures!

After a fainting fit, which lasted some minutes, he sat up, but was too weak to remain long even in that condition, and he fell back; and while thus prostrate, with his eyes upward, thought was busy with the pleasures he had been obliged to leave, and the more his body suffered the more his thoughts loved to revel in the luxurious scenes he had known. Groaning from sheer agony of body, he cried aloud:

"Ah, for one sight of the foaming wave of the Zangian Sea, which curled at morn into graceful wreaths like liquid flowers as the monsoon gently kissed it! One glance, if nothing more, of the snowy strand whereon I have sported often with my playmates, little Suleiman, and Isa, and Abdullah before we plunged gaily into the foam and spray with which each moment the sea drenched the margin of the island. How oft, as nude I lay stretched on the warm sandy shore, the great sun descending towards the continent, have I watched the great ships idly rocking on that sea which in its deep dissolving bosom of blue depths reflected as a mirror the spotless azure of the sky! Happy days! Memory recalls so much that a thousand years would never obliterate. My dear father's happy household gathered under the shade of the towering mangoes, whose rich fruit, golden, and purple, and brown, hung so temptingly over my head; the evening zephyr wind gently brushing by the light leaves as it rustled through from one tree to another with its welcome whispers, bending, as it flew, the tops of the kingly cocoa and the fragrant cinnamon, wafting the rich green bough of the orange, whose precious fruit was as a balm to my soul. Now could I but feel one in my fevered hand! What ample wealth does not my mind bring before my sickened eyes! The amber-coloured stalk of the sugar-cane and its luscious juice; dark green leaves of orange and mangoe; great cocoa-nuts, with their nutritious milk; the brilliant pome-granate, with its sweet soothing odour and thirst-assuaging pippins; the soft, rich guava, with its health-giving meat; the lime, with its yellow, golden fruit, at the mere sight of which fever and thirst are forgotten; and melons, whose deep green skins cover such crisp, sweet treasures. Ah! there is no place on earth to me like the beautiful island of Zanzibar. It is blessed by the beneficent God with Eden's wealth. Streams laugh with gladness and murmur with joy. Fresh, healthy winds blow over it, laden with the fragrance of earth's dearest and best treasures. God has blessed it with abundance, and has caused its warm bosom to heave with triumph. Lo! its gardens pass by me one after another; happy homes stand in their midst; the pride of my race sit happy under the shade of their orange trees, surrounded by their dependents, whose faces seem kindled with the quiet rapture which fills them. Trees and flowers, houses and gardens, men and women, hills and valleys, the sea and streams,—all of Zanzibar,—come nearer to the unhappy and forsaken son of great Amer bin Osman.

"Come nearer, nearer still, to your kinsman Selim,

Let me embrace ye before my destiny is accomplished!

"No! no! Ah, ye are unkind! Gaze in pity upon my abject condition! Look down upon me, ye that are elated with pleasure. Mark my surroundings! This great, silent wilderness of forest, to which there is no end; it stretches from sunset to sunrise, from sea to sea; it excludes light and air; it smothers the earth with its limitless length and breadth. Through its thick, heavy drapery of leafage—I may not breathe, neither be warmed, by ever a single sun-ray.

"Hark to the storm of wind sweeping over the tops of the giant trees! How it expends its might in attempting to open even a slight gap, that one of the true believers might see a glimpse of heaven before he dies! But it may not be. Nature took ages to build this rampart and construct this impregnable palisade, and the baffled tempest retreats, and leaves me hopeless and despairing.

"The air is pregnant with deadly vapours; gigantic trees, fallen from extreme age, lie prone on the ground, infested by myriads upon myriads of creeping things; withered branches strew the ground thickly, and their leaves, long since dead, lie damp and sappy, reeking with every insect abomination. From afar, like the indistinct and distant sound of thunder, is borne to my ears, after traversing aisles upon aisles, the hungry lions' roar, suggestive of what may happen if relief comes not early to the lonely Arab boy; and my quickened hearing catches strains of a still fiercer meaning, the voice of the leopard calling to his mate, mingled with the growls of the hyæna.

"Ah, cruel chance, that my fresh young life should be thus beset with dangers which menace it. What sin has my infancy committed that my youth must be punished so severely? What wrong have these boy-hands performed, that their owner merits death? What guile has ever my childhood's heart conceived for which my youth must pay the penalty? What crime has ever my brain meditated, that I must be reft of my life at so early an age? None—none. I but ever acted as I knew how; not wantonly, not recklessly, but just as instinct and nature, untutored, impelled me to.

I would my father had never passed the years of boyhood, and that he had never met my mother. I would that I had never seen the light of the sun, then had I not encountered such evil days. From the evil day Khamis bin Abdullah kindled in my father's breast knowledge of his comparative poverty I date the birth of my misfortune; from that time hard and evil days innumerable have I seen; mischance has succeeded mischance, danger succeeded danger, one suffering has produced another.

"I saw my parent die as became the chief of his tribe. The friendly shields, which endeavoured to shelter him from harm, averted not the death which sought his lion heart; his companions in arms fell thickly around him in heaps upon heaps of unnumbered dead; while I stood alone, first to wonder at the strange phase of nature—death, then to mourn for the great loss that had befallen me, then to suffer torture like that to those who visit Eblis, and, finally, to wish that I had never seen the light which animates the earth,

or had died upon that fatal field of battle. I, the son
of great Amer, was made a slave by those hideous
Watuta, who are but monstrous apes, was stripped of
my clothing to have my modest youth shocked by the
unbelievers' rude gaze. When, blushing at their imper-
tinence, I resented the rough behaviour, they bound
and scourged me, and they laughed and mocked me as
the tortured flesh gave way and hung in gory tatters,
and the red blood dyed my limbs crimson. Probed and
pricked by their spears, they drove me to the journey
amongst a herd of other slaves, while the relentless
sun streamed its rays upon my naked and defenceless
body, and I thought that all the agony of the damned
was not to be compared to that which I suffered. Ah,
the suffering that followed! The long, long days of
marching, which seemed to be interminable, the protracted pains from thirst, the weary, leaden limbs that
refused to be moved at my command, the long, long,
immeasurable road, the poor victims that fell never to
rise again, whom, nevertheless, I envied for their
eternal relief from misery and poignant pain. Their
stolid faces upturned to heaven, blank and unmeaning;
the unwinking eyes, that must have once reflected
domestic joys, gaped wide, but were dim and glazed,
and nothing more on earth would ever cause them to
cover that horrible, steady gaze on emptiness and
vacancy; the greedy vulture might peck at them, the
kites might satiate themselves on their entrails, the
hyæna might gorge himself on their flesh, yet those
once sensitive eyes would never wink their discontent.
This is death! It is real death. It is the death which
threatened me until, rendered desperate by the keen

terrors which filled me one night, I deserted that ever-moving caravan, to find myself after a time in this strait, and the terror of death has followed me hither. Every thought, and moan, and cry speaks of it. For ever present is the fearful sight of death; it is in this stagnant, oppressive air which I breathe; and the tomb which God has raised above my head—in these lofty columns, bearing far up their leafy roof—I see.

"Fit tomb for an Arab chief's son. A sultan of the Arab tribes might envy me mine. But where are the mourners? There should be my kindred weeping hot tears over Selim's early death. My mother, with her maids, should be present to wash my limbs ere shrouding them with snowy shash.* There should be my playfellows to chant a dirge over my early departure from this life; and the holy Imam to repeat the prayers for the dead. There should be my kinsmen to dig my grave, and women to weep. But I am alone, to die without bidding farewell to my friends,—to die without taking with me to that other world that last enduring look of love from all who esteemed me, which must ever thrill the souls of those who leave sympathising friends behind. Then come and welcome, cruel, cruel Death; wreak thy will on me; my limbs are already chained to that earth of which they are a portion; thou hast hedged me around with thy terrors and affrighted my soul long enough; thou hast advanced and receded, as though it were child's play; I have alternately felt strong and faint, felt brave and weak. I may not balk thee longer!

"Farewell, happy island, with thy purling streams,

* Fine bleached domestic, or cotton cloth.

thy orange groves, thou home of my happy childhood, home of my kindred!

"Farewell, thou solemn earth; aye, bend thine head with shame for the frown with which thou hast regarded thy innocent child!

"Farewell, thou monster DEATH! Thou tyrant! I am conquered; and I—I must—yield. I come, father, dear fa—ther!!"

CHAPTER VII.

Ferodia's Triumphal Approach —His reception by Katalambula – The
King praises Ferodia—Abdullah is given to Kalulu—Abdullah
meets with Simba and Moto—Kalulu's plan of search for Selim—
A Gun found—Selim found—The senseless form of Selim carried
to the Village - Selim recovers—Kalulu fraternises with Selim—
Kalulu's Friendship for Selim.

ON the twenty-ninth day after the battle of Kwikuru,
Ferodia, the chief of the Watuta, made his triumphant
entrance to Katalambula's village. Messengers had
arrived the night before at the King's house to an-
nounce the approach of the victorious chief; and when
next morning, near noon, a great cloud of dust was
perceived on the left bank of the river, then the women,
posted on every advantageous point for a good view,
began the glad lu-lu-lu-ing, and the welcome tones,
when heard by the Watuta, were answered by them with
a shout which might have been heard at the great lake
into which the Liemba ran.

Long before Ferodia had emerged from the leafy
corn-fields on the left bank of the river, the vicinity
of the great gate of Katalambula's village was thronged
by a multitude of men, women, and children gathered
from the rich plain around, who were the brothers,
cousins, nephews, wives, sisters, and children of the

warriors whose return was now so enthusiastically, nay, frantically, welcomed. Two thousand voices sounded the happy "lu-lu-lu;" four thousand hands were clapped together; four thousand legs, brown and black, and black and brown, danced, leaped, moved, and wriggled as the emotions of their owners moved them.

And Ferodia was all this time slowly approaching, while the drums, with tremendous thunderous volume of tone, ushered him into the presence of the assembled multitudes. Note him well as he approaches. What civilised monarch ever acted the triumph he felt so well as Ferodia? What civilised king ever possessed that gait? What actor could have imitated Ferodia? Mark his steps, his lion strides, with his legs encumbered with one hundred rings of fine wire. Watch how negligently he lays his arms, heavy with broad ivory wristlets, on the shoulders of the supple-bodied youngsters, who are jealous of this high honour conferred on them. Note the toss of his head with its wealth of braids! It is the majesty of triumph impersonified. Happy men would those actors be who could but imitate that regal air!

The procession is in the following order, as it appears before the gate and the multitude. Two hundred warriors in front of Ferodia, file after file, each head adorned with feathers in huge, dancing, waving tufts, each man solemnly marching through the gate into the quadrangular square surrounded by the King's quarters to occupy one side of the square in line. Then Ferodia himself, supported by two stalwart young warriors, one on each side. Then two hundred warriors, each warrior's face surrounded by the black, stiff hairs

N

of the zebra's mane, stripped entire with the hide from the zebra's neck, which gives each warrior a fierce appearance, much fiercer than the black bearskin caps give to English hussars. Then the adult captives in gangs of twenty, bearing the plunder Ferodia had taken from the Arabs. Then the boy captives, at the head of whom was Abdullah, whose white face and body obtained universal notice. Then five hundred warriors bringing up the rear, each head decorated according to the caprice of its owner, with feathers, and red, white, and blue cloth.

The nine hundred warriors were formed around the square, while the captives, after depositing their loads near the great tree in the centre of the square—the cloth bales by themselves, the beads in a separate pile, the boxes by themselves, the kettles, pots, pans, and miscellaneous goods by themselves, the powder barrels and bullets by themselves, and the guns by themselves —formed a circle around the tree.

Katalambula was seated on his mud bench or sofa, which was garnished on this occasion with over a score of lion and leopard skins. In his hand was a short rod, to the end of which was neatly fixed a giraffe's tail, with which he negligently whisked the flies from his face.

The multitude which we first saw outside the gate had climbed upon the roofs of the square tembes, and looked down now intent upon the warriors, the slaves, the plunder, and the king, seated with Kalulu and the grey-headed elders and councillors of the tribe under the tree.

Ferodia stood with spear in hand alone in the centre

of the inner circle formed by the ring of slaves, and close to the great heaps of spoil he had taken from the camp of the Arab traders. His attitude was unmistakeably grand, and spoke the proud chieftain. A broad robe of crimson blanket cloth, which trailed to the ground, was tied in a knot over his left shoulder, leaving his right shoulder free. There was a dead silence; not a word was heard from the warriors or from the multitudes. Then the mild voice of Katalambula was heard, saying:

"Ferodia, we have expected thee. We have heard of thy great success; how thyself and the Watuta warriors have triumphed over the Arab traders. Speak, our ears are open."

Then Ferodia replied: "O King, and ye elders of our tribe! I was sent by Katalambula to bear presents to his friends, the Warori chiefs; and, as I had concluded, I was thinking of returning to Ututa, when Olimali sent word to my camp that the Arabs—the traders from the sea—had come to his country with an immense store of cloth and beads. He said they were of those who had slain Mostana thy brother, O Katalambula."

"Eyah! Eyah!" greeted the speaker from the king and his elders, in which Kalulu joined.

Lifting his voice higher, and adopting a more energetic strain, while his spear was used to describe gestures, Ferodia continued:

"When I heard the words of Olimali, the King of the Warori, I became as a hungry lion, even as a roaring lion before his prey. I said aloud, 'Lo, Malungu (the Sky-spirit, or God) has put the Arabs into my

hands, even the slayers of Mostana, thy brother. I
will arise and avenge Katalambula and Mostana's son
on them. I will make strong drink from their bodies,
and give their entrails to the fowls of the air, and
their heads I will raise before Olimali's gate to the
terror of all other Arabs who come, and murder, and
steal, and make slaves, from near the sea.'"

"Eyah—eyah!" shouted the multitude.

"When the morning came, the Watuta warriors were
in the bush and in the corn. They heard the horn of
Olimali, they heard the noise of the Arabs' guns, they
heard the shouting and the battle, and, at my signal,
the Watuta warriors rose as one man. They came
with the swiftness of arrows, like the flash of a bright
spear. We saw the foe in the village of Olimali, we
hemmed them round, we closed the gates, and we
began to slay. Before our arrows and spears the foe
fell in numbers, in heaps, until those that were left
cried aloud for mercy, and fell on their knees. Then
we made slaves of hundreds of men and boys, and
bound them captives for Katalambula. We took guns,
and powder, and bullets; we gathered a heap of wealth,
of fine cloth and beads. Of the cloth, and beads, the
guns, and powder, and lead, I have given half to Olimali, the King of the Warori. Then each Mtuta
warrior received his due, six cloths to each man; the
Watuta chiefs received their due, and Ferodia took a
share. Fifty slaves died on the road to Ututa, two
Arab slaves died, and one white Arab ran away to die
in the forest. We have two hundred and fifty men-
slaves, and seventeen boy-slaves left, one of whom is
the son of an Arab chief. The cloth, and the beads,

and the other plunder from the Arabs lie before you in these heaps. O King, and ye elders of the tribe, I have spoken."

"Eyah! eyah!" burst out in applausive accents amid clapping of hands and lu-lu-ing from all the people.

Then Katalambula spoke and said, "O Ferodia, great chief and warrior! thou art like a right arm to me; thou art a very lion in war. Who is stronger than thou in the battle? The Wabena, the Wasowa, the Wakonongo, and even the Wajiji, have felt thy spear. Verily thou hast spread the name of the Watuta and the renown of Katalambula to the ends of the earth.

"Let the people hear, and let the elders open their ears. What king has a warrior like Ferodia? He goeth forth with empty hands, but returneth full. He goeth from the village poor, and returneth rich. His warriors are beggars when they depart from us, but they return with Merikani, and Kaniki, fine Sohari, and Joho cloth, and their nakedness is hidden under heaps of finery. Who is like unto Ferodia? Were not our maidens in tears when he and his warriors left us? Lo, and behold, they are now laughing, and their hearts dance for joy. Were not our children hungry when he departed? Lo, and behold, they cry no more, for their bellies are full. Katalambula — even I — was poor, whereas who is to be compared to me now in wealth? Verily thou art great and good, Ferodia, and Katalambula is pleased with thee. I have spoken."

Then Katalambula got up and examined the slaves, while Ferodia walked by his side and commented on such as exhibited extraordinary qualities; and in going around the circle, the King came to the boy-gang, and when he came to Abdullah he could barely contain himself for delight and gratified curiosity.

"Verily," said he, "the Arabs are strange people, and this is one of that race. Strange people; all white!"

Katalambula put out his finger to touch the pale skin of Abdullah, and he instantly drew it back as if the skin had bitten him, laughing at himself for his timidity. But, encouraged by Ferodia, he placed his hand on his shoulders, and marvelled at their softness; and then toyed with the boy's hair, remarking that it felt like goat's hair. Then the boy was obliged to open his mouth while Katalambula peered down his throat, as if he were in search of some hidden treasure, or as if he expected something would jump out, since the white boy was such a wonderful creature.

"But what are you going to do with him?" asked Katalambula.

"It is for the King to command," said Ferodia, in an insinuating tone.

"Well, I will give him to Kalulu; but I thought there were three of them; or were there four?"

"Only three white," said Ferodia; "one died on the road, a little fellow, and the tallest ran away, about five days from here."

"Why did he run away?" asked the King.

"Because he was a fool, and the son of a fool," responded Ferodia. "I never saw such a stubborn ass; his mouth was full of words, but his back had no work in it; therefore he preferred to die in the woods, as he cannot live. Yet had he spirit enough for two warriors, and he would have made a fine slave by-and bye."

"Who art thou speaking of, Ferodia?" asked young Kalulu.

"Now, hold thy tongue, boy, and do not thou interfere with the affairs of men; but rather see how good Ferodia, thy uncle, is to thee; he has given thee that white slave for a playmate. Take him, cut loose his bonds, and teach him to be a warrior."

"Nay, let Ferodia answer me," persisted Kalulu, "and I will then see about the white slave. Who is he that has run away?"

"If thou must know," said Ferodia, looking on Kalulu kindly, "'twas a young Arab slave, about thy age, who ran away. He was the son of a chief, and I half suspect he was driven to run away by Tifum's unkindness."

"Tifum Byah!" cried Kalulu; "no wonder he ran, Ferodia; Tifum has not a gentle hand; but I will see thee again, uncle. I must look after my white slave now, and teach him to eat first."

And Kalulu, leaving the King and Ferodia to pursue their examinations into their property, turned to Abdullah with a curious look, and then, taking his spear, he proceeded to cut the rope around his waist; then, beckoning to the astonished Arab boy, he walked away towards his own quarters, followed by him.

When he had Abdullah in his own apartment, all to himself, he again turned to take a look at him, and silently surveyed him from head to foot. Then, walking up to him, he stood with his back to Abdullah's, and, putting his hand over his head, he seemed desirous of knowing whether he was taller than him; and having satisfied himself, he turned round to him again, and, smiling, said to him in Kituta—the language of Ututa:

"Son of an Arab, canst thou speak Kituta?* No? is
that what thou meanest by shaking thy head? Canst
thou speak Kirori? No, again? Kibena, perhaps?
No? Canst thou speak Kinyamwezi? No? Then what
language dost thou talk? But, never mind, thy head
must think of thy belly now; I will go fetch thee some
food. Sit down on this bullock-hide until I return."
And Kalulu vanished, having pointed to the hide on
which he desired Abdullah to seat himself.

Presently he returned with a female slave bearing
some roast kabobs (small pieces of meat), rice, honey
pombe, or native beer, and a thick porridge; and pointing to the food and to his mouth, he intimated to him
his desire that he should fall to and eat; which Abdullah,
casting a grateful look on him, was not slow to understand and to avail himself of.

After watching the Arab boy eat for some moments,
he left the hut again, but soon returned with two men,
whose faces immediately attracted Abdullah's attention
and made him cease eating from surprise. When he
opened his mouth to speak, he ejaculated —

"Simba! Moto! how came you here?"

"Abdullah! poor boy!"

The two men having spoken, Abdullah sprang to his
feet, and, throwing his arms first around Simba's neck,
then around Moto's, he embraced and kissed them both,
and shed floods of tears from joy, while Kalulu, looking
at them all, smiled with fraternal pleasure.

"I am not alone, then, as I thought; I have still some

* *Ki* placed before Tuta means, the language of Tuta; *U*, the country of Tuta; *Wa*, people of Tuta; *M*, a man of Tuta. This rule is the
same with other African names.

friends left," sobbed Abdullah. "I thought all had left me."

"Nay, weep not, Abdullah," said Simba. "Allah is good. Tell me, son of Mohammed, where are Selim, and Mussoud, and Isa?"

"Ah! Simba; evil days have been our fate ever since we came to Urori. Isa died of the small-pox soon after starting for Ututa; then, some days afterwards, Mussoud, my dear little brother, fell ill of the same disease and died; and Selim——"

"Yes, tell us where he is!" said Moto, eagerly.

"The same night that Mussoud was dying, Selim asked me to go with him to the forest; he said he could not live longer, while Tifum was beating him all the time; and to see the men and boys die on the road, and left to be eaten by beasts of prey, sickened his soul. I could not go while the fate of my little brother was uncertain, but I gave Selim my prayers, and after I had fallen asleep he must have gone, for he was not by my side when I awoke, and his yoke-tree was empty. I think he took with him a gun and some spears, for the Watuta who lost those things made a great noise about their loss."

"Run away!" said Simba and Moto, looking at one another blankly. "Selim gone! but, Abdullah, did he tell you which way he was going after he would leave you?"

"He said he intended to try to get to Zanzibar, but while I was dropping to sleep, or whether I dreamed it or not I can't say, I thought I heard him mutter something about you, and Moto, and Katalambula."

"Ay, that's it, more likely," said Moto. "He re-

membered our warning. The boy, if he is not here
now, must be in that forest still. Did he say, Abdullah, whether he would go north or south first?"

"Oh, south, because the camp was on the southern
side of the road, and our part of the camp was the
most southerly; so it was easy for him to slip away
unperceived."

"And how many days from here, Abdullah, is the
spot from whence Selim disappeared?"

"We came here in six or seven days—I forget the
exact number," answered the boy.

All this time, Kalulu looked from one to the other;
and seeing the looks of anxiety and uneasiness on the
faces of his friends, he asked Moto what the matter
was, upon which Moto explained that his young master
was missing—he for whose sake he had sought out
himself and Katalambula.

Then he asked what Moto purposed doing, and was
answered that he did not know, but would consult with
Simba; upon which Kalulu promised that, whatever they
did, he would assist them.

Simba and Moto, sometimes assisted by Abdullah,
consulted together for a few minutes, at the end of
which Moto informed Kalulu that they had decided
that it was their duty to hunt up their young master,
who was by this, perhaps, perishing from hunger, or was
captured again by some other tribe of the Watuta.

Young Kalulu had expected this would have been
the answer; for, being sharp-witted, and knowing how
great was their affection for their young master, he
could have divined nothing else. And he replied that,
if his assistance was wanting, he was ready with his

influence to promote anything necessary for the restoration of Selim to his friends. "For," said he, "since I have seen what the Arabs are face to face, I begin to like them. At least, I think I shall like this one and Selim; besides, my uncle has already given me this one for a slave, and he will give me the other one, if I can catch him. But, Moto, they both shall be thine when thou wilt demand them from my hands."

When this was translated into Kisawabili, the language of Simba, by Moto, Simba said to Moto:

"Tell the young chief that if he can get fifty men from Katalambula, on the pretence that he has heard there are elephants in the forests, we can start at once, and by spreading out through the woods, either find him ourselves there, or hear some news of him, or rescue him from those who have already got him."

After expressing his approval of the scheme, Moto conveyed it by translation to Kalulu, who replied immediately that he would set about it at once; and while saying it, he left the hut.

In half an hour he returned, and informed Simba and Moto that the men were outside the gate waiting for them, though it was unusual to start on a hunting expedition without the ceremony of the magic doctors. "However," he added, "I have explained that it shall be done at the village nearest the forest, where we shall arrive to-morrow at noon if we travel well. So come on, Moto; I want to do something too, or Ferodia will be on everybody's tongue, and Kalulu's name will never be heard; besides, I want to see this young master of thine, and see if he is as good as you say he is."

While he had been talking, Simba and Moto had

snatched up their guns and declared themselves ready, and Kalula, after giving orders to have Abdullah sleep in his hut, and to be well fed and looked after, accompanied by Simba and Moto, hastily left the hut.

Kalulu was very proud as he showed his friends his warriors, and was sure that with such people the lost Arab boy would be found. Then, putting himself at their head, with his friends next to him, he rapidly led the way along which Ferodia had arrived from Urori.

As it was noon when they started, they could continue their march until late at night, which they did; and a couple of hours before dawn next morning found them *en route* again.

At noon, as Kalulu had said, they saw the forest darkening the western horizon ahead; but between them and the forest was a village, whose corn-fields were then reached, situated about a mile south of the road, from which Simba supposed it would be best to spread out, and keep a sharp eye for anything that promised to furnish a clue of him for whom they were about to search.

They soon came to the village, and when the inhabitants recognised Katalambula's adopted son, they manifested great delight, and immediately set about furnishing him and his men with the best they had, consisting of bananas, and porridge, beans, and rice, and pombe.

The chief of the village was very assiduous to please Kalulu, and sat down close to him, imparting local news; and, as he began to impart it, he remembered an incident which had occurred that morning, which was, that one of his men, searching for wild honey, a couple of hours off in the forest, had found a gun.

"A gun!" said Moto.

"A gun!" echoed Kalulu.

"Yes, a gun; and the medicine was in it—the medicine powder and bullet—for when the man who found it was playing with it, boom! it went, almost killing him with fright."

"Yes, yes, that's very funny; very funny," said Moto, trying to curb his impatience; "but did your man find nothing else near it?"

"Nothing else, my brother. What do you mean? Was not the finding of a gun strange enough in a forest which, for aught I know, never saw one before? Can many more miracles happen to us like this?"

"But, my brother," urged Moto, with anger in his tones, "how could the gun have come there if some one had not left it?"

"The Mienzi Mungu (Good Spirit) placed it there for me. It was not many days ago since my father, the chief, died; and when I had put him in the ground deep, and covered him with earth, I collected all his property in a heap, and thanked the Mienzi Mungu, who had been so kind to me, and prayed to him to make me rich and strong. The good Mienzi Mungu has heard my prayers, and has sent this gun, with its strong medicine, from the skies, for me."

"Chief, be silent," said Kalulu, holding up his hand; "the heir of Katalambula commands thee. Knowest thou the spot where thy man found this wonderful gun?"

"My lord, thy slave is silent when Kalulu speaks. I know not the place, but my man must know."

The man was called, and when he was asked if he had searched the vicinity for further treasures, he replied that he had not, as he had hurried away with what he had found to his chief. He was then told to prepare himself to accompany Kalulu and his men to the spot where he had found the marvellous treasure.

Within two hours they had arrived, and stood under a tree in a dense part of the noble forest. The trees grew around thickly, with many towering columns, supporting a mass of leafage, impenetrable to glare of sun or the white light of day.

On the man pointing the exact spot to Kalulu, Moto, and Simba, the warriors of Katalambula were formed in line, and one half was ordered to march northward, each distant from his fellow fifty paces, and the other half was ordered to step out, with their faces to the south, in like manner. The men having thus been posted in skirmishing order, were then ordered to front towards the east and march forward, observing closely everything strange they might see.

The men had not advanced far—not more than two hundred yards—when one of them gave a shout, which instantly attracted the attention of all. He was seen pointing with excited motions at some object lying on the ground. Simba uttered a roar of joy, when, bounding upward to catch one glimpse of the object, he perceived it to be the pale-coloured and apparently inanimate body of his young master. Moto, also, labouring under no less joyful excitement, shot forward with the speed of an arrow, and Kalulu's light and graceful form was seen cleaving the air as he sped with nimble feet towards Simba. The men soon shared in

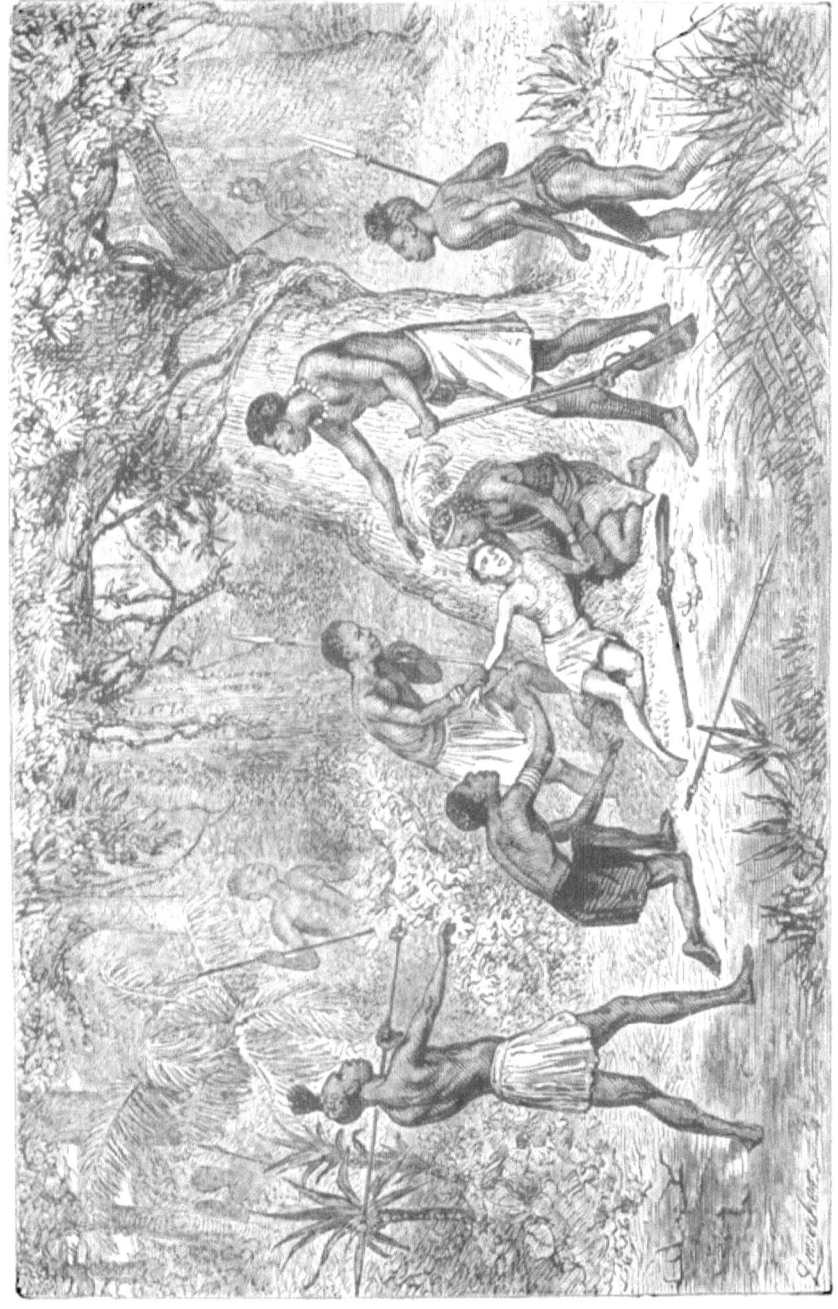

the excitement, and came running up to know the cause; and, among the first, was seen the peasant who had found the gun in this same forest, little dreaming that its owner lay so near.

But the joy of the leaders was soon turned to sorrow. The giant Simba stood nerveless and speechless at the head of the body, Kalulu looked on with deep sympathy on his face, at the side, while Moto threw himself on his knees with clasped hands, at the feet, keen anguish written in every line of his face. The positions of the others, as they came up one by one to obtain a view of the prostrate form of the boy, indicated sorrow, mixed with curious awe; but that of the man through whose aid the body had been discovered was the most remarkable.

When he had approached the curious object which attracted such attention and elicited such shouts, he stood stock still, as if he had been suddenly petrified; but seeing that the pale object bore the semblance of a man, and that it remained motionless, he advanced slowly on tiptoe, while his face underwent remarkable changes as his emotions moved him.

"What is it?" he asked of the nearest man to him. "Is that the Mienzi Mungu who left the gun?"

"No," answered the man, shortly, "this is not the Mienzi Mungu, thou fool; 'tis but an Arab boy, who has died from hunger," he added, proudly, and with the compassionate tone of one who pitied such woeful ignorance.

"An Arab boy!" he uttered. "What is that?"

"He is one of the white people who live in the middle of the sea," the warrior answered.

"Well, what makes him so white? Is his skin like the shell of an egg? Is he hard or soft to the touch?" he asked again, with a strange curiosity.

"Art thou afraid of a dead boy? Go to the body and feel it, fool."

The peasant smiled foolishly as he was thus rebuked; but presently he was seen to crawl towards the body and timidly put his hand on the boy's chest to feel it; but he suddenly removed it with a cry.

"He is not dead! His skin is soft, and I felt it move!"

Moto and Kalulu sprang and knelt down by the boy's side, and a joyful sparkle was seen in Simba's eyes as he also bent down and placed one hand within that of the motionless boy, and the other on the chest. Moto felt the head, to see if there was internal warmth in it, and Kalulu seemed desirous of knowing the truth by reading it in the eyes of Simba and Moto with his own.

"He lives! my young master Selim lives! Allah be praised!" cried Simba fervently.

"But he will not live long if we don't carry him away to put something into him," said Moto, anxiously and hurriedly. Dost thou see Simba, how thin he is? he is nothing but skin and bone—and look here, Simba! Wallahi! what sheitan (bad man, fiend) has done this? See the bruises on his shoulders, and—turn him over on his side—there!—look at his back, Simba!"

"Moto," answered that great and tender-hearted giant, "Tell me, what could have done this? Is it a man? A man?—no! No man could have wounded and striped that back so, because Selim—poor innocent Selim!—could have done nothing to deserve it. This is the work of a pure mshensi (savage), and I will tear out that man's heart, so help me Allah! But let us bear him quickly but gently to the village—and, Moto, ask Kalulu to send the man back running to tell the people to have some very thin ugali (porridge) boiled in goat's milk ready by the time we reach there."

The order was given by Kalulu immediately, and Moto, laying hold of his shoulder-cloth, which he had thrown away from him at the first burst of excitement, began to spread it out on the ground. Simba aided Moto then to lift the wasted form of their young master on the cloth, groaning from sheer sorrow and grief at the thought of what he must have suffered, and murmuring to himself, "Selim will tell me if he lives, and if he dies, little Abdullah will tell me, and then, you sheitan, you mshensi dog! I will treat you in the same way as you treated Selim—sure, sure."

When the senseless form of Selim had been placed on the cloth, Simba and Moto took hold of each corner of it at the head while two other men were ordered by Kalulu to take hold of each corner at the feet, and in this manner they proceeded on their return to the village.

When the party arrived at the village, they found the inhabitants loudly and excitedly discussing the strange events that had occurred, and the report which Kalulu's messenger, the peasant, had made concerning the discovery of a white boy, nearly dead from hunger, in the forest. The report that a white boy had been found created an unprecedented surprise and excitement; no

o

stranger news could have been given in a village where
white people had never been heard of or dreamed of
before; the wildest imagination could not have produced any shape or human figure so wonderful. A boy
all white! white skin—as white as the yolk of an egg!
They might have imagined black men with horns, or
black men with two heads, six arms, and as many legs
as a centipede, or any other monstrosity; but a white
boy, with skin so soft and smooth that the slightest
pressure with the finger produced an impression on it,
—this was wonderful and excelled all tradition. No
wonder, then, that when the party which bore the white
boy was seen advancing, the people made a general rush
to see the curiosity.

But Kalulu, warned by Moto, had thought of this;
and his warriors had been so skilfully arranged that the
excited people found themselves balked; and Moto,
Simba, and the other two men bore their burden into
an empty hut which the village chief, at Kalulu's command, showed them.

The ugali, or porridge, which had been prepared, was
then taken by Simba, and while Moto gently forced the
mouth of the boy open, Simba, with a small wooden
paddle, which he had soon scooped out into a shallow
spoon, began to drop some of the nourishing gruel into
the open mouth. The effect was almost instantaneous,
although to the anxious Simba it appeared a long time;
the open lips closed and a slight movement of the
throat was observed. Again the lips opened, and the
watchful Simba poured a few more drops of the warm
and grateful restorative, and soon, as fast as he poured,
the thirsty mouth received it, with other agreeable

effects which the friends were quick to perceive. Kalulu, who knelt at Selim's head, pointed Simba to the minute beads of perspiration which had formed on the previously dry forehead, and Moto, placing his hand on the chest, gladdened the ears of all with the news that the heart throbbed quicker and stronger.

Presently, Selim heaved a sigh, and the eyelids, hitherto closed, opened, revealing the lustrous orbs which give light and the sense of seeing to the body.

"Ay, what eyes! so large and beautiful!" ejaculated Kalulu, with wonder.

"Hush—sh," said Simba, warningly, as he bent his ears to the lips which now were whispering words which brought the tears to Simba's eyes.

> "And sons shall mourn for Arab fathers slain,
> And Arab wives shall shed their tears like rain."

"Poor boy!" said Simba; "he repeats the words his mother said before son and mother parted." And then in a louder tone he said, "Selim, young master, dost thou know me?"

The head turned round, and the eyes of his young master rested on him full, with the light of intelligence in them.

"Ah, Simba! Is it thou?" asked Selim, in a faint but glad voice.

"Yes, I—thy slave Simba. Praised be Allah for his goodness! my master knows his slave."

"Where am I?" Selim then asked. "I have had such a fearful dream. I thought I was dying from thirst and hunger. But this is not that awful forest I saw. I am in a house, and Simba is at my side. How is this, Simba?"

"Dost thou not know Moto, master?" asked Moto, who had risen to his feet.

"And thou too, Moto, here? Then I am happy. I am not alone, as I dreamed I was."

"No, master, thou art not alone; but take some more of this," said Simba, as he industriously stirred the porridge. "It is good for thee, and thou wilt be quite strong by-and-bye."

And Selim obediently opened his mouth and permitted himself to be fed without demur, though his eyes worked and looked about to aid his mind in resolving the remarkable change of circumstances which had taken place since he fell down in the forest from fatigue, hunger, and thirst.

When the gruel was exhausted and he had eaten his fill, Selim found his strength much recovered, his mind firmer, and he asked Simba to tell him how this change had come about. Simba related briefly all the facts already known to us, to Selim's infinite surprise and joy; and Selim, in answer to a question from Simba, related what occurred to him, from the time Simba and Moto disappeared at Kwikuru to the time he laid down as he thought to die.

Kalulu came round now, and kneeled in front of Selim, and Simba introduced him as the adopted son of the King, who had been so good to Moto, and as the young chief through whose aid they had been enabled to discover him.

Selim lifted his hand, and grasped Kalulu's fervently, and asked Moto to tell him how grateful he felt to him for his kindness, which was no sooner done than Kalulu said:

"Let the son of the Arab chief eat, and rest, and get strong. Let neither hunger nor thirst approach him. Kalulu is his brother. With Kalulu my white Arab brother may tread the forest glades in safety; for the forest is kind to Kalulu; the trees nod their tall heads to him as a friend, the birds make music for him, and the honey-bird finds sweet treasures for him. The forest is full of beauty and richness, and Kalulu's heart is glad when he can roam through it alone. Neither the lion nor the leopard harm him, and the wild boar starts in fear when Kalulu is near him. Get well, my brother, get strong, and fear harm no more."

To which Selim answered, while grateful tears filled his eyes:

"The voice of Kalulu sounds in my ears as the living waters of a fountain in the ears of a thirsty man. My soul responds to his kind words as the closed petals of the lotus to the warm light of day. Fear and distrust fly from me as the gloom of night and early mist before the sunshine. When the heart is tranquil and sadness does not disturb the mind, a man sees joy in all things; even the sombre forest is reft of its terrors, and becomes beautiful, the ground is found to be clothed with sweet grass and pretty flowers. The waving grain and tasseled corn does not bend more easily to the breeze than a man's heart does to his emotions; the dark past will be forgotten by me, and with Kalulu as a brother I shall find beauty in all things, music in birds, pleasure in the fields, joy in sunshine and night."

Kalulu replied: "Thy voice, my white brother, makes Kalulu glad. His heart grows under its pleasant sounds, and is moved like the foliage by the soughing breezes. I will teach thee what the Sky-spirit has taught the children of the Watuta, and thou shalt teach me what the Sky-spirit has taught the pale-faced children of the Arabs. Thou shalt show me what the great sea is like whose waters are salt, and to what it is like when the angry pepo (storm) blows on it; and I will show thee the brown Liemba, where, among the thick matete brake, hides the long-nosed mamba (crocodile), and where the hippopotamus loves to bathe his great body. I will show thee the pretty islands, silent as the night in their loneliness, which are guarded by scores of crocodiles, for me to roam when I like. I will teach thee how to hunt the swift ante-lope and the leaping spring-bok; how to pierce the thick hide of the pharo (rhinoceros); how to laugh at the fierce bellow of the wild buffalo; and how a Mtuta boy meets the lion. Eat and get strong. But tell me, my brother, how comes thy back so scarred and wealed?"

"Kalulu, my brother, thy words have made me strong already. Heed not my bruised body; thy words are a medicine for it. The music of thy voice has healed my sores. I feel them no more."

"Nay, but tell me the name of the man who made them. Was it Ferodia?"

"No. Ferodia has not struck me; it was the man they call Tifum Byah."

"Tifum Byah! the cruel dog; but never mind, I will stripe his back for him."

"Nay, please trouble him not, for my sake, Kalulu; the dark days are over."

"Well, we shall see," said Kalulu. "But now we will leave thee to sleep and rest. We shall stay two days here, when thou wilt be strong enough to be carried before Katalambula. I marvel at the friendship I bear thee; but Moto was good to me, and when he told me thou wert his master, I loved thee then. Now I love thee for thyself. The Watuta know how to love and hate, how to like and dislike."

Then, turning to his warriors, who had crowded into the hut, Kalulu said, "Come, let us leave Moto and Simba with the pale-faced boy; they will watch him."

CHAPTER VIII.

Ceremony of Brotherhood — Ceremony of Blood-Drinking — Selim brought into Ferodia's presence — Simba to the Rescue — The Warning to Kalulu — Kalulu speaks for Selim — Where is Paradise? — Selim and Abdullah are clothed — Down the Liembra — The Hippopotamus — Overboard — Fighting the Crocodile — How Kalulu fought the Crocodile — Securing the River-horse.

ON the third day after his discovery in the forest by his friends Simba, Moto, and young Kalulu, Selim was sufficiently strong to begin his journey to the village of Katalambula. Had Kalulu not assured him of his friendship, and that he would be a brother to him, it is doubtful that Selim would have looked upon the idea of meeting Ferodia and his obsequious servant Tifum Byah—to whose tyranny he owed so much misery —again with pleasure. But it was agreed between Kalulu and Selim that the ceremony of brotherhood, of which he had heard much before, should take place the evening before they arrived at Katalambula's village.

The party travelled by easy stages, and on the fifth day of the journey, the day set apart for the ceremony of brotherhood, they found themselves close to the Liemba stream, at a village called Kisari, distant but eight miles from the capital of Katalambula.

Here the author may remark, for the benefit of the

younger readers, that a close brotherhood among men or boys, unrelated by blood, birth, or marriage, is in no way singular. I need but mention David and Jonathan, Achilles and Patroclus, Damon and Pythias, as examples among men; and what boy of any nation, in any public school, has not some friend who is as dear to him as a born brother? It arises from a similarity of dispositions generally, from the desire to relieve ourselves from little anxieties, and to have some one in whom we have thorough confidence. There were two things singular about this ceremony of brotherhood about to be enacted between Selim and Kalulu. First, was the ceremony of blood-drinking connected with it; and, secondly, was the fact that a Moslem boy—a true believer—was about to become a brother with a Pagan boy—an unbeliever—and to drink his blood. For it is expressly prohibited by the Kūran that blood shall be drunk by the true believer; next, it is expressly prohibited that a true believer shall make any such close friendship with an infidel. But it may be argued for poor Selim that he was yet but a young boy; that he was driven by necessity to this as the best method of assuring his freedom and safety from re-capture, and this the Kūran, whose laws are not cruel, permits when there is necessity; and it might be said that Selim was, perhaps, not aware of the Kūran's prohibition in this small matter; otherwise, I doubt that a boy so generally pious would have erred against the law of the Prophet consciously.

On Kalulu's side, nothing could be said against the ceremony. It was a common custom with his tribe, when any of them met anybody they liked better than another, to go through the ceremony. Sometimes the chiefs did it with neighbouring chiefs, to strengthen their alliance from motives of policy, for the same reason that European monarchs contract—or rather did, for it has lost long ago its former significance— advantageous alliances among themselves for their sons and daughters. Kalulu wished the ceremony to proceed, because he had a strong liking for Selim, born of gratitude to Moto; because Selim was of his own age; because he had pleasant ways with him, and friendship having grown out of the accidental circumstances under which they met, he desired to assure himself, with the ardour of a boy, that real friendship existed between them. Once his brother by this ceremony, no one of his tribe could injure Selim; and Ferodia and Tifum Byah might storm and fret in vain, for the ceremony of brotherhood with Kalulu could not be disregarded. We shall see, however, what came of it.

At sunset, Kalulu was asked to seat himself side by side with Selim on the ground, which he did, taking hold of Selim's right hand, each with his profile half turned to the other. Simba was the master of the cere- monies on this occasion, who held a knife with all the solemnity of one who was about to offer a sacrifice to some horrid deity who delighted in the blood of youths. Moto stood by as a supernumerary, and to interpret the words of Simba for Kalulu. The people of Kisari had also come to witness the ceremony.

Simba advanced as the sun was setting, knife in hand, while the two boys retained each other's right hands, and said to Kalulu:

"Art thou willing to be a brother to Selim, to be

more than a friend to him, to share what thou hast with him, to defend him against all enemies to the best of thy power, and to stand by him until death?"

Kalulu answered, "I am."

"With what wilt thou seal thy word?"

"With the blood of my right arm."

"And what wilt thou give him as a sign?"

"I will give him a sheep."

"Art thou willing further to drink his blood, that his blood may pass unto thee, that the bond of eternal brotherhood may be made strong and sure?"

"I am."

Then turning to Selim, Simba asked:

"Art thou, Selim, willing to accept Kalulu as a brother, to be more than a friend to him, to share what thou hast with him, to defend him to the utmost of thy power against all enemies, and to stand by him to the death?"

Selim answered, "I am."

"With what wilt thou seal thy promise?"

"With the blood of my right arm."

"And what wilt thou give him as a sign?"

"I will give him my gun."

"Art thou willing, further, to drink his blood, that his blood may pass unto thee, that the bond of eternal brotherhood may be made strong and sure?"

"I am."

"Then let it be done!" Simba said; and with that he made a small incision in the arm of each, and as the blood began to flow, he shouted, "Drink!" and immediately the youths seized each other's right arms, and left their right hands free, and putting their lips to the wounds, sucked a small quantity and swallowed it, and the ceremony was concluded by a fraternal embrace. During the exchange of presents which followed, men, women, and children shouted and clapped their hands; and the youngest of them, in the exuberance of their childish hearts, kicked up their heels and danced, as they do upon most great occasions in Africa.

The next morning, a little before noon, the party arrived at the capital. Selim's arrival caused a great sensation: but Kalulu immediately took him and his two friends, Simba and Moto, into his own hut, where Selim, to his great joy, met Abdullah, who was quite recovered from the severe punishment he had received and the fatigues he had undergone. The meeting between the two Arab boys was very affecting, as they could understand each other's feelings and interpret them faithfully one to the other.

After a short time, Simba and Moto left the two boys to themselves and retired to their own hut, while Kalulu, after seeing Selim attended to and supplied with food, started for the King's house to acquaint the King with the events which we have just detailed.

It was not long after the two Arab boys were left alone that a rustling of many feet was heard at the door, not noisy, but hurried, and somewhat alarming; and immediately there stood before the astonished boys the form and malevolent face of Tifum Byah, his former tyrant, accompanied by other warriors, armed with spears and knob-sticks.

"Oh, ho! hee, hee!" shouted Tifum, with a wicked leer on his face. "This is my runaway slave. Ha, ha! thou art caught like a sneaking jackal in a trap. Come, my pale-faced slave, you must follow me;" and he advanced and laid a rough hand upon his shoulder.

"Why with you?" asked Selim.

"Come, no words. Ferodia, the chief, calls."

"But I am now Kalulu's brother," said Selim, attempting to release himself from his grasp, "and I am no longer a slave."

"You the brother of Kalulu! Since when came you to be the brother of Kalulu, you son of an ass?"

"Since yesterday; and if you do not let me go, Kalulu will punish you for entering his hut."

"We'll see about that. Warriors, bear him to Ferodia!" said Tifum, turning to his companions.

And Selim was borne away, despite his remonstrances, to Ferodia's presence, who happened to be seated under the tree in the middle of the square.

"Here is the runaway," said Tifum, laying a heavy hand on Selim's shoulder, to Ferodia.

"Ha! pale-faced dog!" shouted Ferodia, angrily. "What made you run away? Did you think to better yourself by doing so? Speak."

"I am not a dog!" retorted Selim in a passion; for he was getting desperate at the prospect of another lease of such cruel bondage as he had experienced. "I am not a dog, but you are a dog."

"Eyah, eyah! hear him! A slave insults Ferodia the chief!" cried the obsequious Tifum. "Fool, do you know what you say?"

"Silence, pariah!" thundered Selim, more passionately. "I defy you!—I spit on you! You are dirt. Do your worst, great chief—the Arab boy will not bend to you!"

As the boy uttered these words, showing more spirit, and such anger, and bitter contempt as none of the Watutu ever had witnessed before, both Ferodia and Tifum were struck speechless for a moment; but Ferodia broke the silence at last with fiery accents, saying ·

"Tifum, dost thou hear me? Lay that stubborn ass down on his face and cut his back for me with thy whip. Beat, beat, and spare not."

But Selim waited to hear no more. Ferodia had but begun his cruel order when the latent Bedouin spirit of resistance electrified him. His arm felt surcharged with the impulse to strike, and his hand, weighted with hate, was shot full in the face of Tifum, who reeled as if he had been struck with a knob-stick. Then with a light bound he sprang from the circle, sending a mocking laugh into Ferodia's ears as he flew towards the King's house, which had been pointed out to him on his first arrival, shouting "Kalulu! Simba, to me! To me, Simba! Kalulu!"

He had reached the threshold of the King's house when he felt an arm on his shoulder. He turned around; it was Tifum! Rage had given the man a quickened sense and speed to his feet, even superior to the fear which hurried the feet of Selim away. The strong hand crushed the weakened frame of the youth to the ground for the execution of the cruel sentence of Ferodia, and his brain was fast whirling with the terror which possessed him, when he heard a shout—a roar of rage—behind him, and at the same time the force with which he was being compelled to the ground relaxed. Simba was seen bearing down upon the party with irresistible power. He saw for an instant now

the gigantic form of his friend and protector dilated,
as he had seen it in the battle of Kwikuru; he saw
the powerful muscular arms, with their wealth of sinew
and muscle, and the eyes glowing with the ferocity of
a beast of prey: only an instant, for Simba was before
Tifum, face to face with the monster who had striped
the son of Amer, and there was no time to think
before he saw Tifum's body in the air, nor time to
utter the thought of pardon which he wished to say,
before he saw the man dashed with the force of a
cannon ball against the body of warriors who had
hurried up to lend assistance to Tifum—laying half a
dozen of them prostrate on the ground.

Ferodia had seen the giant form of Simba hurrying
to the rescue of the white slave, and comprehending at
a glance that something would happen, he snatched his
spear and started after him. But he had never imagined
that such a thing as he saw could have been done by
living man; and the wonder of it all paralysed his arm,
which tingled but a moment before to send his spear
through the man's body. While Ferodia thus stood,
lost in wonder at such human power, three new-comers
had appeared on the scene—Moto, who had hurried
after Ferodia, and stood behind him, seemingly careless and unconcerned; Kalulu and Katalambula, the
King, who appeared on the threshold, the former of
whom had dragged Selim behind him.

Katalambula, though old and on the verge of in-
firmity, could demean himself royally enough upon
occasions; and this was one of them evidently; for he
advanced and stood before Simba and Ferodia, spear in
hand, with a bearing seldom witnessed.

"What means this, Ferodia?" he asked in a cool, quiet tone.

"It means, O King, that I sent Tifum to catch that runaway slave who deserted me in the great forest; that the slave ran towards thy house, and Tifum ran after him, only to meet with this man, who caught up Tifum as if he had been a piece of wood, and sent him flying against those warriors of mine, who are now picking themselves up."

"Indeed! Who art thou? Oh, I remember, thou art the friend of the stranger who saved Kalulu in Urori! Thou art very strong."

Then turning toward the group which had been prostrated, he asked if any of them had been hurt. One replied that he felt a pain in the chest, another that he could not breathe; one felt his head swim, another a pain in the abdomen; one felt a lump in his throat, another replied that he had a sore back; while Tifum declared he felt bruised all over, and all looked at Simba with terror.

Ferodia now advanced, and made as if he would lay a hand on Selim; but Kalulu interposed his slight form with a drawn bow and fixed arrow in his hand, and a dangerous glitter in his eyes.

"Keep away, Ferodia; or, by the grave of Mostana my father, I will send this arrow through thy body."

"What ails thee, boy? Is not one white slave enough for thee, that thou wouldst deprive me of the other? I made him captive with my bow and spear at Olimali's village. Stand aside."

"Go away, I tell thee! This 'slave' of thine is now my brother. The blood ceremony has been made.

Who injures him injures me; and I am Kalulu, adopted son of Katalambula."

"Well, if he is thy brother, keep him; but give me the other white slave in his place," replied Ferodia.

"Thou hast given him to my father. My father has given him to me. I am too poor in white slaves to be able to give thee any. I have but one slave, for the other is my brother."

"Katalambula," said Ferodia, "this is injustice. White slaves are not caught every day. I must have one of them."

"We may not disregard the laws of brotherhood, Ferodia," said the King, mildly. "When Kalulu made the white boy his brother he made him a Mtuta, and all the Watuta are free men. Thou gavest me the other, and I gave him to Kalulu. It is not our custom to return gifts, thou knowest, Ferodia. But take thou three Wabena men at my hand instead, and be friends with Kalulu."

"No, no, no!" said Ferodia, in a burst of anger. "Thou art unjust, Katalambula, to one who fought for thee with such success, and brought thee so much wealth. I depart at once; and thou," said he warningly to Kalulu, "do thou beware of me; eagle's wings have been clipped ere now, and young lions tamed. Ferodia is king over his own tribe."

"Ferodia," said Kalulu with a sneer, "I fear thee not. I know thee for a bad man; and were it not for my father thou shouldst not leave this village, for I should garnish the gate with thy skull."

"Peace, boy!" cried Katalambula, "and do not

P

make bad worse with thy saucy tongue. And thou, Ferodia, heed him not; remember, he is but a young boy. But it is thou who art unjust, not I. Hast thou not received a fourth of all thou didst bring me? Hast thou forgotten the slaves, the cloth, the powder, and guns I gave thee? Whose were the warriors with whom the battle was won at Kwikuru? Who sent thee there but I? Go home if thou must, and peace be with thee."

Ferodia left the party, but not before he had again menaced Kalulu, which menace that young chief returned with interest. Within an hour he had departed from the village with his warriors, slaves, and property, breathing revenge and hatred, fuming and storming at the slaves, and sarcastically bitter to the bruised and discomfited Tifum Byah.

Katalambula was angry also with Kalulu; but the latter, though forward enough when Ferodia, of whom he was intensely jealous, was concerned, knew the ways of the old man well; and, unmindful of his frowns, he went up and embraced him, and accompanied him towards his house.

"Oh, my uncle, and father!" cried Kalulu, "why dost thou not say a kind word to my white brother? Is he not a handsome brother? Look at his eyes; they are like the young kalulu when it looks at the hunter in fear. Speak to him, ah, do. Think of that horrid Tifum Byah beating him! I am so sorry I did not drive an arrow through him. He is a wicked man, verily, and is properly named Byah. He would cut my head off readily if Ferodia commanded him.

"And thou art the new brother of my boy Kalulu,

art thou, pale-faced boy ? " asked Katalambula, stopping
in front of Selim.

"Kalulu has been very good to me," said Selim, looking up gratefully towards that youth. "He has been
pleased to call me his brother."

"Yes," said Katalambula. "Kalulu is a good boy—a
good boy—he loves the old King, too. I believe he has
a kind heart for those he loves, but he is hot, hot as
fire, when anybody crosses him. Take care he does not
kill and eat you," he added, smiling, and passing on
towards his house.

"But, father," said Kalulu in a whisper, "thou seest
he is naked, except that rag. He is the son of an Arab
chief, and is not accustomed to our ways. Thou art
rich in cloth. Canst thou not give him something to
cover his nakedness ?"

"What need he cover his nakedness, boy ? He looks
fair and clean enough without anything. He is not a
girl. I am sure if I had a white skin I would rather
be naked to show it," chuckled the old man, looking at
Selim.

"But, father, he has told me himself that he feels
ashamed of being without cloth. His people never go
out unless they are covered from head to foot. It is
against their custom, and there is a book written by the
Sky-spirit, which tells them not to be without clothes."

"Well, well, do as thou wilt. Give him four doti
(sixteen yards), and let him cover himself from head to
foot if he wants to, though I think it all folly, all non-
sense."

"Thou art good, very good, father," cried the delighted Kalulu, leaping about the old man.

"Ah, yes, I know I am good," replied Katalambulu, "especially when I let thee have thy own way. There, go now. I am sleepy and tired."

Kalulu left the old man, and, proceeding to the store-room, extracted the four doti he was permitted to take; one of blue cotton, one of white, one coloured barsati, and one fine sohari, which he rolled into a bundle, and covered with a goatskin, and conveyed to his hut, where he found Simba, Moto, Abdullah, and Selim.

When he had seated himself, he asked Selim:

"What book is that thou wert talking of to me yesterday?"

"It is the Kūran," replied Selim, "written by a holy man, sent by the Sky-spirit to tell men how to conduct themselves on earth, so they may enter the good place called Paradise."

"What is the Sky-spirit like?"

"No man, since that great man, has seen him; he is a spirit, and cannot be seen," replied Selim.

"Why do the pale-faces obey a thing that cannot be seen?"

"Because the holy man, Mohammed, who wrote his words down, has given us all we want to know. The holy man saw him, and wrote his words faithfully down."

"Is Mommed alive now?" asked Kalulu.

"Oh no! He has been dead ever so long, many, many years. So many as one hundred sultans of Ututa have lived and died since Mohammed—not Mommed—died," answered Selim.

"Where is this Paradise to which the good men go? I am good. Shall I go to Paradise?" asked Kalulu, with a smile.

"Paradise is away, up, far, far above the clouds. No man is permitted to go there except he is a true believer, who believes in God, Mohammed, and the Kŭran."

"And where shall I go when I die?"

"If thou diest without believing, thou shalt go to the place which is reserved for such as were ignorant, and were not taught the true word. It is far from Paradise."

"Hum! it is not as good as Paradise, then?" asked Kalulu.

"No."

"The Sky-spirit is wicked," said Kalulu. "He sends a holy man called Mommed to tell good words to the white peoples, and prepares a nice place for them. For it is easy to believe, when people are taught what to believe. But the black peoples, they see no holy man. Nobody comes to tell them anything; but because they are ignorant they are sent to a bad place. Bah! the Sky-spirit is very wicked; he is unjust; I don't want to see him, because I shall not die; I won't die."

Selim had here a fine chance to deliver a sermon, and make a proselyte, but he was too young to take advantage of the opportunity; besides, he did not want to make his new brother angry or more rebellious than sheer ignorance made him already.

"But, Selim, tell me; why do thy people wear clothes? Why do you not go about without clothes, as we do?"

"Because it is wrong; it is not decent. The good book says 'Thou shalt restrain thine eyes, and do no immodest action.' It is immodest to expose the person.

Beasts are clothed with fur and hair, fowls with feathers; men cover themselves with clothes. Is man so poor that when he sees all things clothed—the rocks with earth, the earth with trees, the trees with foliage, the beasts of the forest with hair and fur, the birds with feathers, the fish with scales, that he himself who owns all these things shall have nothing?"

"Well, Selim, thou shalt not be immodest any more while thou art with me. I have brought thee and Abdullah cloth. Am I not good now, and shall I not go to Paradise?"

"Thou shalt have all things, Kalulu, when thou wilt become a true believer," answered Selim, clapping his hands with joy and gratitude at Kalulu's delicate kindness. "What dost thou say, Simba? and thou, Moto? Abdullah? We shall be sons of Arabs, and true believers now, eh?"

"I shall be so proud of these clothes, I will not know myself," said Abdullah, as he folded around his body a brand new shukkah (two yards) with the skill of one who knew the art of wearing shukkahs. Another shukkah was thrown over his shoulders, while a piece of snowy cloth, a foot wide and a yard long, was folded around his head, and he stood up to be admired, his pleased and sparkling black eyes mutely inviting his friends to express their pleasure at the transformation.

"Why, Abdullah!" exclaimed Simba. "Wallahi! but thou lookest better in the negro costume of Zanzibar than thou didst in the braided gold jacket and embroidered shirt of Sheikh Mohammed's son; and thou too, Selim. I think I see my young master once more himself. Fine sohari and fine barsati in Ututa! Who would believe it?"

"Ay," said Moto, "my young master and Abdullah, having covered themselves, will forget their misery and vexation, and grow fat and happy. After this I shall always look out for young chiefs in danger, to help them, hoping they will all turn out to be as good as Kalulu has been."

" Now that we are all so happy and good, I propose to my new brother Selim and my white slave Abdullah, who is now no more a slave than I am, that we take a canoe to-morrow, and go down the Liemba to spear hippopotamus and crocodiles; for you must see the Watuta at home in their sports, and we must, by and-bye, go to the great forest several days south of where thou wert found, Selim, to have a grand elephant hunt. What do ye say, Selim—Abdullah?"

"I shall be delighted," answered Selim.

" And I too," responded Abdullah.

" Then it is settled; eh, Simba and Moto?"

" Yes," those faithfuls replied.

At dawn, the time prescribed, the party set out for the river, two warriors accompanying them, bearing the paddles for the canoe. Simba and Moto carried their guns, Kalulu carried the one given him by Selim at the brotherhood ceremony, besides his spear, while Selim and Abdullah carried guns which Kalulu had procured them from the King's store room, with the King's permission.

Arriving at the river, the party found a large number of idlers there already, who had collected to see their young chief and his white slaves, as Selim and Abdullah were called, set off. Some of them wondered that Kalulu should so soon take his slaves away on a pleasure excursion, but they said nothing, the majority of them thinking that he took them with him as gun-bearers. Several of the Watuta offered to accompany Kalulu in his canoe, but he waived them off peremptorily, saying he had enough with him.

Soon after Kalulu had taken his seat in the stern with Selim and Abdullah, Simba, Moto, and the two warriors, taking each a paddle, shot the canoe into mid-river; then with dexterous strokes they pointed her head down stream, to the music of a boatman's song. Each man industriously plied his paddle, and Katalam-bula's village receded from view.

This mode of journeying the two Arab boys, having nothing to do but to sit down and enjoy the scenery, thought much preferable to the continual march of the caravan; and the contrast was certainly great to that bitter experience they had endured on the journey from Kwikuru in Urori to Katalambula with the heavy-handed and callous-souled Tifum. They looked on with delight at the brown river and the tiny billows of brown foam which the stout canoe made with her broad bow; at the dense sedge and brake of cane which lined the river's banks, wherein, now and then, was heard a heavy splash, as the drowsy crocodile, alarmed by the approaching crew, leaped into his liquid home; at the great tall trees which now and then were passed, out of which the canoes of the Watuta are made; at the enormous sycamore, with its vast globe of branch and leaf, affording grateful shade to beast and bird; at the brown cones, the habitations of men, encircled by their strong palisades; at the grain-fields, which shimmered and waved gaily before the tepid southern wind; and at lengthy, straight, far-reaching vistas of river and wooded banks which were revealed to them as they glided down the Liemba.

"Happy hour!" thought Selim. "Would it might last ever, or at least until I reached my own home and mother at Zanzibar!"

"Hail, joyous day!" thought Abdullah. "Give joy to all men, as I have joy. Be still joyous, to-morrow and the day after, until mine eyes shall once more rest on the blue waves of the Indian Sea."

The two boys looked into each other's eyes; the look was interpreted aright by each, and tears crept into the corners of their eyes, and rolled down their faces in still drops - still as the joy which caused them.

About two hours before noon the canoe touched an island; and, disembarking, the party proceeded to select a nice place to rest for an hour, and to refresh themselves with the lunch, consisting of dried meat, smoked fish, and a potful of cold porridge they had brought with them.

Just as the hour had transpired, a hoarse, deep bellow was heard close by, which caused the entire party to start to their feet and glide to the edge of the island, whence they saw a herd of hippopotami quietly enjoying the cool deep waters near a place where the river began a sharp curve at the other end of the island.

"Good!" cried Kalulu; "one—three—five hippopotami! Now for sport. My white brother, canst thou swim?" he asked Selim.

"Yes; why?"

"Because, if thou cannot, 'twere better that thou shouldst stay here. Can Abdullah swim?"

"Very well," replied Abdullah for himself.

"Then come on to the canoe at once. But stop; ye both had better doff your shoulder-cloths, and roll the lower cloths far up the hip; ye may have to swim, for a hippopotamus sometimes charges on the canoe, or kicks it viciously, and then down ye go to the bottom. If it should happen this time, dive down to the bottom of the river at once, and make off under the water towards the island. The hippopotamus is very apt to cut a man in two if he catches him. The animals are now coming up the river; we will wait for them, and when they have gone above us a little way we can sally out from our hiding place, and give it to them. Do ye understand?"

"Perfectly," both answered; while Simba and Moto, rolling their cloths tight around their hips and loins, nodded their approval of what Kalulu had said.

Having done what the sage young chief had advised, Selim and Abdullah accompanied him to the canoe; Simba and Moto took their paddles in their hands, while the two warriors, who were famous for their harpooning, prepared the instrument which they intended to drive into the first animal nearest to them.

This instrument was similar in shape to the harpoons which whalers use for destroying the whales, except that it was not half as neat or sharp. It had a long, heavy staff, and had once been used to pound corn into flour by some woman, as was evident by its close grain and polish, showing that it was hard and heavy, and had been of frequent use. To its pointed end was a broad, heavy, and barbed spear, well sharpened and polished, around the handle of which was fastened the end of a long rope, of native manufacture, made of the bark of the baobab tree.

While the harpooneers were quietly preparing themselves, Kalulu pointed the two Arab boys through a thin edge of cane which hid the boat from the approaching animals, as they came up slowly and unsuspectingly abreast of the place where they lay.

What magnificent beasts they were! What splendid and powerful necks they had! The best prize-bull ever fattened on English grass might have been ashamed of his breadth of neck had such as these been exhibited side by side with him. Unaware of the danger that lay in wait for them, they came up to breathe quickly and boldly, and by so doing exposed nearly all their heads and necks. On the backs of their powerful necks the colour was that of a bright reddish yellow, which also tinged their heads over the eyes and the ears, and broad patches of this colour were also seen on the cheeks. In appearance the head bore a striking similarity to the head of a large and powerful horse; especially did the bold and prominent eyes, the short pointed ears, and noble curve of neck aid the comparison; but at the nose it was more like that of an ox.

The name of this enormous and apparently unwieldy animal, by which he is known to us, is hippopotamus, from the Greek words—hippos, a horse; potamos, a river. Had the Greek travellers been better acquainted with the appearance of this animal they might have called it river-cow, or river hog. It is only when his head is half submerged that we can correctly designate him as a river-horse. Once we see his nose and mouth, we are apt to call him a river cow; but when he is once well out of the water, and we see his heavy body and short legs, we would say immediately that he was more like an over-fat hog than either cow or horse. The hippopotamus has four equal toes on each foot, inclosed in hoofs.

The unwary beasts rose and sank not many feet from the canoe for the last time while they were abreast of the canoe ; and, at the word given by Kalulu, Simba and Moto dipped their paddles, and sent the boat into the stream bow forward, the harpooneer entrusted with the duty of striking standing rigid with uplifted weapon, ready for the blow.

A minute thus he stood, and all eyes were fixed expectant, when at the bow rose the monstrous head and neck of a bull hippopotamus, and at the same moment the harpoon was shot straight and deep into his neck, while the bright blood gushed upward in streams. The stricken animal sounded immediately, while the water was lashed into foam by his struggles, and soon the canoe was moving up the river at terrific speed, while the water rose in high, brown waves at the bow. Presently the speed slackened, and the canoe began to float down the stream.

"Pull back! pull back!" shouted the harpooneer, and at the same time he tossed the buoyant gourd, to which he had fastened the end of the rope hitherto attached to the boat by a round turn around a cleat, into the water. Responsive to the cry, Simba and Moto dashed their paddles into the water ; but they were too late, for they felt the boat lifted up bodily out of the water,

UPSET BY A HIPPOPOTAMUS.

and the crew, losing their equilibrium, staggered on one side, which completely turned the canoe over, and precipitated them into the water.

The three boys, Kalulu, Selim, and Abdullah, instinctively, as they felt the canoe lifted out of the water, rose to their feet with their guns in their hands, and when it was assumed beyond doubt that it would turn over, sprang into the water in different directions, and dived to the bottom, dragging themselves toward their island beneath, by clutching the tenacious mud. For some time the wounded hippopotamus remained master of the field, and no enemy appearing in sight, he sank, uttering a horrible bellow as he disappeared out of sight.

Immediately after, Selim appeared above the surface, more than twenty yards from the scene of the disaster, and swimming vigorously towards the island, which he soon gained in safety. Then appeared Abdullah, about ten yards from the bank; Kalulu close to the shore, with Simba, and Moto, and the two warriors close to him. In a second they stood on the shore, Kalulu minus his gun, but having his sharp spear in his hand; the two warriors had also retained their spears, while Simba and Moto had their guns in their hands, and their long broad knives in their waists.

As soon as they had regained the shore, and stood on dry land, the party began to cheer the youthful straggler, Abdullah, and to encourage him to greater exertions. He was within five yards of the bank, and Simba and Moto were already stretching their guns to him to grasp, when suddenly Abdullah's smiling face assumed a look of terror, and a wild, thrilling shriek was uttered by him, which was silenced instantly by the brown waters closing over his head; and the calm, placid river flowed on, and no swimmer was seen disturbing its surface.

For the shortest possible instant, all hands seemed turned into stone; not a sound nor a breath was heard, until Kalulu was heard uttering the terrible and awful word, " mamba !"—crocodile.

Simba and Moto then breathed, and confused murmurs were heard from all. " Save him !" cried Selim ; "oh, save poor Abdullah !"

There was no need to utter the prayer; for young Kalulu had divested himself of his wet loin-cloth, had broken the staff of the spear he held short off, close to the sharp head, and with the latter grasped firmly in his hand, had plunged head-foremost, unconscious, as it were, of the imminent danger of the hazardous undertaking, into the water, where Abdullah was last seen.

Kalulu's feet had but disappeared beneath the water, when Simba and Moto, dropping their guns, divested themselves of their loin-cloths, and, grasping their long heavy knives, sprang in likewise, and the river, disturbed for but a short second, flowed on as before, with its silent, still flow.

It seemed an age to Selim, who stood on the bank with clasped hands, and cowering form, a prey to the keenest anxiety for the fate of all his friends, who had disappeared beneath the treacherous face of the river.

Yet thirty seconds could not have passed before the deep, brown water was again disturbed, this time in a violent manner, while it began to be slightly discoloured with blood, and the crocodile's tail shot suddenly above the surface, lashing the water into foam, and immediately after, Abdullah's head ; then Kalulu, Simba, and Moto simultaneously appeared above, making for the shore with all haste. As they reached the shore, Kalulu was seen supporting, with his hand beneath the hip, the body of Abdullah, who seemed to have lost consciousness. The ready hands of the two warriors dragged the almost lifeless body, as it reached the bank, and laid it carefully a few feet from the river, on the ground, while Kalulu, wringing his long braids clear of water, and drawing the draggled ostrich feathers from his head, uttered a ringing peal of laughter, and then said in a triumphant tone to Selim :

"We were too much for the mamba, Selim. He did not get my slave Abdullah this time!"

"Ah, thou art so brave, so good, Kalulu!" while grateful tears ran down his cheeks, as he sprang forward to embrace the young hero. "I shall never, never forget thee! I would not miss thy friendship for the world! Thou hast twice saved me—once from death, and another time from the hands of the cruel Tifum. Thou hast still more increased my love for thee, my brave brother, by rescuing Abdullah from the jaws of that horrid mamba. How shall I thank thee, my Kalulu? How shall I praise thee? Thou art swifter than an eagle, braver than a lion, comelier than any of the sons of men! Thine eyes are more tender than a gazelle's to thy friends, fiercer than the greedy leopard's, when it scents the blood of its prey, to thy enemies. Thou art tall as a palm-tree, straight as the hardened shaft of a spear, grace breathes in every

movement of thy limbs. Thou hast saved the life of
my playmate—even the life of Abdullah, the Arab boy.
The dark grey waters had closed over his young head,
his voice had been silenced in the deep, when thou,
O Kalulu, didst leap in—a true hero!—to do battle with
the scaly monster in behalf of Abdullah, my friend, and
playmate of my happy childhood. I saw the waters
hiss and foam, as the monster battled with thee for his
prey. The victory was given to thee; Allah made thine
arm strong, thine heart brave; for Abdullah, my friend,
was brought back from death to life, from the dark
waters to the sunlight, from the grave to the light of
day. O Kalulu! if a fatherless boy is beloved by
Allah, my prayer shall go up to God night and day
for thee; if a true believer may intercede with Heaven,
then wilt thou be blessed, and the soul of Abdullah's
dead father shall cry for thee before the holy footstool
of Allah!"

"Ah, Selim!" replied Kalulu, embracing him in
return, "has Kalulu, the son of Mostana, pleased thee?
then is Kalulu rewarded. Kalulu is thy brother, and
his heart is soft towards Selim, and to the Arab boy,
for thy sake. Thou art good—there is no guile in
thee. Kalulu is also good, but he has seen wicked
men; and when a wicked man draws nigh to him,
Kalulu's heart is black, and bitter, and his spear comes
quickly to his hand. His eyes search out the good;
they found the good in thee, and Kalulu's heart went
to thee as thou didst lie like an antelope stricken to
death in the forest. I shall love all Arabs for thy
sake for ever. There shall be bad blood no more
between us. For as good as thou art am I good, and

as I am good, so art thou. Where I shall be, there
shalt thou be, and where thou wilt be, there shall I be,
until thou canst return in safety to thine own land.
And when thou goest, do thou but remember thy
brother Kalulu, and but whisper his name, then our
Sky-spirit shall send the wind to bear thy whisper to
me. Come, let us see how poor Abdullah fares."

Proceeding to the spot where the still unconscious
form of Abdullah lay, they found that the crocodile
had snatched the young swimmer by the right leg, just
below the knee, where his cruel sharp teeth had pierced
to the bone, leaving ugly marks behind him.

"How didst thou find the crocodile, Kalulu?"

"Oh, I sprang to the place where I saw thy friend
sink, and by good luck I came upon the crocodile's
back. The crocodile having dragged the boy down, let
go of his leg, and laid on top of him. When the
crocodile felt me on his back, he turned round
savagely, but without leaving his prey. I had no time
to stop talking with him, or to ask him to give me
Abdullah back, because I knew he wouldn't; and
besides, I didn't go to ask him, for it is very close
down there, and there is no air. So I felt for his fore-
leg, and while I stabbed him behind, I felt my two
friends, Moto and Simba, who perhaps thought that I
was the crocodile, though my hide is not quite so
rough as the hide of him. When the fellow felt the
keen point of my spear in his heart, he rolled off
Abdullah, and began to kick and lash with his tail in a
dreadful way, and losing my spear, I caught hold of
Abdullah by the leg, and came up. That's how it
was."

Q

"And what didst thou, too, Simba?" asked Selim, turning to his friend.

"When I went down, I caught hold of Moto's hand, and diving, I touched Kalulu, but I knew at once that he was not the crocodile, for his skin is as soft as a child's; the next minute I got hold of the crocodile's leg, though he was kicking and laying about him furiously, and I let go Moto's hand, who got hold of another leg. I buried my knife in the crocodile's belly several times, and he swam away, leaving his inside dragging after him, while I came up to find Kalulu, Abdullah, and Moto right close to me. I think the crocodile has got more than he thought he would get, and that he will leave Abdullah alone in future."

"Do you think Abdullah will come to soon?"

"Oh yes," replied Simba; "he has swallowed a little too much water, or he has fainted from the pain. See now, Master Selim, he breathes! There, his eyes are open!"

Abdullah had only fainted, as Simba said, and this was the reason why the crocodile had so soon released his hold of his leg, and had lain on him. When he opened his eyes, Abdullah gave a long sigh, and asked where he was, to which a cheery answer was returned; and presently he talked, and discussed the event calmly, but not before he had endeavoured to kiss the feet of his saviour, which Kalulu had too much manliness to accept; but he knelt down by him and embraced him, while Abdullah availed himself of the opportunity, and kissed his forehead.

Abdullah having in a measure recovered, the two

warriors were sent to hunt after the canoe, which fortunately was found, stayed in its progress by the reeds, at a point of the island projecting into the current; and, to their great joy, close to the canoe was the gourd to which was fastened the harpoon rope. Giving vent to a loud halloo, Simba, Moto, and Kalulu rushed towards them, and by their united aid they dragged the body of the dead hippopotamus to shallow water, and setting vigorously to work, they soon loaded their canoe with the luscious flesh, it being a food highly prized by the tribes of Central Africa.

By the time this work was despatched, it was night, and the hunters, lifting the wounded Abdullah into the canoe, and having a clear course up the river towards home, they started on their return journey, feeling as proud as men who have been successful in a dangerous exploit only can feel. They sang over and over again exciting hunting and boat songs with vociferous chorus, until midnight, when the fishermen's fires, near Katalambula's village, gladdened their eyes and made them rejoice as home-returned wanderers generally do.

CHAPTER IX.

SELIM was now happy; and next to being able to reach
his own Zanjian Isle, and revisit the scenes of his
childhood, and romp, as of yore, with the playmates of
his youth, and enjoy walks through the orange-groves
with young Abdullah, he could not have chosen for
himself a more tranquil life than that which he now
enjoyed with his friend and new brother, Kalulu.

For the bright Liemba River was beautiful, though
brown; its crisp little wavelets, where they washed
over stone and pebble in the shallower parts, had music·
for him, though he never forgot that horrible scene
near the island, when the smiling face of Abdullah
changed into one of horror and sank down into the
depths, with his shriek echoing through the woods.

The banks of the Liemba became for him a frequent
resort, for Kalulu had made it generally known to all
that he was his brother, and no Mtuta under the King
Katalambula might molest him. Hence, he wandered
where he pleased, finding charms in the wild woods,
and in the depths of waving grain, in the peaceful,

still life that reigned around, in the music of the birds, and even in the harsh cries of paroquets.

The Selim, the brother of Kalulu, was not the Selim of Zanzibar, but was the product of him, refined and pure from the fiery crucible of the unusual hardships he had endured. It was the same boy, but not the same heart. He, whom we knew at Zanzibar, the gay, light-hearted, sunny youth, playing with the females in the harem and his playmates on the beach, but ever listening in wonder to the great, wise words and say-ings of white men, was changed for the dreamy boy with the poet's heart, who chose solitudes, forests, and the depths of tall corn-stalks to indulge in reverie, which we are too apt to ascribe to melancholy. Perhaps it was melancholy, a tender, soft melancholy, engen-dered by many reminiscences of a mournful nature, crowding together in the mind of a boy who had suffered much, but who had seen but few years. There was the death of a loving father and loving kinsmen, the tragic fate of Isa and Mussoud, the most narrow escape he had himself from death, and poor Abdullah's narrow escape from a horrible fate. These were not the best kind of subjects to dwell in the mind of a boy of Selim's years; but what aided to soften all these, and did much to lighten his burden, was his present position, the tender friendship of Kalulu, the company of the gentle Ab-dullah, the calm tranquillity of the life he was now en-joying, and the consciousness—which his perfect trust in the goodness of God created—that there was a God above, who was both good and great, and who would bring him in his own good time out of all trouble.

For many days Abdullah suffered from the wounds

which the crocodile's sharp teeth had made in his leg.
High fever set in, during which time he was attended
by Simba, and Moto, Kalulu, and Selim.

All sport was at an end for Selim and Kalulu while
their friend Abdullah was thus suffering. Nothing of
enjoyment was thought of, nothing could be thought of
but their poor young patient, whose constitution was
battling vigorously against the fever which threatened
often to terminate his life.

And what a time poor Abdullah had! Instead of
the soft, silken counterpane and feathered bolsters,
and the fragrance of lime and orange of his own comfortable home at Zanzibar, here were a mud-hut, low
roof of straw and mud, a goatskin for his bed, a low
door of cane-stalks, through which the white sunlight streamed hot and glaring, voices of a thousand
rats for music, and the bad smells caused by the inde-
cent habits of savages, for the perfume of ripe orange
and cinnamon. All these aggravated the fever and
created hideous dreams at night. For food he had a
thin gruel, which Simba made for him to the best of
his ability; for drink, the muddy water of the Liemba
or some pombe-beer. Despite these, however, his constitution triumphed; the fever left him, and the
wounded leg, carefully bathed each morning by Simba,
began to heal.

When convalescent, Abdullah would leave his hut at
evening, pale and thin as a ghost, leaning on the arm
of his true friends, Kalulu and Selim, to enjoy the mild
air, and to listen to the songs of the Watuta, and the
sonorous music of the drums. The sight of the pale
and thin Arab boy touched the heart of many a ma-

ternal bosom, and many were the expressions of condo-
lence which he received from them. He often heard
these dark-faced women utter expressions which he had
never thought at Zanzibar could ever be uttered by
black women ; and he was rapidly beginning to learn
that women are the same all over the world, whether
they are white or black, and that human love and kindness belong as much to the black as to the white, and
are as often practised. And the outcast, despised
negro race were rising daily in his estimation. Neither
was Selim indifferent to the tones of sympathy he
heard from them ; not only did Kalulu win his friendship more and more each day, but the whole negro
race was being admitted into his brotherhood.

These were really happy days. Abdullah was improving each day, and Selim was fast becoming as
joyous a companion as Kalulu could desire. Inspired
by the invigorating sound of the drums, and the lively
chorus, he was compelled to leave the side of Abdullah
and join in the dance. A favourite song of the Watuta
was the boatmen's song, which seemed interminable ;
but the chorus was so pretty, and had such a sweet,
pathetic melody, that Selim joined with pleasure in it
for its pathos.

The first and second verses ran somewhat in this
strain :—

> Down the brown Liemba,
> The home of fierce Mamba,[1]
>> We are gliding.
> With sudden stroke and song
> The boat is sent along,
>> Swiftly gliding.

---

[1] Crocodiles.

> We fear no fierce mamba
> In the deep Liemba
>   While we are gliding;
> Nor bush nor thickest brake,
> Nor foe that would us take—
>   Swiftly gliding."

The fifth, seventh, and eighth verses are descriptive of the scenery on the Liemba :—

> By waving fields of grain,
> With song and loud refrain,
>   We are gliding ;
> While women hoe the corn
> Till eve from dewy morn—
>   Swiftly gliding.

> Lo ! Isle of Ihata,
> Blest Isle of Liemba,
>   By which we are gliding.
> The isle was long ago
> Blest by great Moshono—
>   Softly gliding.

> Near that tree on yon plain
> Died Moshono in pain,—
>   We are gliding –
> Burnt by dread Warungu,
> Who fear no Malungu—
>   Softly gliding.

The ninth verse is somewhat superstitious :—

> Sole on that lofty rock
> Lives Moshono's sacred cock.
>   We are gliding.
> Now, boatmen, here cease to row,
> Bad luck, to hear no crow !—
>   Softly gliding.

As I have said, the boat song is almost interminable ; it describes every view on that beautiful river, each tradition that surrounds the hills, and memorable sites of battles fought and victories won ; for it is thus that our history was kept before writing was known to us.

Another song, which was a favourite with the young men and maidens of Katalambula's village, describes what love-making is known to the Watuta. For this reason only is it valuable, as illustrative of the mode of marriage. The following verses are sufficient as an example :—

> Canst thou love me as I love thee?
> Wilt thou not come and live with me?
> My father talked with thine to-day,
> Thy father did not tell him " Nay."

> Said he, " Bring me two score of sheep ;
> Bring me pombe in pots thus deep ;
> Bring me ten goats of the best class,
> Thy son may take my pretty lass."

> I've built my hut of sedgy cane,
> The well-thatched roof keeps out the rain,
> The floor is spread with river sand,
> The latch waits lifting by thy hand.

> Thy husband calls, do not delay ;
> Come to his house ere end of day ;
> Put now thy hand in mine and come,
> Come to Kiranga's heart and home.

Selim and Abdullah heard numbers of these during the period of the latter's convalescence, and were constantly amused by them. To sit under the great tree in the centre of the square, to hear the music of the drums, to hear the songs sung, and to see the people dance, was like going to a theatrical entertainment with us. Kalulu often sat with them, but not for long ; the exhilarating influence of the music produced such an effect on his feet and legs, that while listening to it he found himself unable to restrain them.

As Abdullah got better and became able to move about during the day, Kalulu used to take him and Selim to the great Maganga, or magic doctor, to enjoy the conversation of the wise man of the tribe.

This doctor must have been at least eighty years old, for he remembered Katalambula as a child, and knew Mostana, Kalulu's father, and remembered the " great, great" King Loralamba, father of Katalambula and Mostana. This was very old history to Kalulu, who could not conceive the number of years that had elapsed since Loralamba's death, though the time could only have been between forty and fifty years. The doctor, whose name was Soltali, knew any amount of things that no other man knew. He remembered the time when the Northern Watuta, who now live north of the Malagarazi River, separated from the Southern Watuta, over whom Katalambula was chief ruler, for some pique that the younger brother had against Loralamba. He remembered many wars that had taken place between the Watuta and Wabena, and remembered well the incident of which the boatmen sang as they travelled down the Liemba, viz., the burning of Moshono, a great doctor, who lived on the island of Ihata. The Warungu came in great numbers, and were conquering wherever they went, until they came opposite Ihata. Then their cattle died, and their warriors died of a horrible disease which Moshono punished them with. Finally, however, they got across the river and landed on the island; the village was taken, and Moshono was carried to the plain opposite the island, and burnt alive near a great tree. But it seemed as if the Sky-spirit heard the words of

Moshono, and stirred up the Watuta—all; every man who
could bear a sword and spear—against the Warungu, and
a few days after, the Watuta, under Loralamba, rushed
on their camp at night, and there was an exceeding great
slaughter. Only a few Warungu escaped, and since
then they had settled quietly in their own country,
south of the Lake Liemba, many days' march from
Katalambula's.

Soltali was rich in this history, which, alas! is never
destined to see the light; a history that were a man
disposed to write it for the mere love of giving it to
the world, and instructing it in the past life of this
obscure corner of the world, might enlighten the
learned of all countries in much that concerns the
great races of Central Africa.

Soltali's hut was a veritable museum; but it bore a
striking resemblance to the rich men's houses in England and America in this respect. What ducal castle
or baronial hall is there in England, but has its collec-
tion of deer, antelope, and buffalo horns; its stuffed
lions; its tigers, &c. &c.? What rich man's house is
there in America which has not some trophy of its
master's hunting prowess? Soltali had his trophies,
though, owing to his pitiable ignorance of taste, book
knowledge, &c., &c., his trophies were not arranged as
a Schwartzenberg of Austria or a Duke of Sutherland
arrange theirs. There were horns upon horns of antelope, kudu, hartebeest, black buck, spring-bok, gems-
bok, gnu, buffalo, and rhinoceros, and tusks upon tusks
of polished ivory. But the great store of curiosities
that he set the greatest value upon consisted of tails of
elephants, horns of giraffes, eyelids of zebras, tusks of

boars, paws of lions, nose-hairs and whiskers of leopards, claws of eagles, beaks of bustards and kites, wings of ostriches, scales of fish, dried eyes of ibis; all wrapped up in pieces of goatskin, each separate the one from the other. He had a great number of little gourds, filled with the calcined heads of the various animals he had ever killed, and smaller gourds, like phials, filled with the burnt brains of men whom he had killed in war. There were so many brains of Warungu, Wabena, Wasowa, Wakawendi, Wawemba, Warori, Wanyamwezi, Wamwite, Wakanyara, Wakokoro, and a number of other smaller tribes; for in his prime, when he fought side by side with Loralamba, the " great, great " King, Soltali's spear was heavy, sharp, and sure.

Poor, ancient Soltali ! who shall sing thy praises? Who shall tell the wide, wide world all the deeds done by thy mighty hands? Where is the Homer who shall arise and sing of thy prowess? Homer, and Virgil, and Tasso, De Ercilla, and Camoens are dead, and we have none left capable of conveying thy name to future generations. But be content, old man; this page, at least, of this little book will tell a few of the growing generation of true-hearted American and British youths, that such a man did once live as thee, oh, Soltali ! and, perhaps, in an obscure corner of the British Museum, thyself and wondrous museum of monstrosities shall, embodied as it were in this page, rest a few years until they become a heap of dead, unintelligible dust !

At the end of about two months, Abdullah was so far recovered as to be able to go about alone, without the aid of any of his friends; but he had an unconquerable antipathy to the banks of the Liemba. The brown

waters of this river, in which he was so very near-
being engulphed, inspired him with a nauseous aversion,
having something of the effect of tartar emetic on his
stomach, and he never dared, as Selim often did, to
wander along its banks alone.   When he became tired
of the village he walked to the fields, or the gardens,
where the pot-herbs, the lentiles, the pig-nuts, and the
beans grew.   Neither forest nor solitude charmed Abdullah; the company of the nursing women, or the
workers in the field, was far preferable.

One day, Kalulu proposed to Selim, and Simba, and
Moto, that they should get up a party to make a grand
elephant hunt, and, as an apology, said to Selim:

"I should have asked thee long ago, were it not that
I knew thou wouldst not come; but Abdullah is so
much better that he travels about the village as if he
had never been bitten by a crocodile."

"To hunt elephants I will surely come with thee.   I
have got my gun, which I saved from the Liemba, and
I should like to try a shot at an elephant.   Moto is a
great hunter, and he shall teach me how to tickle the
tail and hams of one; thou hast never heard him tell
the story.   Oh, it is such an incredible one! but he
never tells a lie to me."

"Does Moto say he tickled the tail of an elephant?
if it is true, he has done more than old Soltali himself.
Soltali has done some wonderful things with elephants
too, but he never did anything like this.   However, we
shall see how he acts before a real wild elephant.   We
shall watch him—eh, Selim?"

"Oh, I shall have my eyes on him, depend on it;
but when shall we go, Kalulu?"

"At daybreak to-morrow. To-night Soltali must sing the elephant hunting-song of the hunters, and must give each of the hunters a charm, since he is too old to accompany us. I shall take fifty men with me, so that we can make a strong party. If Ferodia catches us in the woods he would make short work of us, and my head would not remain long on my shoulders if he caught me; for then he knows he would be king."

"Why, thou art not going near his country, surely, because I would rather stop here, if thou art. I want to see no more of Ferodia," said Selim in alarm.

"Be at ease, my brother. I go not near him with the best fifty men that the Watuta can count. I go in a different direction, south-east; he lives south-west, south of the Liemba Lake."

"All right; but really thou didst frighten me. My back fairly tingles at the thought of Tifum, and Tifum is with Ferodia."

"Yet, my brother, thou didst hit him a blow in the face, and Moto—cunning man—said he saw it, and said it was well done."

"I wish the blow had gone through his head, then my mind would be at ease, for that man is my bane— my Afrit.* Even when I am at Zanzibar I shall think of that man."

"There, enough, my brother; I will put one of my barbed arrows through his throat the first time I see him, for thy sake. Go and prepare thy gun, and bullets, and medicine powder, and to-night thou must attend to the song of the doctor, or thou shalt have bad

* Afrit is a bad spirit with the Moslems.

luck with us in the hunt." And Kalulu turned away with light bounding steps, which soon carried him away from his Arab brother.

At night—probably at the hour of nine with us, the moon being up—a long, low, rumbling roll of the largest goma brought the destined hunters, together with Kalulu, Selim, Simba, and Moto, running and chasing each other towards the drum stand. There were ten drums, and a boy for each, ascending in height from the smallest to the biggest drum; so that the boy who beat the smallest drum must have been about ten years old, and the boy who beat the largest drum was a sturdy youth of twenty, or thereabouts.

Pots full of pombe and plantain-wine were ranged a little distance off, from which the dancers and the singers could regale themselves when they felt disposed. For the eve of a hunting party's march is considered a great event, second only to the return of a successful party with plenty of ivory.

The hunters formed a select circle round the drummers and the pombe pots; a larger circle, made by about three hundred people—men, women, boys, and girls—surrounded the hunters.

Each hunter had on a capricious head-dress. One tall fellow was very conspicuous by wearing a pair of buffalo horns; another had a rhinoceros horn on the top of his head; another had his head draped with a piece of zebra skin, which gave him quite a remarkable appearance by moonlight; one had a zebra crest, which made him appear as if he wore a Greek helmet; another had a goatskin over his head. Kalulu wore three magnificent snowy ostrich plumes

on his head. Selim wore a turban. Simba and Moto
also wore turbans. One fellow, next to Moto, wore
an enormous black earthen pot on his head; another
had a broad, wooden dish; but it would be wearying to
enumerate all the strange things they wore.

The drummer boys struck up an interlude, which
was a verse from the boatmen's song—the chorus,

> We are gliding,
> Softly gliding,

seemingly giving them immeasurable enjoyment as
they lingered over the word "gliding." While they
were busy with feet and lungs, moving about in a circle,
a sudden silence prevailed;—the great Soltali, the
greatest elephant hunter and doctor of magic of the
age, arrived upon the scene.

A loud murmur of approbation greeted the extraordinary old man. The most remarkable of all head-
dresses was on the head of Soltali, for he had the skin
of an elephant's trunk, the base of the trunk fitting
his head, as if it had grown there, while the trunk,
filled with grass, was stiff enough to stand perfectly
erect, though perhaps it was stiff enough without.
The weight of this must have been considerable; but
the ridiculous vanity of men causes them to do strange
things sometimes, and this act could have been nothing
else than absurdest vanity. Hanging around the old
man's neck was a string of giraffe tails, whose hairs
were blacker than ink. On his arms he wore wristlets
and armlets of pure white ivory. In each hand he
carried a gourd half full of pebbles, which he rattled
every now and then with a horrible noise.

He first, after he entered the inner circle, walked

around three times, staring at each man, rattling his gourds alternately, as he passed round ; then walking to the centre, while the bass drum began to hum and murmur its deep sounds, he began to move his body to the right and left, each hunter sighing deeply in sympathy with the now fast rising murmur of all the drums in concert. Loud and louder beat the drums, until the noise was deafening, and the voices of the singers became a demoniac din ; then lower and lower descended the voices and the drum-sounds, until nothing was heard but the pacific and low murmur of the bass drum and the low sighs of the dancers.

Then Soltali opened his mouth and sang, in the heroic vein, of his doings in the elephant hunt in the far southern lands, the streamy land of the Wama·rungu, in the hot swampy lands of the Wawemba, and on the broad plains of Ututa ; of his mishaps and fortunes, his narrow, hairbreadth escapes, and his wonderful adventures, out of which the author of the present history might make his fame and fortune were he gifted with the power to translate into some kind of verse what Soltali said.

Though demurring somewhat at the necessity of translating at all what the old man said, the author feels compelled to give the gist of the charge he gave the hunters concerning their conduct when they should meet an elephant. He spoke authoritatively and well, and it is a pity that a better translator is not at my side to assist me in the translation of some of the Kituta polysyllables.

" Let the warrior Watuta and the hunters bold
Heed and mark well the words of the Mganga old ;

B

Let them behold these charms, these trophies of my might;
Each of them reminds me of many a hard fight.
Should ye meet the elephant alone in a plain,
Seek not too hastily to give him the death pain.
Singly let none attack him—'tis an unequal fight;
For the elephant is strong, the embodiment of might;
But surround him coolly, and carefully all,
Be ready to obey your leader's slightest call;
Then charge on him, all shouting, and charge with your spears;
Let the stoutest and best of you aim behind his ears.
Watch well the unfortunate on whom he turns round!
He must run this and that way, and oft change his ground;
Ye others must tease him, and invite him your way,
Hamstring him, and spear him, and do what ye may.
Beware of his front! range on his sides and his rear,
Go all together, and let each man heave a sure spear.
Fast as he veers round, hasten at right angles away
To 'scape the elephant's first charge is no child's play,
For his stride is so long he swallows the ground:
One stride of his is as long as a hunter's bound.
After a while he will get tired—heed well what I say,
He is never so dangerous as when standing at bay;
For the hunter too often thinks he is dead game,
And advances too near him, too eager for fame;
But be ye guided by me, and stand off afar,
And your good hunt so well done, ye will not mar.
Let the elephant bleed, let him fall to the ground,
Let him gladden your ears with his fall's heavy sound!
Then think of the Mganga, the words he has said;
Be sure that his services to you are well paid!
Then will ye succeed in your hunt on the plain,
Succeed without loss, and succeed without pain!"

The author may not attempt further translations from the speech, or song rather, of this old Mganga or magic doctor, the Kituta polysyllables having tasked his powers to the utmost; but from his knowledge of hunting in Africa, he feels bound to admit that the old man had a sound head on his shoulders; and the band of hunters having heard his lengthy chant to the

end, declared that they felt eternally grateful to him.
On the conclusion of his chant, he delivered to each
hunter a small portion of whitish powder, which we,
who have been in his museum, feel confident consisted of
burnt brain, mixed with wood ashes.   But this charm,
consecrated by the magic doctor, could not fail to render
each hunter highly successful in his enterprise.

The pombe, or beer, next attracts the attention of
the singers, and each singer incontinently sets to the
agreeable task of guzzling, where the author leaves
them until the morrow—the Kituta polysyllables and
the pombe having fairly upset him for the time.

In the morning, at daybreak, without any of the
formalities of muster or calling the roll, Kalulu, Selim,
Simba, and Moto, left the village by the principal gate,
followed by about fifty strong active young warriors,
not one of whom could have been over thirty years old.
The horn of the leading hunter sounded merrily as he
blew his ringing blasts of adieux, while the party dived
into the depths of the gigantic corn-stalks, and their
friends at the village listened long and attentively,
until the horn could be no longer heard.

Kalulu had a couple of broad-bladed spears, and
half a-dozen assegais, much lighter than spears, with
long flexible shafts, besides a bow and a quiver pack-full
of arrows, which was slung over his shoulders.

Selim, radiantly happy, walked next to Kalulu, as
the path was so narrow that but one could walk at a
time on the smooth, hard road, and carried his own
gun—the "gun from London," which Kalulu had found
among the plunder, with its own special ammunition.
It was probably a fine "Joe Manton," as the barrels were

of fine steel, short, of large bore, and a heavy price
had been paid for it by Amer bin Osman through his
Bombay agent. It was one of those fortunate accidents
that occur sometimes. Olimali might have had the
gun, had not Ferodia, seeing its great beauty and superiority, specially reserved it for a present to Katalambula; and the king not caring, or not having any
use, for it, had placed it among his treasures in his
store room; and Selim, accompanying Kalulu to the
store-room, as a privileged brother, to pick out a gun,
suddenly saw the beautiful little masterpiece of the
English gunmaker, which his father had presented him
with, and with which he had shot the greedy crocodile
on the Lofu, while his sharp teeth were lacerating his
slave Mombo's leg. Could anything have been more
fortunate? "Impossible!" thought Selim, as he had
hastened to secure it, with the ammunition and the
percussion caps. "Impossible!" thought he now, as
he strode on after Kalulu, laughing and chatting gaily,
and sometimes turning round to Simba and Moto with
a gay remark, which permitted them to see his bright,
happy face and sparkling eyes.

Simba had his own bright-barrelled gun, which he
had as yet never parted with, besides a ponderous spear,
which might have made Goliath of Gath faint with the
carrying of it.

Behind Simba strode nimble-footed Moto, who also
had his own gun, besides a couple of long keen-pointed
spears.

Behind Moto strode the Watuta hunters, one after
another, some of them armed with shields, besides
their handfuls of spears and quivers full of arrows.

Merriness is what distinguishes the conduct of all hunting parties, whether white or black, while on the way to the chase or the hunt. Pleasures unlimited are anticipated, and happy sport is expected, and this anticipation and expectation are what produce so many good jokes, and wit, and fun, and raillery, or, as the English call it, "chaff," when the hunting-field has not yet been reached and all feel bright and fresh. The hours that precede the chase or the hunt form the flower-time which men's minds love to remember and dwell upon for the unalloyed happiness which it furnished.

It is needless to describe in detail the ground the party traversed. Once out of the corn-fields, the pastoral plains spread before them, where young Watuta boys were seen indulging in the excitement of a mimic battle or hunt while they tended their fathers' flocks. Here and there were little tracts of cultivation where women were at work hoeing the corn; and as they passed some isolated village, near the gate, under the trees, sat the nursing mothers, lullabying their babes to sleep, or the snowy crisp-haired elders sat on short three-legged stools retailing to each other the experiences of their lives, dwelling with fondness on some particular episode of their generally uneventful lives; while chubby, abdominous little children listened in wonder at what they heard, as chubby, abdominous little boys of white men's lands do when a particularly interesting tale is told.

Beyond the plains and corn-fields, the cultivated tracts and villages, heaved into view the dark blue line of forest—that forest which Selim knew, where he suffered, where he fainted, and laid unconscious. Finally, the party entered it, and they were involved in its twilight gloom.

A week's marching through the forest brought the party to the elephant hunting-grounds of the Watutu. The broad tracks, pounded and pressed, trodden compact and smooth as an asphalte pavement by the elephants' broad, heavy feet, indicated too clearly that this was a common resort for the ponderous beasts.

Lengthy sinuous hollows, overgrown with thicket and shrub, tufted grass, and tall cane, spoke of clear but stagnant water being plentiful here, their ridges, clad with dense brush, ran in serpentine directions, and separated these swampy hollows from each other. Overhead were the leafy crowns of gigantic columnar trees, forming as they met close together a thorough shade for the locality, under which, undisturbed by any enemy, the elephant might cool himself during the fervid noon.

Pressing further on out of this swampy region, they came, about sunset, to a thin jungle, where here and there rose a giant baobab, the monarch of all woods. Choosing one of these great trees, whose foliage was denser than ordinary, the party proceeded to cut down the smaller trees and brush, to form a brush fence around their camp, for the centre of which they chose this great baobab. They built the fence solid, secure, and high, as an efficient protection against wild beasts and nomadic freebooters. They then erected their huts —placing four short pronged poles in the ground, one at each corner of a square of six feet; then two taller poles dividing the square into halves; over these two

taller poles and the two shorter poles on each side
they laid transverse poles, which rested in the forks;
and over these again they laid laterally light sticks,
sloping down each side, which they covered over with
long grass, and in a short time they had a perfect
miniature house. There were other kinds of houses
or huts being constructed; but the following illustra-
tion will best describe the architectural knowledge of
the Watutu.

After constructing their huts, some roamed into the
woods to hunt for wild fruit, others to look for flat
stones to grind their corn upon, others to procure sticks
to make their fires with, others to get water; while
others, again, scoured and prepared their pots to boil

their porridge in. There were about fifteen huts in the encampment, some huts having as many as five for a mess, others only three, while others had but two. It is a noteworthy fact in African camps that, where the mess is large, the more important of the party are together; or that the most popular are those who prefer each other's society to that of any of the rest; though in each large mess one may be sure that one of the members has been admitted only for the sake of utilising his services; and his folly and ignorance, or cowardice and unworthiness, are forgiven and borne with, so long as he is industrious and not idle.

Thus in Kalulu's mess were Selim, Simba, Moto, and an ignorant and timid fellow, who was only too glad to be near the great, and who industriously strove to please them for the sake of the patronage which he received for his labour. Kalulu, of course, as chief, could command the services of all if he chose to do so, but none would have worked as well as the timid fellow who voluntarily offered to cook for him.

After the suppers were cooked and eaten, and their limbs were somewhat rested, and earth had drawn its sable mantle, chequered with the diamonds of heaven, over its head, and the dark foliage of the baobab began to be peopled with formless shapes and shadows, and the fires burned bright, and cast their tongued flames with splutter, and hissing, and crackling, the dispositions of each began to be exhibited. They squatted around a blazing pile, listening to an exciting tale of adventure, or a funny story, which makes men's sides almost explode with laughter. What can be more enjoyable? Nothing. People, for the time, forget everything but the interesting present. Not one in such a position can be left to himself; for his little world is before him, and he must be drawn into its vortex of pleasantry and enjoyment, and forget what he selfishly thinks belongs to himself.

The desire of slumber came on by-and-bye, and each man crept into his hut, and on his own little pile of straw or leaves, drowned in kindly, healthy sleep, forgot not only himself, but his neighbours, his friends, and his tribe.

At dawn, five of the likeliest fellows were sent by Kalulu to reconnoitre the vicinity and the open, swampy ground near which they had camped, and where they had obtained their water for cooking the night before.

They had not been gone fifteen minutes before one of them returned, who, with a warning finger, imposed silence, and whispered the words "Kūmi tembo"—ten elephants!

You might have seen then how quickly the looks of indifference were changed into one of exciting interest, how eyes danced gladly, and sparkled at the joyful news; how Kalulu's hunter-soul kindled into raptures, and how Moto and Simba looked significantly at one another, and how Selim even felt a throb and a warm glow stealing over him.

Moto advanced to Kalulu, and reminded him of the advice given by Soltali to hunt one at a time, and said that while he and his warriors should single out one, it would be better that those armed with guns, viz., he and Simba, and Selim, should engage another, and so kill two. Kalulu at once acceded to the proposal.

The hunters, as soon as they got outside of the boma or camp, deployed in a long line, while Selim, Moto, and Simba stole quietly and quickly away on their own venture, in a direction considerably to the left of the Watuta hunters. All the natives had denuded themselves entirely; Selim and his two friends had but girded their cloths about their loins.

The natives thus deployed, and ready at a signal, moved forward silently, and soon they were joined by the four remaining scouts, who, ensconced behind the bushes, had continued to watch the elephants, who were seen slaking their thirst at a pool, and playfully tossing the water over their backs.

As the hunters emerged from this jungle into the cleared space near the pool, the elephants turned short round to look at the strange intruders, who were thus boldly appearing in their presence.

The hunters stopped also with one accord to survey the ponderous animals they had come to kill. What a sight this was! Ten such noble beasts, clothed with bluish-grey hides, with uplifted trunks, and great ears standing out straight in array before those fifty naked pigmies, who, had they not their sharp spears and their barbed arrows, would no more have dared to approach these magnificent creatures than they would have climbed up to the highest tree and jumped off, expecting to be able to fly.

They stood thus a minute opposed to each other; then Kalulu advanced to the front in the absence of the magic doctor, as the chief hunter, and with uplifted spear in hand, chanted the death-song of the elephant he chose should be killed. This was a picture also

"YOUNG KALULU IS HERE!"

worthy of a great artist—the warriors in the fore-
ground, the slight and nude form of the young chief
in the centre, with his ostrich plumes waving above
his head, as his body oscillated from side to side while
he sang; and fronting him, about thirty feet off, a
monster elephant, with his herd behind him, all looking
astonished at the scene.

The words ran after this fashion:—

> " Thou monarch of beasts, thou king of the woods,
> Thou dangerous beast in thy angry moods,
> Thou elephant strong, thou form of great might,
> Behold Kalulu before thee for fight!
> I've come from the green groves of Liemba,
> From the country of old Loralamba,
> With magic from Soltali Mganga,*
> The surest and best of his Uganga †
> Then look at that sun, look at the pool
> In which thou didst revel, and think so cool;
> Look on that forest, and look on this grass,
> The sweetest and best of this wide morass:
> No more shalt thou see the sun or the pool,
> No more shalt thou revel in waters cool,
> No more shalt thou walk in the forest's shade,
> No more shalt thou delight in forest glade,
> No more shalt thou daintily feed on the grass
> Of the plain, or jungle, or this morass!
> Soltali the Mganga cannot lie:
> Young Kalulu is here! prepare to die!"

As he finished his song his head was violently thrown
back, the right arm was drawn to its length, and the
bright spear-head, flashing once, twice, white sunglints,
was buried deep in the elephant's chest.   A loud shout
greeted the brave effort; and at the instant the elephant
felt the keen sharp iron in him, he uttered a loud

* Magic Doctor.   † Magic Medicine.

trumpet-note of rage, and charged, clearing at one bound several strides of a man.

"Be off, Kalulu, thou brave prince of the Watuta! Hie away young hero! Stay not to count thy steps, thou dusky chief! Spring out, my boy; run as thou didst never run before! Impel thy haunches on—lift thy feet clear from the ground; out with thy chest—set thy head far back! Let thy lungs inhale free the rushing air! Beware of a stumble, else the tale is ended! Ha! well done—at right angles now! So; see the elephant charges the empty air, and runs headlong after vacancy! Now, warriors, is our time, with a whoop, and the shrill cry of the Watuta!"

Such were the words that could be distinguished from the noise and tumult produced by the charge. Twenty spears had been launched into the elephant's body to distract his attention, and had it not been for Soltali's good advice to "turn at right angles away," the elephant would soon have overtaken the daring young chief; but, by his dexterous and easy movement to the right, the monster had charged on far ahead before he became aware that his enemy had escaped him.

When he turned round he found the hunters like a cloud about him; he found himself isolated from his herd; the other elephants having charged in another direction in fury and fright to meet an enemy in another guise, and with different weapons. While the elephant seemed to take this all at a glance, a loud report was heard, which sounded like a volley of fire-arms; but he, unheeding the sound, charged again, with irresistible power, at his nearest foe, only to be foiled

once more by the ever-evading, ever-shifting figures of
his remorseless enemies. Again and again he charged,
only to receive new wounds, an additional shower of
spears and barbed arrows, which tormented him cruelly;
until, fatigued with the unusual speed, faint from loss
of blood, he stood stock still, confronting his enemies,
defiant and still dreadful, though the spears and arrows
in his body might have been counted by hundreds.
Heedful of the prudent counsel of old Soltali, the
Watuta drew back, but still surrounding him, awaiting
his fall. They had not to wait long, before they saw
his body oscillate from side to side, and the left knee
bend, as if he were getting weak; then he staggered
forward, rose up again, and finally rolled on his side—
dead, crushing the spears in his side like straws in his
fall.

Leaving the Watuta to indulge in their self-glorifica-
tion, let us proceed to see how the other three, Selim,
Simba, and Moto, fared.

Moto, as the three left the Watuta, drew alongside
of Selim, and whispered some words in his ears, how to
conduct himself, to reserve his fire, and to fire at the
last elephant which would pass him, aiming behind his
ears, which, of course, would be standing straight out,
giving him an ample opportunity and a good target to
fire at. Selim, faithfully promising, was placed behind
a tree at the furthest end of the cleared ground in the
neighbourhood of the pool. Simba chose one a few
yards off, further still to the left, and Moto another
tree twenty yards to the left of Simba; and in this
position they waited the denouement.

Selim could see the swaying form and nodding

plumes of Kalulu, could hear the death-song, and with his finger on the two triggers of his gun, which was heavily loaded specially for this purpose, stood behind his tree waiting. Soon he saw Kalulu launch his spear, saw the charge and flight, heard the deafening noise, and while his heart palpitated fast, and his pulses throbbed, and his ears tingled, came the affrighted animals of the herd, charging in fear and fury by him. Obediently he waited, according to orders, until the last elephant was passing his position, then, stilling the heart's palpitation and the wildly beating pulse, full of trust and confidence in the powers of his English gun, he deliberately aimed behind the elephant's ears, and fired both barrels at once. The concussion knocked him down; but, while falling, he saw his elephant stumble and fall on his head in a motionless heap, stone dead.

Picking himself hastily up, and snatching his gun, he stayed a moment to take in how matters stood; and finding the elephants in full flight, two limping laggards behind, and Simba and Moto following, he began to load his gun again with equally heavy charges as those he had in it previously; and having placed the caps carefully on, and taking a glance of pride at the game he had "bagged," he ran after Simba and Moto. His two friends he found firing, running, and loading as fast as they could; not a very hard task when the animals were so badly wounded. His nimble feet soon carried him nearer them, and after dodging and running as he had been directed to, as he was pursued by one or the other of the elephants, he had the satisfaction at last of seeing both stand still. Retreating a little distance from view, he took a circuit round, and then returned, taking advantage of every tree, and by great caution succeeded in coming behind a large tree at the distance of twelve paces from one of them. Lifting his gun, already cocked, to his shoulders, he took aim again behind the ears, and fired the two barrels once more, which was met with the same fatal result, for the elephant, after beating the air with his forelegs for a short time, swayed pitifully, and fell over, dead.

But Selim had no time to make these observations, for the other elephant turned short round and charged at the tree. Selim stood his ground until the tree had almost been reached, when, dropping the gun on the ground, he started off for another tree, the elephant in hot pursuit after him. To the right, to the left, forwards and backwards, from tree to tree, Selim ran, until the elephant, to his astonishment, suddenly stopped, the hind-legs doubled under him, the fore-legs bent, and his head came to the ground heavily, and in this kneeling position the poor elephant breathed his last.

Selim had his gun brought to him by Simba, who lavished praises, almost fulsome, on his bravery and accuracy of shooting, in which Moto, who now came up, joined with heart and spirit. Simba, while he embraced his young master, would have it that Selim was the best elephant hunter known; there never was such an Arab boy before, who shot two elephants dead one after another. "And thou must consider, Moto," said he, apologetically, "Selim is but sixteen; if he shoots two elephants, one after another, when he is sixteen, what will he do when he is a grown man?"

"True," answered Moto, "when he is double his age he will shoot four one after another. Selim is a great hunter truly. I wonder what the Watuta have done. Whisht! hear their cries! Their elephant is dead. We must go to see them. Or do thou stop with Selim to watch these whilst I go to tell them what our young master has done. Say, Simba, how much money would the ivory of these three elephants bring at Zanzibar, dost thou think?"

"I know not. How many frasilah dost thou think there are in the three?" asked Simba.

"Somewhere about twelve, I should say? Twelve frasilah of ivory at 50 dollars the frasilah (35 lbs.) would make how much?" asked Moto.

"I don't know—plenty, I suppose," said Simba; "but Selim knows."

"Twelve fifties will make 600—six hundred dollars," answered Selim.

"Six hundred dollars! What a pity we cannot carry it to Zanzibar!" said Moto. "I shall be back directly."

Moto bounded away lightly towards the pool, and in a short time in the middle of the plain beyond he saw the Watuta in a group cutting and slashing at the dead elephant, with noise and excitement enough to frighten every elephant for miles around.

When he approached, the Watuta gathered about him, and Kalulu pointed exultantly at the dead beast into which he had driven the first spear, and Kalulu then asked what luck they had had.

Moto answered: "Selim has killed two, and I have killed one"

"Selim killed two!" echoed Kalulu, with surprise. "What! little Selim my brother?"

"The same," answered Moto.

"Eyah, eyah!" murmured the group, while Kalulu seemed lost in astonishment, and could not utter a word more.

"Selim stands waiting to shew them to his brother, Kalulu," said Moto.

"Oh, I shall come. Why Selim is a hero, a lion, an elephant! Is he not, Moto?"

"He is a brave young Arab, and the son of an Arab chief," answered Moto.

When the young chief started off, all but a few Watuta, who remained to extract the tusks, followed him to see the wonderful three dead elephants.

In the same position in which he had first fallen lay Selim's first prize, with his tusks half buried in the ground. Kalulu gazed at the wide wound in his head, put his fist into it until it was buried up to the wrist, and then turned to Moto with wondering eyes, and said:

"Kalulu has seen dead men in his father's village, pierced to the heart with the leaden balls which the rifles of Kisesa threw, but what gun is this that makes such big holes in the elephant's head?"

Then Moto told him that Selim had fired the two barrels of the gun at once, at such a short distance from the elephant, that the two big bullets went into the head as one, and that this was the reason there was such a big hole, which quite satisfied the young chief.

Leaving ten men to extract the tusks, Kalulu proceeded to where Selim and Simba stood, close to the

S

former's second prize; and here, again, Kalulu saw the wide rent and savage wound in the same spot as that found in the first elephant.

Kalulu sprang on Selim's neck, and embraced him warmly, while the Watuta gazed at Selim as on one they had never seen before, with surprise and unlimited admiration.

By evening the tusks had all been extracted from the elephants, and great portions of the meat were carried to camp, especially the feet, the hearts, and livers, and ribs, where, before blazing fire-piles, the meat was set to roasting, while the adventures of the day were rehearsed over and over, with new additions each time, until midnight of that eventful day came and sealed all eyes in deep slumber.

They moved further south, and in less than two weeks the party had killed twenty elephants, which so loaded them with ivory, that they were obliged to return towards home, unable to carry more.

CHAPTER X.

The burial Song—Kalulu becomes King—Long live King Kalulu—
Kalulu's Oration—Selim asks permission to depart—The dis-
satisfied Minority—Ferodia's Ambition—Tifum the Wicked, and
his Advice—Ferodia visits Kalulu—The treacherous Guests.

AFTER a march of two weeks without a single incident,
they arrived at Katalambula's village, to hear the sad
news that the King had died the day before, and that
everybody was mourning for him.

This was a great shock for Kalulu, for the King had
loved him dearly, and the young chief bore him great
affection in return.

When at first the news was conveyed to him, he
seemed to be suddenly stricken dumb, his face assumed
a livid hue, and he trembled all over. Then, giving
vent to his sorrows in a long, sad cry of sorrow, he
hastened to the King's house, where the doctors were
found attending the corpse, and at once threw himself
on the body, uttering the most doleful lamentations,
crying, "Awake, thou King! thou chief of the Watuta,
awake! Behold me, thy son, Kalulu, returned from the
chase! Open thine ears, O Katalambula! Listen to
the voice of thy son! Open thy eyes, O Katalambula!

stretch out thine hand, and feel the form of him thou
didst so love! Speak, Katalambula! Say, whither
hast thou gone, that thy voice may no longer be heard,
nor thy ears may longer hear Kalulu's voice? Kalulu, the child of thy brother Mostana, calls unto thee!
Come out with me, O Katalambula! Come out under
the tree! come and tell Kalulu of thy prowess when
thou wert young! Ah! Katalambula, I shall die if
thou wilt not wake up!" and thus he kept calling on
the dead, until he found his cries and tears were of no
avail. He rose then, and went to his hut, and closed
the door, and on his rugged bed, his tears flowed
silently and swiftly, until it seemed as if his soul would
melt in tears.

When near sunset, the grave being ready, under a
hut erected over it at the corner of the square, and the
ceremony of burial was about to begin, Kalulu came
out of his hut to do honour to the body of Katalambula.
All the Wa-mganga* from the neighbouring villages were
gathered together; all the elders, the councillors, and
principal men of the tribe were assembled, until the
great square of the capital was crowded with warriors,
women, and children. In order that the ceremony
might be allowed to proceed in due form, they had
arranged themselves around a large circle, having the
great tree for its centre. In this circle were assembled
the doctors of magic and the chief mourners, and near
them were the fattest, finest bulls that could be procured, black in colour and without a single blemish,
which were to be killed over Katalambula's grave; near
by, also, were enormous earthenware pots of pombe

* Wa-mganga—plural of mganga—magic doctors.

(beer) and plaintain wine, which were to be poured over the grave as a libation to his manes.

The drummers were in their places, the wa-mganga (doctors) were ready, painted and striped with white chalk all over, with the gourds, half-filled with pebbles, in their hands; and the chant began.

The author, in order to do something like justice to the pathetic death-song of the King, finds himself compelled to give as literal a translation as possible. The tune was most mournful, the chorus most pathetic, being drawn out into a long, sweet-toned wail; and the voices of the women and children, mingling with the deeper voices of the warriors, were effectively impressive:

> The son of Loralamba,[1]
> The conqueror of Uwemba,[2]
> The Sultan of Liemba,[3]
> > Is dead!
> The brother of Mostana,
> The wisest Manyapara,[4]
> The King of the Watuta,
> > Is dead!
> > *Chorus.* Is dead!
> > Oh, he is dead!
>
> He who fought Wamarungu,[5]
> The great lord of Kwikuru,[6]
> The wise son of Malungu,[7]
> > Is dead!

---

[1] Loralamba, father of Katalambula and Mostana.

[2] Uwemba, a country bordering Lake Tanganika.

[3] Liemba, the river which sometimes gives its name to a portion of U'tuta.

[4] Manyapara is a Kituta term for councillor, wise elder.

[5] People of Marungu.

[6] The capital.

[7] Sky-spirit.

He who slew Tamaniro,
Chief of the Wakhokoro,[1]
By the river Ambenuro,
             Is dead!
     Chorus.   Is dead!
             Oh, he is dead!

Who triumph'd o'er Kansala,
Near the Mount Amboella,
In the land of Kinyala,[2]
             Is dead!
     Chorus.   Is dead!
             Oh, he is dead!

The uncle of Kalulu,
The sire of Koranilu
And pretty Imamalu,
             Is dead!
He who married Lamoli,
The daughter of Soltali,
By the woman Zimbili,
             Is dead!
     Chorus.   Is dead!
             Oh, he is dead!

The lord of Mohilizi,
And the land from Rufizi[3]
To the River Zambezi,[4]
             Is dead!
The bravest, wisest Mwenni,[5]
Of the tribe of Meroeni,
The dauntless Simbamwenni,[5]
             Is dead!
     Chorus.   Is dead!
             Oh, he is dead!

---

[1] A tribe north of Urori.
[2] A small country south-west of Ututa.
[3] A river.
[4] Known as Chambezi.
[5] Lord.
[6] Lion lord, or Lion king.

He was fear'd by Wagala,[1]
By the fierce Wazavila,[2]
Was great Katalambula,
   Who is dead!
But the mighty Mtuta,[3]
Bravest of the Watuta,[4]
The Sultan of Ututa,
   Is dead!
  Chorus. He is dead!
   Oh, he is dead!

Ah! the King we did adore,
We shall see his face no more,
And our hearts are sad and sore,
   For he is dead!
Kindest, best, and wisest King,
On thy head the dust we fling,
And in sorrow do we sing,
   Our lord is dead!
  Chorus. Our lord is dead!
   Alas! our lord is dead!

O King! why didst thou thus die?
Deep in the grave thou must lie,
While we will for ever cry,
   Our chief is dead!
O'er him pour libative wine,
O'er him slay the fattest kine,
O'er him make the magic sign,
   For our King is dead!
  Chorus. For our King is dead!
   Alas! our King is dead!"

When the chant was ended, the body was laid on a long, broad piece of stiff bark, and four wa-mganga (doctors) carried it to the grave, where it was laid on the right side, with the King's shield, spears, bow, and quiver of arrows. A pot, full of millet-flour, mixed with water

[1] People of Ugala.
[2] People of Uzavila—a scattered tribe north of Ututa.
[3] A man of Ututa.
[4] The people of Ututa.

was placed, closely covered, by the head, and the stiff
piece of bark, which served to convey the body to the
grave, was placed over the body; then the plaintain
wine was poured over this, the black bulls were brought
up and slaughtered, the blood pouring into the grave;
then the earth was scraped in and stamped close
and hard; and, finally, ten potfuls of pombe were
poured over the grave, and the ceremony was over.

Then the elders, the councillors, and the doctors
gathered together under the great tree, and began to
discuss the question who should be King. A large
number proposed that Ferodia should be sent for, as he
was a relative of the King; but the majority, though
small, were for Kalulu, who, not only was nephew of
Katalambula, but adopted son, and the choice of the
old King. Besides, Kalulu was a brave lad, and would
in time be a greater warrior than Ferodia, perhaps
greater than Katalambula, and the equal of Loralamba.
His youth was full of promise, and he had already won
everybody's regard for his amiability and good heart,
said they. Whereupon the discussion grew fierce;
those for Ferodia threatened to leave Katalambula's
tribe and go over to him, and would return with spear
and sword to cut Kalulu's head off. Finally, when all this
was at its greatest height, and wordy dissension came
near ending in bloodshed, Soltali rose, and, by his elo-
quence, succeeded in calming the turbulent and winning
over to Kalulu's side several of the adherents of Ferodia,
until there remained but a small, contumacious minority
for the latter.

While the majority waited for the messengers sent
to inform Kalulu of the honour conferred on him, the
minority rose and departed out of the village, mutter-

ing threats, and promising to return with Ferodia, who
would punish all with a terrible vengeance.

Kalulu received the deputation, and when told its
mission, rose at once and followed them to Soltali. This
old man—the principal magic doctor of the tribe—was
not only one of the chief councillors, or chief manyapara—to give the technical Kituta term—but had also
had the honour of having Katalambula for his son-in-
law, as the King had taken his daughter Lamoli for
wife, and Moto's wife, Lamoli, was granddaughter to
Soltali. But, aside from this relationship to Kalulu,
the old man dearly loved the amiable prince, and
rejoiced that he was now permitted to inform Kalulu
that he was elected King.

Some of the *dowa*, or uganga (the millet-flour mixed
with water, a most potent medicine or charm), was
placed near Soltali, and as Kalulu stood before them in
the now bright moonlight, graceful as a dusky Gany-
mede, the magic doctor rose, while the elders and councillors sat around, and, taking some of the potent medicine in his hand, he touched the boy's forehead, each
cheek, nose, mouth, and chin, crying in a loud voice :
" Be thou King ! Be thou brave ! Be thou strong ! Be
thou good ! And let all thy enemies run before thee !"

In succession each elder rose, dipped his hand in the
medicine, and touched Kalulu's forehead with it, saying,
" Be thou King ! Be thou brave ! Be thou strong ! Be
thou good ! and let all thy enemies run before thee !"

Then the warriors were summoned by the drums to
the square, and all the women and children gathered
also, and old Soltali, the high priest and magic doctor,
sang to them the new King's good qualities, his birth,

his troubles, his arrival at Katalambula's village, the
joy of the old King; how Kalulu became henceforth as
his son to him; and how Katalambula had solemnly
sworn that Kalulu was his choice for his successor to
him, Soltali; what Kalulu had already done towards
winning fame; ending with a solemn injunction to all
that they should honour and serve Kalulu as they had
served his father, so that the glory of the Watuta
would become known to all nations, and their bravery
be sung in all the corners of the earth.

N.B.—The author extracts such portions of the chant
as he deems most interesting; but refuses positively to
disfigure any more of his chapters with the uncouth
Kituta polysyllables; and refuses, furthermore, to touch
upon such ceremonies as have verse or chorus in them,
however interesting they may be; for he finds his
patience sadly exhausted with being compelled continually to render into barbarous rhyme words which
grate on his sensitive ears :

> The hero and lion chief, Loralamba,
> King of Liemba and the streamy Wemba,
> Lord of all the pasture lands of broad Usango
> From West Urori to far Ukonongo,
> Whom the unnumber'd tribes of Tuta and Sowa,
> From hilly Lobisa to the lake-land Itawa,
> Obey'd without scruple, him who in each campaign
> Had slain his foes by hundreds on each hill and plain,
> When dying, bequeathed his youngest son Mostana
> The lands of Rori from Wiwa to Kantana.
> While to his eldest son, our King, Katalambula,
> He gave all wide Ututa, including Kinyala.
> Our King died heirless, but in Rori's Kwikuru
> His brother Mostana was blest with Kalulu.
> When, years ago, the Arabs fell 'pon Kantana,
> Destroyed Kwikuru, and slew brave Mostana,
> Young Kalulu came, and sought his father's brother,

And in our King, his uncle, he found a father.
Ye recall the day when the King this orphan met;
How on his head our King's infirmed hands were set,
How fondly he clasp'd the youth to his aged breast,
And, in endearing accents, bade him there find rest.
Ye know what delight this boy has since to him been,
And the King's paternal love ye have also seen.
Oft have ye heard the King make mention of his name,
As one born to win a hero's long-enduring fame.
'Tis needless to rehearse the deeds already done
By the stout arm of dead Mostana's princely son;
They are known to all the Watuta tribes around,
And all our most ambitious youths his praises sound.
Morala, King of Ubena, fell by his hand,
So died the false and cruel chief of Bemba land.
The rebel Bongo, tribal chief on Chuma plain,
Fell by Kalulu's spear, was by Kalulu slain.
When the Arab boy sank in the deep waters brown,
Gripped by the greedy crocodile, and sank deep down,
Who div'd to rescue him? Who but young Kalulu?
Who but the noblest, bravest son of Malungu!
The King swore to me,—the Mganga Seltali,
I,—who to him wedded my daughter Lamoli,
"None shall rule as King over Tuta's Kwikuru
But brave Mostana's son, my princely Kalulu!"
Now in council, your priests and elders do maintain
That o'er the Tuta tribes none may aspire to reign
Save brave Mostana's son, and the choice of Malungu.
We now proclaim him King. Long live King Kalulu!

The warriors gave a great shout, the drums thundered, and all the warriors, the women, the children, the doctors, the councillors, and elders cried "Long live King Kalulu!"

When silence prevailed, Kalulu stood up before the people, and while the body swayed and the hands made gestures, according as his emotions governed him, the young King might, by a stretch of fancy, have been taken for a demi-god-visiting a favoured people, teach-

ing them the ways of the wise, and urging them to
abandon savage habits. While all listened intently
and admiringly, the elected chief spoke as follows:—

"Warriors of the Watuta, and ye elders and councillors! Ye have elected me King, because I, the son of
Mostana, was beloved by Katalambula, and because he,
being heirless, said to Soltali, 'Since I have no son,
Kalulu shall reign in my stead, when I am laid in the
ground.' Katalambula has gone to his fathers; he was
old, he was weighed down with the burden of years,
and loaded with honours; he is no more; the cruel
earth covers him. The King is dead, but ye have
chosen me to fill his place. I am young, I have not
seen many moons, and I am not yet a full warrior.
How, then, shall I fill Katalambula's place? I will
tell you. Katalambula was good; he loved the good
and hated the wrong. So do I love the good and hate
wrong. Katalambula was just. As Katalambula was
just, so shall I be. When Katalambula was young, he
was strong, he was brave, he was a lion in war. When
I shall be a full warrior, I shall be strong, I shall be
brave, I shall be a lion in war. Katalambula was
wise. Ah! I am young, I am not wise; but I have
Soltali, Katalambula's friend, with me. I have the same
elders, the councillors, and the magic doctors; their
wisdom they will give me when trouble comes, and by
their wisdom shall I be wise. There is peace in the
land to-day; the Watuta are rich and prosperous.
There is no sickness amongst the people, neither is
there disease in the herds, or in the flocks. But the dark
days may come, when a strong enemy shall come upon

the land; yet not before Kalulu shall know it. Sickness
may come; but who can prevent the bad spirits that
visit us with baleful disease and thin our warriors, and
make us poor in flocks and herds? Yet Kalulu shall
be ready with his sacrifices and his potent medicine to
soften the hearts of the bad spirits. It is well. The
Watuta love Kalulu; they have made him their King.
When the time comes, and necessity demands, Kalulu
will die for the Watuta. I have spoken."

Having finished his oration, Kalulu retired from
amongst the people, and went into his own hut, where
he found Selim and Abdullah, Simba and Moto, con-
versing upon the events of the last two days.

The four rose to receive him courteously, and offered
him a clean ox-hide to sit upon, and began to condole with
him upon the loss of the King who loved him so much.

"Ah! yes, he was a dear, good man. My going out
and coming in he watched like a lioness her whelps.
He was proud of me, too; for he said I had the eyes of
Loralamba, his father, and carried my head like him.
He often said that I should make the Watuta a great
nation, greater than it was in the time of Loralamba.
He told me, a little before I went away after the elephants, how to behave myself when I should become
King, and advised me to travel with a great many
warriors all around Ututa, and see for myself how
great my country is, and who pay the tribute and who
do not; because, he said, when Kings forget their people
their people forget who is their King, and set up for
themselves. Then quarrels begin, and war follows, and
tribes rise against one another, and a nation becomes
weak. I mean to follow his advice; and when the next

moon is full, begin the journey. Say, Selim, how wouldst thou like it?"

"Oh, Kalulu! thou art King now of all this great nation, thou art rich and powerful; there is none like unto thee in all the lands of Africa. Thousands of warriors are ready to do thy bidding; armies of great, strong, fierce men are under thy feet. If thou wilt but move that little tongue of thine, there is war everywhere; men will begin to hate one another and to lust for each other's blood; villages will be destroyed, and whole tribes shall be known no more. Thou, who art but a boy like me, art dreadful in thy sudden power. But a few days ago, under the tree where the dead elephant lay, thou didst embrace me, thou didst say all manner of kind things unto me. Wilt thou do Selim a favour, Kalulu?"

"Will I do thee a favour? Oh, Selim! dost thou think that, because I am King of the Watuta, I can forget our brotherhood? Dost thou think that Kalulu's friendship changes like the antelope, which roameth about for the sweet grass, now here, now there? No; Kalulu's friendship is like the water of a river, always flowing in the same direction, true and constant. Ask me anything thou wilt, and I will give it thee! Dost thou want a wife? Take pretty Imamalu, and if she is not enough, take Koranilu; and if thou wouldst like another, ask for her, and thou shalt have her. Dost thou need a gun? Ask for as many as thou wilt. What is it thou wouldst ask?"

"I would ask," answered Selim, " that, now thou art King, thou wilt permit Abdullah, Simba, and Moto, and myself to depart to our own land."

"Depart!" echoed Kalulu, "and leave me alone! What has Kalulu done unto thee or thy friends, that thou wouldst leave him?"

"Nay, my brother—if thou wilt permit me to call thee by that name still—thou hast done nothing of wrong unto us," replied Selim. "Thou hast been too good, if anything. What should we have done without thy friendship? But thou must remember, Kalulu, we left our own land to trade for ivory and slaves. We came as far as Urori, intending to go to Rua, on the other side of Lake Tanganika; but at Kwikuru of Olimali the caravan was destroyed, our fathers and friends were killed, others were made slaves along with ourselves. But we were happy in finding a friend in thee. We were released from slavery, and in my master I found a brother. But, Kalulu, at Zanzibar, Abdullah and I have mothers, who are sorrowing for us. I have a rich estate, and plenty of money waiting for me; Simba and Moto have wives and children. If Kalulu permits us to go, would it be well for us to remain here?"

"Ah! poor Katalambula is dead, he has been but just buried; and now Selim wants to go away, and leave me. What evil spirit is this, that makes me suffer so? What have I done, that all should leave me? Why should I suffer, when all other men are happy? I wish I were in Katalambula's place, and he in mine. Thou wilt not want to go at once, Selim, wilt thou? Surely, thou wilt have pity upon me, and remain a few moons longer; then I myself—though I know I shall die—will take thee with a thousand warriors to where thou wilt find thyself safe, and among thy friends."

"Oh, Kalulu, I did not mean to go away at once. I meant after one moon. Wilt thou not let me go after one moon, my brother? Think of my poor mother, what she must suffer all this time! It is this that makes me wish I had the wings of an eagle, to fly to her, and tell her how safe and happy I have been with thee. It is this only which could make me wish to leave thee so soon after thy great loss."

"Then, Selim, let it be as thou wilt. Kalulu has not the bad heart to keep a son from a mother; sooner would his own heart burst in his own body, than my brother should suffer. Thou hast said thou hadst intended to have gone to Rua for ivory and slaves. No need to go so far. I have here two hundred of the Arabs' people Ferodia took at Kwikuru. They shall be thine, and each man shall be loaded with ivory, one hundred of which shall be thy portion, and the other hundred for Moto, and Simba, and Abdullah. Art thou satisfied?"

"Satisfied!" said Selim, in a wondering tone.— "Satisfied! I should be worse than dead clay, if I were not. Nay, thy kindness must have some reward; for the same Sky-spirit which has touched thy heart with soft kindness towards me, has now touched mine: I shall stay two moons with thee, and I then shall ask thee to let me go. But thou art so good, Kalulu; I shall never meet thy like again, when I depart from thee," and Selim wept grateful tears, as he threw himself upon the neck of the noble young savage, while Abdullah, in a transport of joy, kissed the generous chief's feet; nor was Simba or Moto backward in expressing their admiration of Kalulu's generosity.

They spent many hours together, until late in the

night, consulting about what should be done in the meantime, and how a new amusement should be furnished for almost every day; after which they retired, each to his bed to sleep, with their hearts full of peace and love towards one another.

We will now leave the young King and his friends to their pleasures, while we note what became of the minority who expressed themselves so strongly against the election of Katalambula's choice for King, and who departed before the ceremony of election and appointment began, muttering threats.

These threats were by no means idle. They were made by men who had accompanied Ferodia to Urori, and fought at Kwikuru, and who were rewarded so handsomely by him during the distribution of cloth. They were warriors who paid respect to courage and success, and to them Ferodia was a hero far more deserving of the chief authority over the tribe than a boy, who, however promising he might be, had not yet distinguished himself more than any other boy would have done, placed in the same position.

Ferodia was a chief, who, were he King, might be able to make each warrior rich in cloth, in ivory, in slaves, and cattle; while with Kalulu as King, many years must elapse before he would think of venturing upon a war unprovoked.

When they left the village, and were safe outside, these feelings found expression, and, consulting and advising with each other, they were not long in coming to the conclusion that their interest lay in proceeding at once to Ferodia's country, a week's march southwest, and acquaint him with their hopes and desires,

T

and invite him to proclaim himself King, with the aid
of all malcontents, and friends, and to march upon
Kalulu's village and depose the boy-king. This duty
of self-interest they at once set about executing, by
commencing their march for Ferodia's country.

Within a week they made their appearance before
Ferodia's village, and when they told their errand, they
were at once introduced before the chief, who sat under
a tree, similar to the one at Katalambula's, obsequious
and villainous-faced Tifum the Wicked standing by his
side.

"Peace be unto ye, my brothers," said Ferodia,
rising, and hurrying to embrace each one in succession,
and, as is the custom in Ututa and in all the lands adjoining Lake Tanganika, rubbing their elbows first,
then their arms, then their shoulders, and then falling
on their necks, slapping them on the back gently with
the disengaged right hand, muttering continually as he
rubbed each part, "Wake, wake, wake, waky"—Health,
health, health, and peace.

Finally, after going through the ceremony of greeting, like an assiduous old diplomat that he was, he
asked :

"Whence come ye, my brothers? and what is your
purpose?"

The chief of the party of chiefs, who was the spokesman, answered, "Why should we come thus far, O
Ferodia, if it were not to greet thee as King of all the
Watuta? Katalambula, the great King, is dead. He
is no more. There is nothing left of him. He is in
the ground. The Watuta tribes have now no leader,
no chief, no king; they are like unto the flocks on the

plain, bleating for the shepherd that cannot be found. They are going astray after one who is not old enough to be their shepherd. They have elected the boy Kalulu, who is but a child, and is not yet a warrior. He is like unto an infant just weaned, who seeketh the pap refused him. Katalambula being dead, Kalulu is drowned in tears; verily, he has lost his head from sorrow, for he is but a child, and has lost his friend and father, and knoweth not what to do. Wherefore, we came unto thee, O Ferodia, to ask thee to be our shepherd, our leader, our king. Say, what is thy answer?"

"Ferodia answered softly: "The words thou hast spoken are words of truth, my brother. Katalambula being dead, the Watuta have lost their leader. Kalulu, in truth, is but a child—but a child completely spoiled. Any of my boy slaves were fitter to be king of the warlike Watuta than he. Who is Kalulu? He is not a matuta, he is not a warrior, he is not the son of Katalambula, he has not won the right to carry a spear, save as a burden. He is a Mrori, the son of Mostana, one of a stranger tribe. Katalambula being dead, the Watuta have no leader. But who has a better right to fill his place than I, Ferodia? Who won his battles for him, but I, Ferodia? Who conquered the Wabena, the Wumarungu, the Wakonongo, the Wanyamwezi, the Wasowa, the Wakawendi, and the Warimba, but I, Ferodia? By my fame I have won the right to succeed him who is dead. By my courage in the field, there is none fitter to take his place. By my victories, I have deserved the honour. Verily, thy words are words of truth, my brother, and thou makest me glad with thy wise remarks."

"Speak, Ferodia, O chief, when wilt thou that we go and punish Soltali, and those who have chosen another in thy place?" asked the spokesman of his visitors.

Whereupon a council was called, to which all the chiefs and all the great warriors, the doctors, the councillors, even all those who had authority were invited.

The discussion was lively, and had a newspaper reporter who understood Kituta polysyllables been there, I doubt not he would have been as much edified as he would be elsewhere amongst councils. "How is Katalambula's village to be taken? How is Kalulu to be ousted out of his right? How are the warriors in the village to be brought to submission to Ferodia, if they have made Kalulu king?" were the questions to be answered.

One chief suggested that Ferodia should visit Kalulu, and offer him the hand of friendship, and in the night rise up and slay; another, that Kalulu should be invited for a grand elephant hunt: when in the woods the young King might be easily disposed of; another, that he should be invited to Ferodia's country, to celebrate his coming to power, when he could be poisoned by the doctors—in short, all things were suggested to aid the daring conspirators to deprive Kalulu of his rights.

"Tifum, what dost thou advise? Thou art cunning as a phizi (hyæna), chary of thy speech as the flying-cat is of its form, wise as a lord of an elephant herd, but cruel as the sable leopard, which letteth not go whatever it seizes upon. Thou art invaluable to me, O Tifum; therefore speak, and give thy chief counsel," said Ferodia.

Being commanded to speak, Tifum the Wicked rose and said:

"Words, words! Who is like unto Ferodia in wisdom? He searches the heart, and penetrates to the hidden and unspoken thoughts. Ferodia knows that Tifum the Wicked can give him counsel, and he forthwith commands him to speak. Who is like unto Ferodia in the battle? He rages about the war-field, seeking the strong arm and the brave with whom he may measure his strength. His feet lift him from point to point, swift as the swiftest quagga in the forest. He springs aloft with his ever-thirsty spear, seeking to drink the blood of the strongest. When his voice is heard his foes stand abashed, as if the roaring lion had come into the fight. I, Tifum the Wicked, have seen him oft in the war, and Tifum knows whereof he speaks. Ferodia the chief commands Tifum to give him counsel. My counsel is this, O chief. Katalambula's village is strong—the warriors are many—the palisade is lofty and close, and the villages round about are more than can be counted. Ferodia's tribe is small and weak; it is like a handful of sand compared to the sand of all the plain. Alone, we may not venture on a war with all the Watuta. Let us, then, send messengers to the people of Kinyala, whose chief Katalambula killed, and who are yet resentful. To the chiefs of Marungu, and to those of Itawa by the lake. Let us send good words to Mohilizi and to the band of Wazavila, who live but a few days' off, and with all these together, and with the aid of these discontented chiefs of the Meroeni tribe, we may hope to make a successful war. The plan is this: Let Ferodia take with him all the warriors of his own tribe, and with them proceed to Kalulu, and if he asks why we have come, say, 'We are come to offer thee our congratulations. Art thou not our King? Wherefore we have come to serve thee.' Then Ferodia, with one hundred of his best warriors, shall go in unto the village and make friends with all, and be assiduous to please Kalulu, while the rest shall remain outside until the tenth night, when the hillmen from Amboella, the men from the soft pasture lands, the leas, and the meadows of the lake-land Itawa, when those of the fierce tribe of the Wazavila, the strong men of Urungu, and the tall men of Mohilizi, shall have been gathered together—then on the tenth night, while the warriors of Ferodia shall seize on Kalulu and some upon Soltali and other elders, some shall come to the gates, and stand there until it is time for those outside to act; then, when all is ready, let all rush in and slaughter and kill. In the morning, when the Watuta shall hear that Ferodia has conquered, they will be afraid, and will come to him in a body, as one man, and be faithful to him, as they were to Katalambula. But Kalulu must die—there can be no peace while he lives; and if it pleases Ferodia, let it be my task to wring off that young cock's head. O chief, these are the words of Tifum the Wicked."

"Good, good!" all shouted enthusiastically; and even Ferodia was as loud as any in his approbation. The excellent advice of Tifum was acted upon; and the messengers were at once despatched in all directions, to rouse the subdued tribes and to enlist all the discontented to rally to Ferodia's standard, and to bid them all march by way of the great forest, and by night through the corn-fields as near as possible to Katalambula's village, and to be outside the village near the morning after the tenth night.

Ferodia, selecting his warriors, out of which he again selected a chosen hundred—men of mettle and might, unscrupulous, and quick with their spears—proceeded the next morning for Katalambula's village, the Kwikuru of Ututa, while the discontented of the tribe of Meroeni hastened, by day and by night, to make ready their men for the great and momentous struggle. Tifum had with him as bearers several of the boy slaves which were captured at Kwikuru of Urori, and who had endured the fatigues of the march with Selim and Abdullah; and among these was found the little negro boy Niani, who had so mysteriously disappeared from our view and our knowledge. These were not in bonds now; they had come to be entrusted by their new masters for their docility and weakness; and Niani had come to be quite a favourite with Tifum, who recognised the little fellow's shrewdness and deftness of hands.

Ferodia, as he drew near Kwikuru, left the larger number of his warriors, and all the slaves and servants behind; and, taking with him only the choice hundred warriors, advanced upon the capital of the Watuta, and made his appearance before the gates, where, coming in the guise of friendship to congratulate the new King, he was heartily received, and admitted to the great square.

Kalulu was disposed at first, when he was informed of Ferodia's arrival, to be resentful, and his mind was crowded with suspicious thoughts; but Ferodia's excessive courtesy and amiability, the warmth of his greeting and congratulations, soon disarmed the mind of the ingenuous youth, and, as well as he was able, he replied kindly, and tendered the hospitalities of the village.

To Tifum's greeting Kalulu gave a cold and haughty nod; but Tifum was a diplomat of the first water, and, as needs must when needs drive, Tifum excelled Tifum's self in deceptive cordiality and genuflective graciosities. He was smiling and chatting now with Kalulu, and anon with Selim, who he declared had wonderfully improved; that he was now but a little less hand-some and but a little shorter in height than Kalulu the new King, who was sure, by-and-by, to become a greater King than his grandfather Loralamba.

He went up also to Simba, who had so bruised his body some time ago, and so purred and fondled that giant that Simba's repugnance became so strong that he told him to desist, that Arabs were not accustomed to carry their greetings with strangers in such a fami-liar way. But nothing could upset Wicked Tifum's equanimity and plans; he roared with laughter, and slapped his thighs so loudly that Moto began to think Tifum had lost his mind.

Tifum, however, while Moto made the remark, caught sight of the sweet, pale face of Abdullah, and at once darted upon him; and, despite Abdullah's struggles, embraced the lad as if in him Tifum had found a lost son; but when he released him finally, Abdullah, while his face blushed crimson at this indignity, slapped Tifum full on the cheek; but the heroic Tifum did not mind that in the least; he only laughed louder than ever, though Abdullah thought he detected a fierce blaze of anger in his eyes.

However, Ferodia and Tifum were inside Kwikuru, and the time intervening between their entrance into it and the night appointed for the consummation of their enterprise passed quickly and quietly enough. On the tenth morning Tifum communicated to Ferodia the gratifying intelligence that their friends were in the neighbourhood distributed among the villages of the tribe of Meroeni, three hours' distance.

The tenth day passed tranquilly, and the night came. Not a single breath of suspicion had been uttered, though among themselves Kalulu and his friends expressed strong misgivings; but this was set down to their dislike to the ambitious Ferodia and his cunning, intriguing, cruel parasite, Tifum the Wicked. Ah! could Kalulu have but known what devilish plans were lurking unseen in his village—what plot was hatching—what evil hung over him, how quickly had he sounded the cry of alarm, how different would he have acted; how he would have sprung as a leopard into their midst, and torn the conspirators into pieces! But neither Kalulu nor his friends dreamed of anything of all this evil, and drowsiness stole over their bodies, and gentle, unsuspicious slumber pressed their eyelids, and stilled their minds into unconsciousness.

CHAPTER XI.

King Kalulu is a Prisoner—Poor Kalulu!—The Magic Doctor is burnt
—Kalulu is told to prepare for Death—The night following Soltali's Execution—The Mouse assists the Lions—The End of Tifum
the Wicked—Is this Murder?—Niani calls it "Justice"—Safe!
and Free!—Selim pleads to Kalulu—Selim wants Kalulu to go
home with him—Simba the Giant pleads—The Head of Tifum the
Wicked—They intend going to Ujiji.

ABOUT three hours before dawn a body of thirty men,
under the leadership of Ferodia, made their appearance in
the square outside of their sleeping quarters, the garish
moonlight revealing them visibly clear. At the same
time an equal number issued from the dark, cavernous
doors of the tembe, and, after a whispered consultation
with the first party, proceeded stealthily across the
square to where Soltali lived ; while forty men, dividing
themselves into two parties, hastened towards the gates.
Ferodia, seeing all at their posts, waited a short time,
until he saw numbers of dark forms glide into the
square, and until he was told that the warriors were
pouring in by the two gates ; he then proceeded towards
the door of Kalulu's hut, and, after taking a quiet survey
of the sleeping forms of Kalulu, Selim, and Abdullah,
beckoned to Tifum and the warriors behind him, and
suddenly sprang in with a piercing cry of triumph
upon the prostrate and unconscious young King, while
Tifum sprang upon Selim, and another warrior upon
Abdullah.

Warrior after warrior poured in, and in a short time the three boys found themselves, while yet not quite recovered from their sleep, bound and helpless prisoners. In the meantime the war-cry of the Watuta, sounded first by Ferodia, was caught up by all the warriors in the square, and was immediately echoed by each new comer, while crowds had hastened to the hut occupied by Simba and Moto, but only to find these wary men prepared for a resolute struggle. Neither Simba nor Moto, however, had had time to load their guns; they could only club them and crush each skull as it ventured into the darkened hut; but the roof was too low for Simba to exert the full power of his strong arm, so that, finally, numbers prevailed, and Simba and Moto found themselves at last prisoners, bound hand and foot.

In a short time Ferodia found himself master of the village. The plan had been too well devised, too skilfully carried out, to fail. And each surprised warrior, when that first dreadful cry awoke him from his dreamy sleep, only awoke to find himself in the power of foes relentless and desperate. Every soul in the village was in the power of Ferodia, so that he found himself in the morning with over five thousand slaves—for prisoners of war are always slaves in Central Africa.

The chains found in the storeroom of the King, which came formerly from the Arab camp near Kwikuru, in Urori, were of use now, and into the strong iron collars attached to them the necks of Kalulu, the two Arab boys, and the most refractory of the captured warriors, were placed; but as there were no locks, or they could not be found, the eyes of the folding iron crescents, which folding together formed the collars, were simply tied together firmly, while the hands of the captives were tightly bound behind. When all were secured with their hands in inexorable bonds behind their backs, they were marched outside by gangs, under chiefs, of ten and twenty warriors. Then the ivory, the cloth, the guns, the powder and bullets, and everything of value, were brought forth and distributed amongst the warriors and conveyed outside at a safe distance from the village.

After all these things had been done the torch was applied to every tembe, and in an inconceivably short space of time the whole village was wrapped and encircled by the tongues of destroying flames; the straw, and the oil and butter found stored in the huts, and the resinous, gummy substance of the wood which formed the rafters and palisade, adding intensity to the flames, which were speedily devouring all.

While the village—the scene of so much merry-making, and fun, and innocent frolic, scene of the ceremonies, the rejoicings, which have found place in our history—was thus being ruthlessly destroyed, being rapidly reduced to black ashes, to be as a thing in our memories alone, to become only as a tradition for those unborn, the great sun arose as usual in the east with his usual splendour and grateful benignity to light the second epoch of misery through which Kalulu, Selim, and Abdullah passed, and to guide the footsteps of the enslaved King and Watuta on their way to slavery.

Ah! ye, my young readers, surrounded by a halo of kindness and love, by the bloom, the brightness, and the happiness of a civilized life, with which Heaven has

favoured you, can ye imagine the deep, indescribable
misery in which the high-spirited young King found
himself when he thoroughly realised the vast change
in his condition that one short night had made in his
existence? Assist me, then, with your imaginations;
describe him to your own satisfaction, with his feelings
all in one wild riot, with his confused senses struggling
to picture himself as not having fallen to this state,
endeavouring to draw one ray of brightness out of the
dark gloom which environed him, and say for him,
" God—the good, beneficent, all-seeing God—pity the
poor prince and King !" And the author shall say,
" Amen, and Amen !"

Once cleared of the immediate neighbourhood, the
captives were divided. The Wa-marungu, with their
gangs of slaves, chose one road, towards Ferodia's village ; the tribe of Meroeni chose another, with their
slaves ; the Wazavila chose another , while Ferodia,
with five hundred warriors driving before them the
gangs in which were found those in whom we have
become interested, struck for the forest where Kalulu
discovered Selim. Ferodia did not trouble the young
King nor his friends, nor did Tifum venture near them ;
they both satisfied themselves from the rear that they
were safe.

After they had made a wide détour for many days
through the forest, and come to a place where there
was no road nor any signs of its being inhabited, and
having completely baffled pursuit had such been ever
made, and when they had made their camp, Ferodia
drew near to the gang where Kalulu and his friends
were found.

Kalulu, as he saw his hated enemy approach, ground his teeth in rage, and foamed at the mouth like one suddenly stricken with madness, while Ferodia burst into a laugh and teased him to further exhibitions of fury, saying :

" That is right, my little crow-cock, shake thy wings, fan the air with them, and utter a lusty crow, that the fish-eagles, whose screams I hear from yonder swamps, may try and vie with thee. I have wrung a boastful cock's head ere this, and Tifum has too. Hast thou not, Tifum ?"

" That have I done, my King !" answered that servile follower, who was close behind him.

" Thou hearest, Kalulu, what Tifum says ;" and, turning to Tifum, he asked, " Dost thou think, Tifum, thou couldst wring Kalulu's neck for me, and do it deftly and neatly ?"

" Try me, O King, nothing could please me better," answered Tifum, with a significant glance at Kalulu.

" Kalulu's neck is slender, not much thicker than a grass stalk. Thou canst easily do it, I think, if thou wilt bury thy hand in those long, gay braids of his. Thou shalt try thy hand on him to-morrow." Advancing closer to him, he struck the boy in the chest with the butt of his spear. " Dost thou hear, boy !" But he did not retreat quickly enough, for the lithe form of Kalulu shot out and flung itself against him, and the boy's teeth were buried in Ferodia's neck, and he had surely strangled him had not Tifum, lifting his spear, struck him a mighty blow full on the spinal column, which almost paralysed Kalulu.

" Thou fiend, and leopard's whelp, thou shalt die by

torture to-morrow at break of day; meantime thou
shalt see Soltali burning for daring to make thee King
of the Watuta, and while he is burning thou shalt be
stretched until thy limbs crack; and thus saying, the
angry chief strode away, rubbing his neck and fuming
with passion, and gave orders that a fire should be built
near a large tree, and that old Soltali should be brought
forth.

In a few minutes a great fire was sparkling and
roaring at the foot of the central tree in the camp, and
old Soltali was brought forth before Ferodia.

"False mganga, seest thou yon tree and that fire?"
asked Ferodia.

"I see it, Ferodia," answered the old man.

"There shalt thou burn, and thy accursed ashes shall
remain there to blacken and curse that tree, under
which perished a false magician. Ho, Tifum! quick.
Bring Kalulu here first, stretch him on this ground,
with his face turned towards the magician, and let us
see if Soltali's black art will save Kalulu from the pain
he suffers, or himself from the fire."

Kalulu was at once brought forth, and though he
bit, and struggled, and kicked, he was pressed to the
ground by overwhelming numbers, and four men tied
cords to his limbs and began to draw them, until it
seemed as if the young body would be torn asunder;
after which the cords were fastened round pegs driven
deep into the ground.

Then the brutish Ferodia used the staff of his spear
on his body, and, taunting him, bade him look up and
see the false mganga, who had made him King, burning
in the fire.

The gang to which Selim, Abdullah, Simba, and Moto were chained was brought up and huddled together close to Kalulu. Soltali was dragged to the fire, and was tied to the tree; and the fire was pushed close to his feet, and new wood piled on it, and the smoke began to rise, and presently changed into flame.

Then Soltali, finding the flames begin to scorch and burn him, raised his right hand and shouted out with all the strength of his feeble voice, saying:

"Hearken, thou Ferodia, and ye savage Watuta. Ye think to triumph now, and make Ferodia king; but the will of the Sky-spirit must be done. Soltali had not made Kalulu king had it not been his will; Soltali obeyed but the voice of the Sky-spirit. Thou hast triumphed only for a time, Ferodia. Kalulu shall be king, must be king. Thou shalt see a bitter end, O Ferodia, to which my sufferings may not be compared; and thou, Tifum, shalt have thy head taken from off thy body, and the kite and the vulture shall pick out thine eyes. Moshono, who was burnt by the Wa-marungu, calls to Soltali. Soltali goes before thee, Tifum; and thou shalt follow me, O Ferodia. I come, great Moshono, I come. Mosh——"

Before he could utter the last word Soltali's aged head fell upon his breast, while still the flames leaped up and embraced him with their fiery arms, until, finally, the green bark cords which bound him shrivelled up and snapped beneath the weight of the superincumbent mass, and Soltali's body fell forward, while the sparks were shot up and the flames blazed anew. The warriors hastened to pile up wood, but Selim and Abdullah turned their faces away, unable to bear the horrid scene.

Ferodia turned to Kalulu and said, "To-morrow thou shalt die, as sure as Soltali has died. To-night lie where thou art, and when the sun rises be thou prepared to follow him. Tifum shall try his hand on thee."

"Ah, Ferodia, thou hast heard the voice of the good Soltali. The Sky-spirit has said I shall be king. Look to thyself, for I shall kill thee yet. Thou robber, cut-throat, and coward, dost thou hear me?" cried Kalulu.

"Talk away, and crow, my little cockling. Talk as long as thou canst, if it give thee any comfort. Nay, thou mayst burst thyself with talking if thereby thou wilt ease thyself, but to-morrow Tifum shall cut thy head off, and I will get strong medicine out of it. I have said it."

So saying Ferodia walked away, but Tifum could not refrain from going up to Kalulu. He encircled his neck with his hand, and, giving it a gentle pressure, said :

"Ah, Kalulu, to-morrow my knife shall sever that head of thine from thy body. The pain will soon be over, for Tifum's knife is sharp, and I will sharpen it still more, Kalulu, to-night, so that thou mayst suffer but little pain. Am I not good, Kalulu? I shall boil those cheeks of thine with my porridge, and think as I eat them how often they were patted by the silly old King Katalambula. Sleep in peace to-night, Kalulu. Sleep well, for it will be thy last night's sleep. Fare-well!"

"Stay, Tifum Byah, stay one moment," cried Kalulu

U

gently, as if he dearly loved the wretch. " Didst thou hear Soltali's words ?"

" Ay, certainly I did. Am I deaf ?" asked Tifum.

" Dost thou not fear the fate Soltali promised thee ?" asked Kalulu, with mock earnestness.

" I fear a mad old man's ravings ! Tifum the Wicked fear what Soltali said ! Bah, bah ; sleep, Kalulu, go to sleep."

" But stay one moment and hear me. Kalulu shall be King over the Watuta, and he will take thy head off surely, and give it to the Kituta dogs. Come here and bend thy head, closer, I wish to tell thee something," said Kalulu, as he nodded with his head. " There, so ! How dost thou like——" but that moment Kalulu buried his sharp teeth in Tifum's cheeks, and held on with the tenacity of a bull-dog, while Tifum, uttering a shrill cry of pain, could only release himself by clutching the boy's neck and strangling him to unconsciousness. Tifum's face bore a frightful wound, for the teeth, filed into a point in front, according to the customs of the Ututa, had bitten a piece clean out, leaving the cheek-bone exposed, which quite spoiled what beauty he had for ever.

As he felt the havoc made in his cheek the man uttered a frightful howl, and seized a spear-staff and began to belabour the unconscious boy. He probably would have beaten him to death had not Ferodia appeared and ordered him to desist, and to reserve his revenge for the morrow, when he might take it in full.

It was difficult to restrain the infuriated man, while his whole head tingled with the most exquisite pain ; but then Ferodia was King, and a King's commands must be obeyed even though his whole body ached, and he at last turned away moaning over his wound.

Soltali, the Mganga, was more feared when dead than when alive, it seemed, for while his body was being rapidly consumed the people had begun to move their camp a few yards off, none daring to erect his hut near the awful ashes of the magician, and as night came, with its sombre shades filling the whole forest with almost palpable darkness, and thick, dark, formless shadows, it was noticeable that they still further retreated from the death tree, and whispered to each other their belief that Soltali's spirit was in the tree, with great angry eyes of fire, looking down at the camp. Thus the mortal ashes of the old doctor, whom they had so cruelly murdered, were left alone by the superstitious people, and Kalulu, helplessly stretched near by, was the only living being within fifty yards of the dread embers which covered the remains of Soltali.

Tifum the Wicked, too much engrossed with the pain of his wound, had seen nothing of this movement, for he had retired to his hut, with his head close to the door to breathe the cool air of the night. In his hut were the spoils from Katalambula's village, which his own particular slaves had carried for him. Among these were two bales of cloth, ten fine ivory tusks, a keg of powder, a bag of bullets, three or four guns, and, singular as it might seem, was Selim's gun, the Joe Manton which Sheikh Amer had purchased for his son, through his Bombay agent. This accident may be attributed to Tifum's cupidity, who had appropriated this gun as his own, on seeing that it was of a superior class to all others, as well as the belt, which contained a large supply of ammunition. Ferodia would very probably have appropriated such a fine weapon for himself had he not been so occupied with the extent of his success and fortune.

The night grew deeper and more sombre. Melancholy sounds were heard at intervals through the forest, and the superstitious warriors ascribed these to the restlessness of the spirit of Soltali, consequently they huddled into their huts, forgot the cravings of their stomachs, and sought in the cosy warm huts a temporary oblivion from their fears and superstitious troubles, and, as the night got still more aged, even moaning Tifum became tranquil and slept.

When the camp had become as still as though no five hundred warriors with strong lungs and a healthy capacity for noise within them slept in that darkness, Niani's light, active, boyish form, who hitherto has been unnecessarily neglected, began to move from the neighbourhood of a fire where, along with other slaves, he had curled himself to rest, but not to sleep, in the direction of the slave-gang to which his master, Selim, Abdullah, gigantic Simba, and Moto belonged. The pale-coloured forms of the two Arab boys were clearly discernible, and choosing the tallest, he crept up to him, and gently placing his hand over the mouth of Selim, whom he rightly judged it to be, he bent his head low down to his ear.

"I am Niani, your slave; be still, master. I have come to save you, for I have heard Tifum swear that to-morrow you shall die with Kalulu. Hush! I have my knife. I shall cut your bonds, and those of your friends, and we shall all go away far." So saying Niani released his hand, and with his knife parted the bark rope that fastened the iron collar, and in a second Selim felt his neck free from the ignominious chain.

Niani crept to Abdullah, and performed the same kindness for him upon the express condition that he should lie still until the hint was given to rise. From Abdullah Niani crept to Simba, and told that wondering giant who he was, and why he was there. Simba understood at once, and slightly turned over that Niani might cut the bonds which confined his hands behind his back, and raised his head that he might be released from the collar. Moto's turn came next, and in a short time he was also free. Each head was now touched, and they at once rose and followed Niani past the sleeping forms, by the fires, and past the open huts confidently, but still quietly, until they came behind the fatal tree at whose base lay the ashes of poor old Soltali.

"Now, Master Selim, speak, what is to be done?" asked little Niani in a low voice.

"Let Simba and Moto answer; but we must not go without Kalulu, for rather than go without him I will go back and die with him."

"I don't intend to go either without him," said Abdullah. "I would count it a deed worthy of paradise to die with him, and by his side. Here, give me the knife, I will go and cut his bonds."

"No, no, master," said Simba, "I want to go back for a particular purpose, besides rescuing Kalulu. Thou, Moto, stay here, and if any alarm is made, then do thou run east, and in the morning turn south. Here, Niani, come with me. Give me that knife."

They both disappeared on the other side of the tree,
and Simba, crawling on his hands and knees, followed
by Niani, made towards where Kalulu lay stretched in
anguish of body and mind. When he had advanced
sufficiently near, Simba whispered the boy's name with
a warning—" Hush !"

Simba was presently close to Kalulu; and, after in-
forming him of his purpose, soon freed him from his
painful position, and Kalulu sat up, though feeling
almost too sore and cramped to move.

Simba waited patiently for the first feeling of numb-
ness to wear away, then whispered to him :

" Kalulu, dost thou remember Soltali's words? Soltali said that Tifum's head should be taken from off his
body. I am going to take it now. Wilt thou come ?"

The instant these words were suggested all feeling
of soreness vanished, and the boy sprang up and was
about to shout his gladness, when the big hand of
Simba was placed over his mouth, and he whispered:

" Nay, not a word, not a breath, as thou dost value
our lives. Our friends are behind that tree ; they are
waiting for us. Thou must obey me now, if success is
what thou dost hope for."

Kalulu clasped his hand, and understood at once what
was necessary, and followed Simba, who was preceded
by Niani, without further remark.

When near Tifum Byah's hut Niani, who was as
cunning as the nature of the mammal from whom he
derived his name, stopped, and pointed silently to the
hut, which stood alone and removed a good distance
from any other that was inhabited.

Simba turned to Kalulu, and, handing him the knife

which he had received from Niani, whispered to him:
"Stay here silent as a dead tree, until thou dost
hear my signal," to which a nod of the head only was
given for reply.

"Now, Tifum the Wicked," whispered the resolute
mind of Simba to itself, "it is either I or thou; I think
thou. Selim's stripes have to be paid for with thy blood;
if not Selim's, then Kalulu's wrongs. But how can I
ever pay thee for all? Sheikh Amer, my master; poor
Isa; little Mussoud;" and the busy mind fanned itself
into a white heat of anger, and churned the deep hate
into a white foam of fury; and the Nemesis, in the form
of this mighty, big-muscled man, stood over him, Tifum
the Wicked. The great form bent, and suddenly drooped,
with two great bony, sinewy hands clutching the sleeping man's throat, crushing, compressing bone, gristle,
sinew, and vein into a soft, yielding, pulpy mass, until
there was no breath of life nor power of motion left in
him.

All had been done so quietly—the deed of stern vengeance so quickly, coolly executed, that Kalulu started
with surprise as he heard the signal; he could hardly
believe it to have been consummated, yet he advanced
determinedly, as if his help was to be needed. Think
of Simba needing help for such an ordinary creature as
Tifum.

"Cut it off!" said Simba, and Kalulu, nothing loth,
bent down and severed the head off without one re-
morseful pang, and the body of Tifum was headless; and
the prediction of Soltali had become thus soon verified.

Simba and Kalulu were about to move off, when Niani
stepped up and whispered:

"The guns in his hut !"

"Ah, true," and Simba turned round and gave Niani a couple of guns, to Kalulu he gave one, he reserved one for himself, then went into the hut, found the powder keg, the load of bullets and ammunition; snatched a bow, a quiver full of arrows, a couple of spears, and a long Arab sword, which Tifum had also appropriated, and with the booty, too valuable to be measured at a money value for such an expedition as he now proposed to himself, he withdrew as silently as he had come.

Once at the tree the guns were distributed, one to Abdullah, one to Moto, the "Joe Manton" to Selim, who hugged it to his heart, while Simba retained another. To Kalulu he gave a spear with the bow, and a quiver full of arrows. Niani got another spear, while he also received the precious powder-keg to carry. Simba carried the bullets and sword. Kalulu still carried the ghastly load, but nothing was said to any of the others of the deed that was done. Simba merely said "Come," and the five followed him obediently.

"Four hours more of night till dawn," said Simba, after they had got a little distance off. "We must march south. Come."

In a hard, dry, trackless forest, when once a fugitive escapes it becomes impossible to find him. Had Kalulu not taken the precaution to strip himself of his cloth, and place the head of Tifum in it, it is probable that the fugitives might have been pursued; but there was no clue to the direction they had taken, for five hundred warriors had trodden the ground all around while hunting for fruit, or sticks, or water for cooking, the day before, even if the hard drouthy ground might have received the impression of a few men's naked feet. And the natural questions the warriors would ask themselves and each other in the morning would be, "Which way have they gone? Is it north, south, east, or west? or any other of the lesser or intermediate points?" to which, of course, no definite answer could be given; while the more superstitious would say, "Ah! it is Soltali who has taken them away!" and would fear to leave their fellows.

Simba, Moto, and Kalulu knew this, and though they journeyed fast, they journeyed confidently. But, as each of the party was busy with his own thoughts, no words were exchanged until it was grey morning, and day had more power to pierce the gloom of the forest than the old moon, which but faintly showed them their way before morning, when Selim saw some mysterious bundle in Kalulu's hand, and asked him what it was.

"Don't ask now, Selim, my brother, we must march," said Kalulu, and nothing more was said until at nine o'clock they stopped at a swamp to refresh themselves with water, when Kalulu setting down his bundle to drink, the cloth fell off one side, and exposed the head of a man.

"Allah!" ejaculated Selim, profoundly astonished; "what is this?" and Abdullah also cried out in astonishment the same words.

"What should it be, my brothers, but the head of Tifum the Wicked?" asked Kalulu.

"But this is murder, is it not?" asked Selim, aghast at the unsightly and livid head.

"Murder!" echoed Simba; "I think not, young

master. It may be with thy people, but with us Washensi — Pagans — it is justice. It was I that strangled him, Kalulu cut off his head. Was Tifum not going to cut off Kalulu's head?—and perhaps thine, for he hated thee enough, Allah knows."

"Yes," said Niani, "I heard Tifum swear he would do it."

"Well, but he did not do it, and I am sorry, Simba, thou hast thus needlessly taken life," said Selim, with difficulty repressing a shudder.

"Selim, son of Amer, permit Simba, the Mrundi, to ask thee if thou hast already forgotten thy dead father, thy kinsmen, thine own miseries? Say, where is Isa? Where is little Mussoud? How was Abdullah treated? What became of Kalulu, thy friend? Where is Soltali? What has become of the village of Katalambula? I tell thee, young master, that if an Arab boy can so soon forget these, I, a Mrundi, cannot; and were Tifum the Wicked possessed of a thousand lives, I would take a life of his at every opportunity. What sayest thou, Moto, my friend? Have I not said well?"

"Quite right, my brother Simba, I should have done the same; and I am only sorry it fell to thy lot to take his life, because I should like to have taken it myself," answered Moto promptly.

"What sayest thou, Kalulu?" asked Simba of the young chief.

"Here is my answer," answered Kalulu, pointing to the head, which he picked up and tossed into the air, smiling as the head fell on its nose.

"What sayest thou, Abdullah? thou who art an Arab, and the son of an Arab?" asked Simba.

"The Kūran says: '*And if thy enemy depart not from thee, and offer thee peace, and restrain his hand from warring against thee, take him and kill him wheresoever thou dost find him, for over him God has granted the true believer a manifest power.*' Since the prophet Mohammed (blessed be his name) speaks on thy side, Simba, far be it from Abdullah, son of Sheikh Mohammed, to say thou hast done wrong in this fearful thing. I think thou hast done right," answered Abdullah gravely.

"Then, if the Kūran says so, I, Selim, son of Amer, am convinced thou hast done right," said Selim, as he hastened up, and, with an apologetic look, begged Simba's pardon.

"I, Niani, the mtuma (slave) of Selim, the son of Amer, do pronounce that Simba did right," cried the little negro, with an assurance which made all smile, and for a moment forget their previous mood.

"But what art thou going to do with the head, Kalulu?" asked Selim.

"I am going to take medicine from it," replied Kalulu, "to make my arm strong against Ferodia, when we get to the camp," folding it up in the cloth again as he spoke.

"Ah, don't, Kalulu, for my sake," pleaded Selim with earnest eyes; "don't, it is bad; only the lowest and most degraded do that. Cast the ugly thing away, and let it be food for the fowls of the air and the beasts of prey."

"It has been the custom of the Watuta to do such things, and if I do not do it Kalulu will never be king," replied the young chief, resolutely moving forward.

" It has been the custom of the Warundi too, and of all the tribes around here that I have met," said Simba. " Let Kalulu do as he will with it, young master."

" But thou art a Moslem, Simba; thou art not a Mrundi infidel now;" urged Selim, whose feelings revolted at such a degraded idea.

" Ay, I am a Moslem in name, but a Mrundi in heart, master; and when I think of all that Tifum the Wicked has done, and would have done, I myself should like to take medicine from it," replied Simba, with a vengeful look.

" But Simba," said Abdullah, "the Kūran says we ' *are forbidden to eat that which dieth of itself, and blood, and swine's flesh, and that on which the name of any beside God hath been invoked, and that which hath been strangled.*' "

" Al Forkan " (the Kūran) "is a holy book, Simba, that may not be disregarded, and he that turneth his back to it shall surely perish," added Selim.

" I am not going to eat Tifum's head; the Warundi do not eat men. They only take medicine from them; but if the good book says it is wicked, I give you my word I shall not do it," responded Simba. " But let us march, we have no time to talk," and setting the example, by vigorous strides, he induced the little party to strain themselves to keep up with him; and from this time until sunset there were few words exchanged, except a remark now and then upon some exceptional feature of the forest through which they were travelling.

At sunset the fugitives were obliged to halt, and seeing a dense jungle clump before them, they sought

an opening which led to it, which they presently discovered, narrow and a little inconvenient, but it led
them into a delicious and secure resting-place. The
camp, which they now intended to make, was surrounded
by an impenetrable hedge, about fifty feet thick and
about twelve feet high, of thorn and cactus, aloetic
plants, convolvuli, all interlacing, embracing, twining
round each other, each leaf, or twig, or branch armed
at all points with a myriad thorns, through which a
boa-constrictor might in vain attempt to pass, a man
never, were he armed in triple steel, least of all a
rude savage; while inside was soft, green, silken grass,
and a small circular depression in its centre like a
"buffalo-wallow," which contained water. Could anything have been more tempting than this? Surely not.
Had the most cunning Moto devised the best protection
he could, he had never conceived anything more formidable against naked man or beast! And the two
Arab boys laughed merrily, and rubbed their hands
together, as they thought how secure they were.

Simba, who had asumed the leadership, as though
leadership was an everyday thing to him, looking
around, said:

"We are safe. No Watuta can find us here, but we
are short of food, and boys become hungry soon. In
the morning we must look for food, as we journey
south. What dost thou think, Moto? is this forest
likely to last much longer?"

"I know not, friend Simba. I should think not;
but the minute it becomes thinner and more open we
shall see game," replied that clever woodsman, with so
much confidence that Selim, Abdullah, and Niani began

to smack their lips, as if they already tasted the luscious, juicy meat of fat game.

"Simba, I know this forest well," cried Kalulu; "but before I say anything about it, I must know where thou dost intend to go."

"Ah! where?" asked Simba, looking at Moto, and speaking in a tone which was more of a doleful echo than a question.

"Where?" said Moto, in the same tone, looking at Simba.

"I must know," said Kalulu. "We are far from pursuit now. Ferodia might as well look for the honey-bird, hiding his head in a hole, as look for us. Speak, Simba and Moto, where do ye both intend to go?"

"Answer thou, young chief," replied Simba and Moto, together.

"I? Well, let it be so," he answered. "I mean to return towards the east, through the forest, and then turn up north and west, and seek out every man left of my tribe, and make war against Ferodia. Make war on the traitorous thief, until every man that lifted spear in his cause shall be even as this carrion is" (pointing to the chilled head of Tifum). "War, until all my enemies shall fall, and be utterly destroyed as the dry grass of the summer is destroyed by a fire. That is what I intend beginning to do at sunrise to-morrow;" and as the young chief said the last few words he sprang to his feet, and dashed his spear deep into the now unoffending head of Tifum the Wicked, and his whole body quivered with the fury that animated him.

While he was thus imagining that he had already

his enemies low at his feet, he felt a soft touch on his
shoulder, and as he turned his head around he saw the
gentle, winning face of Selim turned up to him with
pleading eyes, and heard him say :

" Kalulu, thou art still the King of the Watuta to
us ; sit down quiet by my side, like my brother Abdullah and little Niani here, and listen to what thy
brother Selim has to say."

The friendship he entertained for Selim came to the
aid of the Arab boy, and this, together with the kindly
tones and sympathising eyes turned towards him, completely subdued him, and he sat down, and for the first
time, to our knowledge, Kalulu wept. Selim's tender
heart could not bear the proud young chief's tears, and
he also wept out of sheer sympathy.

" Kalulu," said Selim, when he had conquered this
feeling, and could command firmness of voice, " when
I was dying of hunger in the forest thou didst
come to my aid, and, pitying me, a friendship grew
in thy heart towards me, and when I opened mine
eyes, and saw thy large black eyes rest on me with so
much pity, so much love in them for me, who until then
was as one doomed to die a lingering death, was as
an outcast from Nature, I learned to love thee as my
brother. The blood ceremony was made, and I gladly
became a brother to thee. When I was in the village,
and I felt Tifum's heavy hand on me, with the cruel
order of Ferodia ringing in my ears, thou didst
again come like a good angel to my aid ; and in my
heart I blessed God and thee. When Abdullah
struggled in the dark waters, and the greedy crocodile
snapped him by the leg, and drew him down out of
sight, down into the depths, I cried out in my agony,

'Oh, save him!' and thou, ever our good angel, didst leap into the depths, and far out of sight thou didst grapple with the monster, and in a short time didst bring him—Abdullah—back to life and to his friend. When thou wert made king, and thou hadst power of life and death over an immense multitude of warriors given unto thee, I did ask thee for permission to go to my own home at Zanzibar, to lift the veil of sorrow from my mother's eyes, and thou didst promise to give me wealth, and abundance, and men under thine own command to protect me on the way. But evil days came. Ferodia, like a thief in the night, came with a great number of men; they took thy power from thee, made thyself, and ourselves, and thy people prisoners and slaves. They bound thee, and made thee—a king—also a slave; and until last night thou wert in bonds, and yesterday thou wert beaten like the meanest, and to-day's sun was to rise on thy corpse. But Niani—good Niani, whom I believed to be created only for mischief and fun—rose in the night, and delivered us all from the power of Ferodia; and we are all here safe from our enemies, and free once more. Allah be praised for ever!"

Kalulu was sobbing violently, and Selim, when he heard his sobs, could hardly refrain from joining him, but, conquering the feeling with an effort, he continued:

"Kalulu, my brother, it is but a little thing that I am going to ask of thee, yet if thou wilt but grant it me, thou wilt make Selim happy—ay, happier even than when thou didst whisper the sweet words in my ear—'Thou art free! Thou art my brother!' I fear to ask it of thee, lest thou wouldst hurt me with a refusal."

"Speak, Selim; what can Kalulu do for thee? Have I not told thee long ago thou hast but to command me. Yet what have I to give thee? Was not Kalulu a slave yesterday? Ha! ha! what has a slave to give?" and the young chief laughed bitterly.

"Thou hast more to give me than ever thou didst possess, Kalulu. Wilt thou promise it me what I shall ask."

"Thou art but mocking me; but I give thee my promise, and a promise is not broken lightly by a Mtuta chief," Kalulu answered.

"Then listen, O my brother! At Zanzibar I have a beautiful home; and all around it are trees, great trees, like those in the forest, heavy with yellow globes of sweetness, called oranges, others borne down with great fruit larger than the matonga (*Nux vomica*) of the forest, which are sweeter than honey, and are called mangoes; and there are tall trees, called palms, which bear nuts large as thy head, full of milky wine, so refreshing when thou art thirsty, that thou wilt recall the time when thy mother suckled thee, and laughed at the greediness of her bright, baby boy, and there are numbers of others, which give both fruit to fill a man's spirit with delight, and others to give perfume, which, when a man inhales it, his senses become suffused with pleasure; and as for the vegetables which my fields and gardens furnish, there is nothing in all Ututa, or the lands adjoining, to compare with them. There are squashes, and pumpkins, and melons, blue and purple egg-plants, cucumbers, chick-peas, and beans, yams, sweet potatoes, white and yellow tomatoes, and plaintains, and bananas, and numbers of things thou dost

x

not dream of. And then my house—ah! there is nothing like it in all Negro-land; it is as high as the tallest tree, and as large almost as the great square of thy village, all of white stone; the floors, instead of being of earth or of sand, are of white stone, smooth and shining as the stillest, whitest water thou hast ever seen; and the beds are of down and of finest, whitest cloth, which when thou dost rest thy body upon them will cause thee to sleep and forget all troubles; and from the upper doors, which we call windows in Arab land, thine eyes rest upon the great blue sea, and the laughing waves, which murmur of love, and beauty, and pleasure all the day. It is to this beautiful home I invite thee, my brother. It is to these scenes of holy love, and God's beauty, which He has given to me, that I wish to take thee; and to my dear mother, who will be to thee as she is to me; who will love thee for what thou hast done for her child, as she loves her own son; to my beautiful mother, whose face is as white as yon white cloud, and as beautiful as the moon, I wish thee to come. Say, Kalulu, wilt thou come, and share my sweet mother's love with me? Say, wilt thou come, and let me show thee the wonders of Zanzibar?"

Kalulu answered not; he never ceased sobbing while Selim spoke; he seemed loth to give the answer in the affirmative, yet he remembered his promise, and he remembered it was Selim who was asking him a favour. A few seconds, therefore, passed in this silence; but when it was finally broken it was by Simba's deep voice, who said:

"Those are wise words, young chief, that Master Selim has spoken. Neither Moto nor I could have thought of them; but the boy's heart has spoken wiser words than Simba and Moto's heads together could have spoken. Young chief, thou shalt yet be King of Ututa; but it will be better first that thou goest to Zanzibar, where thine eyes may see strange things, and thy head learn wisdom. I, Simba, a servant of Selim, could not have invited thee to Zanzibar, because Simba has but a very little hut, not bigger than a camp-cote, where the hunter has to coil himself up like a serpent. My hut would then have been no place for the King of the Watuta; but Master Selim has got a big house, bigger than any king's house in Negro-land; he has numbers of servants, cattle, goats, donkeys, gardens, fields, and fruit-trees, and his riches are beyond my knowledge. Oh! I see light and hope now, young chief. I know what is best for all of us. I know how thou, by going to Zanzibar, may come to Ututa a greater king than Loralamba even. I'll tell thee how. Through the aid of Selim thou wilt become acquainted with numbers of rich Arabs, whom thou wilt like when thou wilt know them better. They are good men at heart, though some are bad, as there are bad men everywhere. This acquaintance will benefit thee and them, for after thou shalt have rested a year or two at Zanzibar, thou wilt be able to induce them to come with thee to thine own country, when for their aid to set thee in thy rights, thou wilt be able to give them back the Arab slaves Ferodia took at Kwikuru, and give them ivory in abundance; and they will make thee rich in cloth and fine things: thou wilt by that time, through the knowledge of such things obtained at Zanzibar, be able to judge of what is good, and what is bad; thou wilt be able to build thy villages strong against every attack of evil men, to conquer Ferodia, and every tribe round about, to make thy country great, so there will be none other like unto it; so that thy name and glory be sung in all the corners of the earth. To be a great king thou must teach thyself and learn many things; and this thou canst do by going to Zanzibar. I have said it."

Then Kalulu, impulsive youth that he was, sprang up and cried, "Enough, Selim, thou hadst almost persuaded me; but Simba has conquered me. I shall go to Zanzibar, I shall learn how to be a great king, and I shall come back to Ututa a strong, big man like thou, Simba; then let Ferodia look to himself. Let him live upon the fatness of the land. Let him enjoy his gains until Kalulu comes back, then by Soltali's ashes, by the grave of Mostana, by the black ruins of Katalambula's village, I shall have fullest revenge. I have spoken."

"Good—good—good," cried all at once, and Selim sprang up and embraced him, while Simba and Moto took each a hand and shook it eagerly, while little Niani jumped and hopped about as though he were a real monkey, whereas he was only a monkey in name, and Abdullah, after Selim released him, insisted also upon the same right to embrace him, and promised upon the Kūran to come back with him to Watuta and see him righted. There was such joy in the little camp, closed in by that impenetrable jungle hedge, such as we are certain was never seen before, and never will be seen there again.

"There is one other little thing I should like to see

Kalulu do," said Selim, smiling, but looking on the ground nevertheless.

"What? anything else for me to do? Well, I will do it. Speak," replied Kalulu, lifting Selim's head up with his hand so that he could see his face.

"Thou art so good, Kalulu, to promise me so many things before thou knowest what it is I am going to ask. Thou knowest that I am very timid and fearful, and I could not sleep to-night quietly with that ugly head so near me, and——"

Kalulu rose immediately, and taking hold of the head by the hair, he tossed it into the middle of the jungle hedge, where, rolling through a little, it remained fixed in the forks of a thornbush situated exactly in the middle of the hedge, where it was more effectively buried safer from all living creatures than were it buried ten feet deep in the earth.

"Good—good," cried Abdullah and Selim, really more rejoiced and feeling safer from Tifum than they liked to confess.

"Now," said Simba, when each person's feelings were calmed, "let us talk of other matters. Kalulu, thou knowest this country. How can we get away to Zanzibar?"

"But where is Zanzibar?" asked Kalulu, surprised.

"It ought to be east directly from here, just where the sun rises every morning," answered Simba.

"I can show the way to Urori; but what lies beyond Urori I do not know," said Kalulu.

"We are too small a party to be able to go through Uhehe alone," said Simba. "That won't do. What do you suggest, Moto?" he asked of his friend.

"If I were anywhere on the track of the traders,' answered that wise and cautious old hunter, "I would soon find out. If I were in Marungu or in Usowa I could soon tell. Did I not hear thee say, Kalulu, that there lay a lake, a large body of water somewhere about here?"

"Yes, Lake Liemba; there is no end to it. It runs towards the north," replied Kalulu.

"Lake Liemba! Liemba!" said Moto to himself, like one trying to remember whether he had ever heard the name before. "I never heard of Liemba that I know of. I have been on Lake Tanganika several times in going from Ujiji to——"

"Ujiji!" said Kalulu, in a surprised tone. "Ujiji! I never heard the Watuta travellers talk about the Tanganika; but I have always heard that Ujiji was on Liemba, not far from Usowa, but further up."

"Wallahi!" shouted Moto. "Then Lake Tanganika is only another name for Lake Liemba, for Ujiji is on Lake Tanganika, and Usowa is only a few days south of Ujiji. First after Ujiji there is Kawendi; then we come to Usowa; and after that is Uwemba—no, not Uwemba—Ufipa; and after Ufipa, Uwemba; then we always went straight to Marungu."

"If thou canst go from Ujiji to Marungu, then," said Kalulu, "or to Wemba or Usowa, the road is easy, if thou knowest the road from Ujiji to Zanzibar."

"Ah! don't I?" answered Moto, in a triumphant tone. "I will find the road from Ujiji to Zanzibar. I have travelled the road five times from Ujiji to Zanzibar, and I ought to know it. I have been guide to Sayd bin Hashid from Unyanyembe to Ujiji; but there is a better and nearer road to Zanzibar from **Fipa** to Usowa; then to Ukorongo and Unyanyembe."

" Well, then," said Simba, " what we have got to do is to reach this lake, whence it is easy to reach Ufipa or Usowa, and from thence to Unyanyembe, after which it will be easy to get to Zanzibar."

" I know the road to the Lake," said Kalulu, " for I was on the lake some moons ago. It ought to lie just where you saw the sun set to-night about twenty days' march from here. But between us and this lake is Ferodia's country. We should go a week further this way (pointing to the south), then turn round and go up, slowly towards the lake."

" Ngema—Ngema" (good, good), all cried delighted.

" To-morrow we will continue the journey south, and after a week we will pick our way toward this lake, and Inshallah! we shall see Zanzibar within five moons from now," said Simba.

" And to-morrow we shall get food—Inshallah!" said Moto.

" Inshallah, Inshallah!" all the Moslems cried.

They now proceeded to divide their ammunition, the powder and the bullets for Simba and Moto and Abdullah; while Selim, on inspecting his cartridge-bag, found a box with a thousand caps and one hundred bullets for his " Joe Manton." Kalulu employed himself in examining the string of his bow; while Niani, seeing everybody else examine his weapon, thought he might as well follow their example, and began to look at the blade of his spear in a wise manner, and delighted everybody with the news that it was sharp.

CHAPTER XII.

As the sky began to flush and brighten, and to be suffused with colour as it heralded the uprising sun, our party of travellers, cosily asleep in their camp, began to yawn and to stretch their limbs until they were finally awake, and sat up.

There were no tents to pack, there were no loads to prepare for the journey; there was nothing for them to do but to shake off the grass and soft earth on which they had slept from their bodies, leave the camp, and march.   This they did.

Nothing is so delightful as an African forest at break of day, where there is no high grass dripping with dew, no cane with its sword leaves to slash you wet with a showering rain as you pass under, nothing but the soft brown leaf-mould on the ground into which the feet sink as into a thick Persian carpet, thus giving you ample opportunities to observe the beauty of a forest at early morn, without inconvenience or anxiety on the score of your health.   The forest, with its countless trees, each loaded with its wealth of leaves and twigs, seems in the first grey opaque light before sunrise to have been planted full grown, and decked with light green leaves during the chaos of night, as they stand in their several positions row upon row in numbers untold, all wonderfully silent and still, awaiting the issue of the morning. And while they stand thus apparently labouring under excitement, though outwardly still as death, in the grey light and opacity through which the trees were first seen, there suddenly dart myriads of bright sheets of brilliant whiteness, which soon alternate with some of the hue of pale gold-and-yellow, and unconsciously the brilliant sheets of colour of glory have become indistinguishable in the general light of day which has at last come. Then, in harmony with the advent of the glorious day, the trees seem to recover from their astonishment, and their leaves begin to rustle and whisper to each other their gentle comments on the great change which the sun has wrought; and from afar, borne by the breath of the wind to the human ears bent on listening, comes the low murmur of wakened life, the songs of birds, the fish-eagle's and paroquet's discordant cries, the hum of busy termites at work, the murmur of lady-birds, the whir of gad-flies and tsetse, the startling "crick" of crickets; and away, almost at your feet, rushes the frightened land-rail uttering a piercing cry, and above your head flies the guinea-hens which, unknown to you, had roosted on the tree-bough just above, with an assumed terror, which provokes your smile; and presently the hyæna is heard uttering his last farewell howl as he hies to his den to shun the honest sunlight, and the lion sends his last farewell roar, filling the forest with its awful sound, and the young fawns and horned antelope are seen browsing on the sweet fresh grass, which is decked with many a minute head, and the elands and the kudu, the sable buck and hartebeest, blue-buck and zebra, are beheld munching and chewing in the glades with might and main, as if they had a task to fulfil before the end of some set time, which we may take as a warning that we have also our appointed work, and must be up and doing.

This beautiful transformation from the gloam of the morning to the full burst of day was seen and enjoyed by the most poetical of our travellers, as they marched as rapidly as their waning strength would permit them after the tireless forms of Simba and Moto.

They had marched an hour, and the whole forest, which to them was a world, was all aglow with insect life, when Simba suddenly halted, with his finger pointing towards an open country bounded by hills in the far distance, and said in a whisper, "Mbogo" (buffalo).

The excitement became general, and the question which first came to each lip was, "Where are they?" but following the direction towards which Simba's finger pointed, they were able to discern with difficulty three or four black specks in a portion of the open country which apparently was the same Ututa plain which had bounded the forest to the right all the time. Simba, Moto, Selim, Abdullah, and Kalulu, at once and instinctively struck for the open plain, followed by Niani, who, with his single spear, looked as important as one could well be, and who seemed to think that all the buffaloes would eventually fall beneath his hand.

Arriving on the edge of the forest, Simba, in order to make sure of one of them, separated his forces, each about forty yards from the other, with instructions to crawl towards the animals and surround them on all but the windward side ; to make no noise, and to wait for a low whistle to rise up and fire. After each of them had promised faithfully for the commonweal to obey such injunctions, which were also impressed on their minds emphatically by the hunter Moto, the laborious task of working their way towards the animals began.

Fortunately the wind was from the westward, so they were not compelled to make any détour to avoid tainting the air, and between the buffaloes and themselves rose several low hummocks, ancient ant-hills deserted long ago, and now covered with dense tall yellow grass. The plain was also covered with the same tall grass, but at their base grew the young herbage—signs of the coming spring and rainy season now fast advancing—which probably was that upon which the buffaloes fed.

To our people it was a serious matter to fail, as their hungering stomachs could not sustain their bodies much longer in their march, without replenishment soon ; besides, the excitement of the escape from cruel bondage had vanished, so that it became a vital necessity to obtain food. This strong, urgent necessity probably compelled their caution, and taught each person the art of stalking much sooner than they had any idea could be learnt before.

Steadily they advanced, crouching close beneath the grass-heads, hiding behind the numberless hummocks

which rose in their front at intervals, behind the tall
mysterious palms whose fan-like leaves kept up an un-
ceasing rustle, and waving as the breeze swayed them
up and down, and blew them with a startling noise
against the tall trunks.

Nearer, step by step, they crawled with bated
breath, and crowds of anxious thoughts running
through their heads, lest the slightest error or alarm
might be made by some awkward companion, every
now and then lifting their heads up to note the progress they made, or the position of the massive and
fierce brutes whom they intended to attack.

Kalulu, more experienced than any other, had found
his task much lighter than either Simba or Moto, least
of all the Arab boys, his lithe, sinewy form had penetrated through the grass with the ease of the young
antelope, from which he derived his name, and had
found it no difficulty whatever to stalk the buffaloes;
so that, long before his companions had gained their
several positions, he had ventured as near a buffalo bull
as prudence would suggest, and one of his arrows was
already resting on the string which his practised hand
would surely send home into the animal's flanks on the
first sound of the signal.

In a few minutes, Simba having kindly waited for his
friends, Kalulu heard the whistle, and as he stood up
he took a second's survey of the field. Moto was far
to the right of Simba, Simba was next to Kalulu,
Abdullah was a few yards behind him, on his left, with
his gun pointed at the same animal he had chosen.
Selim was the furthest on the left, about thirty or forty
yards from a young bull buffalo. This was taken in at

one glance, and probably Simba and Moto had taken the same precaution. The next second Kalulu's bow twanged. Selim's rifle and the muskets of Simba and Moto were heard together, and there was confusion and momentary dismay among the animals, as they heard the startling reports of the fire-arms. The lord of the little herd, in whose side Kalulu's arrow was buried up to the feathers, had already lowered his head, and was preparing for a charge, when Abdullah's gun rang out sharp and loud, close behind, it seemed to Kalulu, who instinctively bent his head, and the formidable bull reeled under the stroke of the bullet, which was flattened in the centre of his head but only for a moment; for, after uttering a frightful bellow, he lowered his head again, and came down, tearing the earth, towards the active young chief.

Pooh! the brute might as well have charged upon smoke, as upon the young Mtuta; for a single bound took him to one side, clear out of danger, and as the buffalo passed by, exposing his flanks, Kalulu drew his bow until it was almost double, and sent a barbed arrow clean through his heart, which rolled him over and over in the agonies of death. Thus Kalulu won the first prize.

Simba and Moto had been engaged with the same animal, which two bullets well aimed soon settled for ever. Selim, on the other hand, had broken a leg, just at the shoulder, of the buffalo to which he was opposed, and with his second barrel had sent a shot through the body, which so sickened the young bull, that he could do no more than roar painfully, and vomit blood, sure signs of his fast-approaching doom. Before he could reload his gun, the buffalo staggered, fell on his knees, and rolled over, still and dead.

Little Niani had in the meantime been skulking behind a tree, watching with a critical eye the battle, and now as he saw it terminated he advanced from his place of security, and gave a shout of triumph, and made as much noise, as though he, single-handed, had laid the three buffaloes low; but, for the good deed that he had so lately done, nobody cared to dispute his assumption, and all laughed merrily as they saw him dance on the body of Kalulu's bull. Not for long, however, for human stomachs were calling for food, and spear-blade, and knife were therefore set industriously to work to carve out the finest pieces of beef. Simba and Moto each carved out a hind-leg of rosy, juicy beef, at the sight of which their hunger grew still fiercer, and Niani, as he saw the rich chunks which Kalulu, with the aid of Abdullah, extracted from his game, could with difficulty summon courage to await the preparations for cooking.

When each was loaded down with beef, the party returned to the forest again, straight towards the east, for its gloomiest recesses, where they might remain in security, while they cooked and ate, should any enemies have heard the reports of their guns.

In about an hour they reached a secure place, a similar clump of jungle almost to that wherein they had slept so cosily the night before. A fire was soon made with the aid of their muskets, by Simba and Moto, while the boys, under the direction and example of Kalulu, employed themselves in preparing slender rods, pointed, with which they pierced small pieces of

beef, to plant around the fire for a speedy broil. In
their great hurry to allay their gnawing hunger, too,
they threw several thin slices into the hottest part of
the fire, which no sooner were warmed than they were
extracted again and eaten with a relish and satisfaction which the poor stomachs alone could have properly
described had they the same power of speech as they
had of digestion.

While they were thus eating, a glance at the fire
showed a regular palisade of slender sticks, on which
numberless pieces of meat were impaled, and Simba and
Moto having thus satisfactorily arranged the cooking
of the rations, began to make other preparations for
the same purpose on a more extensive scale, while
Abdullah and Niani were detailed to procure wood, and
keep up a regular scorching fire, as the march was to
be resumed after noon. The men selected four sticks
with prongs, which they planted at each corner and
outside the beefy palisade, and laying two slender poles
lengthwise, with their ends resting in the forks of the
upright sticks, and over these poles they laid shorter
sticks crosswise, and apart from each other, which
structure, when completed, had somewhat the appearance of a gridiron. On this platform were laid long
strings of meat, and the object of their preparations
was soon explained to Selim, who in this knowledge
perceived where he had been at fault, when he escaped
from Ferodia on the march to Katalambula's village.

It was really wonderful how much these heroes of
ours managed to eat. The palisade on which the
kabobs were roasting, and hissing, and spluttering, was
rapidly disappearing before the veracious attacks of the

gourmands. Some hand was constantly stretched out
to take and uproot the defences round the fire, and
fingers were incessantly employed in extracting from
the sticks the juicy and luscious pieces, and one mouth
or another was continually opened to receive, while the
jaws of all were perpetually grinding meat with their
lips emitting a chorus of "auch," "auch," "tlap,"
"tlap." Though there has been an omission to mention that, over the body of each buffalo, before its
throat was cut, the blessing of God was invoked, it
must not be taken for granted that such pious sons of
Islam as Selim and Abdullah were, could have done
such a deed without going through the grateful
ceremony which the Kūran has enjoined on all true
believers. And in the feeling of plenitude which was
at last felt, they found their reward My young
readers who have never experienced the pangs of
hunger and thirst will have perhaps some difficulty in
comprehending the fierceness of appetite and voracity
which these children of nature exhibited.

About two o'clock in the afternoon, the meat was
taken from the platform, "done brown," and was bound
into a light bale of provisions for each person, with
bark rope, and with a perfectly satisfied feeling, the
party sallied out, and continued the journey south.

At sunset they encamped near a pool of water, and
after surrounding themselves with a stout brush fence,
they set to work upon some more meat, with an enjoyment and gusto few can realize outside of those who
have gone through similar experiences. Jokes were
freely made; Simba uttered his dry, crisp remarks,
which set them all laughing. Then, when the supper

was over, and Moto had taken out from some extra-ordinary recess of his loin cloth a leaf of tobacco, and some lime, and handing a bit to Simba, who received it with joyful gratitude, and placed it in his mouth, with a pleasure which lit his face up. Moto called out to Niani for a story. Little Niani was taken aback by this, and blushed as much as he could blush, for his face seemed to burn, and tingle, as he felt the high honour conferred on him. He answered, he did not know how to tell a story. But Moto having explained to him that he only wished to know what had become of him after he left Katalambula's village, Niani said:

"Oh, it is soon told. Tifum the Wicked, after we came to Katalambula's, took me to his own hut, and made me wait on him, fetch water, and light his pipe for him, and when Ferodia left Katalambula's that night, when he was angry because Simba and Kalulu would not let him take Master Selim with him, I was marched off by Tifum. On the road, Tifum beat me several times, and once threatened to cut my head off, if I did not hurry my steps. I was sorry, and I felt as if I did not care much what he would do to me, since I was parted from Master Selim, who was always so good to me. One of the Arab slaves was caught as he was trying to run away, and Ferodia ordered him to be killed. He was thrown on the ground by six men, and while one man drew his head back by the hair, another with a knife that was not sharp, began to cut his head off. The blood of that poor man spouting up in the faces of the cruel men, while his body was shaking, and moving about as he tried to breathe, I shall never forget; and if only for that savage work of Tifum, who

x

stood by laughing, I think Tifum the Wicked has been served right. Nothing else happened on the road, except that every day some poor slave was badly used, and beaten until he died. I think that more than twenty people died on the road. We got at last to Ferodia's village, which is not near so big as Katalambula's was, though he has plenty of cows, and sheep, and goats. Tifum had four wives, all ugly and cruel, and when Tifum told them to make use of me, those bad women treated me worse than he had done; they pulled my hair, pinched my ears and face, slapped me on the back, made me run after water, to tend their goats, and bring them back at night. Indeed, they nearly killed me, while Tifum laughed as if he enjoyed it. I then thought it better to be very good, and do my work quick, which, when Tifum saw, he took me away from them, and made me work for him only; but he was all the time saying he would cut my throat some day, and eat me—and he used to open his mouth so wide! I think I could have jumped down into it, if I tried hard. I heard him say often, too, how sorry he was he did not have one of the white slaves—meaning Master Selim and Master Abdullah—the Pagan dog! for he thought he could have been much more thought of by his people if he had one of them. Then we heard, one day, that Katalambula was dead, and Kalulu was king, which made Ferodia fearfully angry, and say how he would chop up into little bits everybody who helped him; and the next day, after plenty of talk, he took a great number of people with him, and came towards Katalambula's. Tifum took me with him, and made me carry his spears, and bag of rice, and a gourdful of water. I was thinking all the time I would tell Simba and Moto what Ferodia was going to do, if I could only get in ; but at the village of the tribe of Meroeni, Tifum left me behind, by orders of Ferodia, and I knew I could not help you. The night it was all to take place I tried again, but I could not ; and in the morning we all left for Katalambula's, only to find the warriors of Ferodia masters of the village. You know the rest. I saw you all slaves, and I came very near crying when I saw it ; but I stopped it, for fear of Tifum. But all the time I was thinking, and thinking how I could help you all, but I was afraid. Then that night in the forest, after Soltali was burnt, I heard Tifum swear that in the morning he would cut Kalulu's head off, and, whether Ferodia liked it or not, he would then cut off Master Selim's head. I became angry then. Yes, you may laugh ; but my heart was black, and once or twice I looked at Tifum's knife hungrily, and I thought how I should like to bury it in his black neck ; but no ; I waited until after Tifum had eaten his supper, and I heard him groan in pain, and I thought he would never stop ; but he did at last, and went asleep. Then I got up, with Tifum's knife in my hand, and came to you, Master Selim. And now you know all that Niani knows."

" *Ngema toto, Toto nwema sana* " (Good child, very good child), cried Moto ; but Simba stretched out his long, strong arm, and laid hold of Niani and lifted him up, and hugged the little mite—until he was almost hidden by the great, strong arms—close to his mighty breast, and poured into his ear such endearing terms that poor little Niani had never heard before, that made his eyes water after a singular manner, which he could not very well have explained but that he felt a great big lump in his throat, which seemed as if it would choke him.

Selim, his son, dear young master, who was so very superior to him, and all whom he had ever seen, his Master Selim, who had such a beautiful mamma at Zanzibar—his Master Selim, whom he had seen dressed in gold and silver raiment, in the beautifullest clothes of blue and red silk, and whitest linen, Niani saw looking at him with eyes full of kindness, and a smile on his face,—for which he would have gone through the hottest fire,—with a look which went straight into him, and kindled within him a feeling akin to idolatry, and heard the sweetest words which were ever uttered in his hearing from him. "Come to me, come near Selim, Niani;" and the little black waif, who hitherto had been neglected and allowed to grow wild unnoticed by a single kind human eye, was clasped by his young master and kissed!

"My own mamma shall thank thee, Niani," said Selim, resting his hand upon his head. "Thou dost remember her, dost thou not, Niani?"

"Ah, when shall I forget her, master, or you?" said Niani; while from under the half-closed eyes and bowed head rolled the tears in streams down his cheeks.

"Nay, Niani, thou shalt not say 'you' to me more; say 'thou,' because thou art no longer my slave—thou shalt be more; thou shalt be my friend. Selim has nc slaves around this fire. Neither Simba nor Moto are my slaves; they are my friends, and now thou art also one."

"Yes, but Master Selim, Simba and Moto are big, and I am little and bad, and some day, perhaps, I shall do something wrong, and you will be no longer my friend."

"And when that day comes," responded Selim, "I shall remember a little boy who crept through a camp of wicked people in the dead of night, while all others were afraid of Soltali's ghost, and came and delivered his master Selim from the sharp knife of Tifum, and the memory of that deed shall be sure to make me say, "Forgive Niani, for the sake of that he did to thee. Forgive him for the life he gave back to thee."

"Niani will always try to be good, because he loves his Master Selim," the little fellow said.

"So be it," answered his master.

"And I," said Abdullah, "want to be Niani's friend; and he must say 'thou' to me, and when we reach Zanzibar, Niani will find how grateful an Arab boy can be."

Simba said : "Niani must look upon me as his father from this evening, because he has neither father nor mother of his own. Master Selim, Abdullah, and Moto are his friends; and when Niani is big like me, Master Selim will give him a wife and garden, and a home, and he will grow up with plenty of little Nianis around him."

This set them all laughing, and the idea of little Niani having plenty of other little Nianis, lasted as a good joke until it was time to sleep.

The fire was allowed to die out; but through the gloom of night in the dark forest, with the broad, shadowy boughs swaying softly over the sleepers, the everlasting stars, the southern cross, glittering Orion, and bright, shining Canopus, searched them out, but they never looked down from their exalted heights on a camp in Central Africa, where were purer fellowship, or greater human kindness than that which those sleeping forms contain within them towards one another.

The march of our party was continued the next day and for six days more toward the south without having once emerged from the forest. They saw plenty of game, and almost every day bagged something for the larder; but they always kept a surplus of dried meat by as a provision for exigencies.

On the seventh day after the scenes just detailed above, Kalulu thought they might now turn west, and after going in that direction for three days, might slowly point their faces toward the north-west, or alter their direction towards Lake Liemba, as circumstances permitted.*

The genial shade and tranquillity of the primeval forest was soon exchanged after they turned their faces west for the intolerable heat and vexation of a low, thorny jungle. Their nostrils became offended with the fetid

* The real direction in which our people journeyed may be found by any reader curious enough to wish to know if he will examine the map of Central Africa as published in the book 'How I Found Livingstone,' when the reader will be able to locate easily the scenes laid here. He will find that the countries are laid down with a fidelity which generally belongs to standard geographical works, that no liberties are taken with the habits, the customs, or the true ethnology of the great country of Ututa, or with the geography of Central Africa, neither with the probabilities of a life in that far region. The chain of circumstances, as here portrayed, alone belong to the romantic and the fictitious, and this fact the author would fain impress upon the minds of his readers.

rank exhalations of the cactaceous and aloetic plants, and black gummy bushes, armed with many a horrid thorn, which struggled with each other for place and air with the wanton luxuriance and spontaneous growth which belongs to tropical plants. These loaded the air with a pungent, acrimonious odour, which set them all coughing, and when they impatiently rubbed the tormented organs of respiration, they but added to their discomfort, for their hands had unconsciously rubbed against some leaves as they passed through, and communicated a burning sensation to their noses and lips like that which cayenne pepper provokes. Long creepers, armed upon all sides with ridges of thorn, evoked many an impatient word, as at an unlucky moment they stumbled against these, and were held fast to the great and severe wounding of the epidermis, and pendulous arms, overhanging the road which they traversed, caught them fast often with their crooked and sharp thorns by the skin of the throat, causing severe and painful wounds. These pains and penalties, which the jungles of that region impose upon the unlucky travellers who are compelled to travel through them, were but a few of the inconveniences and discomforts which our friends suffered. The whole ground seemed strewn with the opened kernel of a seed thorn, which is armed outside with as many straight, sharp thorns as there are quills in a porcupine's back. Fancy men with naked feet walking over a ground strewn with miniature porcupines, and you will agree with me that the pain and torment would be as great almost as walking over hot embers. At least such were the opinions of our friends, as they were compelled, while their faces were wrinkled with pain, to stop every other minute to extract the vile thorn kernels which had wounded their feet.

Apart from these miseries of the jungle were those which the heated and cracked earth furnished. The red, drouthy ground was full of wide and unsightly seams, rugged rents, which gaped open to receive the incautious foot, and many a stumble and cry was elicited from the unwary Arab boys, who, instead of watching against these mischances, permitted their eyes to rove over the inhospitable scene.

And over all these shone the sun with a true tropic fervour, where, untempered by the slightest breeze, with no friendly tree intervening with its thick foliage between their heads and the full power of the sun, their nude bodies seemed destined to be baked while they yet had the power of locomotion. These several things, the heat of the sun, the hot vapour from the earth surging upward like steam, the prickly bush and the frequent stumblings, engendered a violent thirst which they all began to feel, while the perspiration streaming from their bodies added more and more to its intensity.

Ah! they may well think with regret of the grateful shade which the luxuriant forest afforded; they may well say that they wished that the forest had lasted for ever, for it furnished many a pool of clear water, the freshness of which the pale yellow lotus flowers, languidly resting on its surface, seemed to enhance. They may well think of the joyous chorus which the gorgeously-feathered birds gave out incessantly from morn until evening; they may well think

with regret of all the pleasures which the primeval
woods furnished, which they have now exchanged for
the steamy plain and acrid jungle. But the road to
home and comfort lies through many a jungle yet,
and these inconveniences ye have to suffer, my friends,
if ye ever think to embrace the friends who await ye
at Zanzibar!

At sunset they came to a shallow pool, whose consis-
tence was that of liquid mud of a chalky colour. The
vicinity showed that it was a frequent resort for such
animals as were benighted in the inhospitable plain on
their way to more northern pasture-grounds, and that
its colour and unsavoury taste had been caused by the
thirsty beasts plunging into its middle in their hurry
to assuage the thirst which consumed their vitals. But
little recked our thirsty heroes for the colour or the
unsavoury taste of the water so long as it relieved in
the slightest degree the pangs which tormented them.

Continuing their journey towards the west the next
day, one of the annoyances which troubled them the
day before abated. The jungle had disappeared, and
in its place stretched a treeless plain before them,
which was covered with tall and bleached grass of the
last summer's growth. This plain, when they had
travelled many hours towards its centre, and took a
survey around, they found to be an oval depression, as
the jungle which they had left in the morning appeared
to be on much higher ground than that on which they
now stood, and Kalulu expressed his opinion that they
had begun to descend towards the lake-land of
southern Liemba, in which opinion Simba and Moto
concurred.

As they advanced still further to the west, the country began to heave upward on the horizon, though they seemed to descend into a yet lower level. Presently walking became a task of difficulty. The firm close ground over which they had travelled, and the dense pasture-grass changed into a tall sedge which formed tussocks, separated and isolated from each other, which they had to span with long strides, and which shook beneath their weight, as they sprang from one tussock to another.

After two hours of this fatiguing work they came to a black spongy ooze, which appeared firm enough on the surface, but as soon as it felt their weight it admitted them up to their waists into the depths of the putrid composition of wet grass and sedgy mould, over the surface of which trickled many a miniature stream of oily slime. The sword leaves of the pubescent reed and sedge slashed and cut their bodies as though razors had been lightly drawn across them, and the blood streamed down their chests and limbs. They presented a miserable spectacle as they finally emerged from the swampy fen, and felt the firm ground under their feet once more, for they were spattered all over with clots of black mud, which, under the sun's heat, were rapidly baked, and formed a filthy grey encrustation.

But heedless of all this they urged their steps until they had reached the ridgy horizon, which, ever since morning, had loomed greyishly blue before them. As it was night when they had reached this elevation, they rested here, completely worn out with the dire march of the day, and so great was their fatigue that they did not pay much heed to the thirst they otherwise would have suffered from.

Long before day on the third morning they were on the way again, looking with dismay at the extensive plain which waved and heaved before them like a sea, and throughout all its prospect promised no amelioration of the fatigue and pain they had endured the day before. Away, as far as the vision could command, the land rose in successive ridges, of a whitish hue, which they knew to be the result of the dry and parched grass which clothed them. It was through such an inhospitable country the march of the third day westward took them.

On the fourth morning Kalulu chose a broad ridge which ran north-westerly, and led the way along its spine, whence they obtained views of all around. Now and then the travellers dipped into hollows, but regained rising ground as oft as they could, and towards night they were gratified by observing dark mountainous masses in the distance, which they were told would be reached in about twelve hours' march the next day.

The night of the fifth day verified the prediction of Kalulu, for they found themselves at the base of a conical hill, near a stream of pure water, close by a bamboo jungle, whose vivid green leaves afforded a grateful contrast to the bleached grass, through which daily grew into greater importance the noisy but clear rivulet, which brawled over pebbles and gravel bottom to the impetuous stream thundering down rocky slopes, past granite and basaltic pinnacles, in foamy sheets and curved round bends, with moan and wail, until it gained the level lea, where it flowed tranquilly on towards its eternity. They plunged through leafy woods, where the sycamore was in its glory and towered aloft in an enormous globe, acknowledged king of trees; through bamboo jungles, through park lands of unusual beauty, by conical hills, and along the base of ridges of gray rock, defiling through deep ravines, until they finally came to a verdant champaign dotted here and there with noble trees, where the swards were as soft as velvet. And all these days they had been descending slowly but surely towards the lake they were in search of, and the vigorous young grass which now gladdened their eyes informed them that they were not far from it. They formed their camp, warmed their last morsel of dried meat, and comforted each other, that in such a land they need not be long looking for game.

About midnight they were roused from their slumbers by the roar of a lion, apparently very near them, and Moto said, as soon as he could collect his faculties:

"What did I tell ye? I knew such a country as this must be full of game, and the roar of that beast confirms it, for a lion is never found except where there is food for him, but, Selim, thou must be ready with thy rifle, for if the fellow is very hungry he will try to take one of us."

"I see him," whispered Kalulu. "There! look at him; do ye not see that dark form slowly moving past that big tree now? There! he stops and looks towards us!"

"Hush!" whispered Simba, "he is coming. Be ready and sure with thy gun, young master!"

"Shall I fire now?" asked Selim in a low tone.

"No, no, no," replied Moto. "Wait until I give the word. Pooh, young master, thou must drive thy ball through and through his head. It will never do to wound him."

The sound of the pulsations in their bodies might almost have been heard, as still as the tree stem under whose leafage they were crouching, they waited the ferocious and powerful thief and prowler who ranges at will, seeking whom he may devour, throughout the long night in the game lands of Africa. Fortunate was it for some of them that he signaled his presence in the forest with that first loud roar, for had he but crept to them, unwarning, as he was now doing, what a terrible confusion he had thrown the panic-stricken people into! Not a sound was heard as he neared them. It was only by the approaching bulk and dark loom of him they knew he was advancing; but presently he again stopped, and they heard the soft brushing of the grass, probably made with his tail, as he twirled and tossed it about wantonly, and through the gloom they saw two specks of luminous light, shine like miniature lanterns, by which Selim was able to take aim. The hand of Moto lightly resting on the Arab-boy's shoulders, warned him and restrained him from firing.

For a moment the lion stood surveying the creatures he knew to be crouched under the tree. He then was seen to move to the left, as if he were about to make a circuit round them, but at every step he took Selim turned his gun, resting on his knee, at him, completely covering him. Suddenly he halted and confronted them, and a loud appalling roar broke on their startled ears, terrible enough in its volume and sound to

unnerve the stoutest, and which caused little Niani and
Abdullah to shrink behind Simba and Moto, who in the
meantime had prepared their guns lest Selim's nerve
might fail him at the critical and trying moment. The
form of the lion, now fearfully plain, came to the earth
with an almost imperceptible downward movement, and
each second as it passed, while he waited for the command, was freighted with keenest anxiety to Selim.

Kalulu warned Moto that the beast was preparing for
a spring. Then Moto bade all be ready, and the word
"Piga" (fire) was heard, sharp and peremptory, and the
three guns simultaneously belched flame and fire, lit up
the form of the then uprising lion, and a savage cry
and dull heavy thud upon the earth announced to these
anxious souls that the lion's spring was cut short, and
that he was either dying or was dead.

They hastily raked the hot embers together, and,
throwing straw on it, soon blew it into a bright blaze
which threw a light over the late scene of terror, and
showed the lion's form stretched on its right side, with
its left fore-paw, vainly beating the air, and the opened
jaws, the gleaming white teeth, and protruding tongue,
and the head almost split asunder, where two bullets
had entered home to the brain, and robbed him of the
cruel life which only endured to rend and devour prey.

"Ah ha, lion! thou greedy beast," cried Niani, hop-
ping about as light as a young springbok. "Thou didst
think to eat Niani, thou cruel one. Father Simba,
rightly called 'lion,' and Master Selim, and friend
Moto have given thee as good as thou didst intend to
have given me. He will roar no more, will he, chief?"
he suddenly asked Kalulu.

A LION SHOT AT MIDNIGHT.

"No, little one," responded that more decorous and dignified youth; "he will haunt the forest no more, nor startle the antelopes with his roar during the gloom of night. Thou mayst sleep in peace now, Niani."

"Ay," added Selim, "and dream of the sweet and sugared hulwa (sweetmeats) and dates of Muscat, and of the pretty jackets with silver lace on them, he is going to get from me at Zanzibar."

"Yes, and the red fez with the gold tassel which his friend Abdullah will give him," said that Arab youth.

"And he must not forget the little wife and lots of Nianis he is going to get by-and-by," added Simba, as he walked forward closer to the dead Simba, after whom he was named.

"He will do there until morning," said Moto. "Let us continue our sleep, or do ye all go to sleep while I watch, because this carrion may bring others in search of him," which good advice was soon adopted, and after some little time had passed all, except Moto, had resumed their slumber.

As the horizon was greying in the east Moto awoke his companions, who set at once to work to make a fire to warm themselves after the chilly night-dew. Kalulu cut off the claws of the lion, which he gave to Simba, Moto, and Selim, while the fourth paw's claws he offered to Abdullah, and when refused by him he reserved for himself.

Simba also stripped the splendid furry mane from the lion's neck and cut it into six equal strips, which he divided amongst his companions, and then suggested that the journey be continued, and that each should keep a bright look-out for game.

Within an hour Simba saw a kudu, and leaving his companions alone, he proceeded after it, and in a few moments the crack of his gun was heard, and his friends, with infinite satisfaction, said that his shot was effective, and, running up to him, were just in time to hear him utter his "Bismillah" (in the name of God), and to see him draw his knife to sever the throat of the fine animal.

Moto, while the juicy steaks were broiling over red coals, and the jaws of his companions were already hard at work, proposed that after the long march they should rest that day and strengthen themselves with meat; but Simba and Kalulu were for prosecuting the journey until they should get a sight of the Lake Liemba, and after hearing Kalulu's reasons Selim concurred in the proposition, though Abdullah and Niani sided with Moto, pleading their fatigue.

They rested until noon, however, and by this time Niani and Abdullah felt so strengthened with the meat they had eaten and digested, that they declared themselves strong enough to march a month longer, which statement was received with pleasure by all.

The same champaign spread out on either side of them as they continued their journey, as beautiful as when it first was revealed to them, and in the far distance they saw herds upon herds of buffalo, giraffe and antelope feasting on the rich grass.

Here and there, to vary the monotony, rose a clump of mimosa, or a tall tamarind, or a silk cotton tree, or a group of stately palmyra, adding grace and beauty to the picture, and now and then they passed a low thicket of brush and thorn.

Above, over their heads, soared the kite and the
bustard, the vulture and the hawk, searching with keen
eyes for prey, while the smaller birds made the groves
and the thickets and the lordly trees merry with their
chirping song.

There was such repose and tranquillity, and a feeling
of perfect security in the scene, that the Arab boys
wished it would last until it was replaced by the happier
scenes of Zanzibar. Poor youths! well they might wish
it, after the disagreeabilities of travel they had encountered in all shapes during their short stay in Africa.
But to make even this pleasant view one of horror, to
transform its peaceful aspect into one ominous and fatal
to them, it needed but fifty warriors of Ferodia to
make their appearance before them, and how quickly
were it all changed, and to make even the jungle and
treeless plain a paradise compared to it!

Kalulu ventured a remark that evening, as they were
comfortably collected around the camp-fire, that he did
not think such a beautiful and rich country could be
without inhabitants somewhere in the neighbourhood.
At least, said he, he had always found it so, and he
thought that on the morrow, or the next day, they
must see signs of cultivation and population, as they
must be rapidly nearing the lake.

The next morning, after they had journeyed a few
hours, Simba, who was in advance, cried out that he
saw a cornfield, which sent a momentary feeling of
terror into the minds of his younger companions; but,
habituating themselves to the sight of it, they became
reassured, as they remembered that Ferodia must be
far away, and that possibly the people had never heard

z

of a man who had made himself a bugbear to them by his ferocious disposition and cruel character.

In an hour or so, after skirting the cornfield, they came to a river, brown and deep, and about twenty yards wide, flowing towards the north, and while they were hugging the thick tall spear-grass which grew along the bank, Niani uttered a low cry, and pointed with his finger towards something that was hidden near the bank. Kalulu retraced his steps quickly to observe what had escaped his eyes, and he saw a canoe with four paddles in it!

He was not long in imparting the tidings, and the party drew together for a whispered consultation; but Moto advised strongly that they should not expose themselves, but that they should retreat at once into the first thicket, a piece of prudent counsel which was acted upon as soon as intimated.

They found, about two hundred yards away from the object of their surprise and concern, a suitable place in a dense bush, wherein they crouched down, after they had posted Niani to observe narrowly from the entrance for any suspicious object, for a discussion about their future movements.

" Who do you think these people are, Kalulu?" asked Simba.

The young chief answered that he thought the tribe was that of the Wa-liemba, and that the canoe belonged to a party of hunters from the village, who were out looking for game.

Moto then suggested that they should wait until near midnight and get into the canoe and float down the river. Simba and Kalulu concurred, and thought it would be a good thing, and an easy way of reaching the lake; but Selim and Abdullah strongly demurred to the proposition, as the act would be one of hostility against a tribe that so far had done nothing to them, besides being dishonest. Simba and Moto, however, aided by Kalulu, brought such powerful arguments to bear against the two Arab boys that they were silenced. They were, said they, escaping from a land where every man's hand was raised against them; where a small party like their own only invited attack from those who felt themselves strongest, against whom, however skilful they managed their movements, they could not expect to be always able to cope successfully. Prudence and safety suggested to them this means to avoid trouble and recapture, and if they did not avail themselves of this happy opportunity, they might, perhaps, in a few hours, be cursing their squeamishness and irresolution, while lamenting their fate in bonds more cruel than any they had undergone while in Ferodia's power. Before such considerations Selim and Abdullah submitted to the superior judgment and craft of Moto and Simba, and said no more, though to each other they regretted that such a step had to be taken.

Night came, without anything alarming having occurred, and Niani was called from his watch, and whatever they said among themselves until the hour of departure was said so low that no one could have heard their voices even had some straggler by accident been outside the bush.

CHAPTER XIII.

THE time to make a bold stroke towards regaining a country where they might meet friends came about three hours after darkness had fallen upon the earth. No sound had been heard to cause alarm: the bull-frogs growled inharmoniously among the wild spear-grass; the bull-crocodile woke the echoes with his hoarse roar; the black ibis had long ago hushed its harsh screams. It was surely time to be astir, for at this time of night peaceful Africans or weak parties seldom venture out of their villages.

They soon found the canoe, and without exchanging a word the men and boys cautiously got in, and Simba and Moto, each taking a paddle, drove the boat out until it reached the flood, and silently dipping their paddles in the water they guided their boat to the opposite side, and under the lee of the tall grass and mangrove trees impelled her along noiselessly.

They came abreast of the village, and they rested on their paddles; they passed it, and the work was resumed with caution. Once beyond the fields, Kalulu and Selim each took a paddle, and the increased muscle soon sent her swiftly gliding down. They were now passing through an uncultivated tract, and Simba exerted his giant strength, and Moto his sinew and muscle to the work, and the rapid progress they were making was seen by the swift flight of trees and branches and tall cane by them.

The stars, in bright galaxies and shiny myriads, lit their course, the river flow aided them, and the rapid rate at which they went exhilarated them. They were probably going down the river at the rate of five miles an hour, thus paddling with the current; nine hours of such work would put them out of reach of danger by morning, even should they be pursued; and provided they paddled on unseen by the natives no trace would be left behind by them.

This was a happy and expeditious way of travelling towards home, thought our people. The longest day's march was nothing compared to the number of miles that may be travelled down stream, for even should they rest awhile the friendly current still conveyed them down towards their destination. So, blessing your stars, and your fortune, glide on my heroes, glide down until morning!

The day dawned and revealed their surroundings, prominent hills, all crowned with tall trees, with slopes descending rapidly to the river's edge, a straight course before them; the current swifter; sometimes racing past the rocks with the speed of a rapid, and not a sign of cultivation about them anywhere. Cheered by the auspicious outlook they bent to their paddles with will and vigour.

Beyond the hill-country the river broadened and became sluggish in its flow; tall matete cane towered above them to the height of bamboo. This also was cheering, for except fishermen no tribe cares to live in such a sickly neighbourhood. After resting a short time and recruiting their strength with a breakfast of dried meat, they continued their course. Low, sandy islands rose in mid-stream, covered with reeds, on which lay, basking in the morning sun, several crocodiles, who rushed to their liquid homes at hearing the sound of the paddles, and on seeing the intruding canoe. On our friends rowed, past mangroves and groups of *Eschinomenæ*, which flung their random roots out in all directions; past sandy isles and patches of sandbars; through narrow channels, along which they raced, whither they knew not, whither they cared not, so they took them to the inland sea they were in search of.

At noon our party halted in the depths of a mangrove swamp, and went to sleep in the bottom of the canoe. In the dark night they woke thoroughly refreshed, and tasked their powers of digestion with some more beef, and then paddled out to the stream once more. Another night was passed under the beamy stars and dark blue sky, while mild breezes bathed their hot brows, and tall cane gently nodded their heads as a token of farewell, and the leaves sighed their regrets at the evanishing canoe. The water broke in wavelets against her side, and formed a foamy wake behind. The bull crocodile sonorously roared, and the bull hippo, at his banquet of tiger grass, uttered his deep base bellow, which strange noises the startled night caught up and pealed across the swampy fens and morasses, rousing the indignant and protesting frogs. Still silent sat the rowers, uttering no words, speechless as shadows; while the canoe cleft the murky-faced river, glided swiftly under the nodding reeds and sombrous mangrove, and halted not for frog or crocodile.

And morning came; and as the rising sun began to drive the mist of night away—lo! the lake at last! Liemba's lake! And the hitherto speechless rowers burst into a triumphant shout and an enraptured "Ah!" as they thought the goal was won.

Let each reader fancy to himself the expanding view of the silver grey waters of the lake; its miniature waves lifting their snowy crests as they felt the force of the gentle gale; the sun reflected a thousand times as, rising above the eastern horizon, it slanted over the heads of the joyous rowers and mirrored itself in the tiny waves and troughs. On the left, the lake-shore studded with many a hummock cone and blue hill, and between each the shadowy forest glades; and along the margin of the shore a strip of white sand, laved by whiter foam. And now the canoe is quite out of the river current, and points up the lake, with glorious scenery awaiting it on the right, brown rock mountains receding from the water's edge to lofty altitudes, while their slopes contiguous are enriched with tier upon tier of luxuriant and green mimosa, and tamarind of darker green. This was the prospect which greeted them after their venturesome flight with a canoe belonging to other people, after rowing over one hundred miles in twenty-five hours, down the river.

But they were not safe yet; their pursuers might be

behind them, and it behoved them to row far and long before they could be said to be quite out of danger. Selim and Kalulu were relieved by Abdullah and Niani, Simba and Moto were tireless.

They followed the right shore of the lake for over eight hours; but at the end of that time they drew in shore under the lee of an island situated in the middle of a snug picturesque bay, and hiding their boat deep among the reeds, disembarked at last on the island to shake each other by the hand, to enjoy in full the happy thoughts and the serenity of mind which the knowledge of their secured freedom had created within them.

"Ah, Kalulu, we are safe!" cried Selim in a transport of joy, as he drew the young chief to his side and sat down to rest with him.

"Yes, my brother, we are safe for the present; but Zanzibar is yet far, is it not?"

"Yes, about five months; but I think, after we reach Usowa we need fear nothing more. Moto tells me the people are kind to the Arabs. But say, is not this beautiful?" asked Selim.

"Yes; but let us go to the top of the island, whence we can see all around," said Kalulu; "and we can sleep in safety, and have the breeze to cool us much better than below here."

In a few minutes they had gained the highest point of the island, and sitting under the shade of a far-spreading mimosa, Selim, having taken at a glance the unusual beauties of the scene, proceeded to point them out to his companion one after another, saying:

"Follow me, Kalulu, and let me point out to thee

what I consider pretty. Look at the water of Liemba,
so beautiful, so clear, so deep; and, does it not shame
the sky with its blueness where it is deep? And look
at the shores dotted with the little hills! They stand
apart from each other, as if each was the abode of some
spirit. They also image themselves in the deep water,
as if they wished to see, as our vain women do, how
pretty they look. Are they not pretty? Seest thou
not how each hill is like a Kituta hut; but, unlike the
straw with which the Watuta thatch their houses, the
great Sky-spirit has thatched these with beautiful trees,
and sent the lake winds to make music among the
leaves and branches. And look between the hills,
Kalulu; follow the winding valleys with thine eyes,
until they rest where the valleys are lost in those grey
mountain folds. If thou wert close to any of those
valleys, thou wouldst hear the brooks sing and laugh
as they race over rock and pebble towards the deep
Liemba."

After a little while he continued, more seriously:
"The music of the trees and the music of the brooks
mingling together speak to us children of the Arabs of
the goodness of the Sky-spirit. If thine hearing was
fine enough, and we two were under those trees of the
valley yonder, thou wouldst be able to hear the voice of
my mind and heart sing in sympathy with the brook
and the trees; and just as my heart sings out of sympathy with their voices, so do the birds sing. Hast
thou never thought how pretty and sweet sound the
songs of birds, Kalulu? I have often, when in the
mangoe grove near my father's house, seated on a
carpet of young and tender grass, watched a little bird

coming with a graceful, easy flight, and listened to it singing as it flew. I have watched it turning its little head about so cunningly to see if I was there, and I have seen it looking for a comfortable twig to rest upon, and when it was satisfied I have heard it utter a wondrous melody, and this it seemed to do by simply opening its mouth and erecting its head, and I could not imitate it, try how I might. But though my voice failed, my heart joined with it in song; and if all the little singing birds sang together, my heart could sing as free, as clear as they.

"Hark, Kalulu! dost thou not hear the deep lake sing? No! I hear it, and understand its song. Look at the minute waves the zephyr rolls on the beach. Listen to the sound of them as they gather themselves up like long bales of white cloth, and rush to lave the sand. That is music to me, and while it sings I think of the deeper, sweeter music which the sea of Zanj makes at eve of day, which it made while my father and his kinsman sat near the foamy waves to watch the sun falling towards the sunset land. Wouldst thou believe it, dear Kalulu, the voices of those tiny waves sounding in my ear like the sighs of departing friends make me better and purer, more like a child of great Allah, the pure Sky-spirit, who made both thee and I, and all mankind. They make me better, because the gentle thought of love to all men fills my mind; they make me purer, because they draw me nearer to God. I have at this moment no hateful, unkind feeling towards any man. To even Ferodia I bear no ill-will. I forget—I have a wish to forget—what misery he caused me and mine. For what am I in the presence of Allah,

whom I see in yon great mountains of grey rock, in
yon boundless forests, in those far-reaching valleys, in
those tall hills, in those wavelets, in the deep, deep
water below us, and that immense roof of cloud and
vapour—so vast, so far above us, above which the golden
throne of Allah rests."

Kalulu had all this time been listening with wonder
to Selim, whom he regarded as talking magic; for the
truth was, that Selim's feelings were so wrought upon
by the beauty of the scene and the gratitude he felt for
his escape from the tribe whose canoe his companions
had taken that his face had assumed a beatified look,
which the more practical Kalulu could not comprehend,
unless he supposed he was talking magic. Magic powers
and gifts Kalulu could understand and appreciate
When he recovered his speech Kalulu said:

"Selim, my brother, thy voice kindles in me a wish
that I were born an Arab's son. Yet for all I have
listened to thee, I fail to see the beauty thou sayest
thou dost see. I fail also to hear the song or music of
the Sky-spirit, or of the brook, or of the trees, or of the
waves. But I am not one of the Arabs. I am of
Urori, and now a Mtuta and a king. I am the son of
Mostana, the Kirori king, whom Kisesa the Arab slew.
I have lived in the sunshine of Urori and Ututa. I
have seen the forests of both countries, and have roamed
over their plains. I have chased the antelope and the
buffalo, hunted the quagga and the giraffe. I have
searched for honey in the woods, and followed the honey-
bird wheresoever he led me. I have trapped wild birds
and guinea-fowl in the jungle. I have been in valleys,
and bathed in the streams that ran through them. I

have climbed steep rocks and high mountains, camped
on the hills many and many a night; but I never heard
music in any of these things.

"Music!" continued Kalulu. "What tribe loves
music better than the Warori and the Watuta. Our
mothers, seated under the shade of plantain or tamarind, sing us to sleep while we suck. They sing of
cornfields, of labour, of gliding down rivers, of war,
of great kings long since dead, and of festal days.
But they never sing of birds, or of the music of the
water. We never hear such music as thou dost hear.
Before we have barely learned to walk, our little feet
keep step to the sounding 'goma' (drum) of the village,
and our hands begin a-clapping with the chorus. When
we are great boys we drum and sing all day under the
shade, and at night during the large moon we often
continue the dance and song until the morning. Our
women, while they hoe in the field, sing; and while
they gather the sticks for the evening fire, or pound the
grain into flower, and while they cook for their lords,
they sing. The warriors sing always before they go
out on the hunt, before the battle, at the marriage, at
a death, and at a burial, they sing. They are ever
singing, and so am I when I may. I love to sing. But
none of our warriors ever said that waters sing, or that
trees, or leaves, or branches sing. Thou mightst as well
have told me that the cattle, when they low, sing; or
that kids when they bleat, or that the hyæna when he
growls, or that the jackal when he hungrily yelps, or
that the lion when he roars. Dost thou call the roar
of the mamba, or the bellow of the hippopotamus, or
the screaming cry of the quagga, or the shrill neigh of

the zebra, singing? Hast thou heard the furious bellow of the buffalo, or the rageful trumpet of the elephant when he charges, or the grunt of the wart-hog, cr the warning snort of the eland, or the noise of the rhinoceros when he plunges at his foe? Would the children of the Arabs say any of these sang? If thou sayest that birds when they chirp, the wind when it moans, the leaves when they rustle, or the waters when they splash and roll over the beach, do sing, then why not say that the noises of the animals are their songs?"

After a short breathing spell Kalulu continued :

"Ah! Selim, my brother, thy Sky-spirit and mine are not the same. Thine teaches thee nothing but lies. Lo! he is afraid to show himself, or perhaps, like the Watuta warriors, he loves to bask in the sun on his throne of gold; perhaps he loves his 'pombe' (beer) like our chiefs. If, as thou sayest, he lives above the clouds, it must be very hot above there, and great heat makes people lazy. Why does he not come down and show himself? Our Sky-spirit comes often to visit us. He is one day like a bird, with white wings; the next he is like a big raven. One day he is a roaring lion, another day he is like a leopard. The Mganga calls unto him with his medicine and gourd, and he either makes us strong in war, or gives us abundance of cloth, beads, and elephant teeth. He kills us, if he is angry, with a bad disease; sends strong tribes, and stirs their hearts against us, while he makes our hearts faint and our arms weak; but he never lies. When a good magic doctor asks him he always answers, and his words come to pass."

After another pause, Kalulu continued once more. " Thou sayest that thy Sky-spirit made thee and me, and

all men. Perhaps he did make thee and the Arabs, for
thou and they are white; but he did not make the
Warori or the Watuta. We are black, born of black
mothers, and sired by black fathers. Hast thou seen
the kidling by the side of its dam? or the young fawn
frisking by the side of its mother? Even as the kidling
and the young fawn came to this world, came the children of the Watuta and Warori. Thou didst tell me
once.that the good Arabs go when they die to a beautiful place called Paradise. Perhaps they do, for they are
white, and have been favoured by thy Sky-spirit. But
good or bad, Warori and Watuta, when they die, go to
the ground, into the deep grave, and there are no more
words from them, because they have no breath; they
are ended. That is what the magic doctors, and those
who know, have told me, and there is no untruth in
what I say."

"Oh! Kalulu, my brother, thou art now like those
who cannot see, because there is no light in their eyes,
or like those who do not hear, because their ears are
stopped. There is no doubt that God, the Sky-spirit,
made the sky like a curtain round about us, and that He
made the earth like a bed spread out for us to live in,
and, though thou art black, He made thee as well as He
made me. He made the birds, the trees, the rocks, the
valleys, and the hills; He hath caused the rain to fall
in its proper season, and all the fruits and corn of the
earth to grow for us, each in its own good time. There
is no lie in all this, it is truth as clear as yon mountains.
Thou art now like a child in the knowledge of these
things, but when thou wilt reach Zanzibar, and shall
have learnt our language, thou wilt know the truth of

what I speak. Thy mind is now like the troubled clouds of the morning, which are yet dark and gloomy, but through them all comes the sun, and the black clouds vanish before his bright glory; so will the darkness which now covers thy mind, and hides the light, for when thou canst talk, and understand what I say, the truth will shine through it all, and the darkness will be no more. Enough for the present; let us rest and sleep, that we may be ready for our journey tonight," and Selim lay down, and Kalulu, after trying in vain to penetrate the meaning of all his brother's words, and to see the promised light before the fulfilment of time, finally lay down, and forgot all about the wonderful Sky-spirit in a deep slumber.

They were wakened by Simba's voice, who stood like a colossal shadow-being of the spirit-land above them, for so his figure appeared to their half-dreamy senses. But a vigorous shake of both by his heavy hand soon dispelled the half-formed dreams, and informed them that it was night, and that their friend Simba was urging them to be up and away.

Lightly they descended the hill and stepped into their dear little canoe, and presently the isle of Mimosas, on which they had rested, was but a dim configuration of a low hill, and, receding still further, it became lost in the general gloom of night.

The canoe was far enough from shore not to be delayed by any fishing-boats; the deep water was all about them, and the lofty, far-upheaving, beaming heaven above them, with its countless myriads of ever-blinking lights, lighting them, poor wanderers, on their way.

Kalulu, to wile away the time and to cheer his

companions, struck up, in a low voice, the boat song of the Liemba, with the chorus

> " We are gliding,
> Swiftly gliding."

And, in the quicker, throb-like impulsion of the canoe which followed, Kalulu knew that the song and music had the desired effect on the crew.

Morning came again, and keen eyes searched the shore for habitations, but, assured that there were none, the crew advanced perceptibly nearer; and Simba, perceiving an opening between two low hills, advised that they should row for it, and try their hands on game, as provisions had run very low.

A happier place could not have been chosen, for all around was clear of cane and rank grass, which generally bordered the lake shore near the river mouths; and instead of this swampy vegetation rose a thin forest, in which there were numbers of fruit-trees, ripe black singwe—an oval fruit of the size of a plum, but which has a more piquant flavour than our plums—and yellow mbembu—a stone fruit, in shape like a small peach; but though I call it the forest peach from this likeness, its flesh breaks off like a pear's, even when ripest, but its taste is a mixture of the peach and the pear—to which our party rushed, like the half-starved creatures they were.

Having refreshed themselves with handfuls of the delicious fruit, Kalulu proposed that he and Selim should venture out in one direction, while Moto and Abdullah should go in another, to look for game; meantime Simba and Niani to look after the canoe. The proposition was agreeable to all.

Kalulu and Selim chose a north-east direction, Moto and Abdullah selected a south-east route.

The first couple, with whom we have most to deal, struck out boldly, Kalulu armed with his spear, and bow, and arrows, Selim with his English "Joe Manton," which had often before distinguished itself on many a hunting field. Thickets were passed by, as well as the thin forest, without meeting with a single head of game; but suddenly the thin forest gave way to a bit of park land, that is, an open country sprinkled with a few noble trees here and there, with its face slightly rolling, thus forming an agreeable prospect compared to what a flat ground would have furnished. In the distance, say at a hundred yards off from the thin forest they were about leaving, the two boys saw a herd of noble zebra engaged in play, in nibbling each other's necks, or, with ears drawn back, were playfully kicking at each other. Selim flung his rifle-barrel into the hollow of his left hand, and aimed at a perfectly regal animal, kingly in his pride and beauty, regal in shape and size, who, foremost of the herd, had seen the intruders, and who, with an erect head and noble mien, was engaged in surveying them.

Crack went the rifle, and the magnificent beast rolled on his side, while the herd, uttering their alarm and sorrow in shrill neighs, scampered off to a safer distance to scrutinize the intruders, who with merry laugh and light bounds hastened to secure their game.

The wounded zebra lay still, and Selim, thinking it dead, could not help laying down his rifle, quite forgetful of the Moslem's duty of severing its throat and

2 A

letting out the blood, to survey the beautiful beast. It was so beautiful he could not help going to it, and striding the back, taking hold of the mane, and saying to Kalulu:

"Ah, what a fine horse he would make! how I wish that such an animal as this would carry me to Zanzibar," and as he said this, while Selim was on his back imitating the movements of a rider, the zebra rose to his feet so quick that the boy had no time to throw himself off, and bounded after the herd with the swiftness of lightning.

Kalulu uttered a cry of horror; but, recovering quickly, he drew his bow and sent an arrow deep into the flanks of the fleeing animal.

This wound but spurred the furious and frightened beast, with his strange rider, to quicker speed. Kalulu heard the glad neighing of the zebra herd as they greeted the approach of their lord; he saw them surround him, then looking suspiciously at the rider; saw them, while furiously galloping over the park land, run at the boy with open mouth and drawn ears; saw them frantically kicking their heels about to the right and left; and, while his heart stood still with fear for his white brother's safety, he saw the herd, still chasing the ridden zebra, vanish in the forest beyond.

Then, waking from the stupor of fear and surprise, Kalulu noted the direction the herd had taken, he hastened back to the bivouac, where Simba and Niani sat waiting the return of the hunters, and breathlessly informed the astounded giant that Selim had galloped away on the back of a zebra into the forest, and urged him to take his gun and follow him; and, without

CARRIED OFF BY A ZEBRA.

waiting to see the effect of his words, he bounded off
again in pursuit of the flying herd.

Niani uttered a cry of sorrow, but Simba, after waiting a second to tell him not to stir from his concealment,
ran after Kalulu. Overtaking him, they both stood for
a moment under the tree where the zebra had lain
apparently dead. Kalulu pointed to the direction the
herd had taken, and without more words the two, Simba
and Kalulu, braced themselves for a run.

The soft ground showed the pursuers the traces of
the hoofs which had been fiercely struck deep into the
ground, as the flanking animals outside of the herd had
charged at the rider of their lord; at the base being
who had audaciously usurped a seat no living man had
a right to claim. The pursuers noted these things as
they ran, and could well have described the fury of the
herd, as they saw their noble king thus ignominiously
treated. What! they! free rovers of the virgin forest
and plain, the untamed creatures of the wilds, whose
gorgeous backs and splendid hides had never been defiled,
within the memory of the oldest zebra, by the bestrid-
ing limbs of any man, to see their noble lord insulted!
No wonder when such thoughts filled them, that their
eyes flashed and their crests bristled, and their flowing tails erected, and their hoofs struck deep with
frantic energy into the yielding turf. Then they
thought of what Selim's feelings must be, surrounded
thus by the indignant creatures, charging, and biting,
and kicking at him, eyes kindled with honest rage, as
they ranged around their monarch—their open nostrils
glowing like fire, and emitting their hot, steamy breath,

while he struck right and left, and shouted to fend them off.

On continued the pursuers, with increased speed, as they thought of the great danger their young friend was in, with their heads resting on their shoulders, and their faces cutting the tepid breeze, and their mouths wide open to inhale the air in short, quick draughts, for the lungs that rapidly exhausted it, with their hands fanning the wind, and their chests rising and subsiding with each breath they took, and the hips urging and impelling the lagging feet, which fain would have spurned the ground.

On, on, my brave, faithful friends! take no heed to yourselves; think not of your growing weariness, or of future pain. Let your livers ache, and the overtasked lungs feel exhausted! Let your heads throb, and your limbs be fatigued; your friend is in need! Be not discouraged. See the large clots of blood that stain the sheeny grass; the zebra monarch must yield to fate, despite his royal body-guard. His life wanes fast, as ye may note by the red blood which dyes the ground. On, on, my gallant souls! Speed on, my agile Kalulu! Confess no fatigue; for thou art a son of the forest, and rightly named after the swift-footed fawnling. On, on, my brave Simba! one effort more; let it not be said that a boy shamed thee! Ha! behold! What said I? Yonder lies your prize stretched on the ground! And see, here is Selim himself advancing towards ye! The Arab boy is then safe.

Simba and Kalulu were so tired after their long run, which had lasted an hour, that they were compelled to throw themselves on the ground, while the throbbing hearts beat wildly, and their lungs laboured hard and fast; but finally, though their heads yet ached with pain, they were tranquil enough to hear Selim's story, which was, in the main, described above, though when the zebra staggered and fell, Selim said that he leaped down, and ran behind a tree, while the herd, neighing shrilly, disappeared in the forest, and left their monarch alone to his fate.

After a short time Simba and Kalulu were so far recovered, as to be able to rise up to cut up some of the zebra that had given them so much trouble and anxiety; then, loaded with meat, they began to retrace their steps along the same road they had ran so fast in pursuit of him whom they now heard laughing as he told some points of the story.

At sunset they arrived at the tree whence the unequal race began, where they found Selim's rifle, which he had unwisely left on the ground, and proceeding to their bivouac, were all heartily welcomed by Moto and Abdullah, who had killed a young buffalo cow, whose generous meat was already cooking on the wooden platform we have in another chapter described.

They rested that night in the same spot, where they were so secure from molestation, to enjoy the abundance Nature had furnished them, and to relieve themselves from the strain the arduous labour of flight had imposed upon them the last few days.

Continuing their journey at sunrise, they hugged the shore, which they had thus a chance to observe more closely. They could see the waves of the surf break on the rocks at the foot of hills rising above them, or playfully toss themselves in wanton glee on the shingly or the sandy beach, their curling caps becoming white foam as they met resistance in the firm land; and at each hollow between the hills they could note the lazy rillets dribble through the tiny sandy furrows into the lake; or watch how the greater streams that continually discharged themselves by every avenue to the great lake, came sailing round the bends of their course from under the sunless gloom of embracing mangrove bough and cane; or look in wonder at the remarkably lofty matete, which they ever and anon passed, whose each stalk was furnished with many a rapier-like leaf, which rustled gently before the wind, and showed a sheen and glister which the finest silk they had ever seen could not rival; or glance with curious eyes at their stalks below, when they came in contact with the black earth that nourished such profuse vegetation, and see how, one after another, these receded to rayless shadow and all-pervading darkness, in which, however their ears detected the movements of busy feet, the quick pattering on the earth, the signals and low triumphant cries of the birds, which seek shelter and have their being in such gloomy recesses—from the sleek-looking diver to the active little kingfisher; from the crested crane, or the towering pelican, to the pretty white paddy-birds.

They passed many and many a bold cape and low-land, whereon grew wild plantains, whose broad fronds offered an impervious protection against the noonday heat, which nourished scores and scores of wild guinea-palms, and dark green tamarinds, and tall trees, too, from whose stems the natives excavate their canoes, and umbrageous sycamores and wide-spreading mimosa. All these headlands and lowlands, head-capes, and far in-reaching bays and creeks, where sported the hippopotami, and lazily floated the crocodile in his enormous length—yea, all were beautiful.

Then the lake contracted; the two shores came nearer, and a strong current carried them safely towards the north, and to a lake of still greater size and extent. They continued along the right shore of the lake, congratulating themselves that they were now in the sea of Ujiji. Now and then they passed villages, which they took good care to avoid, and at night they rested on the shore in the deepest recesses of a cane-brake, or on some lonely island far removed from any habitation; day after day they continued their journey unmolested; and each person of the party now came to think that Usowa would certainly be reached in safety.

But on the sixth day after they had entered the great lake a storm arose, accompanied by lightning and a great downpour of rain, and the furious waves arched their white crests, and were driven wilder and higher above their heads by the angry wind; while the canoe which had carried them so long became tossed about and pelted by the maddened water, until it seemed as if they must all perish. Simba and Moto manfully laboured at their paddles, and endeavoured to direct her head to the shore, but the strong wind laughed at their efforts, and blew her on before it, and the waves dashed their heads against it, and drove it on—now on their topmost crests, and now into the engulfing troughs which opened to receive it as it was precipitated down to them. The lightning played in all directions, the heavens seemed rent with the deafening thunder crash, and the rain poured like a deluge and while the wretched boys were compelled to bale the water with their hands, the wind and waves carried the half-submerged canoe where they listed. Thus through the mist, and fog, and blinding rain, while Simba and Moto continued to keep her before the wind, the canoe was being driven towards an inhabited portion of the shore. The rain ceased for a moment, and the mist cleared away, only to allow the crew in the canoe to see whither they were drifting, and to allow a number of people crowded under a temporary shed on the shore to see them.

"Who were these people?" thought the fear-stricken fugitives. "What would be their reception?" But they had no time to think more before they were in the surf, and a mighty wave came and struck the paddle from Simba's hand, and spun the canoe round broadside to a second wave which lifted it to an immense height, and dashed it upside down; while a third came on irresistibly, and sent it and its late crew far on the beach, stunned and bruised, where, before they could arise to their feet, they were pounced upon by the shore people, to be enslaved once more. Oh, misery!

The shore people turned out to be a nomadic tribe of Wazavila—or Wazavira, as the Arabs pronounce the name—who erect their huts anywhere between southern Unyamwezi and Liemba, from Usowa to the borders of Ututa. Had Simba and his companions been able to travel three days longer they might have reached friendly Usowa easily, but here, almost on the threshhold of the friendly region, they had fallen into the power of the disreputable Wazavila freebooters.

Simba struggled desperately, but neither he nor any of his companions had the slightest chance against the numbers that surrounded them. They were bound hand and foot, and carried under the roof of the shed, where the white bodies and straight hair of the Arabs elicited many a wondering comment, and provoked as much surprise as they had done amongst the Watuta when they were first captured.

The chief of these rovers was called Casema. His people, including women and children, numbered about three hundred. About four months before the period at which they are introduced to us by this capture of our unfortunate heroes, they had started from their home, Benzani, a district which lay somewhere north of the Rungwa River, and east of Usowa, to which they now intended to return, having secured such prizes.

Simba and Moto heard these remarks, as the chief consulted with his people about the plan of action, and felt convinced they need not despair, that the prospects of an escape eventually from these people were exceedingly bright if they were only prudent in their behaviour. They could govern themselves, but they were not so sure of the fiery young Kituta chief, Kalulu, who would probably before long commit some act of imprudence; nor were they quite sure of the indomitable young Arabs, who would be naturally inclined to despair at so many reverses; for Niani, poor little fellow! who was a slave by birth, they need fear nothing, as he could relapse at will into that state of frigid, stoical apathy a slave with no promising future before him so soon assumes.

The sky soon cleared up, the wind went down, and the waves abated, and the captors became more lively in their behaviour; but fearing that some aid might come to their captives in some shape by the lake, at sunset they broke camp, and started for the interior, but not before their miserable slaves had been tied together by the neck, with stout thongs of green hide.

The general direction they travelled was east, but the caravan filed by bends and curves so numerous, that it was with great difficulty Moto could settle in his mind in which direction they were going.

At midnight they bivouacked in the depth of a forest, and warriors were detailed to watch the captives, but the latter were so fatigued with the exertions of the day, that such precautions were needless. They had soon fallen asleep, despite the unpleasant thongs that encircled their necks, or the more unpleasant bonds which confined their hands behind them.

CHAPTER XIV.

The Slave Hunters meditate Another Attack—A True Picture of the
Slave Trade—The Inundated Plain—A Terrible Catastrophe—
The Joys of Liberty—Simba fights with a Leopard — Kalulu
sympathizes with wounded Simba—Kalulu shows Abdullah the
Art of making a Fire—Niani punishes the Dead Leopard—How
a Mtuta Chief fights—Kalulu victorious—Simba thinks Kalulu
a Hero—Spearing the Lepidosiren—How a True Son of the Forest
acts—What Kalulu found in the Arabs' Camp—Kalulu is kid-
napped !—A Victim of an Atrocious Deed.

The unfortunate captives were wakened rudely at sunrise by smart taps applied to them by the warriors
with the butts of their spears. Kalulu felt very much
like resenting this rough behaviour ; but Moto entreated
him, as he saw him raise his flashing eyes, not to urge
them to greater violence, as, whether he liked it or not,
he was compelled to bear it.

They were soon on the road, for savages and slaves
take but little time to make ready for their journey.
After they had marched a little while, Moto heard the
warriors nearest him talk of an attack Casema had
determined to make upon a village some time during
that night, as he had found out that most of the fighting men had gone south on a hunting expedition,
leaving only a few able men to guard it, while there
were numbers of women and children within. The
village belonged to an isolated tribe of the Northern
Wabemba, sometimes called Bobemba.

Towards the decline of day the Wazavila halted in

a thick grove; and as they would not permit the captives or their own people to kindle fires, all were compelled to eat the grains of Indian corn doled out to
them unroasted—a task which the stoutest jaws would
find excessively hard. In the meantime it was noticed
how the warriors sharpened their spears, and critically
examined the strings of their bows, and made other
preparations for war upon the defenceless village of the
Wabemba, which must have been near, else why all
their preparations?

About three hours after darkness, after leaving
twenty men to guard Kalulu and his companions, the
Wazavila, to the number of one hundred and fifty,
started to put their murderous purpose into effect.

Though Kalulu, Selim, and their friends listened
keenly for the sounds of the strife, they heard nothing;
but at the end of a couple of hours they saw a red
blaze over the tops of the trees to the south, and they
knew that the work of the devil was being enacted, or
that it had been consummated, and that fearful glare
of fire seen against the sky was only the final com-
pletion of the craven and wicked deed. About midnight the fiends returned with about two hundred and
fifty women and children, and a few old men, the
ablebodied having perished to a man, as they afterwards found out, in the defence of their homes. The
order to march was given, and through the pathless
jungle and forest the Wazavila urged their slaves with
spear, blade, and shaft, so they might be far out
of reach before the vengeful Wabemba came on their
trail.

The morning rose and found them still tramping on

in a direction considerably north of east, and showed the scene with all its horrors to the sympathizing Selim and Abdullah, though to Kalulu, Simba, and Moto such scenes were not new.

On this and the following days, for nearly a fortnight, the two Arab boys had this accursed evil of Africa brought vividly before their minds, and they saw to its fullest extent the immeasurable vastness of the sin and crime of which the Wazavila freebooters were guilty. They had wantonly attacked an unoffending village, and reduced to servitude and misery the poor people, whose homes had been fired, the flames of which had made the sombre night lurid with the red glare, and had exhausted themselves among smoking embers and the scorched bodies of the men who had lost their lives in disputing the advance of the Wazavila assassins and midnight robbers, who had stealthily entered this village to make the night hideous and awful with their crimes.

Step by step, through that pathless jungle and forest, which seemed interminable, did the poor people moisten the ground with their bloody sweat; step by step did they vent their miseries in hot tears, in groans, which were answered by vicious blows on their backs from their relentless captors. Each day saw an infant, which had been until then full of promise of lusty life, laid down by the side of the path cold and dead; for the mother, under the load of her miseries and privation, could not sustain the young life with her emptied breasts, and too often for detailed recital, she herself resignedly knelt and died by her starved offspring. Too often, alas! did the wretched mother, lacking proper sustenance, first fall dead in her tracks, with her little baby vainly sucking at the chilled breast, while a blank look of hopelessness stole over his little face as he wonderingly looked after the departing caravan, and trembled with an unexplained horror at the dread silence and loneliness of the forest. No mourner was left behind to bewail the fate of these hapless ones; only the moaning winds sang their monotonous requiems until the voracious hyæna and the hungry jackal came to consume that which had become as a blight and ugly spot on nature.

Nothing was better calculated to cure Selim and Abdullah of the desire of ever making money by buying and selling slaves than these scenes, even if the unutterable wretchedness of their own condition had not taught them the full meaning of the term "slave" before this.

Day by day every good feeling within them was shocked; for day by day new victims to human lust of gain were left cold and stretched in death along the road—old and young seemed to perish alike from the same cause — starvation and fatigue. Neither the patriarch nor the child was absolved from the dire fate.

About the fifteenth day they came to a populated plain, where the Wazavila, by the sale of two slaves, obtained sufficient food to distribute a week's rations to each man of the caravan; and in order that their human cattle might recuperate somewhat, they rested in the plain two days. The Wazavila had still nearly one hundred and seventy slaves, over eighty having perished since the night of the attack.

When they continued their march the direction which they took was nearly due north, as they were now about a hundred and forty miles due east of the Sea of Ujiji, the great lake in whose troubled waters Kalulu and his companions came so near to an untimely end. During nearly the whole march rain had fallen, and the plain through which they now traversed added by its marshy character to increase the fatigue of marching.

In two days the plain had sensibly declined to a lower level, and the water rushing from the higher ground had inundated the whole of that part of it they now traversed to the depth of about six inches; in some places it was still deeper. This portion of the plain the Wazavila told Moto was called Rikwa; and from general conversation that he heard, he knew that shortly they might expect to see a river called the Rungwa, which every year during the rainy season flooded its banks. It was for the purpose of giving their starved slaves strength to cross this terrible plain that the Wazavila had halted two days, as it required a long day's march to traverse the inundated part and to cross the river, on the other side of which was higher ground; while, had they been compelled to travel to the eastward, three days would not have sufficed to get over the swampy plain.

Moto communicated his opinions to Simba, declaring that he thought the time to try to make their escape had arrived. It would probably be night, or nearly so, by the time they would reach the river, and, in order to save their slaves from drowning, the Wazavila would be compelled to free them. Simba coincided with Moto, and they passed the word to their friends to hold themselves ready for any contingency that might arise.

What little strength the wearied women and children had gained by their two days' rest was soon exhausted in the passage of the Rikwa swamp. The quagmiry road, trodden into tenacious paste by the long file of human beings ahead, soon rendered travelling by those behind them a work of unconquerable difficulty, and some unfortunate woman or child was momentarily struggling for life in the muddy waste, never to rise again. And as the day rapidly passed away, and no signs of the river were yet seen, the anxiety of the Wazavila became evident. But a little after sunset, as the dying day was being rapidly exchanged for night, the head of the caravan arrived at the ford of the Rungwa, which river, as was expected, was emptying an immense volume of water to spread out and inundate the plain.

Two or three warriors cautiously ventured into the stream to ascertain its depth and force. As soon as they got in it was evident, by the effort they made to keep their feet, and by its depth, which rose up to the tops of their shoulders at times, that the crossing of the river would be attended with appalling loss of human life.

Our party were close to the bank when this experiment was made, watching it with intense interest, and as soon as the warriors had safely crossed, Moto asked a warrior to cut the bonds which bound his hands behind his back, that he might have a chance to save his life. As this was but fair, the warrior complied with his request, and released his hands, as well as those of his companions, and then generously severed the thongs which bound the party neck to neck.

Simba led the way into the water; and, being tall and strong, he took Selim by one hand, and Abdullah by the other, into the raging flood. Moto took Niani, Kalulu, lightly touching his lee shoulder, was able to avail himself of Moto as a breakwater, and at the same time assist him with Niani. When Simba reached the middle of the river the feet of both Arab boys were swept from under them, and the same happened to little Niani, while Kalulu could with difficulty keep his feet—so strong was the flood.

It was a long and anxious task, even for Simba and Moto; but they finally emerged on the bank in the darkness, and sat down, apparently worn out.

Closely following Simba's party were about twenty of the warriors, each leading a woman or a child by the hand; but the first of these warriors happened to be unfortunate, for the woman he led, feeling herself unable to resist the flood, uttered a terrible cry of alarm, and sprang forward, and, being swept against the almost submerged head of the warrior, carried him down with the rapid current. The warrior dived to release himself from the woman, and swam bravely for the shore—two of the warriors on the shore alongside of Simba's party running down the bank to assist their companions.

The cries and screams of the drowning woman threw the women and children then in the stream into a panic, and so confused the men leading and assisting them, that they staggered and allowed themselves to recede downwards, step by step, which soon took them

2 B

into deep water, and the men themselves had to begin struggling for their lives, while the poor women and children were carried down, far beyond aid, by the impetuous current, uttering their drowning cries, which were heard far above all, until they ceased to struggle, and were silenced by the watery grave they had found.

Casema's voice was heard commanding that every two warriors should lead a woman between them, and while the shouts and the screams of the terrified females announced that this course had begun to be tried, Simba nudged Moto as a sign to be ready, and to seize the bows and arrows of the two men who had gone down the bank, while he himself would snatch the spear of the warrior who was still standing by as a sentry over them. Moto conveyed the intimation to Kalulu and the other three to hold themselves ready, and hinted back to Simba to begin.

Quick as a lightning's flash, Simba rose, and snatching the spear on which the warrior leaned, lifted him high in the air, and tossed him head foremost into the river before he could utter a cry. Meantime, Moto had collected the three bows, and three quivers full of arrows; and each, taking hold of one another by the hand, ran from the bank before a single alarm could be given.

Our friends were far out on the plain before a chorus of shrill cries for help announced that another calamity had taken place at that awful ford; and were it only for being relieved from witnessing the many more calamities that must take place before all those living could reach the hither bank, they conceived that they had just cause to congratulate themselves.

Once clear out of sound of the disastrous ford, Moto suggested that they should strike to the north-west, lest, by going too far to the north, they might fall across more of the predatory Wazavila, a suggestion that Simba thought prudent and thoughtful.

Kalulu breathing free again, after his escape a second time from slavery, felt light as air, and was for the moment as happily disposed as he could well be, while Selim and Abdullah felt in their hearts an overflowing gratitude to Allah for his protection and deliverance from vile bondage, and breathed prayers to him to continue in his care of them.

Long before morning dawned, they felt that the character of the country was changed; for rounded shadows heaving upwards gave them an idea that hills were becoming frequent, and that these they saw were but the vanguard of some range they were approaching. The morning and its welcome light confirmed this opinion; for before them rose a majestic ridge of mountains, clothed from top to base with greenest verdure.

Prudence counselled them to seek the mountains by the most unlikely way, and they accordingly adopted the precaution, and were soon scaling a steep slope, overgrown with the feathery bamboo. From the eminence they attained, they turned their eyes to note the plain they had left, which was now spread out before them in one grand prospect, while it spoke or revealed nothing of the misery and sorrow which they knew existed in some part of it, among the human beings driven to hopeless bondage by the cruel Wazavila. Unable to dwell upon its false and treacherous beauty, they turned towards the mountains, which, so far, had nothing of the ominous or fatal in its features for them.

The sun seemed a long time coming out, they thought, as they looked towards the east; but then it was the rainy season throughout Central Africa, which had been heralded in by that awful storm on the sea of Ujiji, and out of which they had escaped to experience the privations of bondage; and the lowering mist and humid fog hovering over the crag-bound ridges above them was the result of the rains that had lately submerged the Rikwa Plain throughout its length and breadth.

About noon, after they had lost themselves in the deep folds of the mountains, our party rested to recover their strength, and to aid the recovery more rapidly by grinding some of their corn rations between their jaws. Simba thought this very dry eating, since they were free, and expressed a decided objection to remain much longer without meat, which, in his opinion, was the only food fit for a free man. Kalulu agreed with him in all he said, and volunteered to accompany any man in a search for game, which, he said, ought to be plentiful in such solitudes. Whereupon Simba agreed to accompany him; but since he did not know much about a bow, he would take his spear, which he could throw as well as any other man, while Kalulu could take a bow and his quiver of arrows.

Matters being thus arranged, Moto promised to be very good, and look after the boys, and see that they got into no mischief during the absence of Simba and Kalulu, upon which Simba thanked him, and bade him surely expect something within an hour.

Kalulu held three arrows in his left hand, and his bow in his right, and descending a deep ravine which opened shortly into a mountain valley of exquisite beauty, he was gratified to observe a solitary eland lying under a tree, with a splendid pendulous dew-lap, moving about as it erected its head to chew the cud and to enjoy in that solitude the sweet repast of grass it had lately eaten. Simba stood hid behind a tall tree, while Kalulu, master of the art he was now practising, began to move through the grass towards it with the ease of a snake. For a moment the young chief debated within himself when to send his arrow, but finally arrived at a conclusion; for he drew his bow, and drove an arrow behind the fore-shoulder, which, penetrating through, pierced the heart, and after one or two spasmodic bounds into the air, the eland stretched himself on the ground, dying.

Kalulu turned round to beckon to his companion, when he saw with surprise that Simba had broken his spear short, and, after stripping himself, had rolled his loin-cloth around his left hand, and raising his shortened spear, had put himself into an attitude of defence against something.

He at once bounded forward to assist his friend, when at the first step he took he saw a leopard spring upon Simba with a terrific cry. Uttering a cry of horror—but nothing daunted by the ferocity of the animal—he placed a barbed arrow on the string of his bow, and came up close to the combatants just as he witnessed Simba thrusting his left hand into the leopard's mouth, and driving his spear repeatedly into his side. The animal's claws were buried in the left hip and knees of Simba, which he was viciously tearing; but his jaws were rendered useless by thick folds of cloth which Simba had thrust into his mouth at the first onset of the brute. It was well that Simba was such a powerful man, else the shock of the onset would have knocked him down, when it would have become doubtful work to save his throat from the gleaming fangs.

Kalulu stayed only to take in these observations, and then stepped deliberately nearer, and drove an arrow through him; and without waiting to watch the results, drove another, and still another, while Simba drove his spear several times deep into his heart, and exerting his strength when he felt the claws relax, he brought his right leg forward, and turning the animal's back on it, pressed down his head with his left hand, and drew the sharp spear blade twice across the throat, almost severing the head. Then the animal, yielding to superior strength and weapons, fell off, shivered once or twice, and lay extended lifeless—dead.

Poor Simba was most grievously wounded; for the claws had penetrated deep into his hip, while the knee-bone was bare.

"Ah!" sighed he, as he heard the expressions of sympathy from his young friend, "if I had only some of that eland thou didst shoot, Kalulu, in me yesterday, to-day I should have bent that beast double, as easily as I would fold a piece of cloth. But grain-food! who can be strong after feeding on grain-food for sixteen days? Give grain to asses, but meat for men!"

"See here, Simba. Do thou rest thyself under this tree, while I go and bring our friends here. It is far

easier for them to come here than for us to carry the
eland to them. Thou mayest take my cloth to wrap
round thy wounds. I don't need cloth while thou art
thus." So saying, the generous, sympathizing youth
hastened to inform his friends of the accident that had
happened to Simba, which they received with surprise
and consternation.

Selim and Abdullah, who had been indebted so often
to the power that lay in Simba's arm, as soon as they
heard of the wounds which their champion had received, now hastened to him to offer their services.

"Speak, Simba! Oh! the frightful beast!" said
Selim, as his eye caught sight of the mangled and
gashed leopard. "Speak! art thou much hurt?"

Simba was reclining under the tree, looked slightly
troubled with his pains; the cloths he had taken to
staunch the blood were lying on the wounded hip and
knee, by no means pleasant to look at. The two boys,
seeing these things, judged immediately that Simba's
case was very grave—that he was going to die; and,
not knowing what else to do, they began to cry, to
sound the praises of their dear friend, and lament his
sudden " taking off."

Simba, however, answered them as quickly as he
could subdue a pang of pain, and command language.

"Nay, weep not, young masters. Simba is but
slightly wounded—flesh wounds—nothing more. No,
_o, Simba is not going to die; he must see his wife
and children, and Selim in his home again, before he
can die. But—Master Abdullah!"

"Yes, Simba, what is it?"

"Dost thou really like big Simba?"

"Oh, Simba, how canst thou ask? Thou hast succeeded my father Mohammed in my affections. Remember the Liemba and the crocodile. I can never forget that awful moment, for the scars on my leg remind me of it daily."

"I thought thou didst like Simba a little; but wouldst thou be very sorry if Simba died to be left in this valley to be eaten by the hyæna and the jackal, Abdullah?"

"Don't, don't, Simba, for Allah's sake, ask any such thing. Thou hast said thou art not going to die, then why torment me?"

"Yes; but I might die if Master Abdullah did not do me one favour, for——"

"Speak; command me, Simba—anything, everything," urged Abdullah.

"If Master Abdullah would only make a little fire, and Master Selim cut a little meat from that fine eland that lies dead by that tree yonder, Simba might eat meat and live."

"Thou shalt have meat, Simba," cried Abdullah, before thou canst count one hundred," and he bustled about, ran here and there; collected bunches of dry grass, leaves, twigs, sticks; brought a good-sized log or two of dead wood, between which a fire should be built; while Selim, after taking the spear which had probed the leopard's heart, had run towards the dead eland, and was slashing and carving great chunks of meat.

Abdullah had his pile of wood ready, but he now turned with a puzzled expression towards Simba, and said:

" Here is the wood ; but where and how can we get fire ? Our guns are in the bottom of the sea !"

Kalulu, Moto, and Niani had come up by this time, and Moto, after examining the wounds of his friend, turned round to Abdullah and said :

"Kalulu will help thee, Abdullah, to get fire ; he does not need a musket-pan or powder."

Abdullah was curious to know how, for he had always seen a musket-pan used, though he had wondered often when a slave with the Wazavila how the natives obtained a fire ; but he had never seen the process.

Kalulu, however, proceeded to show Abdullah how the Watuta obtained fire by other means than a musket-pan. Selecting a piece of stiff, dry bark, he placed it between his feet on the ground, and sprinkled it with a little sand, which he first rubbed dry and warm between the palms of his hands. He now chose the strongest arrow in his quiver, and, cutting off the feathers and the notch, he pared the end until it was level. Then gathering some dry leaves and grass straw on the sanded bark, rested the end of his arrow in the centre, and began to twirl the arrow round with the palms of his hands with a steady downward pressure. In a short time smoke was seen to issue, and, continuing the operation, two or three sparks of fire shot out among the straw and leaves, which, being blown, was soon nursed into flame.

" That is how the Watuta obtain their fire," said Kalulu to Abdullah, with an air of superiority, which the latter thought was quite pardonable, since Kalulu did really produce a fire on which meat might be cooked for the benefit of his friend Simba.

"O Selim! Selim! O Selim!" cried Kalulu, "haste hither with the meat."

Abdullah, in his impatience to see Simba's jaws at work, reiterated the cry, "O Selim! Selim! O Selim! come with the meat, come quick."

"Coming!" was the answer which that industrious young Arab gave, as he turned his face toward the group with a shoulder of eland meat on his back.

"Now, Niani, haste to get more. Think of poor Simba, thy father, suffering for want of it; there's a good boy, bring plenty," said Abdullah; while in the meantime Kalulu had chosen an arrow-blade, and with it was preparing the slender sticks to impale the meat when it would be cut into kabobs for broiling, and Moto had bound Simba's wounded knee with bandages made out of Kalulu's loin-cloth, and had staunched the blood that had been pouring from the wounded hips. Moto also set to work at erecting a shed, which might shelter the whole party, and made a luxurious bed of grass and leaves on to which his friend was assisted.

Kalulu then, while the meat was broiling, and the most pressing duties of the camp had been performed, turned to skin the leopard, whose hide, he thought, would make an admirable loin-covering for himself.

Simba, after he had managed to eat as much of the eland as any two ordinary men would have eaten, began to feel his strength returned to him, and said:

"Ah! there is nothing like meat for medicine, after all. It makes a man look kinder towards his fellows, and if he has his stomach full there is nought that he cannot bear. If I had always plenty of meat in me I would as soon fight a leopard every day as not; and if I had a good knife I would be willing to fight a lion rather than run away from him."

Such sentiments, noble and worthy of the great man who spoke them, met with hearty approbation from his repleted friends, and Moto was of the opinion that after a stomachful of good meat he might also, if hard pressed, do damage to either a leopard or a lion. Selim, following suit, suggested that he, being but a boy, ought to have his English gun in his hand before he could be expected to fight a lion or a leopard; while Abdullah and Niani gravely expressed their fears that if they met either of those beasts of prey they would think of climbing some tall tree before doing anything else.

Kalulu, after skinning the leopard, proceeded to spread the hide out on a piece of spongy sward for the sun to dry it, putting a number of small pegs around to stretch it. The leopard, being denuded of his splendid dress, was not so much an object of fear to little Niani as it had been; it was no more fearful than a skinned dog would have been, though the canine teeth still looked formidable. But knowing the injury it had caused Simba during life, he could not help seizing the broken spear-shaft, and belabouring the dead brute with it in a vicious manner, which no doubt the leopard would have resented, could he have felt the blows showered on him. Having taken his fill of this mild revenge, Niani seized it by the tail and dragged it far out of sight.

The valley wherein these adventures occurred would have been deemed by our friends exceedingly pretty at any other season, but almost every other moment the wind drifted great dense masses of rain-cloud across its face, which completely blurred its beauty, and added more volume to the streams that constantly poured down the slopes from above.

Safe, however, for the time under their shed, they could . contemplate their little annoyances with liberal philosophy, and could readily adapt themselves to the circumstances without great sacrifice of comfort.

Simba was too sore to move for two days, but on the third day they broke their miniature encampment, and continued their journey through the mountains in a direction nearly north-west.

Tropical mountains are always grand, but during the rainy season their grandeur is enhanced. Why? Because wherever you turn your eyes you see some pinnacle, or crag, or summit buried in the angry clouds, which are a dirty grey, and ragged at the edges, but are an impenetrable mass behind of inky blackness, as if the night had been gathered and compressed into an enormous black ball ready to be hurled upon the valleys and plains by some vengeful fury. These black balls of clouds, poised upon the topmost mountain, are a feature in Central Africa; they seem to stand a moment in their precarious position, when a furious wind, which flurries everything in its way, tears along with a mighty sound, reaches the monstrous ball, lifts it up a moment above the mountains, and then hurls it upon the quiet sunlit valleys with thunder-crash and lightning, and great floods of rain.

These were of daily, sometimes hourly, occurrence, while our travellers journeyed slowly to where they conceived friends might be found. Owing to Simba's wounds, their progress was necessarily slow, and this gave them ample opportunities to watch the phenomena we have described.

At the end of a week they were not forty miles from the Rungwa Plain, and at the termination of that period Simba declared he felt as strong and as well as ever, and the eighth day he led the way as formerly, and twenty-five miles were marched.

This day's journey brought the travellers to a long, straight, narrow valley, which was converted through alluvial deposits and vegetable mould of centuries into a quagmire of extraordinary profundity. On the opposite side of the oozy valley to that on which they stood, there was some cultivation, and in a circular jungle they descried a few huts, probably a village. On their side the ground rose up gradually to an ancient clearing, from which disused roads ramified in all directions, which were a sufficient evidence that at one time the country was well populated.

They were striking up one of these roads leading to the old clearing, called Tongoni in the language of Zanzibar, when an arrow whistled close to Simba's ear, followed by another and another.

Kalulu's trained ear detected the sound at once, and casting his eyes hastily around he saw a group of men wearing cloth round their loins, hidden in a thick bush; how many men he could not tell, nor did he wait to count them, but shouted to his friends :

"Up, up! Simba—Moto—up, my brother! up, Niani! run towards that peak beyond the clearing. I will follow you. I shall stop to bring these fellows out, and to show them how a Mtuta and a chief can fight."

"No," said Simba, "we will not go up without you. Come with us, Kalulu."

"Fear not for me, but think of the Arab boys and yourselves. They cannot catch me. Go on to the peak. Go, Selim, Abdullah; Kalulu begs of you."

"Let him be, Simba," said Moto; "Kalulu knows what he is about;" and without waiting to see whether Simba followed him, he snatched hold of Selim's hand and ran with him up the hill. Simba followed with Abdullah and Niani before him.

As soon as he saw his friends start off, Kalulu limped most painfully towards a tall tree that stood near him, and crawled as if he were grievously wounded behind it. But the minute he felt himself safe behind the tree, he fixed an arrow in his bow, while he held three others in his left hand.

Kalulu had not to wait a second before six men came from behind the bush and rushed towards his hiding-place, until they had come within about fifty yards from the tree, when they surrounded it, and one of them seeing him, hurled his spear at him. The spear fell short, about a yard from the feet of Kalulu, but the boy never made any sign of movement. Encouraged by his silence, another spear was hurled at him, which just missed his body, for it fell quivering at his side, not six inches from him. Then an assegai, or a long javelin came, and grazed the bark above his head, and still no answer, from which they surmised that he was wounded too much to make any reply; but immediately one of them, bolder than the rest, made a forward leap to advance towards him, Kalulu drew his bow and sent an arrow through his chest, and before the others could seek shelter again he had shot another through his side. Then, snatching the two spears and assegai which had been thrown at him, the young chief uttered the Kitutu war-cry and bounded, light as an antelope, through the thin jungle.

On seeing the lad run the others rose from their shelter and gave chase. On reaching the top of the rising ground, Kalulu threw himself behind a thick bush of thorn and waited, with eyes and ears on the alert, and fingers on his bow-string, until catching sight of the foremost he took a deliberate aim at him and pierced his throat with an arrow; and, before a sound could have been uttered by the dying man, he had fixed his arrow again and was aiming at a fourth, when the fellow turned about to run, but too late to escape the arrow which, following him, buried itself up to the feathers in his back.

Emerging from his hiding-place, he retraced his steps, deliberately took up the arms, the bows and arrows and spears of the two last he had slain, and seeing the two remaining in full flight, turned round, and sought his companions, who were anxiously waiting for him on the summit of the peak.

In a few moments he had come up with them, and they listened in wonder to his tale, how he had slain four of their enemies, to which his trophies bore ample testimony.

Simba began accusing himself of cowardice, and everything else that was bad, when the young chief stopped him, and said :

" Not so, Simba ; thou art big and a good target for an arrow ; but I am small and thin, and if there had been twenty I could, by being prudent, have escaped easily. None of these people like to come out to the open to fight, and so long as there was but one to fight they would never have chased anybody else; and by dodging through the bushes, shooting the most forward of them, I could have so thinned them that when they reached us on this peak they would not have been able to take us without losing many more men, and perhaps losing all. If we all had been together those fellows might have killed two or three of us, and whom could we have spared?—Selim? Abdullah? Niani? No, Simba; thou seest that I could not have acted otherwise."

"I saw that when you told us to go," said Moto. "Who of us knows much about arrows? Master Selim and Master Abdullah know nothing; Niani is too small even if he did know. Simba says he don't, and I am sure I know but very little compared to a man who all his life has shot with nothing else but his bow. Now, with a gun——"

"Ah, yes; if we had but three or four guns," sighed Simba, "thou wouldst not have been left alone, Kalulu."

"If I had only my English gun here now,—two barrels,—always true—not one of those men would have escaped," remarked Selim.

"But, my brother, surely only two have escaped as it is," replied Kalulu, laughing; "and they are too scared to trouble us any more, I think, though it is time for us to be off before others from the village on the other side of the valley come after us. Here is a spear for thee, Moto; and a spear also for thee, Simba. I will keep one spear, and Selim and Abdullah may keep the bows and arrows. We shall have something for Niani by-and-by, perhaps."

"I hope not," said Simba, "before we get amongst friends."

This feat of Kalulu's in killing four men raised him highly in Simba's estimation, and the consequence of it was that he came to pay great deference to him, far greater than he ever had paid to him before; for thus far, except that he showed himself capable of bearing great fatigue, could run well, was lithe and strong for his age, he had looked upon him as a boy merely. Now, however, as he turned to seek the deep woods, on the ridge leading from the peak to the low range of hills beyond, he furtively eyed him from head to foot, and then shook his head, muttering to himself.

"What is the matter, friend Simba," asked Kalulu, "that thou dost eye me so, and shake thy head?"

"Thou hast a quick eye, Kalulu; and it is as true as thy wrist and arm. I have been thinking," he said in a low voice, "that when thou art a few years older thou wilt be almost as strong as I am now, and that when thou returnest to thy country, Ferodia will be sorry for what he has done, for he will find thee a very lion in his way."

"Thou mayst well say that, Simba," said Moto. "The little boy who pinned my arm to the shield I held when Kisesa attacked his father's village, is improved wonderfully. Wallahi! if he kills four men now when he is but a boy, how many will he kill when he is a man. Ferodia will wish that he had never thought of being king."

"Wait, my friends, wait! Wait a few moons only; I

will show you what Kalulu can do. Killing four men is nothing. I have killed chiefs and many men in our wars, as Soltali said in his song. Ferodia shall see Kalulu's face again; but I do not think it will be as his slave."

"I wonder," said Moto, "what country this is; and what tribe did that village belong to. Hast thou any idea, Simba?"

"Not I; I never was here before."

"Dost thou know, I think those were Wazavila too. They are scattered everywhere about this country since they were driven from their own by Simba, son of Mkasiwa, of Unyanyembe. Ah! that chief is such another as thou art, Simba. A lion by name and a lion in war. He has been the only one able to punish these thieves of Wazavila.'

"In what direction is his country? dost thou know?" asked Simba.

"It ought to be north of where we are—two or three days yet. He is chief of a country called Kasera; but we ought to come to the Unyanyembe road, that goes from Usowa and Fipa, before we reach Kasera."

That night our friends camped near the base of a reddish range of mountains, by the side of a small stream, and in the morning they breasted the most feasible part of the range, and made their way with considerable difficulty through a tangle of bamboo, tiger grass, and thorn bush.

Emerging out of the depths of a stony ravine, they at last stood upon the topmost height of the red mountain range, the colour of which they perceived came from the vast quantities of hæmatite of iron, of which the mountains principally consisted.

By using their observation, they were also enabled to ascertain that this range was the watershed of the Rungwa River, for it ran so far east and west that no springs issuing into the plain of the Rungwa could rise further north of this range, for as far as they saw north the country trended north and west, while south of the range on which they stood the country trended west and south. Moto took this as a good sign of their approaching Unyamwezi, and raised the spirits of his friends considerably by delivering this as his opinion. He also advised that they should now bend their steps east of north.

After a very long march that day, they camped near a lengthy but shallow pool in a forest several leagues to the north-east of the red range. Kalulu thought that, from the numbers of birds about—of fish eagles, cranes, pelicans, hornbills, kingfishers, ducks, and curious geese armed with spurs on their wings, that there must be fish in the pool, and accordingly took his spear and stationed himself near it. In a very short time he saw a movement in the muddy water, and darting the spear straight for it, brought out of the slimy depths a specimen of the Lepidosiren, or a bearded mud-fish, weighing about ten or twelve pounds. His success was hailed with delight by his half-famished comrades, who, though they had bagged a small antelope since the eland, had been much stinted in their meat rations lately. Each member at once constituted himself a harpoonist ; but, excepting Simba and Moto, no luck met the efforts of the others, as they could never throw their spears straight downwards, the spear always swerving to one side when near the bottom, owing to the over-firm hold with which they held their spears. But the success of Kalulu, Simba, and Moto proved ample to furnish the entire party with sufficient for a good supper and breakfast.

They found the meat of the mud-fish very good, though very fat; but being half starved, their stomachs were not over delicate.

Continuing their march next day at sunrise, they came to a park-land, agreeably diversified with noble sycamores, and islets formed by dense growths of aloetic plants and thorn-bush; and about noon they came to a well-tramped road, which, after noticing its direction, Moto declared would take them to the Unyanyembe road.

Inspired by this news, which certainly, after all they had gone through, was well calculated to produce joyous emotions within them, they tramped along this road at a rapid rate, and visions of home, though still far away, came vividly to the minds of the Arab boys, and they unconsciously pictured their mothers looking out of the lattice-windows of their homes, ever-gazing towards the continent and ever-wondering where their absent boys were.

A couple of hours before sunset they arrived in a thin forest. They formed their camp, and surrounded it with brushwood to guard against beasts of prey, and proceeded to warm what fish they had left. It was such a very small morsel for hungry men that Kalulu proposed that he should sally out with his bow and endeavour to pick up something more. He was strongly

dissuaded not to go by Simba and Moto; even Selim
and Abdullah begged him to remain with them, as they
could well afford to be without more food until morning; but Kalulu laughed merrily, and told them not to
be alarmed, he could take good care of himself. Seeing
that he was determined, they said no more.

As Kalulu left the little camp, he threw out, for a last
remark, that they might expect him shortly back with
something fit to eat. He chose the road before him—
the road that his companions would have to take next
morning. He looked keenly to the right and the left,
searched every suspicious place, and allowed nothing to
escape him. The thin forest thinned once more to a
small plain sprinkled with dwarf ebony and a species
of blue gum-thorn. Numbers of ant-hills also dotted
the plain, whose grey tops presented a strong contrast
to the young grass of the plain. Beyond this loomed
a forest thickening again; it was but ten or twelve
minutes walking; success might meet him there, he
thought, and he proceeded towards it, arriving there
by smart walking a few minutes earlier than he anticipated.

He still marched on, hoping that something might
meet his eye which might be broiled over a comfortable
fire, and enliven the little society of wanderers with
whom he found himself; and thus arguing with himself,
he proceeded still further. Suddenly he saw smoke.
There is nothing specially dangerous in smoke, he
thought; but what smoke could this be in the forest?
There was no cultivation about, therefore it could not
be a village. What was it? Kalulu was a true son of
the forest—a true hunter; his instincts were on the

alert. The curious phenomenon of a smoke in the
forest during the rainy season must be explained.
What could it be?

He began to glide from tree to tree, from clump to
clump; now crouching behind a wart-hog's mound, that
that beast had raised above its burrow, then wriggling
along the grass like a snake, and presently leaping up
with the activity of a leopard, until he drew nearer to
the smoke, so near that he heard voices.

"Voices!" The very fact of a human voice being
heard in the forest, except his own, had something por-
tentous in it; for had not all voices lately been those of
enemies? He was ten times more cautious now; and
something like a half-regret for venturing hither came
into his mind. Why had he come so far at all? Why
had he not listened to his brother Selim and his friends,
who begged him not to go out?

He watched from behind the tree, and saw people;
men wearing cloth round their heads, long cloth clothes
leading down to their feet, like those (he heard from
Selim often) the Arabs used at Zanzibar. He listened;
and while trying to distinguish the language heard
words such as Selim, Abdullah, Simba, Moto, and Niani
used. The language was not of the interior of Africa
around Ututa, nor Uzivila, nor Uwemba, surely; and
these people going about the camp in white cloths and
long white clothes were not natives. He had never
heard of any natives wearing such clothes. They must
be Arabs! Did not Moto tell him that they were on
the Unyanyembe road, and that they might meet an
Arab caravan going to Fipa, or catch up an Arab
caravan going to Unyanyembe from Fipa. Of course

these were Arabs ; people of Simba, and people of Selim,
Moto, Abdullah, and Niani! They were his friends,
since he was a brother of Selim!

What should he do? Should he go back at once and
gladden the hearts of his friends with the good news?
Ah! the suggestion came near being acted upon; but
it was not, for immediately it was replaced by another,
" Why not go to them, make thyself known, and they
will be good to thee for Selim's sake ?"

Poor boy! Innocent youth! He judged all Arabs
to be good, like Selim and Abdullah, and he stopped
out of his hiding-place and walked deliberately to the
camp. He was soon seen, addressed, and invited to
come up to them.

" Hi, Ndgu! njo (Hello, my brother! come here.")

This was a fair beginning, to call him " my brother,"
the English reader will think. Not at all; it is an
ordinary hail to a stranger, in the same way that
" Rafiki," my friend, is. But Kalulu advanced, and
many men—probably thirty—hurried to meet him.
Three men, apparently chiefs of the party—but they
were not white, like Selim or Abdullah—were talking
together as he came up to them.

The oldest of them—marked with the small-pox, a
man with very small eyes—who had a light bamboo
cane in his hand, turned towards him, and asked him
who he was, where he came from, what he was doing in
the forest all alone, to which Kalulu answered as well as
he was able in broken Kisawhili—the coast language—
smiling all the time, and wishing he would testify some
pleasure at seeing him. The man turned round to his
companions, and talked with them rapidly a language

he did not understand, but it was horribly guttural. It was Arabic; and as the harsh words were heard Kalulu almost shuddered. The man with the stick pointed to Kalulu often, the others nodded, apparently agreeing with what the pock-marked, small-eyed chief said.

The chief Arab—he was not an Arab, but a half-caste, half-negro, half-Arab—sat down and pointed to Kalulu to seat himself by him. This, thought Kalulu, was friendly; and in pure guilelessness he asked him:

"Are ye Arabs?"

"Certainly. Mashallah! What did you take us for?" replied the chief.

"I don't know. I thought ye were Arabs, but I was not sure."

Then Kalulu looked round, more at home. In one corner of the camp he saw a large gang of slaves, chained and padlocked safe. No chance of running for any of those, he thought. Simba could not break that chain, nor any of the strong iron padlocks which confined each collar.

He was about to ask another question, when, without warning, without the least suspicion having been raised in his mind, he was pounced upon by half-a-dozen men from behind and disarmed. The slave-gang was brought up close to him, an iron collar was handed to the chief, who encircled the young neck of Kalulu with it, slipped an iron loop over the folding crescents, introduced a strong padlock into a staple after it, locked it, and then stood up to survey his captive. He nodded to the men who had hold of him. They released him, and the boy stood up, and the captor and captive looked at each other.

"Did ye not tell me ye were Arabs?"

"We are Arabs," answered the chief, laughing at his simplicity.

"Then if ye are Arabs, what does this violence mean?"

"It means you are my slave."

"Slave! I a slave?"

"Certainly, and worth over fifty dollars at Zanzibar."

"I a slave! Do you know Selim?"

"Selim? What Selim? I know plenty of Selims."

"My Selim. Only my Selim. A white Arab boy, of my size?"

"What of him?"

"He is my brother."

"Your brother! A white Arab boy your brother. Dog of a pagan!"

"The blood ceremony was entered into between us. I am the King of the Watuta."

"You a king of the Watuta! Ha! ha! ha! We have plenty of kings with us. Do you see that woman before you? She is a queen in Uwemba. Kings sell well. If you were king of all the devils, and brother to all the Arab Selims, you are my slave now, and the likeliest, best looking I ever had. I will not part with you under one hundred dollars. Wallahi! There, go. Men, take them away. Strike camp. Ho for the sofari" (journey.)

"But listen, chief, I am not your slave. Let me go. Simba and Selim will be angry with you if you keep me. Let me go, chief. Oh! let me go to the camp; it is right close here."

"Silence! No words, not one word. You are my

slave.   Arabs know how to keep slaves.   For the bad
slaves there is a yoke-tree, besides chains.   Be wise,
and keep silence.   You shall go to Zanzibar with that
chain around your neck; if you are bad, you shall go
with the yoke tree around your neck.   For those slaves
who talk too much we have sticks.   Be wise, I tell you.
Drive the gang on, men."

Kalulu was desperate; the blood rushed to his head;
he got furious.   His senses and feelings were one wild
riot.   He could not describe how or why he leaped
with frantic energy at the villain.   He was possessed
with fury.   He therefore struck at him, caught hold of
him, tried to beat his brains out with his chain, and
would have done it, no doubt, or so bruised his features
that they would have become undistinguishable; but
he now had to deal with clever men, who knew what
the spasmodic, despairing energy of slaves newly captured was.   Before he had given the man more than
three blows he was dragged off, kicked, pounded, cuffed,
bruised, and almost strangled.   Then a systematic
flogging took place; such a flogging that a villanous
half-caste, enraged, would be likely to give, while he
fought with all his might, and gave half-a-dozen of
them work enough to hold him.   When the punishment was over, he was not left to meditate upon his
position, but was marched off in the direction of
Unyanyembe, the last of the slave gang !

The Arabs were about making what they call a " tiri-
kesa "—that is, an evening journey—in order to reach
water before noon next day, by which time they would
probably have made a march of thirty miles.   They
had camped deep in the woods, about half a mile from

the road. Had it not been for the smoke of their fires,
Kalulu would never have seen them, probably. When
once their fires went out it would be difficult for anybody to know that a slave-gang had been there, or that
such a cruel deed as the kidnapping of Kalulu had ever
taken place. If the Arabs but continued their journey
until noon, and started again at night, and left no trace
behind, how would it be possible for those who would
seek Kalulu to find a trace of him?

What a change of feeling came over the outraged
youth! What a sudden and complete transformation
was this! He left a camp of Arabs to enter another.
In one, he was beloved, esteemed, idolised; in the other,
he was a slave, beaten like a dog, chained! In one
camp the Arabs were good, kind, brotherly; in the
other, they were robbers, kidnappers, enslavers, villains.
In one camp he esteemed, he admired, he loved; in
another, he brooded over his injuries, and he hated with
all the hate with which one wronged is able to hate.

If he was treated so harshly at the beginning of his
slavery; if he was the victim of such damnable atro-
city as that which he had suffered, by what rule or
system could be measured that which he would have to
suffer before he reached Zanzibar; and at Zanzibar, with
that iron collar perpetually about his neck, how could he
ever advantage himself? Wou'd there ever be an end
to the indescribable misery he suffered now? Had he
parted for ever from freedom and friendship? Would
there ever be hope for him more?

These were the thoughts that filled his mind as he
was marched off to slavery with that inflexible iron
collar about his neck, and the horrid chain swinging

from one side to the other, with that long file of slaves before him, and the long file of flinty kidnappers behind him.

Ah! poor Kalulu! Thou art but one of the thousands upon thousands of wretched men, women, and children who have trodden that road to its present hardness and smoothness; whose wild delirious thoughts have never found speech as thine have; whose hopeless looks have never been portrayed in any book; whose silent prayers have never seen the light, nor have been rehearsed in any hall where kind Christian men and women would hear them and commiserate their sufferings; whose indescribable agonies have never been touched upon by a kindly pen! But go thou on to slavery, as the thousands who have gone before thee, until English readers shall meet with thee again!

CHAPTER XV.

The alarm of Kalulu's friends—The search for Kalulu—O Kalulu,
Kalulu!—Shall we never more see Kalulu?—Only trees, trees,
trees—Kalulu is Lost!—The march to Unyanyembe—Why come
ye in this guise, children?—Among friends at last!—Selim and
Abdullah in Arab Costume—The Lion Lord's City—Home again!
—Selim embraces his Mother—Kalulu discovered!—The Slave
Market. How much for Kalulu?—Kalulu restored to his Friends
—Kalulu introduced to Abdullah's Mother—My Kalulu!

RETURNING to the camp of our friends, we find the sun
has set, and darkness is settling fast over the earth.
Simba stands at the gate of the camp with an anxious
face, for his young friend Kalulu has not yet returned.
Moto, Selim, and Abdullah are just within waiting,
and listening eagerly for the slightest sound of footsteps.

" What can be the matter with the boy?   Dost thou
think he could get lost, Moto?" asked Simba.

" No; Kalulu could not lose himself if he tried.   He
has slain something, and is coming with a heavy load
of meat, so as not to make two journeys.   It takes the
like of Kalulu to know how to kill game."

" I wish he had not gone away," said Selim, " because it would be a pity if he came to harm when we
are so close to friends."

" What harm can happen to him about here, except
from a lion or a leopard?   But if he met either beast
I would set Kalulu against him.   There are plenty of

trees about here for him to climb up, and I should like to see the monkey that would excel him in climbing," said Moto.

Still the night grew deeper and deeper, and the anxiety of the friends increased.

"What road did he take; dost thou know, Moto?" asked Simba.

"I think he took the Unyanyembe road; but he may have gone after something in the forest. If he saw any game he would not be likely to remain in the road. He would go after it, of course," replied Moto.

"Well, I am going to look for him. Wilt thou come? The boys can keep a good fire up to let us know where the camp is," said Simba.

"What a soft fellow thou art, Simba! Dost thou not know that in the night we can do nothing to hunt him up, when he may be anywhere but in the place where we are looking for him? If we had a gun we might signal him; but by going out in this darkness we would only tire ourselves to no purpose. If Kalulu has been taken too far away by following an antelope or something else, the boy has a thousand ways of passing the night. He could sleep in a tree bough, in a hollow tree, or in the burrow of a wild boar, just as well as he could sleep in the camp. I am no hunter like Kalulu, yet I could do it, for I have been lost many times in the woods. What we must do, is to sleep in the camp to-night, and the first thing at daybreak we two shall go different roads, and wake all the country round with our cries."

"Thou art wiser than I am, Moto, yet it is very

hard. If any harm comes to him, I shall always accuse myself for a poor silly fellow who did not know how to take care of a boy. I am sorry I did not stop him, for something tells me harm has come to him. I would I knew where he was. I would soon see whether a good friend at his back could help him or not. We shall rest here until daybreak, and may Allah grant that we find him!"

"Amen, and amen," responded the Arab boys fervently.

At break of day Simba woke his friends. He had not slept a wink, though he had lain down. With a heart that had palpitated violently at every sound, he had lain listening acutely to every noise that broke the silence. It might have been a light-footed antelope, or the rustling of a fan palm, or the fall of a branch, or the shuffling feet of a hyæna, yet each of these, as he heard it, had inspired a momentary hope that it was the footstep of the returning Kalulu.

Simba was impatient to be off and to use his strong lungs; and when the sun was up, he was brusque in speech to Moto, when he said:

"Come, man, art thou never going to stir? Let us be off. Which way wilt thou take, south or north?"

"Oh, any road will do for me; do thou take the south, I will walk towards the north, and let each of us strike towards the east. We must be back by noon, for if Kalulu is not here by then, and neither of us have found him, then he is——"

"What, Moto?" said Selim, now really alarmed. "Oh, do not say he is lost! We must find him. We

cannot give him up. I will go along the Unyanyembe
road as far as I can, and return here by noon."

"Young master," said Simba, "don't go away from
this camp, I beg of thee. To lose Kalulu is as much as
I can bear; but if thou art lost too, then may all the
bad things of this earth happen to me, I do not care
how soon."

"But, dear good Simba, it is now day. I cannot be
lost, for I will not leave the road. Whilst thou and Moto
go north and south, I will take the eastern road, and
after going two hours on the road, I shall return along
the road to the camp. Who knows what has happened
to my brother Kalulu? He may be wounded, and I
may find him waiting for us. He has done enough for
me; I ought to risk something on my part for him. I
shall go, Simba—there. Abdullah and Niani shall stay
in the camp to watch."

"Well, well, as thou wilt. Thou art master here,
and wherever I be. Come, Moto, let us be off."

"Now, Simba," said Selim, running up to him,
"thou art angry with me. Seest thou not it is but my
duty to search for him? Is it nothing, what Kalulu
has done for me all these months? Be good, Simba, as
thou hast always been to me. Let me go without
feeling that thou art offended with me."

"Nay, go, my young master, and Allah go with thee.
Simba knows not much about Allah; but Simba, while
he looks for Kalulu, will pray to him to be kind to
thee, and look after thy safety. Come, Moto, let
us go."

"God be with thee, Simba, and with thee, Moto,"
cried Selim, as he turned to depart.

"And with thee also," replied Simba and Moto, as they strode off in their several directions.

Soon Abdullah and Niani, left alone in the camp, heard the shouts at intervals of each of their friends as they wandered off,—

"Kalulu! O Kalu—lu! Ka—luuu—luu!" was the cry they heard repeated until the sounds were lost by distance.

Selim strode on, uttering the name of his lost friend over and over. He made the thin forest ring with its liquid sounds until he fancied that every tree lent its aid to cry out the sweet name.

"O Kalulu — Kalulu — Ka — luu — luu — u!" was uttered on the desolate plain among the dwarf ebony and blue gum. The thick forest beyond was reached, and here again the stunted woods re-echoed to the name of "Kalulu." There was no reply. There was not the slightest trace of any Kalulu in the grim solitude. The forest was as calm and silent as though no one had ever ventured within its gloom since it grew. He looked down on the road; the road was smooth and compact, though now and then he thought he saw traces of human toes; but there were so many of them, one person could never have made so many marks with the toes of his feet. Was it not the road on which caravans journeyed to Unyanyembe?

After he had gone many miles through the forest, Selim began to retrace his steps towards the camp, but still shouting the beloved name of "Kalulu;" but there was no reply to it, and sorrow, alarm, and gloom settled down on his heart, and in this state he reached

2 D

the camp, a little before noon, to wait the arrival of Simba and Moto.

His friends soon returned, as unsuccessful as he, without having seen the slightest trace of him whom they now began to lament as a lost friend.

The sorrows of Kalulu's friends were deep. Selim wept copious tears, and all his imagination could not lighten the gloom he felt over the fate of his friend and adopted brother, who had been so good to him; no fancy could alleviate for one instant the overwhelming misery that the unexplained absence of Kalulu now caused. Continually he asked himself what could have befallen him, but all in vain. He had gone away in the full vigour of his youth; his lithe, slender, but sinewy form seemed so indurated and so protected against all mischances by the clever head to plan, the muscular arm to execute, and the clean-shaped limbs and swift feet to run, that he appeared invulnerable. And he had gone away smiling, but since then there was no clue, and his imagination and fancy were paralysed.

Selim turned to Moto, and asked:

"Oh, if thou canst give me the slightest hope that I shall see Kalulu again, I will bless thee?"

"I can't think of anything. A lion may have followed him and sprang on him, and carried him away bodily—though it is unlikely. A buffalo may have gored him, and left him dead. Savage men may have found him and made him a captive; though as this is a 'polini' (a wilderness) I don't see how men could be here. Thou knowest what he has done already, how quick and cunning he was with his arm and feet. He was a true son of the forest ; and if danger and death overtook him, it must have been very sudden."

" What dost thou think, Simba ?" asked Selim.

" I can't think of anything, young master, except that he is not here, and we don't know what has become of the brave young chief without whose aid none of us would have been so far on our way home ;" and the generous-hearted man wept aloud, and his weeping had a sad effect on all.

" And shall we see—never more see Kalulu?" sobbed Abdullah ; " never more see him who saved me from the jaws of the monster in the Liemba, who freed us from bondage, who was our friend and brother, who has been everything to us, the kindest, best, the noblest Pagan child that ever breathed ?"

" He who saved me from death in the forest, who made me his brother, and stood by me through many troubles—who on my account threatened Ferodia, and from that lost his kingdom—with whom I have roamed through plain and forest, and have talked so often with as a brother—the dearest and best brother I can ever have !" cried Selim.

" Stay, young masters, do not give way to such tears. Kalulu may not be lost. He may return to the camp this afternoon. I am going out now to look for him again, and to see if I cannot get something for us to eat," cried Moto. " Meantime, hope ; stranger things than his return have happened."

The boys and Simba looked their gratitude, as, next to Kalulu, they knew that Moto was the best woodsman of the party. Moto strode off in the direction of the Unyanyembe road.

At night he returned, bringing on his back a fat young antelope, and news which made all start.

Said he, while he and Simba turned to prepare some of the meat: "I went along the same road that master Selim went this morning. I crossed a 'mbuga' (small plain), and came to a thick forest. Soon after entering the wood I saw on the left-hand side of the road a yellow heap of earth which a wild boar had made above his burrow. I went up to it, and what do ye think I saw?—the marks of two feet of a boy. They were small and narrow, not broad and large, like a man's foot — Simba's or mine—would be. They must have been Kalulu's. He had jumped on that yellow mound, for the toes had sunk deeper in than the heels. I went on, where the leaves had been disturbed, but all marks were soon lost. However, I went further on in that direction, and in about half an hour I came to a camp, not fenced round, but where fires had been kindled. The ashes below the surface were slightly warm. If Kalulu is anywhere, I feel sure that Kalulu is with those people. But who are those people? Are they Waruga-ruga (bandits)? Are they Wanyam-wezi? Are they natives? Are they Arabs? This is a 'polini' (wilderness); there is no village near here. Where have those people gone to?"

"Let us go on, then, and find out; let us follow this road until we come to some village where we can ask?" said Simba.

"Yes, yes," said Selim, let us go."

"I am ready now," said Abdullah.

"Wait, young master, and thou, Simba. Eat first

as much as ye can, then we can go," said Moto, in the tone of one who knew what he was about.

In an hour a full meal had been despatched, and about an hour before sunset they started towards Unyanyembe; but before they reached the camp which had excited Moto's attention it was dark, and prudence insisted on them stopping there.

All kinds of suggestions were made as to Kalulu's fate, and they fondly called up, by retrospective glances at the past few months, all they knew concerning Kalulu, all he had done, his amiability, his kindness of heart, and the generous character of the young chief, until each sighed for morning.

There was but little sleep that night, and the next morning they were early afoot on the road. The narrow path which they trod led to Unyanyembe, and had been tramped to hardness and compactness. It ran around bushes; sometimes it went straight ahead; then it made great curves like a lengthy brown serpent. There seemed no end to the road or to the forest. It was ever woods, woods, woods, in their front—woods to the right of them, woods to the left of them, woods behind them, and not a sign of cultivation or of population anywhere. Only trees, trees, trees. Trees of all kinds—the candelabra kolqual, the prickly cactus, spear-leafed aloes, thorn bushes, gummy woods, silk-cotton trees, sycamores, mimosa, plane, or the silvery chenar, tamarinds, wild fruit-trees, but no fields or villages.

Darkness coming on at fall of day, they sought a place to make their camp.

Another day dawned, and again they were on the

road; the forest thinned into park-land—the park-land gave place to a sterile bit of chalky-coloured plain —the plain was succeeded by a thin forest—the thin forest by a jungle—the jungle by a plain again, and still there was no sign of living man or of men. They seemed to be the only inhabitants living in the world. Yet the road still ran before them in serpentine curves and long, straight stretches.

At night they rested again near a broad river. They were eking out their meat as much as they could, and at dawn they continued their march. At noon they saw fields of young corn, and beyond the yellow tops a village, and when they came to it they saw natives standing outside the gate.

"Ho, my brothers, health to ye!" cried Moto.

"Health, health to ye!" was the response.

"What country is this?"

"Manyara."

"Manyara!" cried Moto, astonished.

"Yes, and Ma-Manyara is king."

"Why, then, Unyanyembe is not far from here?"

"About nine days off."

"Was not that the Gombe River we passed?"

"Yes, if you came from Ukonongo along the road."

"We did. We have been hunting, and have had a misfortune on the road. We are going to Unyanyembe. What news?"

"Ah! Good news. Manwa Para is dead."

"Dead, is he? Have ye seen a caravan lately going by here towards Unyanyembe?"

"No--none for many days."

"Health, health to ye, my friends!"

"Health, health!" was the response.

Our friends strode on until they got beyond the cultivation and were deep in the forest again, when Moto turned round and said:

"Kalulu is lost!"

"Lost! Oh, Moto! must we give him up for ever?" asked Selim.

"I fear so. I thought that caravan belonged to Arabs. If they were Arabs they would have come this way, and those people at the gate would have seen them. But I think now that camp belonged to the Waruga-ruga (bandits). And where have they gone to? Are they from Ugala or Ukonongo? Were those people Wazavila or wild Wanyamwezi? They were not Arabs, or they would have come this way. We are too far away to go back, and we might hunt for Kalulu years and years among the tribes about here without finding him. The bandits kill all men as soon as they catch them, if they cannot make slaves of them. They are never seen. They are everywhere, but nowhere when ye desire to see them. No; Kalulu is lost, and unless we want to lose ourselves, we must go on to Unyanyembe."

This was a sudden shock to the Arab boys and to Simba. They had nourished a lively hope that their friend might be found, but they were now sternly told that their friend was "lost."

"Poor Kalulu!" said Selim. "He is not lost to me. I will build him up—from his feet to his head, with all his fine high courage, quick, generous temper, and his warm heart, in my memory, where he shall dwell as the noblest and best I have ever met. Until I die

I shall remember him as the truest friend and kindest brother."

"And so shall I, Selim," said Abdullah. "Thou and I shall often talk of him as one to whom there was no equal in worth. When we meet our mothers, we shall remember his name as one without whom they never would have seen us again, and our mothers shall bless him. His memory shall be to me like a plant nightly watered by the dew of heaven, never to die, and whenever I hear his name mentioned I will pray that I may be like him. For Kalulu's sake, all black people who call me master shall be well treated, and shall never be abused." As he said these words, little Abdullah wept copiously, as the worth of his friend rose so vividly before him.

"And I make a vow," said Selim, "for my brother's sake, never to purchase a slave for my service while I live; and when I die my slaves shall all be free. No black man in my service shall have cause to regret that I met with Kalulu in Africa; but they shall rejoice, and know that their treatment is due to Kalulu alone, that they may sing his praises under my palms and mangoes."

"Allah be with ye both!" cried Simba. "If all Arabs were like ye, the Arab name would become beloved throughout all the tribes of the Washensi." *

"Ay, so it would," said Moto; "so it would; and the people of our race and colour would not be bought like sheep and goats, and driven with sticks to the market to be sold. A great wrong is done by the Arabs every day in this country, and it is no wonder

* Pagans.

that the tribes treat them badly when they can. Tifum treated Masters Selim and Abdullah cruelly, because he heard that they did the same to the black people. We, thou, and I, Simba, should not have been so good as we are had any other than Sheikh Amer bin Osman been our master."

" I believe thee, Moto," replied Simba. " We would not be going back to Zanzibar either, if noble Amer's son was other than he is. Master Selim is the best Arab living. Prince Madjid's sons are worthless, compared to my young master. But let us go to Unyanyembe, before some evil overtakes Selim and Abdullah, and we have no hope of pleasure left to us more."

Moto started at the suggestion of evil to his young master, and at once put his best foot forward, until they came to a plain, where he strove to obtain an additional supply of meat, and was so successful with his arrows, that he brought down a zebra.

The march to Unyanyembe lasted fifteen days longer, owing to the lack of the cheery presence of Kalulu, and to the frequent stoppages they had to make to procure food, and to nourish their strength ; but on the morning of the sixteenth day, the well-known features of the hills around the Arab settlements greeted the eyes of Moto and Simba, who had seen them before. To their left rose the table hill of Zimbili, at their base were the Arab houses of Maroro, and stretching nearer to them, was the fertile basin of Kwihara ; and soon rose before them the Arab houses of Sayd bin Salim, Abdullah bin Sayd, Sheikh Nasib, and of the redoubtable Kisesa. But passing by these, and walking rapidly along a road which led through Kisiwari, and between two hills which separate Kwihara from the larger settlement of the Arabs, the great tembes of Tabora greeted them, each surrounded by plantains and pomegranate trees.

Upon asking some of the people who were passing from Tabora to Kwihara—and who stared at Selim and Abdullah as if they had never seen Arabs before—who lived at Tabora, they were given a long list of names, and among these was the name of Sultan bin Ali!

"Where does he live?" asked Selim.

"Yonder, by that big tree. The first tembe ye come to."

Selim and Abdullah gave a shout of joy, in which they were joined by Moto, Simba, and Niani, and as they passed on, Selim proposed that they should break in upon the old man suddenly, who would no doubt be found on his verandah, chatting with half-a-dozen other Arabs.

In a few minutes—minutes that were never counted, but which glided by swiftly—they found themselves pushing their way through crowds of well-dressed Zanzibar slaves, who looked upon the Arab boys with surprise, mingled with awe, but who made way for them immediately, but eyeing them as if they had never seen Arabs.

Selim and Abdullah passed on, however, and came at last before the spacious tembe. They saw the white-bearded Sheikh, seated with his back to the wall, leaning on a pillow which was covered with gay print. On each side of him sat several other Arabs. All started up as they saw the strange Arab boys, undressed and naked, with the exception of ragged pieces of dirty cloth about their loins, walk up to them, and heard the unmistakable Arabic of Muscat, as the boys said ·

"Salaam Aleekum!" (Peace be to ye.)

"Aleekum Salaam!" (and unto ye be peace), responded the startled Arabs, rising to their feet.

"Are ye Arabs, children?" said the old Sultan bin Ali, gazing at them sternly.

"We are children of the Arabs of Muscat," answered Selim, with a tremulous voice.

"How is it, then, in the name of Allah," said the aged Sheikh, "that ye come in this guise, naked, into the presence of true believers?"

"Our fathers are dead. They were rich merchants of Zanzibar. They were slain in battle, and we, their sons, were made slaves. After many months we have escaped—praised be Allah for his mercies!—and have sought ye, our kinsmen."

"Slain in battle!" echoed the Sheikh. "Who are ye? In what battle were your fathers slain?"

"This," said Selim, pointing to Abdullah, "is Abdullah, son of Sheikh Mohammed bin Mussoud; I am Selim, son of Amer, son of Osman; thou art Sultan, the son of Ali, my kinsman and friend."

"Oh, blessed be the compassionate God! Praised be the Lord of all creatures—the most merciful, the King of the Judgment-day!" cried the aged Sultan, as he rushed to Selim and Abdullah, and brought them together, and embraced them both at once, and kissed their foreheads, and would not release them for a moment, but continued to pour his kisses on their faces, and endearing terms into their ears, while hot tears poured down his cheeks as he said, looking at them with a memory which carried him and them to that fatal day in Urori, "And thou art Selim, the son

of noble Amer, my kinsman! and this is Abdullah, son
of Mohammed! Ah, wondrous are the ways of God,
and merciful is He to true believers! I see Amer and
Mohammed in your eyes, children; how came I to
forget that fatal day of Kwikuru? But enter, children.
Enter, in the name of the Most High. Amer's kinsman
cannot forget his duties to Amer's son!"

But the other Arabs could not permit Sultan, son of
Ali, to take the boys away without being permitted to
embrace them, and while scalding tears fell down their
cheeks, they cried out, "Blessed is the Most High,
the merciful and compassionate God!" and poured
their congratulations into the ears of the escaped
captives.

Before quite going in at the door of the tembe, Selim
turned to Sheikh Sultan and said:

"Sultan, son of Ali, let not the son of Amer be called
ungrateful. Lo! here are my friends. Thou hast not
thanked them for what they have done to us. This is
Simba, and this is Moto! Dost thou not know them?"

"Ah, who does not know Simba and Moto?" said the
old man, as he rushed at them and gave them a warm
embrace, and kissed, out of pure gratitude, those rugged
and dusky men of Africa. "Enter, men, in the name of
God. Command the kinsman of Amer, what ye will
eat, and drink. But who is this little fellow—thy son,
Simba?"

"No, Sheikh Sultan; he is Niani, Master Amer's
slave."

"Is he the little fellow who used to play tricks upon
Isa, son of Thani, Selim?"

"The same."

"Come, child, to an old man's arms!" said he, as he caught him up, and gave him a warm kiss.

Simba, and Moto, and Niani found themselves embraced by the other Arabs in turn, and Sultan bin Ali's slaves, hearing who they were, came rushing up by the dozen to embrace their friends, whom they had given up as lost for ever, on that fearful day, when four hundred Arabs and their people met with such a sad fate.

But Sultan bin Ali, seeing them thus engaged, turned to his slaves, and bade them prepare the best at once for food, and then ushered Selim and Abdullah to his own cosy, carpeted room, and, inviting them to rest a moment, hastened out again to an Arab of middle age, named Soud bin Sayd, who was seated on his verandah, and said to him:

"Soud bin Sayd, thou hast two sons of the same age as these boys. Hasten, my friend, bring two dresses for these children—the best thou hast—name thy price for them, but bring them."

"Do not name price. Sheikh, thou hast them. I will but mount thy riding-ass and be back before thou canst say, Bismillah!" and the good-hearted man hurried off as he said it.

Then Sultan bin Ali called to his barber, and bade him bring his basin and razors directly to him, then joined the young Arab boys, who had been weeping continually for joy, fast locked in each other's arms.

The barber soon came, and Sultan told him to shave off the boys' hair, which was grown almost to their shoulders. Before the depilatory process was completed, Soud bin Sayd had returned with two complete dresses — shirts, handsome embroidered dishdashchs (robe), and embroidered skull-caps, two fine blue cloth dāmirs (jackets), wide-flowing linen drawers, and slippers.

Then, excusing the barber of the kind-hearted Soud, Sultan ushered the boys into the lavatory with their new dresses, where there was abundance of water, soap, and towels for them; and after telling them, when dressed, to come out to him and his friends on the verandah, he closed the door on them, and joined the Arabs, who were still in a high state of excitement, consequent upon the unexpected appearance of the Arab boys, and their marvellous escape from slavery.

"Sultan, son of Ali," said Soud bin Sayd, " this is a great day."

" Thou mayst well say so.   How rejoiced the widows of Amer and Mohammed will be, and Leila, who is to be Selim's wife when he gets old enough!   My friends, ye must join me in eating the noon-day meal with the poor children, that they may feel that they are among kinsmen and friends once more.   Poor boys! what they must have suffered!   But there is a great deal to be told yet; we shall hear their story presently.   I am glad ye are here to welcome them with me."

" It is wonderful!—wonderful!   I feel impatient to hear all they have to say," said a swarthy-faced young Arab of about twenty-five.

Within half-an-hour the two Arab boys, Selim and Abdullah, came from their room, dressed, and so changed they could barely be recognized as the wild-looking, long-haired boys who had so electrified the old man with their unpresentable appearance.   Selim

came first, Abdullah behind, the Arabs rising respectfully as they came near, the former advancing to Sheikh
Sultan, with his handsome face all aglow at the change
he felt in him, took hold of the old man's right hand,
and raised it respectfully to his lips, and went on to
the other Arabs to do the same to them, but they would
not permit this, but saluted him on the cheek, as well
as Abdullah.

The Sultan bin Ali invited the boys to the seat of
honour near him, and had pillows brought for them, so
they would not feel chilled by contact with the wall,
and invited Selim to tell his story, with which he at
once complied, and gave them a succinct but brief
account of all that happened to them from the battle-
day to their appearance at Unyanyembe. He never
had such an attentive audience before in his life.
The Arabs were deeply interested in it, and often broke
out into exclamations, which showed the two Arab boys
that they were really amongst friends at last. Kalulu
received great praise, and Sultan bin Ali expressed his
fears that the boy was either murdered or carried into
hopeless captivity and slavery.

Presently food was brought in such quantities that
made the hungry boys stare; one dish was expressly
for Simba, Moto, and Niani, who were called from
among their friends to partake of it. Water was poured
over each person's right hand, and as Selim and Abdullah saw the great dish of snowy rice, and the dish of
curried meat, they could not help uttering one great
long sigh of satisfaction. Sultan assisted the boys to
the best portions, placed more curry over their rice
than he placed over any other, though he did not

neglect his guests. Then hulwa (sweetmeats) and sweet cakes were brought, with honey, and the boys were continually urged to eat, until they at last declared that they had had enough.

The next day the two Arab boys were taken to all the tembes of Tabora, Kwihara, and Maroro, where they were heartily received by everybody, and were invited to feasts, which followed one another in quick succession, until, at the end of a month, Selim and Abdullah had fed so well that they got quite rotund in figure, and appeared none the worse for their privations.

After two months' stay at Unyanyembe, Selim and Abdullah were placed in charge of Soud bin Sayd, who was bound for the coast with a caravan consisting of two hundred slaves, loaded with ivory. Sultan bin Ali and a dozen other Arabs accompanied Selim and Abdullah as far as Kwikuru, three miles from Tabora, and after fervently blessing them, and wishing them all sorts of success, and a long-lived happiness, parted from them with saddened faces.

Tura, on the frontier of Unyamwezi, was reached within five days, and crossing the wilderness of Tura they merged in New Ukimbu. Within three weeks afterwards they were travelling through arid Ugogo, which they passed safely in two weeks; then the friendly wilderness of the Bitter Water — Marenga M'kali—burst upon their view, and the next day, after a march of thirty miles, they were defiling by the cones of Usagara.

Continuing their march, ten days more brought them to the Makata Plain, and on the eighth day after leaving Usagara they camped near Simbamwenni, or the "Lion Lord's" city, which both Selim and Abdullah remembered as the scene where Niani had a disagreeable incident with Isa. Poor Isa! he is dead.

After a rest of two days at Simbamwenni, the caravan of Soud bin Sayd continued its march, and on the seventieth day from Unyanyembe the Arab boys, Selim and Abdullah, and their friends, Simba, Moto, and Niani, looked at the sea of Zanj, from the ridges behind Bagamoyo, and pointed out its ever-smiling azure face to one another with emotions too great for utterance. They feasted their eyes on it until they lost sight of it, as they plunged into the depths of the umbrageous groves and gardens of the sea-coast town of Bagamoyo, into the streets of which they presently emerged, to be welcomed, as wanderers generally are, with glad cries, embraces, smiling countenances, and hearty claspings of the hand.

The next day Soud bin Sayd embarked his caravan in two Arab ships, and accompanied by the young Arabs and their friends he had the anchor hoisted, and the lateen sails sheeted home, and the ships began to move, as they felt the influence of the continental breeze, towards Zanzibar, across the strait which separates Zanzibar from the mainland.

"Moving towards home!—glorious thought!" cried the enraptured Selim, as he turned towards his friend Abdullah, and fell on his neck overpowered by his feelings.

"Home!" said Abdullah, "at last! We have been frequently tried, Selim, but we have been taught good lessons. Thanks be to Allah! He has been but trying

2 E

us, to make us better and purer, and I mean to profit by what I have learned. Wilt thou, Selim?"

"With the help of God, I will," he replied.

"Dost thou know what chapter of the Kûran fits our case better than any other, Selim?" asked Abdullah.

"Which?"

"That entitled the BRIGHTNESS, wherein the Prophet, blessed be his name! says: '*By the sun in his meridian splendour, by the shades of night, thy Lord hath not forsaken thee, neither doth He hate thee. Did He not find thee an orphan, and did He not take care of thee? And did He not find thee wandering in error, and hath He not guided thee into the truth? And did He not find thee needy, and hath He not enriched thee? Wherefore oppress not the orphan, nor repulse the beggar, but declare the goodness of thy Lord.*'"

"Beautiful!" said Selim; "oppress not the orphan may mean oppress not the slave. He found us fatherless, and He took care of us. He found us needy, ailing, perishing in the wilderness, and He hath enriched us. Praised be God, the one God, the eternal God, He begetteth not, neither is He begotten; and there is not any one like Him."

"Amen! and Amen!" responded Abdullah. "There is only one God, who is God, and Mohammed is His Prophet."

"Amen! and Amen!" exclaimed Simba and Moto, who were as powerfully affected by their present and coming happiness as were either Selim or Abdullah.

The shores of Zanzibar at last were seen to rise from the sea, like an emerald set in the centre of a circular sapphire, and the lovely isle was hailed by vociferous shouts by the wanderers, while their hearts beat faster and faster. They neared the shore steadily, and each point became an object of interest, and every well-remembered house received due attention. Finally, the ships rode in the harbour, and Selim, and Abdullah, and their friends, bidding a kindly farewell to Soud bin Sayd, after inviting him to come and see them, got into a boat called by the kind Arab, and were rowed ashore.

As they stand at last on the island where both of these boys were born, on the threshold of their own homes, how much money would, we wonder, induce them to return to Africa without ever having seen their homes? Judging from their faces, we should think the world would not be sufficient, not even to induce them to return to Bagamoyo. What bright, joyous faces they wore! What flashing eyes! Men turned round in the streets to look at them, and talked to their companions, with smiles, about their looks. They saw several whom they knew, but they were too impatient, so near home, to stop to talk to any one, and they paced determinedly towards home; they passed the Arab, the Hindoo, the Negro quarter; crossed the bridge, and were among the gardens of the rich Arabs. Once outside the city, the capital of the island, they broke into a run; but as they drew near their homes they sobered down, became exceedingly agitated, and pale in the face.

Abdullah suddenly shouted, "There, Selim, is my home! As thou hast to pass it, come with me."

Selim consented, and accompanied his friend to the door, gave him one last embrace, bade him come round and see him soon; and then bounded off towards his own stately mansion, accompanied by Simba, Moto, and Niani.

He saw the mangoe trees, the orange groves, the cinnamon and the slender clove trees. Soon he saw the house itself, looming large and white between the trees; he saw the latticed windows, which he had often pictured to himself in the depths of the African wilderness; he saw the cupola of the Arab temple, which his father, Amer, had erected; he saw the walls of the courtyard; he cast one glance at the blue sea, and the spot consecrated by happy associations, where his father and kinsmen had often sat, gazing upon the sea; and then burst through the door of the courtyard, dashed breathlessly across it, and through the great carved door of the mansion, up the stairs, and into the harem, where he saw a woman seated on the divan, near the lattice, looking out. One penetrating glance assured him that she was Amina, his mother! She looked up and saw her son, Selim! returned to her heart and love! from Negro-land.

Let us drop a kindly veil over the solemn and affecting meeting of mother and son, feeling assured that the joy of both was indescribable; that they interchanged the most endearing phrases; that they embraced each other as loving mother and loving son, long parted, would; that while he sat by her side he poured into her ears the sad tale of woe, bereavement, suffering, privation, difficulty, disappointment; the account of the marvellous adventures, hair-breadth escapes; of true friendships formed; the sacrifice, the courage, and the constancy of one whom he could never forget, Kalulu; and that his mother gave him an account of all that she had endured for the last two years; how his uncle had attempted to manage the estate himself, but she would not permit him, knowing his character; how everything had prospered during his absence; how rich he was; and how, with Leila's portion, which Khamis, her father, had given her, he might consider himself one of the richest men on Zanzibar Island. But she begged of him not to think of marrying yet, as he was not yet eighteen—a mere boy—to which Selim gave his promise.

What wonderful things they had to tell each other! things which do not concern the world to know, but concerned both mother and son; which they appreciated, and enjoyed, and could repeat, and laugh merrily over together, without caring one jot what the world outside thought.

On the third day after his arrival at Zanzibar Selim, accompanied by his factor, a smart, shrewd, clever, honest Hindoo Mahometan, by Simba, Moto, and Niani, went towards the city to purchase clothes for his faithful servants and their families. On the way he turned to Abdullah's home and called out to him to ask if he would like to go with him. Abdullah was only too happy, and forthwith appeared outside, dressed in the very height of Arab fashion, and as gay as could be.

Arriving within the city, the factor drew for Selim's use the sum of two hundred dollars, and then, before making any purchases, Selim called upon the sons of the Zanzibar Sultan, his old playmates, who warmly greeted him, and who detained him to hear his story about his sufferings and escape from slavery, all of which the factor had already known from Selim and his mother. Several other friends living in the neighbourhood of the Sultan's palace, were called upon, all of whom expressed the greatest surprise and pleasure at seeing him.

Selim, accompanied by his friends, was about crossing to Shangani Point, when they suddenly came upon the slave-market, crowded with the miserable beings about to be offered to the highest bidders. The buyers were there in considerable numbers, stout, portly Arabs, and well-to-do half-castes, besides Mohammedans from India, who bought for other people, all of whom were examining critically the subjects to be sold. These "subjects" were of all ages, and of both sexes, almost entirely nude. Hardly one of them had a healthy look, mostly all appeared half-starved and sick. There had lately been several importations from Kilwa, Mombasah, Whinde, Saadani, and Bagamoyo, which had eluded the searching eyes of the British cruisers and the agents of the British consulate. But here they were almost under the windows of the house over which the flag of England waved, examples of human suffering, subjects of human brutality; the most hapless-looking beings, the most woe-begone "human cattle" that the sun had ever shone upon.

Selim was about departing, disgusted with the brutal scene, when, casting a last look at the auctioneer, he saw the face of the slave whom he was about to sell. With a frenzied look and pale face he said to the factor, to Abdullah, and his other friends:

"Come this way—come this way—quick, for Allah's sake," drawing the factor away after him until he was hidden from the auctioneer's gaze behind a group of sightseers.

"What is the matter, Selim?" asked Abdullah. "Art thou sick?"

"Sick! No; but listen all of ye. Do ye see yon slave about to be sold now?"

"Yes," answered all.

"Then that slave, as sure as Allah is in heaven, is my adopted brother KALULU !"

"Kalulu !" exclaimed the startled friends.

"Yes, Kalulu !"

"Wallahi, he is !" exclaimed Moto in an excited tone. "There is not another here present who can hold his head like that, be he Arab or African. He is the King of the Watuta! I swear it;" and as he said that he was about to rush off, followed by Simba, when Selim shouted, "For Allah's sake, don't stir !"

"Why? He is not a slave," shouted Simba. "He has been stolen by that Arab caravan, which travelled by night, because the chiefs feared the day, like thieves. Moto, thou wert right. I see it all now. Wallahi! but I will break the back of the thief, even if the Sultan of Zanzibar cuts my head off. Let me go, Selim !"

"Silence, Simba," said the factor. Thou wilt draw attention to the young master. I see what Selim wants. He wants me to go and buy him. Ah, ha! Africa has taught thee cunning, Selim !"

"Yes, go," said Selim. "Offer anything; but don't let him be bought by anybody else. Give a thousand dollars for him, but bring him to me. We will wait thee here."

"Fear not; but there is one thing thou hast not

observed, Selim. I know I shall get him cheap. Dost thou not see that he is handcuffed? He is dangerous. Simba, be thou ready. Watch me nod my head, do not stir until I do so, then go to him and catch him. When I have paid the money he becomes Master Selim's slave. And thou, Selim, keep guard over this big fellow, or he will ruin the game I am going to play. Abdullah, Moto, do ye hear?" asked the factor.

"We do; we understand," they answered.

From their position they could observe everything without being seen. They saw the factor make his way to the front among the buyers. They heard the auctioneer, a sturdy, strong-voiced fellow, conspicuous from an enormous turban he wore round his head, bellow out:

"Ho, Arabs, children of Zanzibar, and ye rich men, look up! Here is a priceless slave from Ututa. He calls himself King of Ututa (a laugh from a bystander). Kings command high prices. ("They make very bad slaves!" shouted Selim's factor.) I am going to run this fellow high. ("No you won't;" Selim's factor.) Look at him well. Watch his eyes; they are living fire. See the pose of his head. Observe his limbs; clean and well-shaped as a Nedjèd mare's. Look at his chest; there's wind, there's hard work there. ("Very little work, plenty of wind to run;" Selim's factor.) Just take a glance at his teeth; there,—open boy. No, dog! take that (buffeting him). Look at his hair; it hangs below the shoulders. Believe me, no slave was ever offered in this market to equal him. Offer; an offer, Arabs. Rich men, who require a good slave, make an offer for the best slave ever brought to Zanzibar."

"Say, auctioneer, why is he handcuffed? did he try to murder his master? And why is the chain about his neck? Has he tried to run away?" asked Selim's factor.

"Silence!" thundered the auctioneer. "An offer is what I want."

"Two dollars!" shouted the factor, smiling sardonically.

"Two dollars!! Only two dollars! for this unequalled slave. Man, look at him, and offer a hundred."

"Five dollars!" shouted a bystander.

"Five dollars! Five, five, five, five, five."

"Six!" shouted the factor.

"Six dollars! Six, six."

"Ten dollars!" from a bystander.

"Twenty dollars!" shouted the factor.

"Twenty dollars. Come, bid up. Only twenty, twenty, twenty, twenty. Who goes beyond twenty?"

"Twenty-five!" shouted the bystander.

"Thirty dollars! He is worth more, but he is a devil. I can see that by his eye."

"Thirty, thirty, thirty, thirty. Bid up. Only thirty! He is worth more. Bid up, Arabs. Thirty, thirty, thirty. Going,—going,—going,—gone!" and the auctioneer nodded to the factor.

The factor walked up, counted thirty dollars in American gold to the auctioneer, who laughed as he put the money in his pouch, and said:

"My friend, this slave will murder thee the first time he catches thee asleep. Be wary of him; I should hate to hear some morning that thy throat is cut from ear to ear."

"Fear not for me, my friend. I have seen worse than he is tamed. Release his neck from the chain. Let go his hands."

"Art thou mad?" asked the auctioneer.

"Not at all. Let him go free," replied the factor.

The neck-chain slipped off, and the hands were about to be freed, when the factor nodded to Simba, who sprang through the bystanders like a very lion, and while the hands were being freed, uttered, with his deep voice, the magic name—

"KALULU!"

The slave, still on the stand, turned round at the sound of the word. He saw the unmistakable face of Simba, and behind him, advancing slowly, two Arab boys, well-dressed, whom he did not know, but he recognized Moto and Niani. He reeled as one struck, but the great strong arms of Simba were round him; they lifted him up from the stand, carried him on the run towards the two Arab boys, and he was placed face to face with the tallest of them.

"See, Kalulu, dost thou not know Selim?" asked Simba.

The astonished boy looked at the face one moment. He saw him advance with his old smile towards him, and he sprang at him, and thus it was how the two friends had met after so many months. Abdullah, Simba, Moto, Niani, were embraced one after another, to the astonishment of the bystanders, who could not conceive how such Arab boys could degrade themselves so low as to hug a slave that a few minutes ago was in chains, and sold for the cheap sum of thirty dollars!

Are not all bystanders in all parts of the world

always wondering why such and such things happen? Is not the world for ever in a maze, and deeming many things of like nature to be incomprehensible? When was the world not shocked at an exhibition of nature?

But our friends paid no heed to the surprise of the bystanders or to their remarks; they left the market-place arm in arm, and proceeded towards a shop where "long clothes" were sold. An Arab shirt thrown over him, and a piece of white cloth folded around his head, made a wonderful change in Kalulu. Then Selim gave orders to the factor to purchase the best clothes he could get for Kalulu, blue cloth jacket, embroidered cap, and embroidered shirt, linen drawers, crimson fez with long blue tassel, and slippers, besides a Muscat shash and Arab dagger, over and above what he had intended to purchase for him, to which the factor promised to pay implicit attention.

Selim turned to Kalulu and said:

"In two or three days, Kalulu, thou wilt be as well dressed as any son of an Arab in Zanzibar; but now I must show thee my mother and my home. When we are outside the city thou canst tell us thy story."

In half an hour they were in the country; and Kalulu, when requested to begin, said:

"I went out to look for game, and coming to the forest I saw smoke, and men wearing Arab clothes. I went to their camp when I found they were Arabs, not thinking they could act as they did. They spoke me fair at first; but while I was seated alongside of the chief his men sprang on me, and they chained me. I struggled hard at first, but they hurt me and abused me as if they meant to kill me. We travelled that night through the forest, and every night until we came to Unyanyembe, where we were kept in a house in a dark room. After a few days we began another journey, which ended at this sea. On coming to the island the chief put me to work in the field; but they could not get me to work. They beat and beat me every day; but I would not work, and the chief, finding he could do nothing with me, sent me with many more to be sold. That is the story."

"Dost thou know that thou art my slave now, Kalulu? But when I was a slave of thine thou didst set me free and protect me by making me thy brother. I do the same to thee now. Thou art free, and I shall be a brother to thee, and my mother shall be thy mother," said Selim.

"And mine too, Kalulu," said Abdullah; "Selim shall not keep thee all to himself. My mother wants to see thee. And here we are at my mother's house, to which I ask thee to come now."

In a few moments they were at the door, and Abdullah invited Selim and Kalulu to walk in. They were led up a flight of stairs, and presently stood in an ante-chamber. Leaving their slippers outside, Abdullah ushered his two friends into a spacious saloon, close to the walls of which ran a luxurious divan, covered with soft silken carpeting, the like of which Kalulu had never dreamed of before; the floor was also covered with Persian carpets of great thickness.

"Ah, Kalulu, my house is not so grand as Selim's; but it is better than most Arab houses," said Abdullah. "Stay here a moment until I go to prepare my mother."

Abdullah was not gone long before he returned with his mother, whose face was veiled by a thin muslin gauze, but who, on seeing that the stranger was but a boy, threw off the veil and advanced towards him, and began to thank him in the sweetest tones he ever heard. She also told him to make the house his home whenever he liked, or whenever Selim could spare him, and after saying all that was required of her to say by her son, she vanished into her own room.

After his mother had gone, Abdullah said: "Thou seest, Kalulu, that our women have customs different from thine. Wert thou a man, thou shouldst never have seen her face? Yet thou art such a big boy now, my mother is even afraid of thee. However, whatever my mother failed to tell thee, her son says. Thou art welcome : come early or late, thou must consider all my mother or I have at thy service. These are the words of my mother and of myself."

"Thou hast done with Kalulu for the present, Abdullah. Come thou with us to my mother," said Selim.

"Nay, Selim ; my brother Kalulu must eat in my house, and then we shall go together with thee."

"Our noon-meal is ready. Come thou and eat with us. I want Kalulu to see my mother. Come, Abdullah, we can return and take the evening meal with thee."

Seeing Selim was urgent, and really anxious, Abdullah, being but a boy, consented, though it was against Arab custom ; but he was consoled by the reflection that the principal meal was to be eaten with him ; and bidding Selim stay a moment, he went back

to his mother, and informed her that they should have
guests for the evening meal; then returning, he sallied
out with Selim and Kalulu. Simba, Moto, and Niani
were at the door waiting for them, and together they
proceeded to Selim's house.

If Kalulu was impressed with the grandeur of Abdullah's house, he was much more so with the splendid
appearance of Selim's. The shining white marble of
the courtyard, the spaciousness, cleanliness, and order
that prevailed; the well-dressed slaves, that came
forward assiduous to please; the broad stairs, the
carved portals, and the roomy entrance-hall, took away
the young chief's breath almost with surprise. He was
speechless with astonishment, and he mentally compared his own miserable clay-floored hut with this
grandeur. He looked for Simba and Moto, but found
they were stopping at the door; they were excluded
from above, whither he was ascending, and Kalulu
reflected upon this.

The ante-chamber was passed, at the door of which
Selim and Abdullah left their slippers, and they advanced into a grand and spacious saloon, larger than
the one at Abdullah's house, more superbly furnished,
with numbers of curious things which Sheikh Amer
had collected through his Bombay agent.

Selim turned round to Kalulu and asked:

"How does the young King of Ututa like his brother
Selim's house?"

"Thou art greater than I, my brother. I have had
thousands of warriors who would have done my slightest
bidding; but I am the first King of Ututa who ever
saw a house like this. I have had plenty of ivory, and

cows, and sheep, and goats that could not be counted for number, but I never had a house like this."

"By-and-by, Kalulu, when we are all men and strong, we shall take thee back to Ututa and see thee righted in thy own; thou having seen these things, thou wilt be able to do likewise. But thou and I have much to learn yet. We are boys, and we cannot fight Ferodia; but until we are men, rest with Abdullah and me at Zanzibar; make my house thy own. Stay here; I go to call my mother, Amina, whom thou must like."

"I shall like everything that thou dost like, Selim," answered Kalulu, seating himself on the divan as he spoke.

Selim knocked at the door of his mother's apartments, who came to the door. Her son respectfully saluted his mother's right hand, and led her into the room; but when she saw a stranger and a black man, she drew back, and said:

"Who is this, my son; and what dost thou mean by bringing a slave into a place where none but Arabs are admitted? And I have left my veil behind. Fie, boy!"

"Nay, dear mother, this is only a boy; and he is not a slave, he is my brother." answered Selim, smiling, as he beckoned Kalulu to advance, who looked somewhat awed at the transcendent beauty of Selim's mother.

"Thy brother! How, hast thou two mothers? My lord, Amer, never told me he had other wives than those who live in this house. What folly is this, Selim, my son? Who is this boy?"

"Dost thou not know, mother? Canst thou not guess? Behold my brother, MY KALULU!"

"Kalulu!" echoed his mother, and immediately she

recovered her smiles, and walking up to him, she poured into Kalulu's ears all a fond mother could say to one whom she considered as her dear son's saviour and deliverer, and she ended with saying:

"This house is at thy service. Command anything thou dost wish, and thou shalt be obeyed. I also, who am Selim's mother—who for so long mourned him as dead—know how to be grateful. Simba, Moto, and little Niani, who shared his troubles with him, have already been rewarded with houses and gardens, and Selim is continually sounding their praises to me. But to thee, knowing as I do that thou hast suffered much, I shall be as a mother; and thou shalt be MY KALULU."

THE END.